Two, maybe three tricks, if it was a good night, and she'd be going on to bigger and better things. A gleaming, new Olds sedan pulled over to the curb and the driver, middle-aged, overweight, and sweating, waved her over.

"Wanna go out?" Holly crooned.

"Yeah," the man said, his voice hoarse with lust.

She slid in beside him, gave him a wide, welcoming smile and chirped, "Fifty for a blow and seventy-five for a lay."

The man looked down at the steering wheel, murmuring out of the corner of his mouth, "I guess I'll have the first one."

Holly gave him directions and as he pulled away from the curb, she began to softly sing along with the radio. It was the Tina Turner song she liked — "What's Love Got To Do With It?"

"What's love but a second-hand emotion?" Tina sang as the driver eased into a lane between a couple of warehouses. "What's love —" this time the soul queen's plaintive query was stopped short as the man cut the ignition and fished two twenties and a ten out of his wallet.

And as the fat man began to grunt with excitement and thrust his fleshy hips at her, she heard Tina's voice going round and round in her head. And she knew.

FATAL CHOICES

FATAL CHOICES

JAMES M. BURKE

KNIGHTSBRIDGE PUBLISHING COMPANY

NEW YORK

ACKNOWLEDGMENTS

The author would like to gratefully acknowledge the assistance of the Manitoba Arts Council and the Ontario Arts Council in the preparation of this book.

Published in the United States by
Knightsbridge Publishing Company
255 East 49th Street
New York, New York 10017

ISBN: 1-877961-23-X

10 9 8 7 6 5 4 3 2 1
FIRST EDITION

Chapter One

"Huh, did you say something?" Larry Chambers lowered the newspaper and glanced across the table at his wife. Jane was wearing the same expression he'd seen so many — too many — times before: anger tinged with just the right degree of hurt.

"As if you care," she said through tight, bloodless lips. "As if you *ever* care."

He sighed heavily and tented the paper over the remains of his breakfast.

"You know what I'm like in the morning," he soothed. "It's a routine with me. I've got to get through the paper so I know what the hell's going on in the world." He ran a hand through his thinning hair. "Do you think it's a treat for me to wade through this stuff? Killings. Fires. An economy that's going down the toilet. But how the hell would it look if Toronto's top radio hot-line host wasn't up to date on current events?"

"It must be hell to live in a pressure cooker." The

mockery in her voice was subtle, designed to disquiet rather than incite. "Well, don't worry about it. You may not have to put up with it that much longer anyway."

He picked up the paper, folded it carefully, and took a deep breath. It was no use. He might as well rise to the bait, or she'd keep at him until something snapped and they had a flaming row. He could almost feel himself being reeled in when he finally replied, "What's that supposed to mean?"

She clapped her hands in feigned delight. "Why, you're actually speaking to me! If this keeps up, we may have an honest-to-goodness conversation one of these days."

Pushing his chair away from the table, he got up. "There are two things I haven't got time for," he said sourly. "Riddles and sarcasm. If you think I'm going to play guessing games . . . ."

"I wouldn't want you to tax your mental faculties, since I know you like to conserve your brainpower for the benefit of your ever-diminishing audience."

He stood looking down at her, watching her take tiny, mouselike nibbles out of her toast. "So that's it," he said finally. "You've heard about the latest BBM ratings."

"You're not the only one who reads the newspapers," she said, cocking her head to look at him. "How much are you down? Ten, twelve points?"

"Don't you know?" he sniffed. "I'd have thought you'd have the story framed so you could gloat over it at your leisure."

Ignoring the gibe, she said blandly, "That guy on CKLB — what's his name, Ferguson? — really seems to be taking off." She smiled innocently. "But I guess that's not surprising, because the public can be so fickle, especially when someone new and exciting comes on the scene." She arched her eyebrows. "And I guess the fact that he's a real hunk hasn't hurt him any either."

"He's a hunk all right," Larry muttered, "but I won't say of what."

Jane gave him a condescending smile and bustled about

clearing away the breakfast dishes. He watched her in silence, thinking how he wanted to be anywhere but here, seeing her glow with malicious triumph. How had it come to this? he wondered. How had their relationship degenerated into a series of poisonous little skirmishes that began and ended in a vacuum? He suddenly felt very tired and old. Forty-four. He knew he looked older. More sleep, he decided. That's all I need. That and fewer nights like the one that had ended at four that morning. There was no doubt about it. He couldn't handle the booze like he once could.

Slipping into his jacket Larry tightened the knot in his tie, and reflexively patted his breast pocket, ensuring that his wallet was in place.

"Can we expect the pleasure of your company at dinner?" Jane asked, slamming the door of the dishwasher.

"Yeah, sure," he nodded absently. "If anything comes up, I'll give you a call."

"That would be a pleasant change," she said icily.

"Look," he countered, "I told you I was sorry. I had to make nice with some of our advertisers. We had a couple of drinks and one thing led to another and —"

"And you got bombed out of your mind as usual," she snapped.

"All right," he conceded. "I had a few too many but I made it home, didn't I?"

"I don't know why you bothered, frankly," she said. "About all you ever do around here is sleep and change your clothes."

"I can't tell you how much I'd like to continue this conversation," he said wryly, "but I've got to get my ass in gear. Time and ratings wait for no man and I don't want to disappoint the few listeners I may still be able to hang on to."

She followed him to the back door, her arms clasped over her ample bosom.

"Well, don't overtax your vocal cords," she smirked. "You know how tired you get after a hard morning in front of the microphone." She ran her hands seductively over her full hips. Her diaphanous nightgown clung to the ripe flesh. "Too tired to do what a lot of other men would pay for."

He gave no sign that he'd heard her. Checking his image in the hall mirror, he ran a comb through his sandy, close-cropped hair, wincing inwardly at the sight of his red-rimmed eyes and sallow complexion. Jingling his car keys out of his pocket, he looked at her expressionlessly. For a brief moment, he felt a twinge of sadness at the hurt and anger in her face. Somewhere, they'd lost it, whatever it was that had taken their separateness and made them one in feeling and purpose. Understanding? Love? What was it? And where had it gone? Time and again, he'd tried retracing the steps of their relationship but had never been able to find the place where they'd stopped dreaming together. He wanted to reach out to her, but the distance between them had grown too great. Instead, he smiled thinly and said: "Well, if anyone makes you an offer, maybe you should take him up on it. That way, when I get fired, you'll be able to support us in the style you've gotten used to."

As the door slammed shut behind Larry, Jane had to check herself from running after him and flinging some choice epithets. Oh, what the hell, she smiled resignedly, there's always next time.

She wandered back into the kitchen and stood looking out the window. She blinked into the brightness of the sun still low in the sky. It would be another scorcher, she thought, another day to lounge around the pool with a tall, cool one. Or maybe more than one. She checked her watch. Time to get the kids up.

But when she went upstairs, it was not to rouse the girls from their slumber. Instead, she padded down the hall to the master bedroom. Sitting down at the dresser, she cocked her head this way and that, cataloguing the telltale signs of middle age. The crow's feet radiating from the corners of her hazel eyes. The puffiness under her chin. The barely detectable sag of her cheeks and the tiny folds under her eyes. She fanned her fingers through her thick auburn hair and sighed at the streaks of grey at the temples.

Then she stood up and slowly pirouetted in front of the mirror, studying her body, instinctively sucking in her stomach, then dejectedly letting it out. God, she told herself, I'm going to have to start going to aerobics again. But what the hell for? I thought it was the *wife* who was supposed to plead headaches to keep an orgasm-hungry spouse at bay. Not in this household, that's for damn sure.

She pursed her lips, silently querying her reflection. I wonder if he's getting it somewhere else? Then she quickly shook her head and chuckled dryly. That would be *too* ridiculous. He wasn't even that interested *before* we got married. And the honeymoon. Well, my dear, an orgy it most certainly was not. He probably would have been just as content to keep knocking back the Scotch and watching the late show.

The booze. Maybe that was it. He'd been hitting the bottle a little more than usual lately and she'd read somewhere — in *Cosmo* was it, or perhaps *New Woman*? — that alcohol was a sexual as well as an emotional depressant. And what was that other article — the one she'd just skimmed through at the hairdresser? Something about stress having an effect on the sexual performance of men, particularly those in their middle years. Promising herself to do a little research on the subject before confronting her husband, she started down the hall to the girls' bedroom.

Larry left his car in the Park 'n Ride lot and hurried toward the subway station, glancing at his watch as he skipped down the concrete steps. Dropping in his token, he surged ahead with the crowd on the southbound platform and was half-carried into the train.

He sat down next to a young, prim-looking woman who had her face buried in a *Harlequin* romance and flipped open his attaché case. He pulled out the sheaf of briefing notes that his researcher, Elaine Steele, had put together. She had done her usual efficient job, providing him with all the information about daycare centres that he needed to be able to discuss the issue with that morning's guests. Although daycare was still a major issue in Toronto, it was one that Larry would have preferred to avoid. It wasn't so much the issue, as the people behind it. If they seemed to many like dynamic, committed women, to Larry they were strident bra-burners who thought it was the government's duty to look after them from cradle to grave, bailing them out of all the screw-ups they'd gotten themselves into.

As the train pulled into the Bloor station, he shoved the notes back into the case and stood up, noticing for the first time the advertisement that occupied the panel just over the doorway. "Tune in Larry's Line. Your choice from nine to noon, weekdays on CKAL, 780 on your dial." He smiled at his likeness hunched over a microphone. It was a good shot all right. Made him look ten years younger.

Involuntarily and with a trace of embarrassment, he glanced around to see if anyone had caught him in his fleeting moment of narcissism. As one, the faces around him were turned toward the sliding doors, as the passengers got set to bolt for the escalator leading to street level.

Larry opted for the stairs. He needed the exercise, he thought. He still felt a little light-headed and needed something to get his blood going before he stepped into the studio. Even after a dozen years as a hot-line host, he still got a rush from being behind the mike and flexing 100,000 watts of muscle. No matter what the goddamn ratings said, he was still the king of the airwaves and the studio was his castle, the base from which he reached out to his subjects, implanting ideas, shaping moods, bringing tears to the eye and heat to the blood of his listeners. He smiled to himself. Almost a quarter of a million people turning their dials to his show, his voice, his opinions. Christ, if that didn't mean something, what the hell did?

He nodded as the receptionist saluted him with a cheery "good morning." His office door was open and as he strode briskly in, he saw that Elaine was already there, waiting for him. Cool, efficient, and not a hair on her well-coiffed head out of place. She had the slim figure and emaciated good looks of a fashion model, and her raven hair and high cheekbones gave her face a faintly oriental cast.

But though attractive and well-groomed, she was no clotheshorse, no pretty package with a lot of fancy bows and nothing underneath. She was bright, tough, and energetic, but these weren't the qualities that caught most people's attention. It was something else — a kind of serenity, a sense of herself and her destiny that made her more than the sum of her parts. And, as she saw it, her destiny was to be successful. She had no illusions that it would be easy, but that wasn't even a consideration. What mattered was that she knew what she wanted and, more importantly, what she'd have to do to get it.

Elaine Steele hadn't always been so single-minded. Her first couple of years out of university had been a time of some heavy soul-searching as she agonized over whether she was prepared to pay the price for success in the high-powered world of mass-market journalism. But once she'd made her decision, there'd been no looking back, at either her choice or herself. No looking back from resigning her position as a co-anchor on a medium-market television station in Hamilton, where she'd had a chance to develop an on-air persona that most people thought reflected her actual personality: warm, outgoing, concerned, and knowledgeable. But not *too* knowledgeable; intellectual women were taboo as anchors.

A female newsreader had to come across as everyone's big sister while still exuding an acceptable degree of sexuality. She had to appear well-informed but not overly aggressive or particularly witty. The constant smile, of course, was *de rigueur*. That was what reassured the audience that all was well in spite of mass starvation, riots, and plane crashes; that life went on and it was still in their interests to go out and buy the sponsors' products.

It hadn't taken long for Elaine to be slotted into her role. When she and the other on-camera personalities engaged in the folksy banter that showed the viewers they were one big, happy television family, Elaine always had to be the foil for the jock sportscaster and the off-the-wall weatherman, the butt of their limp jokes, whether they centred on her attire or hairdo or her legendary helplessness when it came to things mechanical. That was the formula the hotshot media consultants deemed most saleable and that currently prevailed on most North American news shows.

In a way, it had been a valuable experience. She'd had to come to terms with her ego, with the insidious satisfaction that came from knowing she'd been recognized on the street or in the supermarket. Ultimately, however, she'd decided that reading someone else's words and mouthing someone else's thoughts was not for her. She'd seen too many pretty faces get old too soon under the cruel lights of the TV studio.

It was different for men. Some old schmuck — so nearsighted he needed his copy in extra-large type — could stay on camera forever. Age gave a male anchor character, the image of an avuncular sage. All it gave an on-camera woman was a premature golden handshake and an explanation that the station needed a new, youthful format in order to remain competitive.

Yes, Elaine Steele knew the game well. She'd seen the winners and the losers and she intended to make damn sure she didn't become one of the latter, even if it meant taking orders from a self-centred chauvinist like Larry Chambers. After all, it wouldn't last forever. As a matter of fact, the way the rumours were flying around, CKAL's star performer might not be giving *anyone* orders for much longer.

Larry murmured a good morning and spread the briefing notes on his desk.

"Good morning," she replied, sliding a steaming cup of

coffee toward him. Black and strong. Just what he needed to get his motor started. He took a sip and stabbed one of the papers with a forefinger.

"What the hell do these broads want anyway? Christ, they're asking for enough bread to look after every damn kid in the city. What do they want to do? Buy Casa Loma and convert it into a nursery school?"

Elaine patiently explained that the money the directors of the Morningstar Daycare Centre were trying to obtain from the provincial government included the cost of renovating an old multi-family home and operating expenses for a three-year period, after which they hoped the facility would be self-supporting.

"Well, it still seems like a helluva lot of dough," he groused.

"Not as much as it costs to keep women on welfare because they can't get out and work for a living."

"You've been hanging around with too many libbers, Lainey my girl," Larry grinned. "That's a pile of horse-pooky and you know it. Give these broads someplace where they can dump their kids and they'll get out all right, but it won't be to work. They'll be out taking a run at anything in pants so they can be like their role models in those sleazy soaps they're all hooked on."

"Watch it," Elaine chided. "Remember, the majority of your loyal audience is made up of those very same ladies."

"Well," he said, winking broadly, "they have to show a little good judgement some of the time, don't they? I mean, even the law of averages would dictate that they couldn't be bimbos every waking hour."

Elaine bit back a retort. She knew better than to debate with Larry Chambers. He had a certain way of letting you know that he not only wanted but expected to have the last word. Well, why not? He had the leverage and he knew it.

"Well, don't you agree? Don't you think that most of these so-called feminist activists are nothing but ego-trippers who just want to stir up a little shit so they can make themselves feel important or get bought off with a government handout?''

Elaine threw up her hands defensively. ''Hey, I don't get paid for having opinions. I just compile the information. Besides, I flunked demagoguery in college.''

Thinking she might have gone too far, she glanced at Larry, but his expression was unchanged as he popped a breath mint into his mouth, muttering half to himself, ''Well, maybe it won't be that bad. Maybe I can get something going — bait one of those lady-libbers into blowing-off some steam.''

''Well, if anyone can do it, you can,'' Elaine said smoothly, hoping he'd take it as a compliment.

Larry shoved the sheaf of notes aside and fished out a cigarette. It would be the first of many. As he suddenly remembered his luncheon date that day, his hand shook as he touched a match to the tip of the cigarette. I wonder what the hell Riley has on his mind? he mused. The big guy himself, Harrison Riley, President of Horizon Investments and owner of radio station CKAL, had requested a meeting with Larry and the station manager, Ken Jessup. Requested, hell. When Riley wanted to see you, it was a command performance and anyone who didn't know that sure as hell soon found out. What was it he'd said when he called last week? Just an informal little luncheon. A few things he wanted to kick around. Nothing heavy. He just thought it'd be a good time for the three of them to touch base. Who was Riley kidding? Larry mused. Not him and sure as hell not Jessup. When Ken had gotten his invitation, he'd hotfooted it right down to Larry's office, his face a concerned question mark.

''What do you think's up?'' he'd asked.

''Oh, nothing,'' Larry had deadpanned. ''He probably just wants us to try out for the station's softball team.''

The pudgy, bearded station manager had sagged into a chair, his expression pleading with Larry to deny what they both knew. "Do you think it's the ratings?" he'd finally groaned.

"Does a bear make big potty in the woods?"

"Well, what's the answer? What do we tell him?"

"We tell him the truth, for Christ's sake," Larry had bellowed. "We tell him that those fucking ratings don't mean a goddamn thing. We tell him that Trent Ferguson's a flash-in-the-pan and I'm going to knock him off just like I've knocked off everyone else for the last twelve years."

Jessup had chewed his lower lip nervously. "Yeah, you're right. Sure you will. But suppose he asks for something specific, some strategy to stop our slide. What do we say?"

"We just say old Uncle Larry is going to start kicking some ass. I'm going to get this town stirred up the way only yours truly can. Remember that time I had that pair of fags talking about how they should be able to get married and adopt children and all that bullshit? Christ, every redneck in the city must have tried to call in. And that was in the days when if someone said you looked like Rock Hudson, it was considered a compliment. That's the kind of stuff we need now — good, hard-hitting journalism that socks it to people where they live, which is about a foot below their belt buckles."

Yeah, he'd been full of bravado with Jessup, but now the cracks in his confidence had begun to widen. You couldn't pull any smoke-and-mirrors bullshit with Harrison Riley. He was sharp and tough and Larry knew he'd have to have better answers than the ones he'd used to reassure Ken.

The throbbing in his right temple grew more insistent. He cursed himself for hitting the bottle so hard the night before. And mixed in with the anger was a deepening fear. Once again this morning, he'd been unable to account for all of his movements the night before. He remembered downing doubles at the press club, then hitting a bar with a couple of public relations types. But this was where the continuity ended and events became jumbled and fragmented. Again, there was a blank spot as though part of his activities of the previous night had been edited out of his memory.

Elaine broke into his thoughts — "Five minutes to show-time, Larry."

He clambered to his feet, clutching the briefing notes. "Time to make nice with another bunch of do-gooders," he grunted.

"And you're s-o-o-o good at it, darling," she crooned.

"Yeah. It comes with the territory."

The territory. *His* territory, he thought, and there was no damn way anyone was going to take it away from him — not Trent Ferguson, nor anybody else. Not after what he'd gone through to get it. He followed Elaine into the studio and was introduced to his guests. A couple of overage hippies, he quickly decided. Into love and sharing and looking as godawful as they possibly could. Why was it that the plainest women were always the ones who had a hard-on against makeup and even halfway fashionable clothes? Denim work-shirts, peasant skirts, and sandals. It was like a uniform with them and yet they were the first ones to prattle about doing your own thing.

After his producer, Bob Grey, got voice levels, Larry told the women they'd be going on the air in two minutes. "Just take a couple of deep breaths and relax. There's nothing to it. Just pretend you're at a hen party with some of your lady friends."

Sarah Alexander winced. Neither she nor Heather Pearson had been particularly enthused about appearing on the show. They were both familiar — too familiar, they felt — with Larry's program. Once Sarah had even called in when she'd felt driven to respond to some of Larry's chauvinistic pronouncements on working mothers.

Oh well, she thought, as she fielded Larry's small talk, maybe this talk-show ordeal would be worth it if they could show that there was public support for their project. But, God, she didn't like this man — neither his theatrical on-air abrasiveness nor the unctuousness he was now displaying.

Now he was turning his phony charm on Heather, summoning up just the right note of earnestness.

"You ladies certainly have your work cut out for you," he intoned. "The public is getting pretty money-conscious, what with the economy the way it is. And, as you know, when money gets tight, the first thing that's chopped is social programs."

Heather nodded. "Yes, that's probably true," she said, "but there is such a need for this type of facility that we just have to keep pushing and doing our best. I think if more people were just aware of —"

Larry silenced her with a raised hand, looking past her at his producer, who was hand-signalling a countdown from behind the glass of the control booth.

"Good morning and welcome to *Larry's Line*, the people's voice," Larry boomed. "And I'm sure we're going to hear a lot of voices with many valuable comments today. The topic for our first segment is daycare. Do we want it? Do we need it? Or are nurseries and preschool facilities just another cop-out for so-called working mothers who put their careers ahead of their kids?"

Sarah and Heather exchanged alarmed glances.

"In the studio with me are two ladies from the Coalition for Better Child-care, Sarah Alexander and Heather Pearson. Good morning, ladies."

"Good morning," they murmured in unison.

"Well, tell us about it, ladies," Larry said. "Tell us why the taxpayers of Ontario should trip all over themselves in a rush to support still another hand reaching into their wallets."

Sarah cleared her throat. Although she had a set speech prepared, Chambers' prosecuting manner had rattled her. She began tentatively, with a vague sense that some invisible trapdoor had been sprung, and she was falling.

"Well, we don't think providing a proper standard of daycare for the children of women who join the workforce, either through choice or necessity, constitutes a plundering of the public purse. And we also don't think that women who want to provide a better standard of living for their kids than they can get on welfare are abandoning their children by taking jobs.''

"Sure, sure," Larry said brusquely, "we've all heard the apple-pie-and-motherhood clichés and the fancy social-work rhetoric, but what it boils down to is that a lot of kids are deprived of a mother's care when they're shipped off to these — these child-care warehouses. You surely can't expect someone who's getting minimum wage and probably doesn't know the first thing about raising kids to give them the love and understanding they deserve, can you?''

"That's why we want to secure an adequate level of funding — so we can get qualified people to provide high-quality care while allowing women to further their careers and give *to* rather than take *from* society." Sarah was at ease now, sure of herself and her argument. She felt she'd scored some points and was reassured by Heather's smile.

"Well, so much for idealism," Larry snapped. "Let's go to the people. Let's hear from you folks out there. What do you think of the provincial government coughing up your hard-earned tax dollars to subsidize a child-care operation that sounds suspiciously like what they've got in Russia where kids are taken away from their parents and raised by the state?

"You know," he went on, his voice becoming husky with emotion, "the thought of some innocent little tyke growing up without knowing a mother's love and care fills me with a pain I can't describe. But that's what appears to be happening in this day and age just so *career*" — he made the word sound like an obscenity — "women can steer clear of changing their kids' diapers and doing the breakfast dishes."

Flushed with anger, Sarah started to respond but, by then, the phone panel had turned into a rectangle of blinking lights as a half-dozen callers were put on hold. Larry punched a button and bawled:

"Good morning, caller. What have you got to say to my guests this morning?''

The voice was creaky with age and tinged with the resentment of one who had been relegated to the role of spectator rather than player in the game of life.

"God bless you for setting these *women*" — her inflection invested the word with the same opprobrium that Larry had earlier attached to "career" — "straight. I've never heard such god-awful claptrap in all my born days."

Larry recognized her voice. She was one of his regulars, a member of his senior-citizen cheering section whose prejudices were her strongest link to a world she neither understood nor particularly cared for. Like many of the show's long-time listeners, she could be counted on to rise to Larry's inflammatory bait.

"Anything else to say about our topic?" he prompted. "As always, you tell it like it is."

"Well, uh . . . I just . . . I mean . . . ." she began haltingly.

"How about the cost?" Larry coaxed. "Do you think Queen's Park should be playing surrogate mother at the taxpayers' expense? Do you think you and a lot of others who put their shoulders to the wheel to make this country great should have to pay for socialized diaper-changing so a gang of part-time mothers can keep from getting their hands dirty?"

"No way," she quavered. "There's too many want something for nothing as it is. Why, when I was a young woman, we all did for ourselves. We cooked and washed and cleaned and made sure our children had proper homes. We made sure they respected their elders and feared the Lord. But these days," she huffed indignantly, "nobody respects nothing — not their parents, their church, or their flag." She paused as though momentarily overwhelmed by the enormity of the tragedy, then rushed on. "And land sakes, the language! You'd think these young people don't know any words longer than four letters. Why, when I was on the streetcar the other day —"

Larry thanked her, his finger poised to terminate the call, but the elderly woman continued her diatribe. "They ought to have their mouths washed out with laundry soap. 'F' this and 'F' that and taking the good Lord's name in vain. And right there on the streetcar. On King Street, it was. Yes, I'm sure it was. But I might be wrong because my memory's not what it used —"

"Well, thanks again for calling," Larry cut in. "Some of your plain, old-fashioned common sense is worth a heckuva lot more than the garbage these social scientists, academics, and bleeding hearts want to feed us."

"Eh, what was that?"

"I was just thanking you for your call, m'dear."

"My . . . ? Oh, my call. You're welcome. Keep up the good work, Larry. Your show is a real blessing to people like me who can't get out much. You stick up for the little person and that's what we need."

"God bless you, luv," he said, breaking the connection and fielding another call all in one motion. It was a male voice this time. Another older, right-wing type riding a tide of righteous anger about "the people who built this country having to pay to bring up other people's brats."

Sounding as if it had been aged in cheap whiskey, the voice railed on. "I already done my duty. I raised my own kids — and damn fine kids they are. Not a one of 'em ever been near a jail or one o' them marijuana cigarettes. Y'know what I mean, eh? No mollycoddling neither, eh? They found out soon enough that a belt can be used for a damn sight more than just holdin' up your pants. Y'know what I mean, eh?"

"Thanks a lot for those words of wisdom, old timer," Larry carolled, breaking the connection and flicking open another line.

It didn't take long for Heather and Sarah to detect the pattern. When Chambers got callers who supported his point of view, he let them ramble on *ad infinitum*. On the other hand, when he found himself confronting people who had opposing views, he either cut them short or infused his comments with generous doses of sarcasm.

With frequent commercial breaks cutting into the program, the two women found that they had precious little time to argue their case and when their segment drew to a close, they felt drained and frustrated. As Larry ushered them out of the studio, he shook their hands perfunctorily and went through a well-practised set-speech.

"I'm sure that you've opened a few eyes and minds with your comments today and that's what it's all about in a democracy — freedom of speech."

Sarah forced a smile. "Yes, you're certainly right about that. Of course, when one particular philosophy controls the lion's share of the media that tends to restrict the dissemination of information, doesn't it?"

Larry shrugged. "Well, that's the way this old world wobbles, isn't it? He who pays the piper calls the tune."

"And so that's the only tune that gets played," Heather interjected.

Larry threw up his hands. "What can I say? I'm just a servant of the people. They're the ones who call the shots and if I didn't realize that, I'd be just another poor schmuck with all the answers but no one to listen to them."

Bob Grey stepped into the hallway and called to Larry. "Thirty seconds, big guy."

"I'm on my way," he replied, giving the women an airy wave as he headed back into the studio. Sarah and Heather exchanged bemused glances, the latter murmuring: "So this is investigative journalism in the big city."

"That's what they tell me," Sarah laughed. "Let's get a cup of coffee. For some strange reason, I have an awfully bad taste in my mouth."

Chapter Two

Jane stretched, arching her body into the sun, as the hot rays washed over her, making her skin tingle. She spread her legs a little and the sensation flowed into her inner thighs. For a moment, she wondered how it would feel to shed her bikini and let the sun work its golden magic over her nipples, down the soft curve of her belly, gliding over the triangle of pubic hair like a gentle hand.

Then, as though awakened from a fitful sleep, she hoisted herself onto her elbows and blinked into the sun. A slow, embarrassed smile spread over her lips. Pretty kinky, she chided herself. The fantasies were becoming more frequent these days, often invading her thoughts at the most inopportune times. Once, she had almost rear-ended a taxi on the 401 when, in her imagination, she had cast herself playing a torrid love scene with her daughter Arlene's riding instructor.

Listening to the soft rock lilting out of Dianne's ghetto blaster, she drained her gin-and-tonic. Housework could wait, she decided. What could be more important at this moment than lounging beside the pool, sorting through her thoughts, and taking stock of her life?

Lately she seemed to have so little time to herself. Either Dianne or Arlene was constantly after her for something or other — more pocket money, a ride to the tennis courts or riding stable, or permission to stay overnight at a friend's house. This morning, however, was sheer bliss, with nothing but herself, the sun, and a tall, cool drink.

The girls had left early for the lake with Jane's sister, Sandy, and her three kids. Poor Sandy, Jane thought, feeling not the slightest bit of remorse at staying behind. Reluctantly, she swung her legs off the chaise longue and got up. She crossed the patio, slid the glass door open, and went into the kitchen to mix another drink. Measuring out an ounce-and-a-half of gin, she carefully poured it into her glass, and then with a smiling "What the hell," splashed in another couple of ounces right from the bottle.

Glass in hand, she returned to the pool and stood there, studying her reflection in the cool, glassy surface. The bouquet from the gin blended with the medicinal odour of chlorine, as she stared down at her full-length image, wondering how long it would be before she looked like the distorted portrait that was thrown back up at her. She sighed. Getting old was such a bitch. Why did it have to happen that way? Just when you started to find out who you were, you began to look like someone else. Why the hell was it that women her age had to spend so much time and money to make sure they didn't *look* like women her age?

She took a deep breath and thrust out her chin defiantly. So I'm not Brooke Shields. I am a mature, sensitive, intelligent, and attractive woman and — she looked down ruefully at her ripe thighs and her self-assurance crumbled — one who probably should go back to aerobics class.

"Hi there! Nice morning, isn't it?"

Jane had no idea how long he'd been standing on the other side of the pool. She felt her face go hot with embarrassment.

Had she been talking to herself out loud? Although she quickly dismissed the idea, she couldn't shake the feeling of having been caught out.

"Oh, you surprised me. How are you, Tod?"

"Pretty good, Mrs. Chambers." In his early twenties, with sun-bleached, long blond hair curling at the nape of his neck, he had the tanned, lean look of a surfer. Faded jeans hung low on his hips and a tightly fitting T-shirt sculpted his hard-muscled upper body. He shielded his eyes and squinted at the sun.

"Looks like it's going to be another scorcher. You're lucky you've got a pool. Sure wish *we* did."

The Welbys and Chamberses had been neighbours for over a decade, sharing barbecues and bridge, and socializing a fair amount. Tod was the Welbys' youngest, attending university in Ottawa but now home for the summer.

"Well, you're welcome to use ours anytime you like," Jane smiled, half-wondering if he'd been dropping a less-than-subtle hint.

He shook his head. "Don't think I'll be able to, at least not today. Mom's got a couple of chores for me. As a matter of fact, that's why I came over. Our hedge trimmer is broken and I've got some yard work to do. I was wondering if I could borrow yours."

By now, he'd skirted the pool and was standing in front of her. She became conscious of his gaze, his eyes only half-meeting hers as they drifted over her shoulders, then lowered, taking in the soft thrust of her breasts. She felt awkward, out of place in her own backyard. There was something else too, a strange feeling, a mixture of resentment and repressed excitement.

Instinctively, she plucked her robe from the chaise longue and draped it around her shoulders. When she turned back to him, whatever darker intent she'd read in his eyes had disappeared. They were clear blue and guileless, looking into hers as he smiled, showing white, even teeth. Returning his smile, she was surprised to find that her relief was tempered with disappointment. And with it came embarrassment at realizing that, all this time, he'd been waiting for an answer.

"Oh, the trimmer," she stammered. "Of course you can borrow it. You can have anything you want, uh, need." She slipped into her thongs. "It must be in the garage. I'll go and get it. You just wait here."

She was glad of the opportunity to flee. What must he think of me? she wondered. Probably thinks I'm some middle-aged airhead who needs daily injections of gin to get through the day.

Squatting at the edge of the pool, Tod watched Jane make a hurried retreat. Wonder what's bothering her, he mused. Looks a little antsy. Maybe — whoa now, Tod boy. That's way too close to home. It's all right to live dangerously, but right next door? Still, he smiled to himself, it would almost be worth it just to shaft that bigmouthed husband of hers.

Before he had enrolled in university, Tod had taken a year off to "find himself" and, during that period, he'd done the entire hippie trip, the shoulder-length hair, drugs, the whole bit. Later he'd discovered that his parents had bared their souls about his antiestablishment lifestyle to Larry, probably figuring that a guy who had all the answers for a couple of hundred thousand listeners could offer a formula for straightening out their kid in no time flat. Old media-mouth had gone even further than giving advice though. He'd gotten on Tod's case himself, giving him the usual, straight-arrow bullshit about getting a good education, selecting the right career, and doing his bit to keep the wheels of Canadian industry turning.

Tod had never gotten over his resentment at this hotshot broadcaster, this megamouth, telling him how he should live his life. Yeah, he'd like to stick it to him all right. Or, if not him. . . .

When Jane returned to the pool, Tod was spinning the dial on the radio. Hearing Larry Chambers' distinctive voice, he stopped and listened for a few moments.

Stereophonic pomposity, he thought, brought into your home through the wonder of modern technology. Jane's voice broke into his interior monologue.

"I'm sorry, Tod. I can't seem to find them. I'm sure they're in there somewhere," she said, gesturing helplessly toward the garage, "but the place hasn't been straightened up in over a year and . . . . . . well . . . . . ." She smiled apologetically.

He stood up and looked directly into her eyes. There was the same disquieting glint she'd seen earlier, a spark of something dark and dangerous. This time though, the flutter in her chest lasted but a few seconds. His boldness no longer threatened her composure. Smiling demurely, just enough to let him know that she knew the game and could play it as well as anyone, she thought of the film, *The Graduate*. Who had made the first move? Mrs. Robinson? Or the kid Dustin Hoffman played? Benjamin, wasn't it?

His eyes hadn't strayed from hers, and the insouciant smile continued to play at the corners of his mouth. But when he spoke, his voice — halting and strained — belied his confident demeanor.

"Uh, that's O.K., I can get them from someone else."

His pectoral muscles heaved against the front of his T-shirt as he took a deep, steadying breath and cast about for another topic of conversation, anything that would keep him there until he could get his head together.

"Uh, while you were in the garage, I was listening to Mr. Chambers' show." Jane almost burst out laughing when he added, somewhat incongruously, "*Larry's Line*. Uh, do you listen to it much?" he finished lamely.

The question was so unexpected that it took a few seconds to register.

"What? Oh, Larry's show. No, uh, that is, not all the time." She gave him a conspiratorial look. "Now, I don't want you to breathe a word of this to anyone, not even your parents, because it may sound a little disloyal but, frankly, after a while, all his shows start to sound alike to me. Same issues. Same people saying the same things in the same way. You know what I mean?''

"Well, I guess it's not easy trying to fill three hours of air time five times a week," he offered. Jane's robe had fallen open and Tod let his glance drop to her breasts, which were only marginally covered by the flimsy top. Hell, he thought, if she doesn't mind showing them, I don't mind looking. Then, cocking his head toward the radio, he asked, "Who's that he's got on now? She seems like quite a performer."

She felt a flush of pleasure. I was right, she thought. I am still one helluva good-looking woman and this kid knows it. She forced herself to focus on the voices wafting out of the ghetto blaster.

"Oh, she's been on a number of times. She's one of those — I think it's fashionable to call them psychics. But, as far as I'm concerned, she's no different from any run-of-the-mill card reader or astrologer."

Tod looked genuinely interested. "You mean people still go for that stuff — horoscopes, crystal balls, and all that garbage? I thought only subscribers to the *National Enquirer* went for jive like that. You know, the kind of people who think aliens are walking among us and using their extraterrestrial powers to neutralize our mental processes and make us vote Conservative."

"Watch it," she said, feigning indignation, "I happen to be a true-blue Tory and proud of it."

Tod made a face. "So are my parents. But like I was saying, I really can't see why anyone would take all this psychic b.s. seriously."

"You'd be surprised," Jane smiled. "Larry says that psychics pull in some of his largest audiences. Every time he has one on, the last thing he has to worry about is filling dead air. It's one call after another."

"Man, isn't that a great commentary on civilized

society," Tod groaned. "I wonder what my psych prof would say about that."

"Probably the same thing I do," she said. "That a lot of people are so desperate for answers — any answers — that they're ready to grasp at any straw that's offered to them whether by a psychic, a fortune teller or —"

"A radio hot-line host?" he laughed.

She shrugged, giggling. His eyes met hers, probing gently.

"How about you? What's your straw?" he asked softly. "Or maybe someone like you, who's so together — looks, personality, the whole bit — never gets desperate."

She raised her eyebrows skeptically. "What are you majoring in at college? Advanced Flattery?" Her expression softened; she seemed to be speaking as much to herself as to him. "We're all desperate at some time or other and it can either be in the middle of an endless, sleepless night or —" she threw back her head and squinted at the sun, "under the hottest sun and clearest sky of a beautiful summer day."

When she turned back to him, Tod was touched by her wistful expression. He could feel her sadness and it frightened him. But in the next instant, the spell was broken, exorcized by her brittle laughter.

"Speaking of desperation," she said, "at this very moment, I am totally, unutterably desperate for another drink. Would you care for something?"

"Yeah, I would," he said huskily.

"Well, you came to the right place," she said gaily. "It wouldn't be very neighbourly of me to let you die of thirst, would it?"

He followed her through the patio door, watching the swivel of her hips beneath the clinging robe. She mixed a couple of gin-and-tonics and handed him one.

"You know," she said matter-of-factly, "I think this is the first time we've ever had a drink together."

"Cheers," he smiled, saluting her with the glass.

"I hope your parents won't think I'm corrupting you."

"I'm not exactly an angel, you know," he said with an air of studied worldliness.

"Oh, aren't you?" she asked, clapping her hands in mock surprise. "How disappointing."

As though in response to some hidden signal, he set down his glass on the kitchen counter and moved slowly toward her. She looked at him uncertainly, then stepped forward, gazing into his eyes, searching for something, as he cupped her face in his hands. He brushed his lips over her eyelashes, then her mouth. She craned her head, pressing her lips fiercely against his. Their hot, ragged breath mingled.

His mouth found her neck, sending a cold rush down her spine. Burying his face in the fragrance of her hair, he ran his fingertips lightly over her shoulders. Their moans and murmurs rose above the steady whirr of the air-conditioner, as her robe dropped to the floor and his strong hands hungrily explored her breasts.

She clutched at him, raking his back with her fingernails, pulling him closer, grinding her hips against him, and feeling him grow hard. His hand stroked her inner thigh and she let out a long, shuddering breath. Then abruptly, she pulled away.

"Wait."

"For what?" he asked hoarsely. He was breathing heavily, his mouth partly open and his wheat-coloured hair was matted on his forehead. She brushed his lips with her fingertips, and then walked over to lock the patio door. When she turned to face him, his eyes glistened with desire and an erection strained against the worn denim of the close-fitting jeans. A smile of pure triumph slowly spread over Jane's face.

"For this."

With a couple of deft hand movements and a provocative shimmy, she stepped out of her bikini bottom and slowly glided toward him. Taking his hand, she began to lead Tod toward the stairs. And as the door to Jane and Larry's bedroom clicked shut, the ghetto blaster continued to play beside the cool, shimmering pool.

A young, female caller: "I was born on October 27th and I'd like to know if I'm going to meet a new guy, like in the next couple of weeks."

The psychic: "I see you meeting someone. He is new to the city and lonely and will be grateful for your friendship. But I must warn you not to rush into a relationship. Like most Scorpios, you are impetuous and tend to leap before you look. I would advise you to examine your feelings very closely before you make any sort of emotional commitment."

Larry: "I'm afraid I'm going to ring down the curtain on today's edition of *Larry's Line*. But I'll be back tomorrow morning at nine with another three hours of entertainment, opinions, and hard-hitting investigative journalism. That's it for my time. Thank you for yours."

Harrison Riley stepped out of his Rolls in front of the Windsor Arms, telling his driver to pick him up at two. That would be enough time to straighten out this talk-show business, he thought. Ordinarily, Harrison didn't involve himself in such trivial matters as ratings, but this hot-line show, was a special case. Even though he had extensive holdings in all facets of the media, ranging from a chain of newspapers to a half-dozen TV stations, CKAL held a special place in his heart. It was the flagship radio station of his nationwide fleet — the number one station in the number one market in the country.

He smiled, acknowledging the effusive greeting of the Courtyard Café's *maitre d'*. He liked the decor and the bright spaciousness of the posh Yorkville eatery although, if pressed to characterize it, he would probably have settled on "Art Deco greenhouse." But the ambiance was only part of the reason, he liked the Courtyard, though. The restaurant's clientele was the other. He enjoyed being recognized by the chic and sleek, the movers and shakers in Toronto's mass media and performing arts establishments.

Of course, not all of those sipping Perrier with a practised nonchalance were on their way up. It wasn't hard to spot the losers — the out-of-work broadcast executives in expensive but outdated suits and the down-at-the-heels actors and directors whose brittle smiles and too-loud laughter were intended to deflect attention from the desperation in their eyes.

The has-beens and never-wases. Their voices rose above the normal buzz of luncheon discussion, trumpeting about deals, projects, and contracts. Producers whose sole credits were a couple of long-forgotten National Film Board shorts. Directors during the CBC's golden age of drama who would now cut each other's throats to get an assignment directing a detergent commercial. He knew most of them, for in his early years, Harrison Riley had dabbled in just about every area of the broadcasting business, including copywriting, producing, and announcing. But it wasn't long before he had discovered where the real power and money lay.

He'd started by buying a small-town radio station and had never looked back. Over the past twenty years, he'd put together a communications empire of such dimensions that he'd had to use all the political clout he could muster to fend off the Combines Branch. A couple of years back, when the economy tightened up and he found himself financially overextended, it had looked as if he might have to sell off some of his holdings. But he'd been lucky. He'd managed to find a backer who was willing to inject enough capital to put Horizon Investments back on an even keel. And if he now had a silent partner, so what? Jack Lexer was still just one of many minority shareholders; it was he, Harrison Riley, who called the shots and would continue to do so.

In his late fifties and with a full head of silver hair, he looked every inch the tycoon. Regular squash games kept him trim and at six-feet-two, his physical presence commanded nearly as much respect as his Bay Street baron status.

The *maitre d'* ushered him to his usual corner table, where

Larry and Ken, already sipping on cocktails were waiting.

"Hope I haven't kept you gentlemen waiting too long," Harrison said, waving them back into their seats as he slid into a chair next to Larry. "That damn traffic is getting worse every day. I think I was better off when I used to take the good old TTC."

Yeah, sure, it must be a real hardship being chauffeured around in a Rolls, Larry thought, laughing politely. Harrison took some cigars out of the inside pocket of his jacket and offered them around. Ken declined but Larry took one and flicked his lighter, igniting Riley's cigar first.

They both took deep, satisfied puffs and, after ordering a drink, Riley lost no time in coming to the point.

"It's probably no secret — both of you fellows have known me for several years — that I take a personal interest in all my holdings. With some guys, the only story they're interested in is the one on the balance sheet. Am I making money or losing it? But that's not my style. As far as I'm concerned, the mass-communication industry already has too many fast-buck artists for its own good."

Larry and Ken nodded solemnly.

"Informing the public is a sacred trust and we should never forget that," he said, wagging his forefinger for emphasis. "So how do we uphold this trust?" he asked rhetorically. "Well, I'll tell you. It's by convincing people — the young, the old, and everyone in between — that we're more capable than anyone else of giving them what they want. Now, I'm not talking about pandering," he said quickly. "But I *am* saying that it's our duty to be aware of, and responsive to, their interests and concerns."

Larry caught Ken's eye and sensed they were sharing the same thought: Why didn't the guy get to the point? After all, it wasn't as if they didn't know why they were here. He tried to convey an expression of interest while across the table Ken Jessup was hanging on Riley's every word as if it were holy writ.

"Yes, we have to fulfil our obligation to the public," Harrison droned on, "because if we don't, we'll soon find there won't be anyone out there watching, reading, or listening to our product. Then we'd really be shit-out-of-luck." He leaned forward and smiled conspiratorially. "Hey, we might even have to go and work for a living."

"Perish the thought," Larry grinned.

"Work?" Ken frowned theatrically. "What's that?"

"We're all too old to want to find out," Harrison smiled. But in the next instant, he was all business again. "O.K., so it looks like we have a slight case of falling ratings, am I right?"

Ken nodded glumly while Larry studied Riley warily, trying to anticipate his next comment and prepare an adequate response.

"Well," Harrison continued, "I've got some ideas about how we can deal with that and I'm sure you fellows have, too." He looked from one to the other as Larry and Ken struggled to convey a semblance of confidence. Taking a deep drag on his cigar, Harrison exhaled expansively. "Yes, we're going to take care of this problem all right." His gaze perched first on Ken, then shifted to Larry and his voice became steely. "And we're going to do it before the next rating book comes out."

Ken cleared his throat to speak, thought better of it, and looked entreatingly at Larry.

"That's a pretty tall order," Larry began slowly. "You know the way things work in this business. People are attracted to something new, especially when it's hyped like the second coming of Christ. We'll get 'em back though. We'll turn it around. I've got —"

"Exactly three months," Harrison said curtly.

"Hey, no sweat," Larry said airily. "We've been through the same schmeer a half-dozen times. But why the panic?" Catching the angry glint in Riley's eyes, he instantly regretted his choice of words.

"Panic?" Harrison smiled thinly. "Did I give you the impression that I'm seized by panic or some other irrational impulse? That's very interesting."

"That's not what I meant," Larry apologized. "What I mean is that I've never seen you so concerned about the results of a single rating period."

"Well, Larry," Harrison said slowly. "It's not so much the fact that we're dropping in the ratings as much as who's gaining."

"CKLB," offered Larry.

"Trent Ferguson," added Ken.

"Wrong, gentlemen," Harrison snapped. "Ben Abelson."

Ken frowned in puzzlement. "Abelson? You mean the guy who owns all those appliance stores?"

"That's right. I just found out that he swung a deal for the majority shares in Select Broadcasting. He's calling the shots over there now and that sonuvabitch has been out to get me for years, ever since I blocked his bid to join the Upper Canada Club." He snorted. "The bloody nerve of the guy! His old man ran a fruit stand in Kensington Market for Chrissake! That pushy bastard paid an arm and a leg to get Ferguson," Harrison continued. "Christ, the guy must have been making well over a hundred thousand with ABC and my sources tell me he's getting a helluva lot more than that now."

Larry whistled admiringly. "Well, that's a good piece of change. But he may as well make hay while the sun shines because its going to be a strictly short-term proposition."

"That's what I like to hear," Harrison chortled. "That's the old CKAL spirit." Then, abruptly his face clouded and he said sternly, "Boys, it's very important that Abelson doesn't get the upper hand and I don't just mean financially. Sure, the more listeners we attract, the more advertising revenue we pull in. Hell, that's a fact of life." He smiled slyly. "I wouldn't want this to get around but I can live with a little less profit. But what I can't live with —" His lips curled in disdain, "is that goddamn Jew-boy putting one over on me. You hear what I'm saying?"

Ken was taken aback by the racial slur but knew enough not to show it. It was Riley's business if he was anti-Semitic. He called the shots. And, anyway, it wasn't up to radio station managers to wage personal crusades against bigotry. Hell, that's why they had all these human rights councils and antidefamation leagues, wasn't it?

Harrison hailed the waiter and the three men placed their orders. Larry was anything but hungry, though. All he could think about was a double-shot of smooth, well-aged Scotch coursing down his throat, igniting the warmth in his belly. But what he felt instead was a sharp pain, like a hand gripping his insides, squeezing tighter and tighter. His goddamn ulcer has sure picked a helluva time to act up, he moaned to himself. Must be stress, and no goddamn wonder. Talk about being on a hot seat. What the hell did Riley want him to do? Carry the flag for the Aryan race? He was smack in the middle of a high-stakes game of one-upmanship and would have to make damn sure that Harrison Riley didn't come out second-best.

"Larry, Ken," Harrison reached over and placed a fatherly hand on each man's shoulder, "I've got a world of confidence in both of you. I want you to know that. That's why I thought we should get together today."

He hooked his thumbs in the vest of his dark pinstripe suit and leaned back in his chair. "Remember when we were in a bit of a valley back in '81 and you guys pulled us out? Some great stuff that year, especially that show where you had those guys from the Canadian chapter of the Ku Klux Klan. Our ratings went sky-high for that period."

Ken stroked his chin reflectively. "Yeah, they sure did. But on the down side, that show sure brought a lot of loonies out of the woodwork. God, it was scary how many of our callers agreed with those wackos."

"Hey, but the dynamics were great, weren't they?" Larry bubbled. "Classic conflict situation. Bleeding-heart liberals on one side and rabid rednecks on the other. Man, it had the same elements — the same clash of philosophies — as the William Buckley–Gore Vidal debates — when was that? 1960?"

Minus the wit and depth, Ken thought to himself. But again, he kept silent. He was forty-three, with a small family and a big mortgage, and station manager jobs didn't grow on trees. He didn't delude himself about his importance to CKAL. He was the manager but Larry was the star, the draw for the advertisers.

Harrison Riley slapped the table in agreement. "That's right. And that's what we need a lot more of. Dynamics. Conflict. Raw emotion. We need issues that'll grab Joe and Jane Lunchpail by their privates, and guests that are prepared to let it all hang out. Forget ideas. Ideas are for books and people who have time to read them. We've got to hit people where they live. We've got to make 'em laugh and cry. That's the trouble with this country — too much emotional constipation!"

Larry winced inwardly as Riley continued his sermon. "Lately, *Larry's Line* has just been skimming the surface. We've got to get underneath, tap the secret fears and simmering anger. We've got to get people to take a stand — to care about themselves, their country and, above all, CKAL." He pronounced the call letters with something bordering on reverence.

The waiter returned with their meals and they ate in relative silence. Ken realized that Riley was expecting not only feedback but concrete answers, but, although his mind had been racing furiously, he kept coming up empty. Finally, as they were finishing their liqueurs, desperation rather than inspiration drove him to take the initiative.

"Well," he began tentatively, "I don't have to tell you that Larry and I —" he looked to his colleague for confirmation, "are just as concerned as you are about our —" He was about to say "slide" but checked himself, substituting "numbers." "But I can promise you that we have no intention of rolling over and playing dead. We've got some dynamite stuff on the back burner that'll blow Ferguson's mind."

Larry's eyebrows peaked in surprise while Riley's expression remained fixed, an amalgam of expectancy and skepticism.

"Well, actually," Ken hedged, "Larry's the one who's been doing most of the brainstorming. I've been spending a lot of time on budgeting these days. And then there's our proposal for changing the FM frequency. . . ."

So that's the game, Larry told himself. The old pass-the-buck, we're-all-in-this-together-but-some-more-than-others caper. He glared at Ken as sweat began to seep into his armpits. Gotta tap dance, stall for time. While his mind darted about like a caged rat, he tried to appear cool and self-assured. Broadcasting executives were like wolves. If you kept them off balance you were safe, but once they smelled your fear you were dead meat.

"As Ken said," Larry began, "I've been looking at a couple of things that I'm sure will help us reclaim our audience share. And I'm sure our illustrious station manager —" he looked pointedly in Ken's direction, "would have made a valuable contribution if he hadn't been tied up with other things." He smiled engagingly and added with an unconvincing earnestness, "I'm sure they were pretty important as well." His face a picture of innocence, Larry gloated inwardly. He'd read it right. Riley's eyes narrowed and his face darkened.

"There is —" his eyes stabbed Ken, "nothing, I repeat, *nothing* more important than shoving it up Ben Abelson's ass and breaking it off. Do I make myself clear?"

Ken nodded vigorously and looked down at the table. Riley shifted his gaze back to Larry and smiled. "Well, I'm glad you're on top of it. How long do you think it'll be before we're back in the driver's seat?"

Larry puffed out his cheeks and thought for a few seconds before replying. "Should be able to pull it off for the next ratings book," he said matter-of-factly. "This Ferguson guy is all glitz. He's the fucking Julio Iglesias of the airwaves. But the man's got no substance. Shit, I was breaking stories when he was sending audition tapes to five-thousand-watt stations in Fargo and Peoria.

"Good stuff," Harrison beamed. "And when we're back on top, I'm really gonna rub Abelson's nose in it." Then he leaned forward, smiling expectantly. "O.K., what've you got? What's the strategy?"

All the while, Larry's mind had been churning, dredging up ideas, only to dispiritedly allow them to sink back into oblivion. But suddenly, like the fluke solving of a Rubic's cube, the colours and pattern clicked into place.

"Well," he said, "I've been thinking it might be time to do some real ass-kicking, law-and-order stuff. You know —" he lowered his voice dramatically, "is it safe for you to take a walk in your own neighbourhood? Are your children walking targets for perverts and punks? Is the inner-city becoming a haven for hookers, purse-snatchers, and winos? Is Toronto the Good rapidly degenerating into Toronto the Bad and the Ugly?"

Larry was warming to his spiel now, the words pouring out effortlessly, his face and hands adding texture to his performance.

"We'll get this town so wired up the politicians'll be shitting bricks and the cops'll have to stop doing their patrolling in donut shops and maybe start wandering into high crime areas once in a while just to make it look good."

Larry completed his pitch and waited. The three men sat like huddled statues while around their island of silence, the sound of clinking glasses and animated chatter hovered like an invisible cloud. Larry and Ken discreetly scanned Riley's face, searching for some sign. Finally, his stony expression softened. First the lips, then the eyes.

"It sounds good," he said cautiously, still not willing to show more than a single card. "But what else have we got, in case this doesn't fly? Don't you think we need more than one arrow in our quiver?"

Larry was quick to press his advantage and build on his employer's positive reaction. "No problem. This abortion thing is still going hot-and-heavy even though it's been off the front pages for a while. We've already had pro-choice groups on a couple of times and we've given equal time to anti-abortion advocates. But we've never had the two sides on together. We put them on head-to-head and it's a whole new ball game — an entirely new dimension to an issue that's already turned average, law-abiding citizens into violent vigilantes.

"A couple of weeks ago, there was a clash between the pro-choice and anti-abortion factions in front of the Harbord Street clinic and if the cops hadn't been there, who the hell knows what might've happened. Feelings are running high and if we can bring that kind of raw emotion into the studio, it would be nothing short of dynamite. Christ, we may even be able to bait the spokesmen for the opposing factions to take a swing at each other."

"Well, there's no denying that abortion is a critical issue," Harrison nodded. "And there's no better way of dealing with contentious issues than giving them a full airing. That's the biggest safety valve we've got in Canada — the chance for people to let off steam. Without it, God knows what mischief they'd get up to." He split his gaze between Larry and Ken.

"Gentlemen, it's apparent that my confidence in you has been well-founded. These programming initiatives seem like just the ticket to knock even the most jaded listener on his ass. I can't tell you how relieved I am," he said sombrely. "We've had a lot of productive years together and I'd hate to have to think about making adjustments to such an enduring part of Horizon Investments' corporate family."

Making adjustments, Larry repeated to himself. A nice antiseptic term for giving the chop to a couple of guys who'd busted their asses for over a decade to make sure that Harrison Riley got a fair return for his investment dollar. He gulped back the bitterness and forced a smile.

"We'll be back on track in no time," he said, turning to Ken. "Right, pardner?"

"You got it, buddy," Ken replied, then turned to Riley with a worried look, "but it's going to kick the shit out of our budget. We're gonna have to do some heavy promotion — TV, print, the whole works."

Harrison waved a hand in dismissal. "Whatever it takes. No matter how much it costs, do it." Then, glancing at his watch, he signed the cheque and pushed himself away from the table. "Gotta run, but it's been great seeing you fellows again. Really great. Just like old times."

He shook hands with the two men and took a few steps before wheeling around and adding, "I'll be checking from time to time just to see how things are going."

To Larry, the comment was redundant. It was common knowledge that Riley had eyes and ears in every part of his corporate empire and there was no reason to think that CKAL was any different. It could be anyone: the controller, the sales manager, anyone. He felt a tightness in his chest. Even Ken.

Ken and Larry watched as the aristocratic-looking executive made his way toward the front of the café, stopping to exchange pleasantries with some CBC upper-echelon bureaucrats in three-piece corporate uniforms. Then, as he moved on, they saw him stop near a window table and extend his hand. The man who took it was rotund, bald, and wore black, horn-rimmed glasses.

"Well, I'll be . . ." Ken shook his head in wonderment.

"What? Who is that guy?" Larry asked.

"None other than our boss' chief nemesis. Abelson. Ben Abelson."

Larry craned his head to look more closely. "That's the guy Riley's got the hard-on over?"

"In the flesh," Ken said, watching the two media moguls pump hands and exchange broad smiles.

Larry turned to Ken, grinning, "What's that saying? It'd be a great world if everyone was as nice to you as the person who's out to shiv you?"

Ken smiled thinly. "Yeah, it's quite a performance, isn't

it? Kind of reminds me of you and Trent Ferguson when you run into each other at the press club.''

"C'mon," Larry said defensively, "I've got nothing personal against Trent. It's just that he's a pretender to the throne and this king isn't about to let himself get deposed by Ferguson or anyone else. You know what this business is like. Second place is a ticket to the boondocks and that's one ride I'm not going to take." His eyes were flinty. "I'm going to be on top again and that's where I'm going to stay, no matter what it costs, no matter what it takes."

They were almost at the station when Ken stopped and faced Larry, "Don't you ever wonder whether it's worth it?"

Larry frowned, genuinely puzzled by the question, "What? Is what worth it?"

"The pressure. The game. The life-and-death struggle for the hearts and minds of people we don't know or give a shit about."

Larry chuckled dryly, "To tell you the truth, I can't say I think about it."

"You don't? You really don't think about what you do or why?"

"You know what I think about?" Larry flared. "I think about how many asses I had to kiss to get where I am." His face reddened and his eyes bulged with anger. "Now, it's my turn. I paid my dues. I've got a house with a pool and a new Cadillac and all those cocksuckers who call me Mighty Mouth behind my back can take a good suck of my left one!"

Abruptly, he wheeled and strode into the station, leaving Ken with a vague sense of disquiet. Ken tried to put a label on the feeling. Was it fear for his job? After all, his ass was on the line as well as Larry's. Or was it guilt at laying the burden of chalking up better ratings on the hot-line host?

Finally, he gave up, shrugging his shoulders in resignation, accepting without being able to explain a premonition that something had been set in motion, some force beyond his control that would have a profound effect on his life.

Chapter Three

Pete Gossett yawned as he ran his hand over his stubbled chin and squinted into the bathroom mirror. He ran a comb through his tangle of dark hair, still wet from the shower that had only partly awakened him. It was mid-morning, but he still felt drugged with sleep. Thank God he didn't have to report for work until noon, he thought, staring at his image, struck by the way the eyes seemed so much older than the rest of his face. Picking up a pair of scissors, he trimmed the thick moustache that was threatening to overrun his upper lip. Then he lathered his face and began to shave. This may well turn out to be the most challenging part of my day, he told himself, cutting a swath through the shaving cream with the safety razor.

"Ow! Hell!"

A little patch of blood seeped through the snowy foam covering his throat. He stared at it fixedly, fascinated by the stark contrast between the tiny splash of crimson and the white shaving cream. His mind flashed on a long-stored image: an effigy of Christ dangling from the cross, the torso milky-white, the hands and feet streaked bright red.

He'd seen it in some out-of-the-way church in the Gaspé, on a backpacking trip right after he had graduated from the University of Toronto. He remembered looking up at the sad, stoical face and feeling the tears flood his eyes — deeply moved but not knowing why. Hell, he still didn't know. He was reasonably sure his reaction had had little, if anything, to do with the suffering and sacrifice of a man who'd given his life to save mankind. Pete had been a journalist for fourteen years and if mankind had been saved, it was sure as hell news to him.

No, the best he could think of was that the plaster effigy symbolized all of society's victims, all the sad, frightened, and damaged people who are chewed up and spit out by the ego-trippers and power-brokers of the world. Yeah, if there was one thing he knew about, it was victims. As a crime reporter, Pete had come face to face with hundreds of them. He'd interviewed women whose infant daughters had been raped and mutilated; men whose sons had been stabbed to death in barroom brawls. Their stories had all been different but their faces had shown the same numb grief.

He'd often wondered why they agreed to talk to the media and expose their agony to the world. He guessed the pain was so heavy that it helped to share it with someone, anyone — even those, like himself, for whom human misery was a product to be packaged, promoted, and sold. Where Willy Loman's stock-in-trade was a shoeshine and a smile, Pete relied on sound instincts, dogged determination, and a strong stomach. The result was the same though: making a sale, whether it was drygoods or hard news.

The crime beat had been a large part of Pete's life, perhaps the biggest part for several years. And, in spite of the constant exposure to every variation of human degradation, it was something he still couldn't get out of his blood. Living on the edge, moving in a netherworld of crooked cops, psychopaths, and dope pushers had given him a rush.

It was like being a war correspondent and having the battle zone within commuting distance. No passport. No overseas flight. Just a twenty-minute subway ride and there you are.

Yeah, there was a war on all right. There was no major theatre of battle, no mass confrontation of opposing forces. It was a hit-and-run, guerrilla style of campaign and it was being waged in every major city in North America.

Pete had done a tour of duty on urban battlefields all across Canada. He'd won his share of decorations, too. In 1980, he'd chalked up a national award for investigative journalism for his exposé of a loanshark operation run as a kind of cottage industry by one of Toronto's top criminal lawyers. Another of his front-page exclusives had generated so much heat that the boys in blue were forced to move against a prostitution ring that had cornered more than half of the city's flesh-peddling market.

But every time he opened a fresh can of worms, whether it involved organized crime, corrupt politicians, or feeble law enforcement, he made as many enemies as admirers. Even within his own newsrooms. There was the endless wrangling with editors who didn't know their asses from their computer terminals and company lawyers who thought the motto on a newspaper masthead should read: "Truth, Justice, and the Avoidance of Lawsuits at All Costs."

After the skirmishes, came the heavy stuff. Requests for his resignation and finally, his outright dismissal from his last three jobs. He slipped into a pair of jeans and a brown corduroy jacket, his post-hippie, quasi-antiestablishment costume, and gulped down some instant coffee.

Well, at least he didn't have to worry about any static now. He was in a safe harbour, covering the sports beat for the *Herald*. He'd come full circle, ending up where he'd begun as a cub reporter over a dozen years ago. And he knew he wouldn't even have this job if it weren't for Jake Botting, the sports editor. Jake had been his mentor in the old days and had put in a good word for him when the city editor bleated that hiring him would be asking for trouble.

After all, Jake had argued, what harm could Pete do reporting box scores and interviewing wide receivers and designated hitters?

So now Pete at least had a steady pay cheque but, God, he wanted to be back on the crime beat so badly he could almost taste it. The scent of a good story in his nostrils. The thrill of the hunt. Digging, sifting, and finally uncovering a nugget of crucial information.

At least he was still in the business, even if he was treading water, waiting for a chance to do what he knew best and cared about most. He'd have to be patient but it wasn't easy, especially now that he'd found someone who'd rekindled his sense of wonderment at how much pleasure one person could give another. He'd met Elaine Steele at the press club a couple of months ago and they'd hit it off immediately. One of the things he liked about her was that she didn't trade on her sex appeal, and God knows she had more than her share. Her large, expressive eyes spoke a language all their own, answering questions he hadn't asked. She was also witty and intelligent. Hell, she had to be. After all, hadn't she been aware of his reputation as an investigative journalist and even able to recall some of the details of a couple of his major scoops?

They'd laughed a lot that first evening. Lunch had led to dinner and casual hours to passionate nights. And the funny thing was, the intensity hadn't waned. There were no valleys, just higher and higher peaks. Last night had been the best yet. Remembering her sweet smell and taste made him grow hard. He yawned and stretched. He was paying for it now though. It must have been after four A.M. when he'd finally dragged himself home. And dragged was the word. Well, that was the way it was when you put on a few years, he guessed. He was almost grateful when she shooed him out of her apartment, telling him she had to get up early.

He cast a baleful look around his own apartment, taking in the scattered clothing, the unmade bed, and the pile of dishes that'd been soaking in the kitchen sink since the day before. He shook his head disgustedly. He had to do something about the place. With every passing day, it was looking more and more like a garage sale.

The strange thing was that while he adopted a *laissez-faire* attitude toward his living quarters and his personal appearance — dressing for comfort rather than style — when it came to his job, he was close to being a perfectionist. His filing cabinet, rooted in one corner of the cluttered bedroom, was crammed with reference material, everything carefully filed and cross-indexed for easy retrieval. And the top of the desk that squatted beside it displayed only his typewriter and some office supplies which were laid out with military precision. But if Pete was aware of the contradiction between his personal and business life, he had long since given up trying to understand it.

Well, what'll it be? he asked himself. Hose down the dishes and whip up a nice nutritious breakfast or head down to Frank's Cafe and give the old digestive system a quick grease job? One further look at the stacked dishes made the decision for him and as he stepped into the hallway, he made a mental note to buy a package of Rolaids — the large, economy size.

Elaine slouched at her desk, wondering what had transpired at Larry's luncheon with Harrison Riley. When he returned to the station, he'd headed straight for his office, leaving instructions not to be disturbed. It didn't look good. The last thing they needed was more heat. The ratings alone had provided plenty. Things were tense all right. The usual easy banter around the studio had given way to gallows humour. Sample: What do you call the staff of a hot-line show with low ratings? Answer: unemployed.

She glanced resentfully at the door to Larry's office. It wasn't fair. She was a part of the show, too. She had a right to know what was happening. If Larry went down in flames, chances were she'd go with him. She could picture him at his desk, chain-smoking and knocking back Scotch from a mickey that he always kept in his bottom, right-hand drawer.

He thought he was so clever, she smiled to herself. He thought no one was wise to the fact that he nipped at the booze from first thing in the morning until he weaved his way home in the afternoon. She looked at her phone console. The tiny white light signalled that Larry's private line was in use. Well, at least he's not just brooding, she thought. The light blinked off and a few seconds later, his door swung open. He stood in the doorway, his tie askew and his face florid.

"Could you come in here for a moment?"

She caught a whiff of alcohol as soon as she stepped inside the room. He waved her into a chair and settled back behind the desk. The flame from his lighter trembled as he lit a cigarette. He took a series of short, jerky puffs and fixed her with a pale, watery gaze.

"Well, Lainie, my girl, the shit has now officially hit the fan." His voice was harsh and bitter.

"Riley?"

He nodded. "He laid it on the line at lunch. Either we kick Trent Ferguson's ass in the next ratings book or that's all she wrote for yours truly." He chuckled dryly. "And if I know Harrison Riley, I won't be the only one walking the plank."

She shook her head in disbelief. "How could he possibly let you go? You've been number one in your time slot for ten years."

"Twelve," he corrected. "But to guys like him, what you've *done* is old news. The only thing that counts is what you're doing *now*."

"But by the next ratings period? That's crazy. We can't turn it around by then. It could take six months, maybe a year. CKLB is still promoting the hell out of Ferguson's show and for all we know, he may not even have peaked yet."

Larry slammed his fist on the desk. "Fuck Ferguson! We've got to stop looking over our shoulders at the competition and concentrate on what *we* have to do. And that's to put on some shows that'll knock this city on its collective ass. We've got to touch off some fireworks, generate the kind of controversy that'll get people talking about us!''

"What does Ken think?''

Larry laughed mirthlessly. "Ken? I'll tell you what he thinks. He thinks he can save his ass by throwing me to the wolves. That's what he thinks!'' Her incredulous expression fed his wrath. "You don't believe me? Well, you should've been with us at lunch. Our friend and protector, that fine, selfless station manager of ours just about turned himself inside out trying to cover his ass and lay the weight on me.''

She stared at the floor. It was all moving too fast. She was good at sorting things out, putting them in their proper places, weighing their implications. But this was different. Instead of standing on the sidelines — cool, detached, and clinically analytical — this time, she was right in the game. She looked at him blankly.

"Well, where do we go from here?''

His shoulders slumped and his voice seemed tired. "Who knows? I've got a couple of things we can run up the flagpole — abortion, incest, coddling of criminals, that kind of stuff. And Riley's given the go-ahead for a promotional blitz — TV, newspapers, billboards, the whole works.'' He shook his head and exhaled heavily, "but it's still a crapshoot.'' He looked at her wistfully. "You know, there was a time when I knew all the right buttons to push to get a rise out of an audience but now —'' he threw up his hands in defeat, "I don't know, maybe I'm losing my touch.''

"Hey,'' Elaine chided, "that doesn't sound like the Ayotollah of the airwaves we here at CKAL have come to know and love. Where's the old fighting spirit? Where's the old get-up-and-go?''

"It got up and went,'' he quipped.

She was amazed at how much pity she felt for this abrasive, overbearing man, who'd never shown so much as a hint of sensitivity toward her feelings. Although he was of average height, he looked so small hunched over his desk, it was as though his body had shrunk along with his self-confidence.

She tossed off a crisp salute. "Lieutenant Steele awaiting your orders, *mon capitain.*"

Managing a feeble smile, he shoved a notepad across to her. There was a name and phone number scrawled across the top.

"O.K., the first thing I want you to do is call that lady and try to book her for a telephone interview at ten tomorrow morning."

Her eyes dropped to the notepad. "I'm sure Erica Jantzen is a lovely lady and all that, but what is it exactly that makes her newsworthy enough to warrant an appearance on *Larry's Line?*"

"She's the mother of that girl who went missing last week."

"Oh, yeah, I remember. The police have been looking for her, haven't they?"

"As much as they usually do in a case like this," he said. "They usually don't get too excited when a fourteen-year-old disappears for a while, especially the way kids are these days. A lot of them are more at home on the street than with their own families."

"What made you think of booking the mother?"

"I had a couple of drinks with Mike Edwards the other day, trying to find out whether Toronto's finest were working on anything particularly juicy. He said things were pretty slow in homicide but that the Missing Persons people were being swamped and most of the cases involved teenagers. That's when I got the idea of focussing on a typical case and exploring the human interest angle — you know, the torment a parent goes through not knowing whether her kid has taken off, been abducted, or is lying at the bottom of a river."

"And Mrs. Jantzen is the lucky candidate?"

"You got it," he smiled.

"But why tomorrow? That's rushing it a bit, isn't it?"

"Maybe so, but the kid apparently had a few problems, so it's my guess she just took off for a while and could show up back home at any time. If that happens, it's scratch one grief-stricken mother and one potentially dramatic segment, so that's why we've got to grab the Jantzen woman while the grabbing is good."

"O.K., but suppose she doesn't want to go on the air? A lot of parents in her situation wouldn't be keen on talking about it."

Even as she was framing the question, Elaine was aware that she was going beyond playing the devil's advocate. But despite Larry's growing annoyance, she couldn't stop herself. She had a feeling — no, it was more of a premonition — that no good could come from treating a mother's anguish as a spectator sport.

"You tell her we'll give her all the time she wants to say whatever she wants." He paused, his expression hardening. "And tell her that looking for runaways isn't a high priority with the cops and if she wants to see her kid again, her best bet is to play ball with us because I can put a helluva lot more heat on the police than she can."

"That's coming on a little strong, isn't it?"

"We'd better start coming on strong," he snapped. "Otherwise we won't be here. So I suggest you start acting like a researcher and leave the moralizing to 'Dear Abby.' "

"Well, excuse me for having an opinion," she said icily.

He circled the desk and put his hand on her shoulder. "Aw, shit. I'm sorry. I shouldn't be taking it out on you."

"Oh, that's all right," she said breezily. "That's what you pay me the minimum wage for, isn't it?"

He forced a smile. "You got it. And I want you to know you're worth every penny." He pulled on his jacket and straightened his tie. "I'm gonna take off now. I feel like the walls are closing in on me around here."

She nodded sympathetically. "I know how you feel."

He chucked her under the chin. "But don't worry," he

grinned, tapping his temple with a forefinger. "This huge, pulsating brain of mine has just kicked into overdrive and when I'm out of the shithouse and back in the penthouse, you're going to get the biggest raise I can swing."

"I'll remember that."

"You got it, kid," he winked and swaggered out of the office.

She sat there for quite a while thinking about what Larry had said. About Ken. About her. And, most of all, about her future at CKAL being tied to the fortunes of *Larry's Line*. It wasn't fair. She'd worked hard. It wasn't her fault that Larry's on-air persona had begun to wear a little thin after a dozen years. Maybe his warning had just been some kind of psychological ploy, an attempt to spur her on to greater effort.

No, that was wishful thinking. She knew the way this business dealt with failure. It didn't just pluck the flower. It pulled out the plant by the roots. She felt hollow and frightened but the sensation only lasted for a matter of seconds. She was now coolly determined, as though having confronted the worst possible scenario, she was now able to work toward the best. She also had no illusions about what it might involve.

Sorry about that, Larry, she mused, but if the lifeboat only has room for one passenger, I'm going to make damn sure it's reserved for Elaine Steele. Then she picked up the phone and began to dial Erica Jantzen's number.

At the station, Larry had felt claustrophobic. Everything seemed to be pressing in on him — the walls, the furniture, even the glances of his co-workers. A few nips of Scotch usually helped him unwind, but not today. Today, he'd felt as if his skin was a couple of sizes too small. He'd wanted out. Out of his body, his feverish mind, and the room that seemed more like a trap than an office.

But now, as he walked down Yonge Street on his way to the subway, the symptoms were still with him. The voices around him on the crowded sidewalk were walls of sound, constricting his movement, blocking his thoughts. Panic was hot in his throat. He wanted to run but was afraid that if he did, there would be even more people staring at him than there were now. He could feel their eyes. They were as hot as the sun sweeping the canyon between the office towers and low banks of restaurants and shops.

He was at the Bloor station now. In twenty minutes, he'd be in his car, waiting for the air conditioning to refrigerate his body and cool his thoughts. Then when he got home, he'd spend the rest of the afternoon in the pool and maybe barbecue a couple of steaks for dinner.

Just as he was about to push through the Bay entrance, he froze as though caught in a field of opposing forces. Then he felt it. The stirring, gentle at first, hardly noticeable, but getting stronger, more demanding. A part of him tried to resist, to force the surge of longing back into its dark prison. But another reached out, welcoming the current of excitement that was now in his blood, pounding in his temples. He was vaguely aware of the bodies rushing past him then felt a foot on his in-step and a hand roughly shoving him aside.

"Hey, what ya doin', sleepwalkin'?" a voice barked in his ear.

"Huh, what?" By the time he turned his head, the voice had fled into the building.

Slowly, he began to walk away, back onto Yonge Street. Stepping into a drugstore, he found a pay phone and called Jane, telling her that he had a meeting and not to expect him for dinner. Her solicitude surprised him when she cautioned him not to work too hard.

The heat shimmered off the pavement as he headed south on Yonge. Unconsciously, he began to pick up his pace, weaving around sidewalk stragglers. Past the fast-food outlets cheek-by-jowl with exclusive bookstores, boutiques, and martial arts studios.

Stopping in front of a peeling wooden door, he glanced around furtively. Then he pushed it open and closed it quickly behind him. He stood in the tiny hallway leading to the second floor, peering through the dingy glass pane in the door and watching the faces sift by. Able to see without being seen, he felt safe in the semi-darkness. Pulling off his tie and shoving it into his jacket pocket, he slowly started to climb the worn wooden stairs.

A musty smell crept into his nostrils, and although he was ascending, he had the sense of going down into an old, damp cellar. Up he climbed, past the scrawled graffiti and peeling plaster. At the top of the stairs, a single, blue-tinted light bulb waged a futile battle against the dark. He wrinkled his nose at the smells, the ghosts of mealtimes past mingling with the sharp scent of disinfectant.

Larry reached the second-floor landing and crossed over to stand in front of the door to apartment three. He stood there, shifting his weight uncertainly, his finger suspended over the buzzer. The sound of rock music blared out through the oak door, as he stabbed the buzzer and waited. No one came. A heavy-metal guitar solo soared in an ear-splitting crescendo. Larry waited for the music to ebb, then tried again. The volume lowered, then died. He heard some muffled movements, then quick, padding footsteps.

"Who is it?"

He shot a quick look at the door across the hall before replying, "Larry. Larry Chambers."

A chain rattled out of its catch and the door swung open. Larry was immediately greeted by the sweet, subtle scent of marijuana. There was a stronger aroma too. Fresh incense, lit to camouflage the grass but too late to have the desired effect.

"Hi, lover," she cooed. "Wow, is this ever a nice surprise." The voice was warm, lilting. She seemed genuinely glad to see him.

He stepped into the apartment, kicked the door shut, and took her in his arms. He kissed her lingeringly, desperately, not wanting to let the feel and taste of her go. Tearing at her negligee, he dropped to his knees and pressed his face into her soft, warm belly. Tracing a pattern with his tongue, he clasped her tight, high buttocks with both hands and pulled her close to him, still closer, as his mouth probed lower, deeper. Her thighs opened, accepting, inviting. He moaned gently as she stroked his hair and crooned comfortingly. His body shuddered. His breath caught, and then was released in a long, tremulous sigh as softly, he began to cry.

Chapter Four

Holly Gains lay back in the tub. The water was almost up to her chin and the foam from the bubble bath tickled her neck. She'd loved bubble baths ever since she could remember, which hadn't been that long, because she was only sixteen now. She could stay in the tub for hours, locked in her own little world where the air was sweet and the bubbles so clean and shiny. It was such a different world from the one out *there*. She scooped up a handful of froth and rippled it with her breath.

With her other hand, she reached for the joint in the ashtray perched on the edge of the tub. Holding the joint gingerly between her fingertips, she took one last drag. The heat from the smouldering fragment seared her fingers and she quickly flicked it into the toilet bowl. She flapped her arms under the water, making the surface swirl. She closed her eyes and the dark silence was broken only by the drip of the tap at her feet. Then colours began to unreel through her mind, changing from patterns to images. It was like watching a cross between a bright tapestry and a Gothic comic strip. God, is this weed great or what? she marvelled. She'd done mushrooms and acid that didn't get her off this much.

She hoisted herself up in the tub and looked closely at her breasts. Firm, upthrust, with jutting nipples. Then she studied the little islands of discolouration on the pale skin. Skimming over them with her fingertips, she felt a mild twinge of pain.

Christ, she thought, this sucker was really turning into a bad trick. It was the booze, she concluded. Whenever he was pissed, it was like all the ugly, violent stuff he usually kept inside came out, she thought, shivering at the recollection. The way he'd squeezed and twisted her flesh, it was like she wasn't even human. Thank Christ he didn't want to tie her up, because he looked so spun out that she would have had to tell him to take a hike. And that would've got her in deep shit with Speedy. She remembered Speedy's orders: give him anything he wants, on the house. She smiled in self-satisfaction. Well, what Speedy didn't know wouldn't hurt him and, more importantly, hurt her.

Even though the john — this Larry what's-his-face — was supposed to get freebies, he'd gotten into the habit of laying twenty or thirty bucks on her each time — a "tip," he'd called it. She stepped out of the tub, towelled herself off, and still nude, walked over to the window and looked out. The sun had dropped behind the office buildings and the street lay in heavy shadow.

In a couple of hours, she'd be at her usual spot on Jarvis Street, waving, smiling, and doing the little hooker dip, the slight bend at the waist that let you make eye contact with the dudes cruising the strip. The competition was tough and a girl had to do everything short of flashing her beaver to connect with a john, she thought, giggling at the idea of the straights with their expensive cars and hundred-dollar hardons. Not that she always scored a hundred dollars a trick. Most of the time, she was lucky to get half that, but, as long as she kept busy, Speedy didn't complain.

She slipped into a pair of black bikini panties, then wiggled into a red form-fitting skirt, slit halfway up her thigh. Pulling on a filmy white blouse, she tucked it into her waistband, cocked her head, and studied herself in the long mirror on the bedroom closet door. Although the blouse was cut low, she didn't show much cleavage — her breasts were too small and firm, but she was pleased at the way her nipples strained against the thin fabric, showing up in dark contrast to her pale skin.

"Oh, shit!" Frowning, she padded over to the dresser, picked up a can of deodorant, and sprayed some under her arms, thankful that the blouse was sleeveless. She set the can down, then, as an afterthought, quickly retrieved it. Hiking up her skirt, she pulled the front of her panties down with one hand while aiming the container at her crotch with the other, and triggered a scented mist. Then, pulling the panties up, she sprayed the front of the undergarment.

Plunking herself down at the battered dresser, she fussed with her dirty-blonde, punkish hairstyle, then heavily rouged her cheeks and smeared on some purple lipstick. She studied herself full-face, then in profile, running a finger over the slight bump on the bridge of her nose. It was a souvenir from Speedy when he was paranoid from cranking crystal meth and thought she was trying to hold back some of the bread a john had laid on her. The doctor had done a good job, but it still bothered her when she thought of how straight it had once been.

Holly splashed some cheap-smelling perfume on her neck, slipped into a pair of platform pumps, and slung her handbag over her shoulder.

"Holly, baby," she purred seductively to the painted child-woman who vamped at her from the mirror, "you are one fine-looking lady. Those fucking johns are gonna cream just lookin' at you."

Then she shoved a large piece of bubble gum into her mouth and swept out of the apartment with the anxious anticipation of a high-schooler on the way to her first sock-hop.

She was going to meet Speedy at the Carousel Lounge on King Street before heading down to Jarvis. He spent a lot of time there, jiving with the other pimps and doing a little dealing. Nothing heavy, grass and hash mostly, with maybe a little coke when someone would take a chance and front him some, which wasn't often. Dealers usually wanted payment in advance, and Speedy seldom had enough bread to swing more than a single gram of blow.

He was seated alone at a corner table when Holly walked into the murky bar. The waitress had just put down a couple of draft, and after draining one of them, Speedy Renner wiped the foam from his drooping moustache with the back of his hand and belched contentedly. Small, wiry, and in his late twenties, Speedy — he earned the soubriquet by virtue of a prodigious amphetamine appetite — was decked out in his usual uniform: scruffy jeans, black T-shirt with a Harley-Davidson emblem, and a pair of hand-tooled cowboy boots which he wore mainly because of the elevator heels that boosted his normal five foot-eight height by a couple of inches.

In his left ear, he wore a gold stud, which taken together with his pinched, sallow face framed by dark, lank hair, gave him the appearance of a minor-league pirate who was down on his luck.

Holly smiled when she spotted the T-shirt. He was always wearing it even though he didn't own a bike or, as far as she knew, had ever even ridden one. But it served his purpose. It helped him cultivate the image of a bad-assed dude who could call upon the assistance of his biker "brothers" if anyone leaned on him. He stopped short of wearing club colours though. He wasn't about to carry the charade that far and risk getting stomped by some Hell's Angels with a hard-on against poseurs who traded on their hard-won notoriety.

She waded through the smoke and smell of stale beer to his table. He got up, wrapped one arm around her waist and gave her a lingering kiss while exploring the valley between her buns with his free hand. She knew that part of his show of affection was for the benefit of the other patrons in the seedy bar. He was sending them the message that this was *his* chick, that he had what it took to have a foxy lady tricking for him. But she didn't mind. Speedy could really be sweet and loving at times, especially when he was off the meth and bennies and they dropped acid together. That was when they opened up to each other and she didn't feel alone.

Alone. That was how she'd always felt when she was a kid. Her mother had always been too drunk to pay much attention to her. Unfortunately, that wasn't the case with her stepfather. When she was six years old, playing in the cellar with an old Raggedy Ann doll handed down from her grown-up sister, her mother upstairs in an alcoholic coma, Holly recollected "Daddy" giving her a chocolate wrapped in gold paper and asking her if she wanted to pet the soft bunny in his pants pocket. Only there'd been no pocket and the "bunny" hadn't been soft. Later, he'd shown it to her and made her hold it in her hand as he moved it back and forth. By the time she was ten years old, he was regularly having intercourse with her. "Don't tell Mommy. This is Holly and Daddy's secret and if you tell a secret, all the people you love will hate you and go away and you'll never see them again," her stepfather had admonished her.

She remembered the first time. It was easy to remember because she still felt the same pain and fear every time she was with a john, even sometimes with Speedy.

At first, Holly had only suspected that her stepfather's furtive assaults on her were wrong. By the time she reached her teens, she knew, and carried her guilt the way her schoolmates lugged their lunchboxes. When she finally decided to resist, he'd left her alone for a couple of years. Then, last year, he'd tried to get it on with her again and that's when she'd freaked out, shrieking at the top of her lungs and raking his face with her nails. That was also when she'd told the whole story to her mother who rewarded her by calling her a liar and kicking her out of the house.

It shouldn't have been a surprise. After all, who would her

mother be more likely to believe? A sullen, rebellious teen-ager who skipped school and was a habitual shoplifter? Or the man who paid the bills, mowed the lawn, and brought her the tall green bottles of gin she sucked on every day? It'd been no contest.

After a couple of days on the street, crashing in abandoned buildings with other kids who had no place to go and too much time to get there, she'd met Speedy. It was in an all-night café. He was at the next table and he smiled and made faces at her until she erupted in giggles. He'd also bought her the first hot meal she'd had in a week and had taken her to his apartment where he held her close and whispered words she'd only read in cheap pocketbooks.

Yeah, Speedy loved her all right. He'd told her so lots of times, even after he'd broken her nose. Holly had convinced herself that she deserved the beating Speedy gave her. He was right, she *had* held back money from him. Not much, just twenty bucks so she could get the new Springsteen albums. But he was her old man; he looked after her, and she shouldn't have done it.

Watching Speedy down his second draft, she smiled, think-ing about the time an old john had gotten her to blow him in his car in a parking lot over on Queen Street. He'd no sooner wiped off his dick when he'd tried to take back his forty bucks. He'd grabbed the bread right out of her purse, but there was something he didn't know. Speedy had been driving down Jarvis in his old beater and had seen her get picked up. Hav-ing nothing better to do, he'd followed them and was parked just outside the lot where Holly and her client had started tussling.

Speedy had rushed to her aid like a knight on a white charger, only this knight was wielding a tire iron rather than a lance, and he proceeded to use it on the john, who was cowering under the steering wheel. After he got through with the guy, Speedy had lifted his wallet and what a time they'd had that night! He'd ripped off almost eight hundred bucks and scored some coke that had really gotten them blasted.

He ordered her a beer and they sat and held hands. Holly looked at him adoringly. Yeah, she thought, he was her old man all right and she was his chick. She belonged to him. It was the first time in her life she had someone who gave a shit if she lived or died.

"Stay with me awhile, babe," he said, "Frenchy's coming by with some shit for me — some hash oil and grass — but the motherfucker'll probably be late as usual."

She nodded and squeezed his arm affectionately. He really was good-looking, she thought. Kind of like that guy who used to be the lead singer for Van Halen, that David-what's-his-face.

"I'll stay with you as long as you want," she purred, dropping her hand onto his thigh.

"Oh, oh," he yelped. "Either I'm gettin' hard or this goddamn table is rising all by itself!"

She'd seen the trick before; He was making the table tilt with his knee. She giggled anyway and grabbed for her beer, which threatened to topple over.

"Here comes your buddy, now," she said, spotting Frenchy coming through the door.

In his mid-thirties, Bernard "Frenchy" Pouliot was a well-known rounder in Toronto's dope-dealing and flesh-peddling circles. He was also regarded as a man on the move. He'd started out like Speedy, a small fish dealing dime bags of grass and hits of LSD, mostly to high-school kids who couldn't tell the difference between Acapulco Gold and alfalfa. He'd cut his grass with everything from parsley to catnip and no one had been the wiser.

Today, if he wasn't exactly in the major leagues of organized crime, he was at least on the fringe. That was why he could dress stylishly in a cream-coloured summer suit and a tan Panama hat and wear fourteen-karat gold chains around his neck. He was tall, slim, and swarthy. With his close-cropped, dark curly hair and neatly trimmed moustache, he could have passed for an over-dressed junior executive.

"Hey, what's happening?" he bawled, as he and Speedy exchanged a soul-brother handshake.

"A little of this, a little of that," Speedy replied.

Frenchy merely nodded at Holly and she replied in kind. She was used to being ignored. It was the same when she and Speedy were at after-hours clubs with some of the other pimps and their chicks. The girls were treated like part of the furniture and they had to be careful not to interrupt when the men were talking.

Holly didn't mind beause all they seemed to talk about were deals and money and stuff like that didn't interest her. She just wanted nice clothes, a place to stay, and that special feeling she got when Speedy told her he loved her and would always look after her.

Speedy pushed himself away from the table. "I gotta go to the can. I'll be right back."

Holly wasn't surprised when Frenchy followed him a short time later. That's the way dope deliveries were usually made — in some back alley or washroom. When the three of them were seated around the table again, Speedy asked, "You sure this shit is top-grade? Some of my customers are pretty heavy dudes and I don't wanna burn 'em." He stuck out his jaw. "Not that I'm scared or anything. It's just that I got a reputation to uphold, y'know."

Frenchy smiled thinly. He knew all right. He knew guys like Speedy only too well. That was how he was able to exploit their fear and their greed.

"Don't worry," he said. "The stuff is prime, baby. It's so good, I use it myself." He leaned back smugly as though this was the highest possible endorsement.

"Yeah? Well, I hope so," Speedy muttered, "because that stuff you gave me last week was like nothing, y'know. A coupla' guys even asked for their bread back but I was tapped so I laid a chunk of hash on them instead."

"Since when did you start giving refunds to customers?" Frenchy asked.

"Since a couple of them happened to be bikers who said they'd stomp my ass if I didn't cough up."

Frenchy fanned out his fingers and studied the well-manicured nails. "Oh, yeah?" he asked disinterestedly, while making a move to get up. "Anyway, I gotta split but I'll tell you what. If you aren't doing anything later on, say about midnight, drop by the Royal York."

"Oh, yeah? What's going down?"

"Only the most humungus fuckin' party you ever saw, that's all. Just ask at the desk for Jack Lexer's suite." As an afterthought, he jerked his head toward Holly. "And bring the chick. She might be able to make some good contacts."

"Lexer?" Speedy repeated admiringly. "He's gonna be there? Far out! Man, would I like to get next to that dude. He's —"

"Outta your fuckin' league," Frenchy cut in. "Hey, you could be standin' beside him in a fuckin' crowded elevator and you couldn't get next to him. That ain't the way it works, bro'. It's kind of like with royalty, y'know. Like, suppose Queen Elizabeth was in the city on a royal tour or something, and you happened to spot her. What would you do? Go up to her and ask if she wanted to get lucky?"

Speedy made a face. "That old broad? Are you outta your mind? I wouldn't screw her with *your* dick!"

"Yeah," Frenchy chuckled, "she's a real two-bagger all right."

"A two-bagger?" Holly asked innocently. "What the hell's that?"

Speedy beat Frenchy to the punch line. "That's where you put a bag over *your* head in case *hers* falls off."

Holly didn't really like jokes that put women down but she laughed along with the two men anyway.

"Anyway," Frenchy continued, "what I'm saying is keep out of Lexer's way and don't say shit to him unless he talks to you first." He paused, smiling knowingly. "And the chances of that happening are slim and none."

"Hey, I wasn't gonna come on strong with the dude," Speedy countered. "I just figured I could buzz in his ear about maybe using me somewhere in his operation. It don't have to be nothin' big. . . ."

"It don't have to be sweet fuck-all," Frenchy hissed, "unless I give the word. As far as you're concerned, *I'm* your main man. I'm the guy you talk to if you want to do business with the organization." His eyes swept the surrounding tables before he went on. "Listen, I've been working for the outfit for almost a year now and you know how many times I've talked to Jack Lexer?"

Speedy shook his head.

"Twice," he snorted. "One time when he asked me to get him some smokes and I asked him what brand —" He squelched Speedy's smirk with a dark glare. "And the second time . . . ." He paused, his face growing stony at the recollection.

"Yeah, go ahead," Speedy prodded. "I'm listening."

By this time, so was Holly even though she'd long since learned that it was a helluva lot safer keeping her face out of Speedy's "business" dealings.

When Frenchy picked up the narrative, he tried for a note of bravado but it didn't fool Speedy. He could tell that just recalling the incident, his friend was more than a little shook.

"I was talking to this chick in a club, not a bimbo either. I'm talking class with a capital C. Sherri, Cheryl, something like that. Anyway, like I said, I'm talking to this chick — not hitting on her or anything — just making nice, and Lexer and a couple of his captains happen to walk by. I say, 'Hi, how are you?' and stick out my hand. And him, he don't say fuckin' nothing. Looks at me like I ain't even there. Then he looks at the chick like she's the lowest scuzz-ball in the whole Jesus world and in this really soft voice tells her to get the hell out of there and go wait in his car.

"Then he turns to me with this same pissed-off look on his face like somebody just puked on his shoes, and says that if he ever sees me talking to her again, he'll have my dick cut off and shoved up my ass."

Speedy stared at him slack-jawed. "What was the story? Why did he lay that kind of shit on you?"

Frenchy shrugged. "You think I asked him? Anyway, later on I cracked about it to Benny Accardi and he laughed his fuckin' head off. Yeah, he thought it was a real riot that I almost got my ass in a sling."

If Frenchy was going to name drop, he could have done a lot worse than use Accardi's. Speedy knew him by reputation, a mid-level mobster and a key man in the organization's narcotics operation.

Speedy shook his head in wonderment. "Man, that Lexer is something else, ain't he?"

Frenchy's smile was tinged with irony. "Tell me about it."

"Anyway," Frenchy continued. "You hear what I'm saying about the man? He's way up here." He held his hand a foot above his head, then, dropping it to table level, added: "And we're down there. The only people he talks to about business are his lawyers who pass his orders down to the captains. That way, all of their discussions are covered by what they call 'lawyer-client privilege,' which means the cops and the courts can't get shit out of them."

"Smart," Speedy nodded. "Very smart. So no matter what goes down, Lexer's clean."

"You got it," Frenchy said. "Man, if you knew how much protection he's got, it'd blow your mind. There's at least three levels between him and his top people and any of the rackets. They got offshore bank accounts, numbered companies, and a whole stable of legit businesses — everything from real estate to waste disposal — to help wash the dirty money. And the beauty part is that the guys they got fronting the whole ball of wax are the top lawyers and accountants in the city. The same guys who represent all these big-name companies and are always getting their pictures on the society pages."

"Oh, yeah?" Speedy asked. "I always thought that mob lawyers were real shysters. You know, shady types."

"In the old days, maybe, but not now. Take the organization, for example. Lexer's got the best legal talent money can buy. But these guys got more than brains. They got something even more important, and that's connections. When the organization hooks up with these dudes, it gets a direct pipeline to Ottawa, Queen's Park, and the boardrooms of the biggest corporations in the country."

Speedy's eyes lit up like one of the pinball machines he was always playing. "Far-fucking-out!" Then, abruptly, his expression became earnest. "See, that's why I want in, Frenchy. Fuck, I'm tired of this nickel-and-dime shit. I can really go somewhere if I hook up with a big outfit and kinda work my way up."

"Well, tonight may be the start," Frenchy said. "I told Accardi about you and he said he'll see if he can find a spot for you."

"He did? That's great, man! Really fuckin' great!"

"Yeah," Frenchy said, "Anyway, he'll be at the party and you can rap to him and see what's shakin'." He let his gaze drift over his friend's seedy attire. "One other thing. . . ."

"Yeah?"

"Do yourself a favour and lose those threads. You're going to a high-class party, not a biker gang-bang."

Speedy fingered his T-shirt. "Hey, ain't nothing wrong with the way I dress. If you wanna look like a fuckin' shoe salesman, that's your problem."

Frenchy shrugged. "It's up to you. But you show up wearing that outfit and they won't even let you into the hotel."

"O.K., O.K., I get the picture," Speedy said sullenly.

"Anyway," Frenchy said, getting to his feet and preparing to leave, "like I said, I gotta take off —"

"Right," Speedy said, "but before I forget, you owe me a C-note."

"Oh, yeah? How do you figure?"

"That radio jerk-off, that Chambers guy, paid Holly a visit this afternoon."

Holly nodded in agreement. "Yeah, and he didn't even phone first."

Frenchy looked surprised. "Hmmm, that's the second time this week, isn't it?"

"Yeah," Holly flared. "And I hope to fuck it's the last!"

Speedy shot her an angry look. "Cool it! I'm trying to take care of business."

"Some goddamn business," she said hotly. "If you don't think that guy's severely bent, case this." She pulled down the top of her blouse, showing a scattering of welts.

Frenchy studied the livid bruises with interest. "I didn't know the old fuck had it in him," he said, almost admiringly.

"Fuckin' creep," Speedy spat, then quickly changing mental gears, added: "Uh, I could sure use that hundred. . . ."

Frenchy pulled out a wad of bills, peeled off a couple of fifties and handed them to Speedy. Then he turned to Holly, "The dude had a good time though, eh? There was no hassle or anything . . . ?"

"Yeah," she said disgustedly. "He had a good time all right. He even said —" Catching herself in mid-sentence, she stared at the tabletop in embarrassment.

"What?" Speedy asked. "What did he say?"

Eyes downcast, she murmured. "I'll tell you later."

He grabbed her wrist roughly. "You'll tell me now!"

"Ow, Jesus," she wailed, pulling her arm free. "Christ, I'll tell ya if it's so gaddamn important to you." She was aware that Frenchy was watching her closely. "He said — you're gonna laugh when I tell you — he said that I reminded him of one of his daughters."

The two men exchanged perplexed looks before Speedy snorted derisively: "Christ, what kinda fuckin' pervert is this guy anyway? What's the story? Is he ballin' his own daughter, or what?"

"No, no. He didn't mean it like that," Holly said hastily. "He didn't crack about that until later when he saw my Springsteen albums and said his oldest kid was a big fan of The Boss."

"Well, ain't that great," Speedy sneered. "What does the old fuck wanna do, adopt you so's he can shag you in his own pad instead of having to come downtown?'' He turned angrily toward Frenchy. ''What's the story with this creep anyway? Why did you steer him our way? Christ, the organization must have a hundred broads they can fix him up with.''

''At least,'' Frenchy smiled, ''but the buzz I got was that Chambers is a close personal friend of Lexer's and he's got a thing for young stuff. Sure, we got some teenage pussy in the rubshops but what with an election coming up, the word is that the cops'll have to get off their asses and start coming down on the parlours again.'' Taking his cue from Speedy's puzzled frown, he continued. ''So I guess the nitty-gritty is that Jack doesn't want to take a chance on having Chambers scooped up in some chicken-shit raid.''

''Yeah,'' Speedy grunted, ''but you guys know when a bust is coming down, don't you?''

''Most of the time. But there's always a chance of a fuck-up by our inside guy at the cop shop and I guess Lexer and the organization's other heavyweights don't want to take a chance on our pal Larry getting his name in the papers. They want him the way he is, with everybody looking up to him like he's some kind of fuckin' hero, eh? If it got out that he's as big a creep as most of the jerk-offs that listen to him, he wouldn't be worth shit to them.''

Speedy nodded, pretending that he grasped the argument but, in fact, he was totally in the dark. All he knew was that Frenchy had agreed to give him a C-note for every john the organization referred to Holly and that — at least, most of the time — was good enough for him.

Sometimes he thought that Frenchy tried to make things seem complicated just to make himself feel important. Anyway, that was no skin off his ass. He had other things on his mind.

''This party at the Royal York. Like, what's it for?''

Frenchy adjusted his Panama hat, trying for just the right tilt of the brim.

''There's a big pro boxing card in Cabbagetown this evening that Lexer's promoting to hype a couple of guys from his stable — Nicky Ventura and some other animal. He wants to fatten their records, so they'll probably be handed some easy touches. So this bash'll be like a victory celebration for the hometown boys.'' He rubbed his palms together in anticipation. ''Lemme tell you, you sure don't wanna miss this blowout. There's gonna be heavy-duty people there like you won't believe. Lotta made-guys from the states and some big names from Hamilton and Montreal.''

''Hey, I'll be there, man,'' Speedy exclaimed. ''That's the kind of action I can really get off on.'' He paused for a couple of seconds before asking: ''You sure it's O.K. if I bring Holly?'' Thinking of all the sharp foxes that were sure to be there, he was almost disappointed when Frenchy replied: ''Yeah, no sweat. It'll give her a chance to meet some of the people you're going to be working with.''

''Working with?'' Speedy echoed. His frown softened into a broad smile as the significance of his friend's words sank in. ''You mean I'm in? I've been accepted into the organization?''

Frenchy returned the smile. ''Let's say you'll be in kinda like an apprentice program. But if you keep your nose clean and don't fuck up, in six months or so, they'll give you a steady spot in one of the —'' he paused, choosing his words carefully, ''branch offices.''

Speedy pumped his hand warmly and after Frenchy left, he could hardly sit still.

''Ain't that great, babe?'' he crowed. ''I'm in. I'm in the fucking organization!''

He stabbed her with a look. ''What's the matter? You don't seem too excited.''

''O.K.,'' she pouted. ''So you're in the fucking big-time now. So where does that leave me? Should I pack my stuff and split or what?''

He gave her a hug that almost lifted her out of her chair. ''This isn't just for me. It's a shot for both of us. You got any idea of all the shit the organization is into? They got fuckin' film studios where they make their own goddamn porno flicks for Chrissake! They put out skin books that sell for ten, twenty bucks a pop. And their chicks must be pulling in a couple of grand a week easy, in those fancy studios with the Jacuzzis and stereos and all that shit. Christ, babe, the sky'll be the fuckin' limit once we find out who's who and what's what.''

''I don't know,'' she began doubtfully.

''That's right,'' he snapped. ''You don't. That's why *I* call the shots.''

''But it won't be the same,'' she said. ''I like it the way it is now, just the two of us. This way, it's not like a business, because what I do out on the street is for you. It's because I love you.''

''And I love you too, babe,'' he said softly, looking deeply into her eyes. ''That's why I want to make something of myself, because you deserve better than tricking on street corners. You got class.'' He held her on the end of his gaze: ''Didn't I tell you that the first night I met you?''

She nodded, smiling uncertainly.

''Yeah. You're too good for this nickel-and-dime shit. We both are.'' He leaned forward, bringing his face so close to hers that she could almost taste the beer on his breath. ''What the hell has this goddamn world given us? Look at me. I'm almost thirty and I'm still selling grass and acid when most of the guys I started out with are fronting nothing but coke and smack. That ain't performance, babe. I know it and you know it. I want bread, you're goddamn right I do. But I want respect too. And this is my chance; it's your chance too. We're gonna move up together.''

''I wouldn't fit in,'' she said in a forlorn, little girl's voice. ''I don't know how to talk to people. I can answer questions all right but I can't think of things to say first.''

''You'll learn,'' he said reassuringly. ''How the hell do you think all these TV stars and rock singers got where they are? It sure as hell ain't because they got anything in their melons. The trick is to use what you got and, babe —'' he dropped his hand onto her lap and gave her crotch a pro-prietary pat, "believe me, you got a lot. Christ, you look at these movie stars today and you know how they started? As hookers or models for porno mags, that's how. Look at fuckin' Madonna for Chrissake! Everytime you turn on the TV, there's someone interviewing her. Johnny Carson, Phil Donahue, even Barbara-fuckin'-Walters. And do you think they dump on her because she flashed her snatch in *Penthouse*? No goddamn way. They kiss her ass like she's a fuckin' queen or something."

Listening to him, Holly heard for the first time the fear and insecurity behind his brave words. Suddenly she realized he needed her, that, by now, even the smallest dreams were too big for him to pursue alone. Blinking back tears of happiness, she smiled and said, "Well, what time are we gonna hit this party?"

Speedy thought for a moment. Ah, what the hell, he finally decided. What's another couple of tricks? Hell, we ain't even officially with the organization yet.

"Tell you what, babe," he said. "Suppose you just do your thing like always for say, a couple hours. Just make sure you're home by eleven. I'll call you then and let you know what's shakin'."

Holly looped her arms around his neck, gave him a big hug, and swished out of the lounge to her last night on the streets. She was excited. She was tired of selling herself in parked cars and hot-sheet hotels. Tired of washing the cum out of her box in the washrooms of service stations and bars so she'd be ready for the next trick.

Two, maybe three tricks if it was a good night, and she'd be going on to bigger and better things. She wondered if Speedy had been snowing her with that stuff about making porno flicks. She'd like that. Turning guys on without having them paw her and slobber all over her.

Her grandma had always said she was photogenic. She shifted the wad of gum in her mouth, shoving her tongue deep inside it and blowing a huge bubble. Just as she reached the corner of King and Jarvis, the bubble burst, plastering her lips with sticky pink strands. Trying to scrape the gum free with her teeth, Holly suddenly got the giggles. And as her slim body swayed, captive to the laughing fit, and her wide blue eyes glistened with child-like glee, a gleaming new Olds sedan pulled over to the curb and the driver, middle-aged, overweight, and sweating, waved her over.

"Wanna go out?" Holly crooned.

"Yeah," the man said, his voice hoarse with lust.

Holly took out her gum, rolled it into a ball, and dropped it on the sidewalk. She slid in beside him, gave him a wide, welcoming smile and chirped: "Fifty for a blow and seventy-five for a lay."

The man looked down at the steering wheel, and murmured out of the corner of his mouth, "I guess I'll take the first one."

As he pulled away from the curb, Holly gave him directions and began to sing softly along with the radio. It was the Tina Turner song she liked — "What's Love Got to Do With It?" She liked the way Tina wailed, like every part of her that mattered was in each word.

"What's love but a secondhand emotion?" Tina sang, her voice a distillation of pain and cynicism, as the driver eased into a lane between a couple of warehouses. "What's love —" This time the soul queen's plaintive query was stopped short as the man cut the ignition and fished two twenties and a ten out of his wallet. As he began to fumble with his trousers, Holly shoved the money into her handbag, at the same time, pulling out a handful of tissues. As she bent over, she thought of Speedy and how much he cared for her. And as the fat man began to grunt with excitement and thrust his fleshy hips at her, she heard Tina's voice going around and around in her head. And she knew.

Chapter Five

Pete tried to focus his attention on the boxing ring. After all, that was what he was getting paid for, but his mind was elsewhere, replaying his conversation with Elaine. He'd thought they had a date to go for a late drink after he filed his story on the fights, but when he'd phoned her to confirm it, she'd acted like the whole thing was news to her. He couldn't figure it. And when she begged off, she'd seemed so distant. Women and their games, he thought. Who could figure either? Not him, that's for sure, and that's probably why he had an ex-wife who called him twice a year to brag about her latest boyfriend and ask if he was still working.

He looked up at the ring, blinking against the brilliance of the powerful overhead lights illuminating the squared circle. He winced as the black man took a heavy shot to his ample belly and sagged to his knees. The fighter's eyes were clouded with pain as he struggled to his feet, holding a gloved hand to his midriff. The referee gave him a standing eight-count, wiped off his gloves, and waved the combatants back into action.

The black man, a ring-wise veteran of over a hundred pro bouts, leaned back on the ropes in a clumsy imitation of Muhammad Ali's rope-a-dope tactic, his gloves shielding his head and his elbows tucked against his rib cage. His opponent, Nicky Ventura, a Cabbagetown kid with no more than a half-dozen pro encounters under his belt, rushed forward like a miniature bull, throwing punches from all angles.

Most of them landed on the black man's gloves and arms, but each pop of leather brought a chorus of o-o-o-o-h's from the partisan crowd. The only shot that did any damage was a roundhouse right to the kidney that drew a warning from the referee. When the bell sounded, the old campaigner shuffled back to his corner on weary legs, collapsing onto his stool almost before his cornerman had it in place.

Another stiff, thought Pete. Another over-the-hill American punching bag brought in to make the hometown hero look good. This time, the old trial-horse was calling himself Mustapha Khalid, but he probably used a different name in every town he fought in.

In his prime he'd probably fought as a welterweight, but he looked close to forty now and was carrying about a dozen pounds of excess baggage, the flab collecting on his chest and waist. The bell sounded for round three and Khalid lumbered to the centre of the ring where he posed with his hands high in the peekaboo style popularized by Floyd Patterson. With his feet seemingly screwed to the canvas, he bobbed and weaved, trying to slip punches while looking for a chance to counter.

Ventura stormed in, banging with both hands. Short combinations. Hook to the body, then to the head. Straight right to the gap between his opponent's gloves. His chiselled upper body glistened with sweat. The heavy body shots brought gasps from both Khalid and the expectant crowd. Smiling around his mouthpiece, Ventura pivoted to his left, poised to unleash a lethal hook. It was the move Khalid had been waiting for. Ventura was just cocking his left, when the pudgy black man fired a cannon of his own, a straight, overhand right, that caught the kid flush on the nose. It burst like a ripe tomato, spraying both Khalid and the referee. From his ringside seat, Pete heard the sound of gristle cracking.

Then the bell sounded and the fighters returned to their respective corners. Ventura's trainer quickly applied some ice to the bridge of his man's nose and the pressure alone almost made the kid pass out from pain. Pete figured that they'd have to stop the fight. One more good shot and they'd be looking for pieces of Ventura's beak in the cheap seats. He looked around for Phelan, the ring doctor, but he hadn't moved, limiting his concern to a questioning glance toward the referee.

A tinny gong signalled the start of round four. Ventura's handlers almost had to shove him out of his corner. He quickly got on his bicycle, using the entire ring. Dancing, circling, he flicked out his jab, trying to keep his opponent at bay. Pete guessed that the broken nose had made Ventura gun-shy because he skipped back a few paces every time Khalid started to load up with his right hand.

Plodding after Ventura, Khalid, or Harry Washington, as he was known to his co-workers in a Buffalo foundry, seemed to be in no hurry. In fact, Pete would have sworn the aging warrior was playing some pugilistic cat-and-mouse game, setting up his opponent for the kill then letting him clinch his way out of trouble.

It was hard to tell with the mouthpiece pressing against the fighter's thick lips but Pete would have laid odds that the old pug was smiling. Why didn't he finish him? he wondered. Hell, it was as obvious as the nose spread over Ventura's face that the kid was shot. All Khalid had to do was cut off the ring, trap the hometown hero on the ropes and start winging. Nicky boy would drop faster than a nymphomaniac's drawers.

But on reflection, Peter understood the veteran boxer's strategy. If he flattened the hometown favorite, he'd be cutting the promoter's throat and that meant his chances of getting paid would range between slim and slimmer. Plus his stock would drop considerably with other promoters who were trying to fatten up their fighters' records.

Pete smiled to himself as Ventura landed a light combination and his cheering section filled the smoky hall with cries of: "Finish 'im, Nicky! He's shot! Kill that nigger!"

Almost as if responding to some secret signal, Khalid swapped his serene smile for a look of resignation. Pawing with his left, he let Ventura snap his head back with a soft jab. Then he dropped his left glove almost to his waist and shuffled forward with his jaw invitingly exposed. Ventura telegraphed the right cross so badly that even the referee could see it coming and stepped back. Still, it was a little wild and Pete almost laughed out loud when he saw Khalid aim his chin to catch it. The black man's choreography was impeccable. He twirled one hundred and eighty degrees, fell back against the ropes, and slid down onto the seat of his black satin trunks.

He shook his head dazedly while the referee hovered over him, barking the count. The crowd was on its feet, roaring with a cathartic vengeance. Shakily, Khalid hoisted himself onto one knee, struggled to get up, then pitched forward on his face. The arena went wild. Ventura's handlers hoisted him onto their shoulders and one ecstatic supporter leaped into the ring and unfurled an Italian flag, touching off another wave of cheering.

As his trainer waved some smelling salts under his nose, Khalid glanced out of the corner of his eye and saw Ventura bounding about the ring, his arms raised in triumph. He made a face as the acrid scent of the salts invaded his nostrils.

"Get that shit outta my face," he growled. "Jes' let me lie here a bit and give them motherfuckers their money's worth."

Pete recorded the time of the knockout in his notepad. His photographer, John Thomson, a young, lanky kid with a bushy beard and hippie appearance, had been snapping away from all angles. Although barely in his twenties, John was one of the best in the business and had already won a handful of national awards.

"Well, what ya think?" he asked, leaning over Pete's shoulder. "Personally, I think he deserved straight nines. That sucker could give Greg Louganis some stiff competition."

"What?" Pete cried, feigning indignation. "You don't mean to tell me that wasn't on the up-and-up?" He shook his head sorrowfully. "You media types are all alike. You're so poisoned by cynicism that you think nothing of defaming a fine, well-conditioned athlete like Mustapha Khalid."

Giving himself a light slap on the wrist, the photographer smiled. "Well, shame on me."

Pete glanced up at the ring where the defeated boxer was being hauled to his feet. As a tribute to his gameness, the crowd offered some sporadic applause. Khalid-Washington stumbled to his corner while his handlers draped his robe over his shoulders and helped him out of the ring.

Pete jerked his head toward Nicky Ventura. "I'm gonna get a couple of quotes, then we'll head back to the newsroom."

"Sounds good," John replied, beginning to pack away his equipment.

The dressing room was wall-to-wall bodies — family, friends, and the usual hangers-on. In one corner, Jack Lexer was holding forth before a coterie of listeners that included some of the leading lights from the city's business and legal fraternities.

The lawyers' presence shouldn't have surprised Pete. They were usually out in full force at most pro fight cards, rubbing shoulders with bikers, pushers, arsonists, forgers, and extortionists, all of whom were either present or potential clients. Hell, Pete thought, they fed off each other, lawyers and hoods. Venality and criminality went together like shit and toilet paper.

Pete shook his head in disgust, watching Lexer's entourage compete as to who'd be the first to second his comments. Pete had had an abiding interest in the flamboyant developer long before the latter had embarked on a massive campaign of corporate acquisition and started turning up on the boards of every prestigious cultural organization and charity in Toronto.

Lexer had come a long way in a short time and Pete thought it strange that no one seemed to know how he had parlayed a small trucking company into a corporate octopus whose tentacles reached into almost every sector of the economy, from real estate to high-technology.

Sure, there was the innuendo, the whispers about his corporate coups being financed by mob money. But where was the proof? Pete sure as hell hadn't been able to find any and he'd looked as hard as anyone. Especially after that caper in the mid-seventies.

Pete remembered the story well. He'd covered it for the *Herald* when he was on the crime beat. The Metro vice boys had caried out one of their periodic raids on the massage parlours on the Yonge Street strip, netting over thirty "attendants," plus a dozen or so managers and a like number of drivers who worked for the outcall end of the racket. The bust had merited a full-scale press conference at which the Chief of Police had declared that the backbone of prostitution in Toronto had been broken and that not only the underlings, but the kingpin himself, had been taken into custody.

It sounded good at the time, but Pete did a little digging and found out that the alleged vice king, one Gilbert Groening, had become President and General Manager of the chain of massage parlours less than a week before the bust went down. Further investigation revealed some even more intriguing information, because the former owner and chief executive officer of Entertainment Services Ltd. turned out to be none other than Jack Lexer.

The plot thickened still more during the trial which saw Groening plead guilty to charges of keeping a common bawdy house and living off the avails of prostitution. The man who, according to court documents, purchased the string of massage parlours for the sum of "one dollar and other considerations" was hit with a year in jail and a hundred-thousand-dollar fine, which he promptly paid, in spite of the fact that before taking over the operation, he'd been working as a four-hundred-dollar-a-week driver for one of the outcall operations.

And Lexer? Well it seemed that neither the Attorney General's department nor the cops felt that it would serve any purpose to even question him since he was no longer the owner of record when the offences took place. How fortunate for him that he got out at the right time, Pete mused wryly. Funny though, how he'd been able to run the operation for almost four years without drawing any heat; then, all of a sudden, he gets out and the fuzz swarm down on the studios like Swat teams from "Hill Street Blues". Yeah, Pete thought, a suspicious person might have all kinds of ideas about a caper like that.

There was something else about the case that had bothered him. Then he remembered. Groening. The punk who took the fall. A couple of days after he had finished doing his time, his body had been found in an abandoned quarry. The job had been neat and professional: one twenty-two-calibre slug in the back of his head and another in his right temple.

The recollection left a bitter taste in Pete's mouth. He looked over at Lexer again, thinking he should get a quote or two from him. After all, besides being the promoter of the card, the guy was Nicky Ventura's manager. But he decided against it, confining himself to a brief interview with the fighter. Pete had wrapped it up and was about to leave when he caught sight of Larry Chambers. The hot-line host was deep in conversation with a striking brunette, whose shapely frame was accentuated by a clinging black silk dress. Pete hadn't noticed him during the fights but he'd certainly spotted the woman. She'd been sitting in a front-row seat, next to Lexer, with her arm twined through his and her head resting on his shoulder. Pete was just about to step into the hallway when he heard his name called and turned to see Larry hurrying toward him.

"Pete! How the hell are you?" he boomed, thrusting out his hand.

"Couldn't be better," Pete replied, shaking hands.

"Glad to hear it." He jerked his head toward Nicky Ventura. "Kid's a real scrapper, isn't he? He's going to go a long way."

"Yeah," Pete said dryly, "he'll probably win the Canadian title unless Lexer commits the unpardonable sin of matching him against someone who is under the age of fifty or isn't an avowed pacifist."

Larry smiled condescendingly. "Still the same old Pete Gossett. Still looking for the dark cloud around every silver lining."

"It's a dirty job, but somebody has to do it," Pete grinned. "But enough of this small talk. Let's get to the burning issue of the day."

Larry's forehead creased in puzzlement. "And what might that be?"

Pete craned his head, searching through the crush of bodies, before finally spotting her. "The gorgeous brunette you were just chatting up and who is now hanging on to Lexer's arm."

Larry tracked Pete's gaze, beaming. "Isn't she something?"

"Yeah," Pete said admiringly. "Who is she, anyway? I don't think I've seen her around."

"Considering the circles you move in, I'm not surprised," Larry sniped. "Her name is Cheryl Batten and she is one high-class lady. Used to be married to David Batten."

"You mean *the* David Batten? Wasn't he just named ambassador to the States?"

"That's right."

"Christ, I've heard of slumming," Pete said, "but this is ridiculous."

Larry chuckled. "Don't worry about Cheryl. She does all right for herself."

"If all right means cozying up to Jack Lexer," Pete countered, "and speak of the devil. . . ."

Pete spotted Lexer heading in their direction, the crowd separating in front of him like the parting of the Red Sea. Cheryl Batten was clinging to his arm and the pair were flanked by a couple of clean-cut young men in dark business suits. Most observers would have taken them for junior executives, but Pete knew better. Their hard, shifting eyes, and tight, ruthless mouths gave them away. He recognized one of them. Danny Kostek had been a top middleweight a few years back and had come within a hair of dethroning the British Commonwealth champ. But after that, it had been all downhill, marked by a succession of scrapes with the law: possession of a restricted weapon, attempted extortion. All kinds of charges — but only one conviction — simple possession of narcotics, a charge that'd been plea-bargained down from possession-for-the-purpose-of-trafficking. Lexer sure knew how to pick his bodyguards all right. Pete nodded amiably in his direction and was rewarded with an icy stare.

"Larry," Lexer bawled, clapping a pudgy hand on the hot-line host's shoulder. "I'm going up to the suite now. Drop up whenever you want and —" he jerked his thumb at Pete, "bring your friend."

Larry made the introductions and Pete and Lexer shook hands. Pete was impressed by the developer's grip. He sensed the man was trying to intimidate him with a show of physical strength and he squeezed back, imitating Lexer's tight smile.

This was the first time in several years Pete had been close to Lexer, and he studied him carefully to see if the remarkable upswing in his business and social fortunes had changed him in any perceptible way. It was a snap judgment but, as far as Pete was concerned, beneath the carefully cultivated image, he was still the same old Jack Lexer: loud, crude, and flashy.

His wiry, salt-and-pepper hair had been permed and looked

like a cross between an Afro and a brillo pad. The face was fleshy with a couple of chins separating it from a bull-neck, and the coarse features included a mashed-in nose that was twisted slightly to one side, bushy eyebrows that met above where the bridge of his nose had once been, and lips so thick that they almost looked swollen.

"So you're with the *Herald*, eh?" Lexer said in an accusing tone. "I hope you're gonna give Nicky a good write-up. The kid deserves it. He's a good boy. Trains hard and there's sure as hell no quit in him. Another half-dozen tune-up fights and he'll be ready for anyone in the top ten."

Yeah, sure, Pete thought. If Ventura ever got in the ring with a decent club fighter from Philadelphia or Detroit, he'd be cut to ribbons. The difference between American and Canadian fighters was like night and day. In the States, a boxer has proper coaching and over a hundred amateur fights before he even thinks of turning pro. In Canada, a kid has a dozen amateur bouts, wins a bronze-medal at some rinky-dink competition, and then some fast-buck promoter convinces him he's ready for the big-time. But he kept his opinion to himself, instead saying:

"When's he going to fight again?"

"Soon as his shnoz heals. I wanna keep him busy. Kid that age, if he ain't busy, can get into a lot of trouble." He turned back to Larry. "Anyway, me and Cheryl are going up now, so I'll catch you guys later."

They watched Lexer's party leave, then Larry playfully jabbed Pete in the ribs.

"Well, what'ya say? You want to go up to Jack's suite and see how the other half lives?"

"I wouldn't mind," Pete said thoughtfully, then shot a look at his watch, "but I've got a story to file and it'll be close to midnight by the time I get through."

"Hell," Larry snorted. "The party'll just be starting by then. C'mon, buddy. Loosen up and live a little. You're not afraid Elaine'll find out you've been a bad boy, are you?"

Pete smiled weakly. "Somehow, I don't think she stays up nights worrying about what I might be doing."

Larry's eyebrows shot up in surprise. "What? You mean you're not — what do they call it — an item?"

"Not even close, pal."

He shook his head sorrowfully. "It looks like I wasted my time introducing her to you. Too bad. I thought you two would hit it off."

"We did, but whether it goes any further than that. . . ." He shrugged, letting the words trail off.

"Well, then," Larry said, "there's nothing to stop you from partying it up a little, is there?"

"No, I guess not."

But even as Pete was heading back to the newsroom, he still hadn't made up his mind about putting in an appearance at Lexer's party, although, in a way, he felt somewhat obligated. After all, he had given Larry a half-assed commitment and, even though they weren't what you'd call close friends, they did go back a long way together. They'd both been reporters at the *Winnipeg Clarion* in the early seventies. It'd been a good paper and, even though Pete had been pretty green, Jeff Reardon, the city editor, had let him have a lot of slack in his leash and he'd been able to break a couple of big stories.

But, like a lot of good papers, the *Clarion* had been swallowed up by a money-hungry chain that would've been content to fill its pages with wire-service copy and press conference pap if it could get away with it. Now, it was some kind of half-assed tabloid, filled with advice to the lovelorn columns, horoscopes, and pictures of any scantily clad nymphet who could be tenuously linked to some pseudo-news event.

Aw, the hell with it. That was all in the past. And so, in many respects, was his friendship with Larry Chambers. Since Larry had gone into radio, they crossed paths no more than a couple of times a month, usually at the press club. So it certainly couldn't be friendship or loyalty that nagged at him as he hunched in front of his computer terminal and fed in his fight copy.

It wasn't until he left the building, that he finally made up his mind to attend Jack Lexer's party. By then, he also had no illusions about his decision. It had nothing to do with obligations or commitments. It was something a helluva lot more compelling; it was Jack Lexer. Not the man so much as what he represented — hidden power. Shadows within shadows and masks behind masks. Pete could not only smell a story, he could taste it. Maybe it was the one he'd missed when Lexer had slid out from under the prostitution bust. Maybe that was what gnawed at him, the feeling that if he'd worked a little harder, dug a little deeper. . . .

Well, that was then and this is now, he told himself. Whatever happened yesterday, today there were pieces to put together. And some of them even had names. Jack Lexer. Cheryl Batten. Larry Chambers. Gilbert Groening. Danny Kostek. How did they fit into the picture? For that matter what *was* the picture?

By the time he reached the Royal York Hotel and strode purposefully into the stately stone fortress, the swarm of questions had receded. All that remained was a feeling of serene certainty, an almost mystical conviction in his head, heart, and guts, that he was on the trail of the biggest story of his career and that this time nothing would stand in his way.

Jane had been so deep in thought that when the phone rang, it was almost like being awakened from a sound sleep. It was Elaine Steele asking for Larry, and she sounded excited. Jane was surprised. She didn't know Elaine that well, had actually only had one real conversation with her but she had been struck by — and if the truth be told, somewhat envious of — the young woman's composure and air of self-confidence.

Emotion certainly wasn't this gal's long suit, Jane had im-

mediately decided. Oh, she had charm all right, but Jane
had the feeling that it was controlled by some internal switch
that could be turned off and on at a moment's notice. Miss
Icewater. That was the name she'd coined for her husband's
researcher and she'd begun to use the soubriquet with
greater frequency once she'd discovered it got under Larry's
skin.

"Larry hasn't come in yet," Jane told her. "He went to
the fights. You know how crazy he is about seeing grown
men trying to beat each other to a pulp."

"What time do you expect him?"

"It's difficult to say. He *has* been known to stop for a few
drinks afterward, you know."

"Well, is there anywhere he can be reached?"

"I suppose you *could* look under bars in the yellow pages
and go through them alphabetically," she said, with a false
brightness.

Elaine could feel the hostility seeping out of the receiver
like a cold fog. She wondered what was bothering Larry's
wife but concluded that she was probably just another bored
housewife who had to put some excitement in her life by
playing mind-games that even *she* didn't understand.

"Well, would you please give him a message for me?"
Elaine said, fighting to mask her irritation.

"Certainly. That's what wives are for, isn't it?"

Elaine bit back a retort. The whining note in Jane's voice
set her teeth on edge like the scrape of a fingernail on a
blackboard. She recognized it as a blatant pitch for sympathy
but she refused to play along with it.

"Would you please tell him that Mrs. Jantzen has agreed
to be on the show tomorrow." She tried to sound crisp and
businesslike but was aware of the undercurrent of excitement
in her voice. "And she's also agreed to be interviewed in the
studio rather than over the phone."

It had been a hard sell. At first, the woman had been
taciturn, insisting that she was too upset and nervous to go
on the air. But Elaine had turned on the charm and had

gradually gained her confidence. She convinced the distraught mother of three that publicizing her daughter's disappearance was the best way of getting information on her whereabouts. The police were doing what they could, she argued, but a lot of kids went missing each year and the authorities just didn't have the necessary resources to carry out intensive searches for all of them.

Although one part of her had been repelled by Larry's suggestion that Mrs. Jantzen's anguish be paraded before a quarter-of-a-million listeners, she'd managed to come to terms with the fact that she was participating in a calculated exercise in voyeurism. Larry had been right and she'd been wrong. Raw, human emotion was a big draw on the airwaves. It was what pulled in the numbers the show needed.

Elaine realized that, despite her credentials, she still had a lot to learn about the business, and she was surer than ever that she'd made the right move by signing on as Larry's aide. She paid him the grudging respect of acknowledging that, while he was currently in ratings trouble, he'd been a hot-line heavyweight for a lot of years. He'd bounced back before. And if he was now too burned-out to pull still another rabbit out of the hat, well, she'd be in the right place at the right time to help bury the corpse.

After hanging up the phone, she set to work preparing questions for the Jantzen interview, stopping only after she realized it was past midnight. I wonder what kind of shape our star performer is going to be in tomorrow morning, she mused. But she knew she was worrying needlessly. No matter how hungover he was, no matter how bleary-eyed and shaky, as soon as he sat down at the mike, a remarkable transformation took place. It was as though the studio had healing properties for CKAL's maestro of the microphone.

As she flicked out the light and slid into bed, she found herself thinking of Pete. He'd sounded so hurt when she'd begged off from meeting him for a drink. She felt bad about that. It was a complication she hadn't counted on when she first started sleeping with him. She liked him. He made her laugh and had proven himself a giving and inventive lover. His passion had been almost therapeutic for her, considering the pressure she was under.

She smiled, and stretched sensuously. Her skin tingled as the satin sheet rustled against her naked body. She rolled onto her back and the silky material settled between her thighs. Feeling a twinge of desire, she wondered if perhaps she shouldn't have kept her date with Pete. A ghost of remorse immediately triggered a surge of resentment; she didn't need him. She didn't need any man playing on her passion, her instincts, or her guilt.

She closed her eyes and sighed. To hell with it. If he was going to fall so hard, that was *his* problem. Why were so many men like little boys? she wondered. Why did they always want to take their marbles and go home if the game wasn't played by their rules? But the questions were either inconsequential or the answers too elusive, for she fell into a sound sleep before arriving at even the threshold of a conclusion.

As soon as the elevator door slid open, Pete was engulfed by a wave of sound. Laughter — soprano peals and baritone roars. Excited, aggressive voices vying for a place in the conversational sun, ebbing and flowing against a constant level of background noise.

Some of the guests had spilled out into the hallway. Young men in yacht club blazers; pampered women in Creeds' cocktail dresses and sculpted hairdos. And everywhere, the rich aromatic scents of the lotions and potions the beautiful people used to enhance their desirability.

And, here and there, clusters of swarthy men with lived-in faces. Men with flashy clothes and even flashier women whom they wore on their arms like trophies. Pete marvelled at the clinging dresses that seemed designed to highlight every erogenous zone known to modern man — not to mention Dr. Ruth — and guessed the dresses were a helluva lot tighter than what their wearers had used to get them.

Pete glanced through the open door into the lavish reception room. A haze of smoke drifted up to the vaulted ceiling, muting the glitter of the opulent chandeliers. The guests ranged from fresh-faced college types to elderly white-haired matrons with hair freshly styled by Mr. Bruce, and whose corrugated necks bore spidery strands of pearls and diamonds.

Most of the men were middle-aged or older and dressed in conservative three-piece suits. There were also a handful attired in tuxedoes, and Pete guessed that they'd probably attended some formal affair earlier in the evening. It was a mixed bag all right. Everything from politicians and captains of commerce to restaurateurs and ex-pugs who greeted each other with feinted hooks to the body.

There was certainly no shortage of food and drink. A contingent of young women, costumed like French maids, right down to the abbreviated skirts and black mesh stockings, patrolled the room, proffering canapés and glasses of champagne from silver trays. And for the real drinkers, there was a complimentary bar in one corner. You had to hand it to Lexer, Pete mused, the guy sure knew how to throw a party.

Opting for the bar, Pete edged through the forest of bodies, ordered a double Scotch, and began to scout around for Larry. He thought he'd just touch base with him, give the party the once-over to check out who was there, and then head home.

At noon tomorrow, he had an appointment to interview one of the Jays' relief pitchers — some poor, underpaid wretch who was pulling in over a million a year and had an ERA of 5.27. It was hard enough to get enthused about talking to some jock whose mission in life was to throw a small round object past a guy with a long wooden object; he didn't want to press his luck by showing up with a hangover.

As it turned out, Larry spotted Pete first, and waved him

over to where he was conversing with a couple of other men. "Do you know Mike and Morley?" Larry asked when Pete had joined their circle.

Pete nodded and smiled. As an investigative journalist he had often interviewed Mike Edwards and Morley Spector, both of them prominent members of the city's legal establishment, if at opposite ends of the spectrum. As a sergeant with Metro's Homicide Division, Edwards made his living by trying to put people in jail. Spector, on the other hand, had paid off the mortgage on his Rosedale mansion by trying to keep them out, and his impressive batting average had made him one of the Toronto's preeminent criminal lawyers.

Their physical appearances were equally disparate. The tall, raw-boned detective with his anachronistic, carrot-colored brushcut, looked like a country boy on his first visit to the big city. And no one knew it better than Edwards himself, for it was an image he'd worked to cultivate. That's why, even though he could afford better, he confined himself to wearing the dark slacks and loud, checkered sports jackets favoured by most of the city's plain-clothes detectives. He knew any rounder with a half a brain could spot him as a cop from a mile off, but, the way he worked, he figured that was an asset rather than a liability.

Edwards was quick to acknowledge that painstaking undercover investigation and high-tech surveillance served a valid purpose, but they took time and money. He had his own way of scooping the human garbage off the streets and into penitentiaries where their stink would only bother each other.

His stock in trade was physical and psychological intimidation. In the old days, when he'd been with Vice, he'd had to work at it, follow through on his threats to lean on informants and suspects. Now, he seldom had to resort to fabricating evidence or kicking the shit out of the scumbags who were turning one of the finest cities in the world into a cesspool. He could get what he wanted just by trading on his reputation.

Spector, on the other hand, seemed anything but threatening. He had a soft, pear-shaped, almost matronly body. His narrow shoulders made his large head seem even more disproportionate, and his heavy-lidded eyes gave a perpetually sleepy look to his round, pale face. The mop of dark brown hair framing the broad forehead added to the out-of-synch image — it was unfashionably long, almost a Beatle cut, and made him look more like a middle-aged academic than a veteran trial lawyer, whose combative style and cunning had made him a legend in his own time. Pete shook hands with the two men and then turned to Spector.

"I didn't know you were a fight fan, Morley."

"Frankly, I'm not," Spector replied. "But I never like to miss a good party and Jack —" he aimed his champagne glass toward Lexer, who was standing a short distance away listening intently to a man Pete recognized as the head of a major trust company, "certainly knows how to entertain."

"Yeah, he's a real fun guy," Pete said dryly. "Also very well-connected from what I hear."

"Well, I couldn't say anything about that," Spector said coyly. "Lawyer-client privilege and all that."

You've already told me what I wanted to know, you fucking shyster, Pete said to himself. So you're still wiping Lexer's ass for him are you? Then Pete said aloud: "You've been representing Mr. Lexer for a long time now. What is it — seven, eight years?"

The lawyer's smile tightened. "Something like that."

"Watch it," Edwards cut in. "You know how these goddamn reporters are. You give them the time of day at a party and the next morning, you see your name on the front page next to a whole load of bullshit."

"Hey,' Pete said, affecting a hurt look, "would I do something like that? Besides, not only am I off-duty, but I'm no longer on the crime beat."

"Oh yeah?" Edwards said. "What happened? They get wise to you and start running your stuff on the comics page?"

"If they did, I'd at least know *you* were reading it," Pete jabbed back.

"That's really funny, Gossett," the detective glowered. "I hope nothing ever happens to you to make you lose your sense of humour."

"C'mon you guys," Larry cut in. "Lay off the heavy stuff. We're here to have a good time." His voice was slurred and he swayed slightly as he made his way to the bar for a refill. It was Pete's cue to slip away.

"Have fun, gentlemen," he nodded at Edwards and Spector.

"We'll try," Spector smiled, adding: "Nice to see you again."

Edwards looked at him stonily, saying nothing. That was the difference between the two men, Pete thought. Spector could hate your guts but he'd keep stroking you, looking for a soft spot to put the knife in. With Edwards, it was different; what you saw was what you got. He was still marvelling at the eclecticism of the crowd when his credulity was tested still further. A thin, bald-headed man passed so closely that his shoulder brushed against Pete's. Pete stared, then addressing the back of the man's head, called out, "Good evening, your worship."

The head turned, showing a long, pointy nose anchoring some black horn-rimmed glasses. The mouth was large, the thin lips curled around a quizzical smile.

"Uh, good evening," he said hesitantly. His forehead creased and Pete could tell that Supreme Court Justice Alan Nadeau was trying to place him.

"Pete Gossett, the *Herald*," he volunteered. "I interviewed you a couple of times when I was on the court beat for the *Star*."

"Oh, yes, now I remember," the judge said, shaking Pete's hand. "I haven't seen you around lately. You're not covering the courts any more?"

"Not right now, but I hope to get back there one of these days."

Nadeau was already looking past Pete, searching the crowd. "Oh, is that right?" he said distractedly. "Well, good luck," he smiled, moving away, "we can always use good, accurate reporting in our court system."

Unbelievable, Pete told himself. Lawyers he could understand, but first a cop, and now a goddamn judge! He looked toward Lexer again and wasn't surprised to see that Nadeau had joined his group and that the developer had a beefy arm draped over the judge's shoulders.

The puzzle was getting bigger. More pieces to fit together. Or maybe, he chided himself, the wall between his paranoia and imagination had finally collapsed and he was seeing connections and conspiracies where none existed.

So there were a lot of powerful, well-connected people partaking of Jack Lexer's hospitality. That didn't mean they were in his pocket. After all, now that he thought of it, Nadeau and Lexer had both served on the board of directors of the Samaritan Foundation, an institute that had raised millions of dollars for medical research. And Spector, well hell, he was Lexer's lawyer. Why wouldn't he be at the party?

That left Mike Edwards. What the hell could a big-time developer with reputed mob connections have in common with a detective sergeant from the Homicide Division? Answer: sweet bugger all. No, Edwards had probably been at the fights — hell, it was only natural that a guy like him would get off on violence — and heard about the bash from Larry, or some other acquaintance. All totally innocent and aboveboard. Oh, yeah? Then why couldn't he make himself believe it? Why was his mind still searching, flipping through the pages of the past?

Suddenly, he snapped his fingers and a knowing smile lit his face. He was aware that a few heads turned in his direction, but he couldn't care less. He had it. The connection between Lexer and the homicide detective. It went back at least ten years. Only Edwards hadn't been with homicide at the time. He'd been a vice dick, and had made a name for himself by leading the raid on the massage parlour chain that Lexer had unloaded less than a week before the bust.

He glanced across the room. Edwards was in a tight huddle with Lexer and Nadeau, and as Pete watched, the trio slipped through a side door into one of the suite's adjoining rooms. His instincts had been right. There *was* a connection. But before he could congratulate himself any further, the door opened again and two women emerged.

One of them was Cheryl Batten and the other Pete recognized as having been at the fights, sitting in the front row with Lexer's cronies. She was a little shorter than Cheryl, and somewhat chunkier, although all of her curves were in the right places. The dark-blue cocktail dress clung to her body like a second skin, and the low-cut neckline flashed a generous display of cleavage. She was also fairer than her companion, with a mane of light-brown hair that reached her shoulders.

The two women seemed to be arguing. Their mouths were contorted in anger, their eyes hot and intense. As Pete started to wedge through the crowd toward them, Cheryl Batten yanked her wrist free of her companion's hand and fled back to the room she'd just left, slamming the door behind her.

The fair-haired woman stood looking after her helplessly for a few seconds, then, with a resigned heave of her shoulders, started in the direction of the bar. Darting and elbowing his way through the crowd, Pete managed to beat her there and was about to order a drink when she brushed up against him. The warmth of her body and the scent of her perfume sent a pleasant tingle through his skin. He turned and smiled down at her, noting the large grey-green eyes, and the strong, almost mannish, chin.

"Can I get you a drink?" he offered.

She was staring pensively at the floor and it took a few seconds for his words to sink in. Then she glanced up at him from beneath her long lashes and smiled.

"Do I look like the kind of girl who takes drinks from strangers?"

"Well, actually, no," Pete said earnestly, "that's why I think I should introduce myself. I'm Pete Gossett and you're . . . ."

"Linda Selden. And I'll have a gin and tonic. But not here," she added as Pete started to hail the bartender. "I've had enough of this place." Her lips curled in distaste as she swivelled her head. "And these people."

"No problem," he said. "I was just getting ready to leave, myself."

She slipped her arm through his and smiled. "Then what are we waiting for?"

He took one last glance around the room and saw Larry Chambers emerge from a shifting mass of bodies. He was reeling drunkenly, his arms flapping loosely at his sides. Pete called out to him as he lurched past, but his eyes seemed fixed on some distant horizon and he didn't so much as turn his head.

"Larry seems to have quite a load on," Linda remarked.

"Yeah," Pete said. "I hope he doesn't try to drive in that condition."

"Do you know him very well?"

"Yeah, pretty well. We worked together a while back."

Her eyes widened with interest. "Are you in radio too?"

"No, newspapers. I'm with the *Herald*."

"A reporter?"

"Something like that. I cover sports."

"We should have a lot in common," she smiled. "I once dated a wide receiver for the Argos."

"A wide receiver, eh?" Pete deadpanned. "Did he have good hands?"

She batted her eyelashes coquettishly. "That would be telling."

As the elevator door closed soundlessly, it sealed in their laughter, making it and them part of a private joke in their own private world. And for a moment, Pete forgot about

Jack Lexer, Mike Edwards, Cheryl Batten, and the exposé that would release him from the purgatory of covering sports. But only for a moment.

"C'mon," Speedy snarled, tugging at Holly's arm. "We're late as it is."

She held her ground, struggling to free herself. "Lemme go! I ain't going in there!"

They were standing in the middle of the sidewalk, directly in front of the entrance to the Royal York, and the steady stream of people entering and leaving the posh hotel was careful to give them a wide berth as though whatever was afflicting this garishly attired and obviously ill-bred couple might be contagious.

Stung by the amused glances they were drawing, Speedy pulled her roughly off to one side. "Well, for Chrissake, will you just tell me what's buggin' your ass? Before, you were just about freakin' out, you were so wired about goin' to the party."

She stared down at the sidewalk for a few seconds before forcing herself to meet his eyes. "That was before. When it was in my head. But now, it's — it's —" she clenched her fists so tightly her hands shook, "here."

He shook his head disgustedly. "You're goddamn right, it's here. That's why *we're* here. Because if it was somewhere else —" Lost in the maze of his own argument, he threw up his hands in exasperation. "Ah, fuck it."

The guilt was like a heavy hand, pressing her down, scrunching up her insides. She was letting him down. Just like she'd let people down all of her life: Her mother with her dead eyes. A sponge soaking up cheap gin. Holly screaming: "You're killing yourself! You're killing us both! I hate you! I hate you!"

The Children's Aid worker who urged her to keep away from drugs. Mrs. Harris, the teacher who tried to get her to stay in school, and now, Speedy. Loving him as she did, it

tore her apart to cop-out on him, but she couldn't help it.
Everything had been O.K. until they got here and she saw
the passing parade of beautiful people going into the hotel.
People with the time and money to have the deepest tans, the
straightest teeth, and the most stylish clothes.

She looked down at her cheap blouse and the red slit-skirt,
certain that a thousand eyes were peering at every tiny
wrinkle, staring at every microscopic stain. She suddenly felt
cheap, and small, and terribly out of place, and she
desperately wanted to be back at their apartment or even out
on Jarvis where at least she knew who she was.

She knew she had to get control of the funny feeling that
started somewhere deep down inside her or she was going to
cry and she couldn't remember the last time she'd done that.
She bit her lip and turned toward Speedy, who was pacing
back and forth and looking at her darkly.

"I'll try," she said softly.

He stopped in mid-step. "What did you say?"

She took a deep breath. "I'll go to the party with you, but
if it's a bummer and it's like, bringing me down, I'm gonna
split, O.K.?"

He smiled indulgently. "Sure, sure. No problem. But
you'll have a ball, babe. This Lexer dude throws parties like
you wouldn't believe."

He grabbed her elbow and started steering her toward the
entrance. Then, stopping short, he eyed her sternly.
"Give," he snapped.

Without a word, Holly put her hand to her mouth and
removed a large wad of bright pink gum. With a look of
distaste, Speedy took it from her and dropped it on the
sidewalk.

It was at that moment that Pete and Linda stepped out of
the hotel. Pete glanced briefly at the approaching couple but
paid little attention until they drew abreast. It was only then
that he recognized Speedy Renner.

Pete had first run into him three or four years back when
he was still on the crime beat. He'd interviewed him about a

police brutality claim. Speedy had alleged that some narcs had busted into his apartment without a warrant and had trashed the place while looking for drugs. He'd claimed that, during the search, the cops had gotten physical, pulling out a clump of his hair, loosening a couple of his teeth, and damaging one of his eardrums.

Pete had done an article on the charge and the subsequent internal investigation carried out by the police department. The narcs' story was that Speedy had attacked them, and that the three dicks, each of whom weighed over two-hundred pounds, were forced to defend themselves against their one-hundred-and-fifty pound assailant.

Although Pete had tried to cover the story objectively, his skepticism had shown through in a couple of places. He remembered writing something to the effect that "each of the three burly vice officers testified that he was forced to be off work for several weeks as a result of injuries inflicted by the short, slightly-built complainant."

Even though the inquiry had whitewashed the episode, Speedy Renner had appreciated the fact that Pete had had the balls to tell it like it was, and he'd called him to tell him so. That, in turn, had led to a relationship that was marked by a little too much suspicion on both sides to be called a friendship. Nevertheless, the two men had met for a coffee or a beer now and again and Speedy had proved himself an invaluable source of information about what was going down in the fringes of Toronto's underworld. Pete had returned the favour by slipping him a twenty now and then when the small-time hustler was down on his luck.

After he'd been dumped from the crime beat, Pete and Speedy had lost contact and, looking at him now, Pete realized that it had been over a year since he'd seen him. Sensing that he was being stared at, Speedy shot Pete a hard-eyed look. Then his thin face expanded around a wide grin.

"Pete! My main man!" he bawled as they exchanged a soul-brother handshake. "What's happenin', bro? Long time, no see."

Pete took in Speedy's dark-brown sport shirt, tan slacks, and his fresh haircut.

"You're looking good, man. Real good."

"Yeah, and I'm feeling good," Speedy grinned. He was a bundle of twitches and his eyes were wild and bright. Pete could see he was flying high, probably on bennies or crystal meth. Speedy waved over Holly, who was standing off to the side, solemnly taking in the scene.

"Pete, this is my lady, Holly," he said, looping his arm around her waist and pulling her to his side.

"You sure know how to pick 'em, my friend," Pete said, extending his smile to include the thin, nervous-looking girl and thinking: She's just a kid. Wonder where he latched on-to her? One question he didn't have to ask was *why*.

By then, Linda was fidgeting impatiently and reinforcing her presence with some discreet throat-clearing. Picking up the cue, Pete hastily introduced her to the pair.

"This is Linda. She's a very good —" He hesitated and looked at her questioningly. "Friend? Acquaintance?" She shook her head negatively after each characterization. "How many chances do I get? How about potential stranger?"

She tried to keep a straight face but there was laughter in her eyes. "How about companion of a potential lunatic?"

"As you can see," he said to Speedy, "the lady is crazy about me."

"Yeah," he replied, "it sure looks that way."

"Anyway," Pete said, "what are you and your lovely lady up to tonight?"

While Holly glowed at the compliment, Speedy smiled self-importantly. "Me and the chick, we got a big party to go to. We got a special invitation, y'know, and there's gonna be a lot of big people there. I mean *big*. You remember how I used to talk about getting with an outfit where I'd get protec-tion and could score some big bucks? Well, Pete, my man," his voice was taut with excitement, "tonight is when it all gets out of the starting gate."

Pete's eyes narrowed thoughtfully. "You wouldn't be going to Jack Lexer's bash, would you?"

"That's right. How did you know?"

"Just a guess," Pete said, his gaze acknowledging Linda. "We just came from there ourselves."

"No shit," Speedy marvelled. He turned to Holly and crowed. "See, didn't I tell you I was real tight with important people? When you're the best goddamn reporter in the city," he beamed, clapping Pete on the shoulder, "you go to all the right places, right, pal?"

"You got it," Pete smiled. "But if you're going up to Lexer's there's something I think you should know."

Speedy's face clouded. "Oh, yeah? What's that?"

"Your old buddy from vice, Mike Edwards, is up there, and you and he never got along, did you?"

Speedy shook his head disgustedly. "Yeah, I told you about the time that asshole busted me, didn't I?" He rushed on without waiting for an answer, including Linda and Holly in his bid for sympathy. "The rat-bastard overcharged me with trafficking to squeeze me into copping a plea for possession. He is one king-sized piece of shit!"

"He also seems to be pretty thick with Lexer," Pete observed.

"Oh, yeah?" Speedy brightened. "Hey, far-out. Now, maybe once and for all, I can get him off my case."

But as the two couples went their separate ways, Speedy Renner had no way of knowing how much irony was about to be packed into that one short sentence.

Chapter Six

Larry sat hunched over his coffee, pretending to read the paper so that he wouldn't have to make the effort of carrying on a conversation with his wife. His barely touched breakfast had been shoved to one side and as he slowly sipped his coffee, he made sure his tremulous hand was shielded by the paper. A couple of aspirins had dulled the pain that started in the back of his head and stopped between his eyes, and now, at least his stomach no longer felt jumpy. But that shouldn't have been a surprise since he'd heaved up its contents a half-hour before, turning up the shower full-blast so Jane wouldn't hear him retching.

He hadn't really had that much either, he concluded, deciding that his downfall lay in mixing his drinks. He should have stuck with the Scotch instead of — instead of what? He knew he'd sampled a wide assortment of booze at the party, but now, he was hard-pressed to recall what he'd imbibed. And the pounding in his head intensified when he tried to remember. Well, that was the last goddamn time he'd get bombed like that. He'd watch himself from now on. All he needed was to get nailed with an impaired driving rap. As a matter of fact, it was a minor miracle that he'd been able to drive home in his condition.

It wasn't that far from the Park 'n Ride lot but he must've been all over the road. Why couldn't he recapture even a slight sense of the event? His palms began to sweat and the paper seemed to be glued to his fingertips.

Again there was a black hole in his memory through which a part of the previous night had vanished. He tried mentally to retrace his steps from the time he'd left the party but something kept getting in his way, something dark and forbidding, and so huge he couldn't see where it began or ended.

Carefully setting his cup on the saucer, he lowered the paper and glanced hopefully at Jane. "I wouldn't mind another cup of coffee."

Eyeing the uneaten breakfast, she bit off the sharp retort on the tip of her tongue: "I guess another dose of caffeine won't do too much harm," she said, filling his cup. Most mornings, she'd have been tempted to tell him to get it himself, but today she felt less combative and more than a little guilty. The inner glow of self-worth generated by being desired by a young, attractive man had worn off, and in its place lay a hard, cold, lump of remorse.

What had happened to the analytical mind in which she'd always had such pride? All it had taken was the brush of Tod's lips against her cheek and the gentle touch of his fingertips on her rigid nipples and she'd been reduced to a mindless being intent on nothing but a few fevered moments of passion. She wondered what Tod had thought afterward. Had he felt triumphant at seducing an older — she made a quick mental edit — a mature woman? Or did he despise himself for spending his passion on someone old enough to be his mother? But then, who had seduced whom? Even now, she wasn't at all sure.

After pouring the coffee, she stood looking down at Larry

for a few seconds, noting the patches of thinning hair and thinking that at one time they'd looked forward to growing old together. Now, she wondered where the years had gone. How could they have gotten so old so fast and have so few good memories to show for it?

"Did you see the note I left you?" she asked.

"Yeah. Thanks."

"It must really be awful for that poor woman, not knowing where her daughter is — whether she's safe or, for that matter, whether she's even alive."

Larry folded the paper and dabbed his mouth with his napkin. "Yeah. And she's not alone. There are thousands of missing kids in this country, most of them runaways. I don't know what the hell it is with kids these days. . . ."

As if on cue, Arlene and Dianne clumped down the stairs and took their places at the dining room table. "Morning, Dad, morning, Mom," they chorused.

Dianne, at fifteen, was two years older than her sibling and by far the more outgoing of the two. "What have us kids done now, Daddy?" Her eyebrows shot up in alarm. "You aren't going to do a show about Arlene and me, are you? About how we listen to "Twisted Sister" and "Rough Trade" and all kinds of other music that's rotting our brains and don't make our beds."

He smiled wryly, "I could do a whole week of shows on you two, but I wouldn't want to wish it on my poor, unsuspecting audience."

He stood up and straightened his tie, gazing fondly at his daughters. He felt lucky to have such great kids. Pretty, too. Dianne was rapidly approaching womanhood — too rapidly as far as Larry was concerned. She had dark, shoulder-length hair, large, brown, almond-shaped eyes that dwarfed the rest of her delicate features, and a lithe ballerina's body. It was no wonder that the voices of a battalion of adenoidal males were constantly conducting an assault on their telephone.

And Arlene. Sturdily built with ash-blonde hair, strong

features, and serene, pale-blue eyes that mirrored her easygoing nature. In a couple of months, the braces would come off and her teeth would be just as perfect as the rest of her.

There was nothing perfect about the way they dressed though, he thought. Faded, stone-washed jeans and misshapen T-shirts, and Adidas that looked like they'd been worn in a coal mine. Larry pulled on his jacket and kissed each of them on the cheek.

"What have you two got on for today? Anything earth-shattering?"

Dianne mumbled through a mouthful of cornflakes. "I'm going over to Deedee's. She's got a new poster of Simon LeBon that's supposed to be just awesome. I can hardly wait to see it."

"I'm sure I wouldn't be able to wait either," Larry smiled, "if I had even the slightest idea who this Simon Bonbon guy was."

She groaned in dismay. "Not *Bon*bon, *Le*Bon. He's the lead singer with Duran Duran."

"The only Duran I know of is Roberto," he said. "They called him 'Stone Hands' because of the way he could hammer an opponent to pieces."

Dianne wrinkled her nose in distaste. "Oh, gross!"

"Barbaric," Arlene chipped in, rubbing sleep and a few strands of hair out of her eyes.

"I'll tell you what's barbaric," Larry countered. "the way you two keep your rooms. I'll bet dollars to doughnuts that neither one of you made your bed this morning."

The two girls exchanged bemused, here-we-go-again looks.

"You can wipe those smirks off your faces, too," he shouted. "I'm your father and you owe me some respect whether you know it or not!"

He saw the sudden shock and dismay in his daughters' faces and the guilt he felt was stronger than the pounding in his head, but something inside him had been uncaged and he couldn't stop the angry thoughts and harsh words.

"Youth centres and foster homes are full of kids who have no respect for their parents. So are the streets. You may not know it, but there are girls out there —" He flung his arm toward the patio door. "Thirteen, fourteen years old strung out on dope, selling themselves on streetcorners. Eating out of garbage bins. Like animals, like refugees from some war that's going on right under our noses and we don't know about!" His voice broke and he stared at them numbly, his arms outstretched as though reaching out for an answer, something to make sense of it all. He felt a hand on his wrist and turned to see Jane's face, calm and reassuring.

"It's after eight," she said softly.

"Yeah, right," he murmured. Picking up his briefcase, he started for the door, then stopped and took one last look at his daughters. Their eyes were downcast and their bodies tense, almost cringing. His eyes burned and he had to bite his lip to hold back the tears. They were his blood. The best part of him. The only part he loved. His mouth opened and closed but no sound came out. Then he turned and stepped into the sunshine of another bright new day.

After digesting Elaine's briefing notes, Larry leaned back behind his desk, staring moodily up at the ceiling. He felt a heavy cloud of doom hanging over him. Oh, sure, Erica Jantzen would make a bang-up guest. Her story was sure to tug at the heartstrings and put the fear of God into those parents who could identify with the desperate mother.

But what could he do for an encore? He had a full slate of guests booked for the next week or so, but there wasn't a bona fide blockbuster among them. Just a collection of social scientists plugging pet theories and politicians trying to chalk up brownie points with the electorate. Deadly stuff. The only sure thing he had was a return appearance by Madam

Tamara, whom he'd decided to keep on for the entire three hours. Thank God for psychics, he sighed.

Every once in a while, he caught sight of Elaine flitting past his door, casting anxious looks in his direction. Eight-forty-five. Usually, just being at the station infused him with energy and a sense of potency, but today he felt tired and defeated. He was losing it, both here at the station and at home, where his kids must be thinking he was some kind of ranting dictator. Well, at least he could do something about that. He'd make it up to them. Get them tickets to one of the upcoming big rock concerts. What was that group they liked? Oh, yeah, the Police. How had they come up with a name like that, he wondered?

You'd think the cops'd be the last thing a bunch of dope-freak rock musicians would want to identify with. Anyway, he'd bury his prejudices and show his daughters that he was prepared to be tolerant and giving and that if he over-reacted from time to time, it was only because he cared for them so much.

Eight-fifty. The throbbing in his head had abated but his hands were still racked with tremors. He butted out his cigarette and was about to reach into his desk drawer for a quick, bracing nip from the Scotch bottle when he sensed someone standing in the doorway. When he looked up, he was surprised to see Mike Edwards' lantern jaw aimed at him.

"Mike!" How the hell are you?" Larry asked cheerily. "I didn't expect to see you again so soon."

"Me neither," the detective said, taking a few steps into the room. His face was drawn and grim and his usually square shoulders seemed to sag with a kind of world-weariness.

Larry shot a glance at the clock on the wall. "Geez, Mike, I'd like to chew the fat with you but I've only got a few minutes. . . ."

"This isn't a social call, Larry."

Larry's eyebrows knitted as he looked inquiringly at the hulking cop. "Oh, yeah? What's up, Mike?"

"I'm here to speak to Erica Jantzen. I understand she's supposed to be on your show this morning to talk about her daughter's disappearance."

"That's right. How did you know?"

"I was just at her home and one of her kids told me."

"Well, she'll be here in a few mintues," Larry said, quickly adding: "She'd better be. Otherwise I'm gonna be interviewing myself for a half-hour."

"You may have to do that anyway, Larry," Edwards said expressionlessly.

Alarm flickered in Larry's eyes, "What do you mean?"

"I mean that it'll be pretty hard for Mrs. Jantzen to talk about a missing daughter when the kid is no longer missing."

"They found her? When?"

"Not *they, we.*" Edwards paused, letting the full impact sink in.

"You? You mean homicide?"

The homicide detective spoke so dispassionately that he could have been reading the information from his notebook. "The body was discovered around seven-fifteen this morning in Rexdale, about half-a-mile southwest of Humber College. There's several acres of undeveloped land there, with a dirt road leading through it. She was found some thirty, forty yards from the road. She was out in the open but the grass is pretty high there and you couldn't see her from the road."

"Who found her?"

"Some guy was out jogging down that dirt road and had his dog along for company. The dog took off and started sniffing around her. Then he started to howl and that's when the guy went over to see what was wrong." The detective smiled pityingly. "The guy must've had quite a breakfast because he left a trail of barf right back to the road and then some."

"How did she die?"

"Asphyxiation, it looks like," Edwards said. "Probably manual strangulation. Appears as though she was worked over pretty good, both before and after she was killed."

"How do you know it's the Jantzen kid? Nobody's postively identified her yet, have they?"

"No. That's why we want the mother. But we found a handbag maybe ten feet from the body that had some I.D. in it and the victim fits Helen Jantzen's description to a T."

"Have you got any leads?"

Edwards shook his head morosely. "Looks like it's gonna be a tough nut to crack. The word is that she was a working girl, although she hadn't been tricking for long — maybe just a week or so. Could be she had a hassle with a john and the guy spun out. Who knows?"

"Christ, it didn't take long for some pimp to turn her out, did it?"

"It never does. A lot of these kids are disasters waiting to happen. They got their heads stuffed with all this shit about how exciting and glamorous it is to be out on the streets, peddling their twats for some loverboy who slips them a little nose-candy now and then.

"The goddamn movies and TV are full of that crap, and even when they show someone who got snuffed, it's all nice and antiseptic so the people watching don't toss their cookies." He smiled malevolently. "Just for once, I'd like them to show it like it is. Did you know," he said to Larry in an oddly pedantic tone, "that it's quite common for a strangulation victim to have a bowel movement when he or she is being snuffed?"

Larry acknowledged with a short shake of his head that this information was news to him.

"Yeah," Edwards continued with a triumphant gleam in his eyes. "They should show that in cinemascope and living colour and maybe they could show a nice closeup of maggots coming out of the mouth of a corpse that's been lying in the sun for a day or so." Larry glanced pointedly at the clock, but Edwards was wound up and showed no inclination to cap the well of bitterness.

"Naw, *they* don't have to put rotting carcasses in body bags. *They* don't have to smell the stink and brush maggots off their shoes. That's for guys like me. We're the ones who gotta pick up all the human garbage nobody wants and haul it away before people find out what's really going on out there." He jerked his thumb in the general direction of the door. "You know," he said thoughtfully, "I've been thinking that the homicide division should do what the sanitation people do."

"What do you mean?" Larry asked.

"Well, you know how you have to put your garbage in plastic bags and have it all neatly tied up and everything? Well, we should insist that killers do the same thing with their victims so the bodies would be a lot easier to handle."

It wasn't until a slow smile began to spread over the detective's face that Larry realized he was joking. At that moment, Elaine Steele swept in, acknowledged Edwards with a smile, and turned to Larry.

"Erica Jantzen is in the studio. I fixed her up with a cup of coffee and told her you'd be right there."

"O.K.," Larry said. "Go back in there and hold her hand. I just need another minute or two with Mike."

She glanced up at the clock. "It better not be any longer." Then she bustled away down the hall. She'd no sooner gotten beyond earshot when Larry stood up and looked straight into Edwards' eyes.

"Mike," he said earnestly, "you've gotta do me a favour."

"What's that?"

"Hold off on telling Mrs. Jantzen that you found her kid."

The detective blinked slowly. "Geez, I dunno. In a situation like this, I'm required to notify the next of kin as soon as possible."

"Yeah, but who's to know you didn't get here until she was already on the air?"

"Nobody, I guess," he shrugged. "But what's the problem?"

"The problem is that she's my lead-off item and I've nothing to slot in if you drag her away." Larry's mind was racing, formulating a strategy while simultaneously anticipating the detective's arguments. "C'mon, Mike, what'ya say? You and I go back a long way together and you know that I'm the biggest goddamn booster you guys have got. Anytime there's static about police brutality or corruption, who's the first guy to editorialize about how you're getting a bum rap? Yours truly, that's who. And whenever the department wants to lobby for more men and more money, I'm the first one to let one of your mouthpieces come on and wave the flag. Right?"

Edwards' nodded agreement was all the encouragement Larry needed to press his case. "O.K. then. Can you do me this one small favour? Just let me have the woman for fifteen, twenty minutes?"

Elaine stuck her head into the room just as Edwards grudgingly agreed. "O.K., fifteen minutes and then we hit the road."

"Great," Larry bubbled. Then, spurred by Elaine's anxious look, he bolted for the door. Trotting in tandem with Elaine down the narrow hallway, he delivered his instructions out of the corner of his mouth. "I want you to bring Mike Edwards into the studio during the 9:18 commercial break."

"Why? What's up?"

He smiled smugly. "You'll find out."

He disappeared behind the studio door and, within seconds, the on-air light flashed red. Elaine looked back down the hallway and saw Edwards lounging in the doorway of Larry's office. As she slowly walked toward him, *Larry's Line*'s musical signature filtered out of the P.A. system, followed by Larry Chambers' familiar greeting.

"Good morning and welcome to *Larry's Line*! Our show today is packed with all the drama and excitement of life in this great city of ours. I'll be back with my lead-off story — and it's one that certainly touched me deeply — just as soon as we hear a couple of messages from those nice folks who pay the bills down here at CKAL."

If she had a few more pounds on her, she'd be a pretty hot-looking piece, Mike thought as he watched Elaine walking toward him. With her dark good looks, she reminded him of a Mexican stripper they'd once had at a Policeman's Benevolent Association stag.

Thinking of the stunt she'd pulled with Danny Stadnick, one of his old partners in vice, he chuckled to himself. When she'd asked for a volunteer from the audience, old Danny had just about bust his balls hustling onto the stage. He could picture him, standing there with his laundry down around his ankles and the Mexican sleazebag giving him head and digging her long, painted fingernails deep into his buttocks. Crazy fucking Danny hadn't known whether to shit or go blind.

Then Edwards thought of the task ahead of him. Notifying the next of kin of a homicide victim was one of the roughest assignments a cop could have, he decided. No wonder so many cops got burned out so early. Thank Christ they had the Benevolent Association where they could let off a little steam, he concluded, or cops could start to become just as bent as those goddamn weirdos out on the street.

Coming out of the commercial break, Larry led off with a brief recitation of the facts surrounding Helen Jantzen's disappearance. Then he directed his attention to the plump, severe-looking woman sitting across from him at the narrow, L-shaped table. She was in her late-thirties, her dark hair pulled up in a bun. A total absence of makeup gave her a washed-out look and her voice, flat, expressionless, with something of a sing-song cadence, reinforced the impression.

"Erica, I believe you've said that Helen has never stayed away from home before, not even overnight with a girlfriend."

"That's right, Mr. Chambers," she said earnestly. "My Helen was always a home-girl. That's why I know she is not, what-you-call-it, a runaway. She would never just up and leave without saying anything. She would have no reason to. We're a very close family and I'd know if anything was bothering her. But there wasn't. She was just as happy as could be, looking forward to a visit from her cousin when she —" The woman's voice broke and she took a deep, steadying breath before completing the sentence, "went missing."

"Perhaps it might help if you gave us some idea about your daughter's interests. For example, did —", he quickly caught himself, "er, does she belong to any clubs or participate in sports?"

"She plays on the volleyball team at school but what she likes to do best is sing. She's a soloist in the church choir and at home, hardly a minute would go by when she didn't have a song on her lips." Her voice quavered. "I guess that's why the house seems so empty and quiet now, what with her gone and all."

During a lengthy discussion of the police department's attempts to locate the girl, Larry kept glancing at the clock: 9:12, 9:15. As they approached the next commercial break, he cast nervous, sidelong glances toward the studio door. Finally, 9:18 came, and with it, Larry's mellifluous "and we'll be back with more right after these few brief messages."

Right on cue, the studio door swung open and Elaine ushered Mike Edwards in.

Larry made the introductions and Erica Jantzen cocked her head, smiling respectfully at this nice police officer with the soft, deep voice, not understanding at first. Then understanding all too well. Her face drained of what little colour it had and her skin looked waxy. She raised a hand to her cheek, digging her nails into the soft flesh. Wincing from the pain, she knew that this wasn't just another nightmare from which she'd be jarred awake, perspiring, clutching at the air, and screaming into the night. This time, the horror was real.

Edwards hovered over her, a large, bony hand resting lightly on her arm as he tried to coax her out of her chair. Suddenly, the on-air light blinked red and Edwards and Erica Jantzen froze, looking anxiously at Larry. Although the idea had been gestating in Larry's brain ever since Mike had told him about the girl's body being found, it had languished on the periphery of his consciousness. Now, the idea had come in from the cold and he had only a matter of seconds to make a decision.

Catching Mike's eye, Larry raised his hand like a traffic cop and quickly placed a cautionary finger to his lips. Then he leaned over his microphone, his voice husky with emotion.

"Ladies and gentlemen, it is my sad duty to report that there has been a tragic development in the disappearance of sixteen-year-old Helen Jantzen, whose mother is with me in the studio at this very moment."

In a split second, Edwards' expression turned from surprise to anger. Keeping his eyes averted from the detective, Larry rushed on. "Mrs. Jantzen has just been informed that Metro police have discovered a body which they believe to be that of her daughter." The sentence was punctuated by Erica Jantzen's low moaning as she repeated: "My baby. My baby."

"This information," Larry continued, "has just been received from Detective-Sergeant Michael Edwards of the Metro Homicide Division. I repeat, the search for Helen Jantzen has apparently ended with the discovery of a body in Rexdale early this morning. Police report that the girl was brutally beaten, strangled, and left in a field a short distance from Humber College.

"This *Larry's Line* exclusive is brought to you in an effort to keep you, the public, informed and vigilant about the safety of your own loved ones. As a further contribution to CKAL's ongoing crusade to keep our city safe and free of crime, I am now going to try to conduct a brief interview with Erica Jantzen, the victim's mother. As you can understand, she is totally shattered by this tragic development and I'm sure she would welcome all your prayers at this terrible, terrible moment of shock and grief.''

Elaine had been on her way to the reception area to corral the guests for the next segment when she heard the soul-crushing revelation over the P.A. system. Stopping in her tracks, she pressed her arms against her sides, tightly clenching her fists. Glaring at the speaker high up on the corridor wall, she softly hissed: "How could you? How *could* you?"

Behind his microphone, Larry leaned forward, looked into Erica Jantzen's eyes, and said: "I want you to know that if there's anything I, or the management here at CKAL, can do for you, either now or in the future, please don't hesitate to let me know."

Her red-rimmed eyes blinked as she sat imprisoned in the thing that was her body. She wanted to get up and run away, back to her little house where she could pull the curtains shut and let all the pain, anger, and guilt flow free.

But she knew she couldn't leave. Thirty-eight years of blind obedience to authority told her that it was her place to be in that studio, listening to this man go on about how important it was to make the streets safe for the citizens of Toronto.

She heard only every second word and understood only every third, but she knew that if she didn't do what was expected of her, she'd be letting a lot of people down. Mr. Chambers was a famous man. His picture was in all the subways and almost everyone she knew listened to his show. Who was she to say that talking about other people's kids wouldn't bring her Helen back?

No, she wasn't about to show herself up by doing something foolish with about a million people listening in. She'd sit there for just as long as Mr. Chambers felt it was the right thing for her to do. But she felt like such a ninny. She'd been watching his lips move but, for the life of her, she couldn't even guess at what he said.

"Erica," Larry pressed, "I know the profound grief you're feeling isn't something you can easily share, but is there anything, anything at all, you'd like to say to all those people out there listening to CKAL who have been so deeply touched by your loss?"

She gave an embarrassed smile. "Well, I've never been much of a talker but I'd like to thank you and everyone here at the station for being so nice to me."

Larry reached across the table and took both her hands in his. "It's hard for us to accept such a senseless, savage act of human depravity but we can take some consolation from our faith in a good and just God."

Tears welled up in her eyes and her lower lip began to quiver. He squeezed her hands tighter and his voice rose in righteous wrath. "I want you know that from this day forward, I and this radio station — the most public-spirited station in this country — pledge that we won't rest until the monstrous killer of your little girl is brought to justice.

"I will personally put up one thousand dollars as a reward for any information leading to the arrest and conviction of this sadistic animal who is roaming the streets of Toronto, and I'm sure that the management and staff of CKAL are prepared to make a substantial contribution of their own."

His voice pulsed with emotion. "I implore all of you out there in *Larry's Line*'s vast listening audience to join with us here at CKAL in giving your full cooperation to the Metro police to help them track down this brutal killer. If anyone has any information, please call me or the Homicide Division immediately. Whatever you do, don't wait! There's a psycho out there and he could strike again. And the next time —" his voice became deep and ominous, "his victim may be *your* daughter."

Edwards tightened his grip on Erica Jantzen's shoulder. "I think we should go now," he said softly, flashing the hot-line host a withering look. But Larry continued to grasp the woman's hands as she stared intently into his face, seemingly mesmerized by his voice and piercing eyes. It was as though the only part of her world that hadn't been destroyed consisted of the broadcaster's soothing words and heartfelt concern.

"Erica, I know you must go," Larry said solemnly, "and my heart goes with you. But before you leave, is there anything I can do to help you through this time of trial?"

He stole a glance at the phone console out of the corner of his eye. It was lit up like a manic pinball machine. Her pale, puffy face seemed to be melting and she made a few false starts before managing to murmur:

"Could you — would you pray with me?"

"I'd be proud to," he said, his voice brimming with humility, "and I'm sure that all my listeners will be adding their voices and hearts to ours."

"Our Father," she began tentatively.

"Who art in heaven," Larry intoned reverently, his vibrant baritone propping up the woman's quavery soprano as they chorused: "Hallowed be thy name."

In her office, Elaine sat staring out the window, her lips moving silently, almost involuntarily in concert with the prayer. Then her mouth formed into a small, brittle smile. Good thing this isn't television, she thought wryly. Otherwise, Larry'd probably use some graphics and have his audience follow the bouncing ball.

Opening her purse, Elaine took out her compact and after touching up her makeup, carefully adjusted her smile. Then taking a deep breath and squaring her shoulders, she told herself that if she still wasn't completely ready to take on the world, she now at least stood a better than average chance of making it through the day.

Chapter Seven

Speedy rolled over onto one elbow and blinked blearily at Holly. It was almost noon but she was still sound asleep, her face, the lipstick smeared and a streak of mascara running down one cheek, was half-buried in her pillow. Her mouth was slack and her bottom lip rippled in concert with her raspy breathing. The raggedy teddy bear that she sometimes took to bed had slipped from her grasp and was spread-eagled on the floor, staring glassy-eyed at the ceiling.

He rubbed his lips against Holly's bare shoulder, at the same time sliding his hand beneath the sheet and tracing a pattern on her back. She stirred and gave a little, muffled moan as she rolled over onto her stomach. Hooking his arms under her armpits, he pulled back, twisting her torso like a rodeo cowboy wrestling a steer into submission. She lay sprawled on her back wih the sheet bunched up around her waist. The sour odour of stale rum wafted out of her half-open mouth as he traced the areolae of her nipples with his fingertips. Then he bent over and kissed her roughly, moving his mouth over hers, cupping her head with both hands.

"Wha — What're you doin'?" she said, looking at him from beneath drooping eyelids, her voice heavily drugged with sleep.

"What's it look like?" he said, nuzzling her neck. "I'm making love to my old lady. Wanna make something out of it?"

"C'mon, eh? Save it for later. I'm fuckin' wrecked."

"Ain't no way I can save *this*," he yelped, grabbing her hand and placing it on his erect penis.

"Aw c'mon, honey," she wailed sleepily. "It was really rough last night, honest."

"Now," he barked, yanking the tangled sheet from her nude body and straddling her. "I'm your old man, remember? I got rights."

Sighing resignedly, she raised her knees and slowly spread her legs. He entered her with a grunt of satisfaction, his eyes shining with lust. She flinched, pulling back her hips and emitting a sharp cry of pain. But if he noticed, he gave no sign, pumping long, deep strokes as she bit her lip and tried to focus on something, anything, so it wouldn't hurt so much.

When they'd gotten to Lexer's suite, Holly had wanted to have a couple of drinks and just groove on the party and the people in their fancy clothes with jewelry hanging all over them like decorations on a Christmas tree. But Frenchy had nailed them as soon as they got in the door, saying he had a job for her. She hadn't wanted to go with him and had said as much to Speedy, but he'd just said she should do as she was told because his ass was on the line if she screwed up.

So she let Frenchy lead her down the hall to another smaller suite. The place was empty. French said she should wait, that someone would be coming in a little while and she should show him a good time; do anything he wanted. She wasn't to ask him for money, though, because now she and Speedy were on the organization's payroll and they'd be drawing regular salaries.

She sat on the soft, gold couch and waited and about fifteen minutes later, the john showed up. He was higher than a kite and Holly had been around long enough to know that it was from more than booze. Coke, she thought, and it wasn't long before he confirmed her perception.

After introducing himself as "Al," the skinny middle-aged man pulled out a small, tinfoil packet and laid out a line of coke on the glass-topped coffee table. Then he got down on his knees and snorted about half of it, inviting Holly to finish it off. It was good blow. Holly hadn't done much high-quality cocaine but she knew that this stuff hadn't been stepped on much, judging from the buzz it gave her.

They did another line each and the guy started to seem like more than just another john. Even though he was a lot older than she and had a bald head and horn-rimmed glasses with thick lenses that made his eyes seem big and spaced-out, he seemed pretty nice. He smiled at her and told her that she looked pretty and sweet. Sweet. She couldn't remember the last time anybody'd told her that. And he said she reminded him of his daughter when she was young, before she got married and had kids of her own.

He asked her what she wanted to do with her life and said there were all kinds of opportunities for anyone who wanted to make something out of themselves. He said that these days women had all kinds of choices that they didn't have years back, when if you didn't get married and have at least a couple of children, everybody thought you were some kind of weirdo.

She'd thought it was kind of funny that he talked about things like that, because almost every john she met had only one thing on his mind and he didn't waste any time getting around to it. But this dude was different. It didn't seem as if he was just making nervous small talk. He seemed really interested in what made her tick.

That's why she opened up, telling him about her dream of having a little house of her own — nothing fancy — but it had to be white with a green roof and matching shutters.

And inside, it'd have nice, new furniture that she'd picked out of the Sears catalogue — a sofa she could stretch out on while she was nursing her baby daughter and a nice, high-backed chair where her husband could relax and watch TV.

On Sundays, she'd dress her daughter in the fanciest, frilliest clothes she could find, and push her in a stroller all over the neighbourhood with her husband at her side, looking proud as hell to have such a nice family. And one thing she'd never do was yell at her little girl or lay a finger on her no matter how bad she was. The most important thing, though, was making sure the kid had a good father who would protect her and make sure no one ever hurt her.

That was when the john got kind of paranoid or something. He started shouting about how he could never hurt his daughter and anyone who even thought that was sick. When he kept on yelling and grabbed her by the wrist, Holly had become frightened and had started to edge toward the door but he had blocked her path, and ordered her to remove her clothes. After she had complied, he quickly peeled off his own. Forcing her down onto the lush, living-room rug, he'd thrown himself on top of her, wedging her legs open with his knobby knees. With his glasses perched halfway down his nose and hot breath blasting out of his gaping mouth, he worked away at her, grinding his pelvis against hers. After several feverish seconds, he reached down and shoved his hand between her legs, stroking her and then himself. Then he was at her again, pounding against her and twisting his hips in a futile attempt at self-arousal. Holly figured maybe the problem was booze or drugs but whatever the cause, it seemed to her that there wasn't much chance that this sucker was going to get it up.

After a couple more half-hearted thrusts of his hips he had drawn back, scowling down at her. Holly's stomach had knotted in fear. Never had she seen so much hate gathered up in one person's face. She started to tell him that it was all right, that lots of guys had trouble getting a hard-on once in a while, but his black look had been as effective as a hand pressed over her mouth. She had remained silent when he got up and shuffled slowly to a corner table. He stood there for a while with his back to her, and when he started back toward her, she noticed that he had something in his hand. She didn't know what it was until he was kneeling beside her and she stole a look out of the corner of her eye. It was a 7-up bottle and she was only mildly curious until she felt the cool, round surface against her inner thigh.

She tried to twist away but the coke had messed her up pretty badly and her legs felt numb. His eyes seemed even larger now and bulging out so much, they looked like they were rubbing right up against the lenses of his glasses. She felt the neck of the bottle enter her, planing against the soft tissue, going deeper and deeper until it felt like she was going to split right in two. Then he started moving it back and forth, slowly at first, then faster and faster, so fast that, once in a while, his hand slipped off the bottom of the container and slapped against her leg.

Fighting against the pain, she pleaded with him. "No, don't. It hurts." But he seemed to be in a trance, his head bobbing and his arm maintaining a mechanical, piston-like stroke with the bottle. God, it had hurt but, finally, instinctively, she had known what he wanted — needed — to release her from his will.

Feigning a powerful orgasm, she'd thrown back her head and moaned fiercely. And he had finally stopped, staring down at her with a strange, triumphant look in his eyes, his chest heaving. He hadn't talked to her again after that. After they'd gotten dressed, he'd looked out into the hall to make sure no one was around, then hurriedly ushered her out.

It had hurt when she'd walked back to Lexer's suite to find Speedy. And it hurt now with Speedy in the saddle. A few sharp grunts and one last shuddering thrust and he was through. She felt raw, burning, as he withdrew and rolled over on his back. He reached over and gripped her hand fondly.

"Love ya, babe," he murmured dreamily.

She closed her eyes, felt the pain pulse deep inside her and tried not to cry.

Larry eased the navy-blue Cadillac alongside Jane's white Rabbit convertible and went into the house. Generally, he had lunch downtown with Bob Gray or Ken Jessup, then did a little paperwork before he went home, but today he wanted to rest up, lie around the pool and recharge his batteries. He had to be at his best tonight. He knew that morning's show would be the main topic of conversation at the press club and instead of letting a bunch of holier-than-thou types slice him up behind his back, he'd decided to go down later and confront them.

All their talk about journalistic integrity was just a pile of sanctimonious horseshit anyway. They were jealous of him — of his salary, which was almost ten times what a beat reporter made, and of the fact that he was the best-known journalist in the city. People talked about him. Some loved him. Some hated him. But they talked about him. He didn't just report news, he *made* it.

Throwing his sports jacket onto the living-room couch, he called for Jane but there was no answer. Following the sound of high-pitched voices and splashing, he walked over to the patio door and looked out toward the pool. Clad in a bikini and reading a pocketbook, Jane was stretched out on a chaise longue. Both the girls were there as well. Arlene, in a dark one-piece swimsuit, was fiddling with the dial on the ghetto blaster, and a bikinied Dianne had just hauled herself out of the pool, her dark hair plastered against her skull and water streaming down her slim body. His smile collapsed into a frown when he spotted the fourth member of the group. Tod Selby. Big shot college man, Larry sniffed. Well, as far as he was concerned, he was still a wet-behind-the-ears punk and always would be. That's the way it was with all these kids who were born with silver spoons in their mouths. Where he'd had to work for every single thing he had, punks like that had it all handed to them on a silver platter.

Larry winkled his nose in disgust. And get a load of those trunks. They barely covered the crack in his ass. Who does the kid think he is? Sylvester Stallone? Seeing Jane get up from the chaise longue and start toward the house, he ducked away from the glass door, went back into the living room, and called out to her as he heard her enter the house. "Jane? Is that you?"

She padded toward the sound of his voice. He looked up from a handful of envelopes, most of them bills. "Can you make me a bite to eat? I'm starved."

"You're home early." Her raised eyebrows turned the statement into a question.

"Uh-huh. Thought I'd find a nice spot in the shade and unwind." He tried to sound casual. "I don't suppose you caught the show this morning. . . ."

"Some of it," she allowed, turning to go upstairs.

"Well, what did you think of it? The interview with the Jantzen woman, how do you think it went?"

Her voice was heavy with resignation. "What do you want me to say? That I enjoyed hearing you dissect her grief over my morning coffee? That your recitation of the Lord's Prayer was a broadcasting tour de force?"

Larry chuckled mirthlessly, shaking his head. "I'll be damned if I can figure it out."

"What's that?"

"Oh nothing much," he drawled, "just how you can despise everything I do to make a living — a damn *good* living — and still manage to swallow your principles when it comes to sharing in the rewards." His face twisted into an accusing sneer. "If you think what I do is so immoral, how come you don't feel the same way about what it's given us? This house, your precious little convertible, and your charge accounts at the best boutiques, and winter jaunts to the Bahamas. Where the hell do you think those things come from? From Larry Chambers putting his ass on the line every morning so every bleeding heart and self-appointed conscience of the community can take a potshot at him!''

"Shhhhhh," Jane cautioned, pointing toward the patio. The sound of splashing and girlish squeals drifted in from the pool.

He clapped his hand to his mouth in mock contrition. "Oh, I'm so sorry. How uncivilized of me to tell the truth in my own home. Please forgive me. It won't happen again." As she whirled and stamped angrily up the stairs, he called after her. "That's all right, honey. Don't put yourself out. I'll make my own lunch." The slam of their bedroom door told him the barb had hit its mark.

As she shucked her bathing suit and donned shorts and a halter, she realized that her muscles were tense with anger. "Bastard," she spat, thinking about the way Larry always twisted things to make it look as though everything were *her* fault. *She* hadn't asked him to badger that poor woman. *She* hadn't asked him to anoint himself as some kind of law-and-order saviour. Sure, she enjoyed the house, the charge accounts, and the holidays, but they were for his benefit too. Didn't he realize how important it was for his career and image to have an elegant home and an attractive, fashionably dressed wife?

She walked to the window, telling herself she was checking on her daughters, but looking directly at Tod Selby. A smiling, golden god, she thought. What a model he'd make for a nude sculpture. Although they'd said little to each other this afternoon, they'd shared little secret smiles and she was certain there was a bond between them that consisted of more than mutual desire. Once, when their eyes met, she had an overwelming sense that they were reliving the identical moment of their lovemaking at exactly the same time.

She drew back from the window and sat down at her dresser. She heard the refrigerator door slam and plates rattling onto the kitchen counter. Distractedly, she fussed with her hair and looked into the mirror with an almost morbid fascination. Squinting at her reflection, she decided the crow's-feet were definitely starting to become more noticeable. Perhaps it was time to start thinking about a little cosmetic surgery. Nothing much, maybe a lift here and a tuck there. She pinched the soft flesh at her waist. A couple of weeks at aerobics and laying off the gin-and-tonics would take care of that.

Suddenly, a wave of hopelessness swept over her. She knew she could change her appearance, make herself look younger, more attractive. But what about inside? What could she do to excise the old scars, to smooth and shape the way she felt about herself and her life? Could a new face and figure breathe life into dead dreams?

She looked at her reflection, projecting it into the future, seeing the lines web her cheeks, the jowls begin to sag, her neck becoming wrinkled and knotted with veins. What young man would enfold her in his arms, then, and banish the boredom and futility that gin-and-tonics only mitigated? How long would it be, she wondered, before she had to start paying for her fleshly diversions?

As she descended the stairs, she heard Larry talking to someone on the phone. She listened, determining that he was speaking to Elaine Steele. He always seemed to have so much to say to *her*, she thought resentfully. They'd been together at the station all morning, and yet he still felt it necessary to call her after work. His voice wafted out of the living room and as she busied herself in the kitchen, she barely had to strain to overhear his comments.

"We've got to keep the momentum building," he lectured. "This morning was just the beginning. We're going to play this Jantzen thing for all it's worth."

"I hope you've got some idea about how to do it because I'm fresh out," Elaine replied, trying to hide her lack of enthusiasm.

"So far, I've only got one but it's a beauty, if I do say so myself," he crowed.

"Shoot."

"*Larry's Line* is going to set up a fund for Erica Jantzen and her surviving children," he said excitedly. "We'll accept donations on their behalf from corporations, private citizens, you name it! But to get the ball rolling we're gonna need her on again."

"Again?" Elaine said incredulously. "The you-know-what is still hitting the fan from this morning. As a matter of fact, I just got word that the Ontario Women's Rights Union is talking about filing a complaint with the CRTC charging that you misused the airwaves by exploiting Mrs. Jantzen's grief and sensationalizing a tragedy."

"That's great," Larry hooted. "They'll be playing right into our hands. There's no such thing as bad publicity during a ratings war."

Elaine racked her brain, trying to think of some argument that would dissuade him but, finally, she could only suggest that, given her initial experience, Mrs. Jantzen might not be too enthused about participating in another media event.

"Well, I don't think something as important as this should be left up to her. There's a very sick person out there. Helen Jantzen's murder may be the work of some psychopathic serial killer and we've got to do everything we can to nail the bastard before more innocent lives are lost."

"I can see how the woman would be a draw," Elaine said, "but how would her appearance help the cops home in on her killer?"

"Simple, my dear Steele," Larry gloated. "Once we get everyone tuned-in to good old CKAL — except for maybe a few people who want to listen to Ferguson purely out of pity — we announce that we've set up a citizens' information line with a special number that the public can call to pass on any tips about who might have snuffed the kid."

"Well, that sounds as if it'll fly," she said, "but I think we'll have to do it without Mrs. Jantzen because I think the chances of getting her in front of a microphone again are slim and none. Why don't we get Chief Ackerman to come on instead. He could give a progress report on the investigation and —''

''The problem with that,'' Larry cut in, ''is that there hasn't been any progress. Even though Mike's still a little pissed-off, he's been keeping me posted, and he says they haven't come up with a thing.''

''O.K.,'' she conceded, ''but you're asking me to put all our eggs in one basket. If she does decline, what do we have for back-up to keep the pot boiling?''

''She won't decline,'' Larry said smugly. ''She can't afford to.''

''What do you mean?''

''I mean that the woman is on welfare. She doesn't have enough money to feed and clothe her other kids and give them a decent roof over their heads. If there's anyone who appreciates money, it's someone who hasn't got it, and Erica Jantzen fits that description to a T.''

''Are you suggesting . . . ?'' Elaine was too taken aback to finish the question.

''Suggesting, shit. I'm telling you. I know for a fact she wants to have a nice funeral for her daughter and she hasn't got two nickels to rub together. So you tell her we'll foot the bill — everything from the casket to the burial plot. All she's got to do is spend half an hour in the studio. She'll never get a better deal.''

Elaine stared at the receiver, first in disbelief and then with loathing.

''Well?'' Metallic and distant, Larry's voice filtered out to her.

''Suppose it gets out,'' she finally said. ''Suppose we get caught in the middle of a chequebook journalism scandal?''

''That's where the fund comes in,'' he said. ''We throw our contribution into the pot with the donations from the public and who's to say who gave what to her? She gets a fancy send-off for the girl, we get a dynamite guest, and nobody's any the wiser.''

"All right," Elaine said dully, "I'll see if I can get her for Friday."

"And one other thing."

"What's that?"

"Put some copy together for the information line and get Bob to record a public service announcement. And tell him I want that PSA to run every twenty minutes for the next couple of mornings."

After he hung up, Larry finished off the ham sandwich he'd prepared. Then he got up and poured himself a double shot of Scotch. Taking a healthy swallow, he kicked off his shoes and sprawled out on the living-room couch. Polishing off the drink, he cushioned his head with his hands and closed his eyes.

"Are you going to the press club again tonight?"

His eyelids shot open and he jerked his head in the direction of the voice. He hadn't heard Jane come into the room and the question, as well as the icy tone in which it was delivered, startled him.

"Yeah. That's right."

"With Elaine Steele?"

"Not *with* her. I'm meeting her there." He smiled patronizingly. "I know how important it is to make these distinctions with you."

"Larry."

There was something in her voice that defused his belligerence. Something soft and vulnerable that he hadn't heard for a long, long time.

"What?"

"Do you ever wonder why we don't talk anymore?"

"What do you mean?" he frowned. "It seems like you've had quite a bit to say to me lately."

She shook her head sadly. "That's not the kind of talking I mean. I mean being open and really communicating instead of just aiming words at each other."

He thought for a few moments then nodded slowly. "Yeah, I guess things haven't been all sweetness and light between us lately."

"Now, that's an understatement," she said softly.

He looked into her eyes, saying earnestly: "I don't know how to say this so you won't think I'm trying to duck the issue but this just isn't the right time. . . ."

She gave a tired shrug. "Maybe you're right." She paused and when she spoke again her voice was steeped in resignation. "Or maybe we've already run out of time."

"What's that supposed to mean?" he asked warily.

She avoided both the question and his eyes.

"I could say I can't go on like this — living with a stranger, and not even a friendly one at that — but that wouldn't be true. I *can* go on like this — I have for the last couple of years but —" Her voice took on a defiant edge, "I don't *want* to."

He stared at her, genuinely perplexed, thinking how little he really knew about this woman with whom he had lived so long, shared so much. He felt as though he was standing on the edge of an abyss while a voice deep inside him debated the merits of taking the final, irrevocable step.

"Does that mean what I think it does?" he finally said.

She nodded. "This isn't good for any of us. There's no love here. Oh, sure, you love the girls and so do I and they love us back. But with you and me, it's an emotional dead-end. It's been so long since we've gotten anything from each other that we've stopped expecting it."

"Christ," he pleaded, throwing up his hands in frustration, "can't this — can't *you* wait? You know I'm up to my ass in alligators. I'm fighting for my professional life and the next couple of weeks can make or break me."

"They can also make or break *us*," she said quietly.

"What do you want me to do?" he asked. "Go back to doing remotes from used-car lots or shilling for the Buy of the Week at Honest Ed's?"

She took his hand. "I just want you to slow down long enough to see what's happening to us."

"You don't understand." His voice was calm and controlled but she saw the flicker of fear in his eyes. "If I slow down, Ferguson will pass me and when you're number two in my business, you don't get a chance to try harder. That's when they start talking about you in the past tense."

Jane had released his hand and had begun to back away when she suddenly stopped. She looked into his eyes and saw that uncertainty had replaced fear. He seemed to be struggling with himself and she smiled encouragingly, hoping it was the breakthrough she'd been waiting for, the chance for her to feel wanted, needed. But as suddenly as it had appeared, the intimation of vulnerability vanished, and as Larry flashed her a broad wink and swaggered over to the liquor cabinet, she was left to wonder if it had existed only in her own imagination.

.

"Christ, do ya have to leave that piece of garbage lying right in the middle of the floor?" Speedy booted Holly's well-worn teddy bear across the room, where, hitting the wall, it ricocheted into a sitting position, the head tilted to one side and the glass eyes aimed at Speedy as though in silent rebuke.

Holly darted over, picked up the over-sized toy, and cradled it in her arms.

"Why did you have to go and do that?" she asked with a hurt look.

" 'Cause I almost broke my fuckin' ankle on that ugly, moth-eaten piece of junk, that's why," he snapped. "I'd toss it into the trash only the garbagemen would probably refuse to take it. The goddamn thing looks like it's got a dose of AIDs."

She looked at the stuffed animal's face wistfully. "I always wanted one of these when I was a kid, but all I ever had was an old Raggedy Ann doll with all the stuffing coming out the back." She frowned regretfully. "It could've been a real nice doll if Mom would've sewn it up and maybe given it a wash, but if she wasn't drinking, she was passed out and —"

Speedy shot her a disgusted look. "Forget about it. I don't wanna listen to any shit about dolls and teddy bears.

Sometimes you act like a goddamn baby. I don't know why the hell I got tangled up with you in the first place."

"Well, I do," she smirked.

He eyed her warily. "So you're a fuckin' genius now, eh? Well, go ahead, tell me."

"Because you wanna live off this," she snapped, clapping a hand over her right buttock.

He came toward her slowly, a tight smile on his lips. She blinked, bit her lip, but stood her ground, trying not to show the fear that was making her chest tight.

"Babe," he crooned, reaching out and fingering her streaked hair. "You know it ain't right for you to talk to me like that and show that kind of disrespect." His voice was soft and soothing as his hand began to gently stroke her hair. Back and forth. Back and forth. Holly closed her eyes, her body relaxing, her chest loosening.

That was what he'd been waiting for. Raising his free hand, he slapped her hard across the face. Her cheek went from white to crimson, as her eyelids shot up and two large tears formed in the corners of her eyes.

Showing her a clenched fist, Speedy glared at her. "Next time, you'll get this. From now on, I want some respect around here. I'm your old man and don't you fuckin' forget it!"

Then, yanking the teddy bear out of her arms, he stomped toward the door of the apartment. Stepping into the hallway, he hoisted it over his head, swung it around by one leg, then hurled it down the stairway. Holly watched in horror, then tried to dart past him, but Speedy was too quick for her, grabbing her by the arm and spinning her around.

With a fierce effort, she managed to pull free, but off-balance, she went sprawling against the door of the neighbouring apartment. Just as Speedy was roughly hauling her to her feet, the door opened a few inches and Anna Janacek peered out. The wizened old woman viewed the scene with fear-stricken eyes from above her safety chain.

Catching sight of her, Speedy screamed: "You want

fuckin' entertainment, go watch TV, you old witch! Shut that goddamn door and keep your face outta my business or you're gonna have big trouble!''

The door quickly clicked shut but the old woman kept her ear pressed against it, listening to Speedy's curses and threats.

''Now, get in there and get ready,'' he fumed, shoving Holly toward the door of their apartment. ''You got work to do tonight and I don't want you lookin' like no two-bit slut. And no more of this mouthing-off shit, you got it? You do that one more time and you're fuckin' dead! Got it? Dead!''

Speedy slammed the door so hard that Anna could feel the vibrations next door. Prying her ear from her door, the elderly window shuffled arthritically back into her living room. Her heart was beating so hard that she was afraid it might burst right through her frail rib cage. At seventy-seven-years-of-age, she couldn't handle such excitement. Suppose she was getting a stroke? she thought fearfully. Suppose something snapped inside her brain like what happened to Nellie Kupchyk that time when she was coming up the steps from the basement with her laundry? Nellie was still in a wheelchair and talked like a little baby.

She wondered if she should call her daughter to come and take her to the hospital. No, she decided, with a firm shake of her head. The hospital was too far away. Nobody would come visit her there. Elsie and Walter, they just lived two, three, miles away and they only came once every two weeks. She shook her head sorrowfully, thinking of how she'd prepared huge meals for her large family at Christmas and Easter. And now? She looked around the tiny apartment. And now, nobody.

Then she thought about the police. But if that crazy man next door found out she had called them, he might hurt her. She slumped into her old wooden rocker, draped a blanket over her knees, and set the chair in motion.

The familiar movement calmed her. The hammering in her chest subsided. No, she told herself, don't do nothing.

Keep your mouth shut. If you don't make trouble for no one, no one makes trouble for you. Her old, pale eyes turned inward. So different in old country. Here, this Canada, I no understand the young people. They are just like animals. And that crazy man next door. All the time hit. All the time scream. Why that girl stay with him? she wondered. She's probably crazy just like him. With her head in her hands, she swayed gently from side to side. "Oy-yoy-yoy," she clucked. It keep up like this, and someday, somebody get killed.

If there was anything Elaine *didn't* want to do, it was to put in an appearance at the press club. She'd already gotten some feedback on that morning's show from some of her colleagues in the media, and the consensus of opinion was that Larry's performance had been the epitome of yellow journalism.

She'd been surprised to hear herself defending the segment, stressing both its news and public service value. But even in her own ears her arguments had rung hollow. The truth was that just thinking about Larry's predatory performance made her skin crawl. And to top it all, now she had to go and beard the lions in their own den just so Larry could put on a show of station solidarity.

She stood looking out the window of her Avenue Road high-rise, trying to steel herself for the ordeal ahead. The hardest part would be facing Pete, she thought. Even though they were poles apart on so many things, his respect for her as a journalist was important to her. She remembered the first time they met. Fuelled by copious amounts of white wine, she'd rattled on about her ambition to become a top-flight journalist without compromising either her principles or her sexuality.

He'd listened patiently, then lectured her about the inherent timidity of the Canadian media. In Canada, he'd pontificated, there could never be journalistic exposés along the lines of a "Watergate" or a "Pentagon Papers." The owners and executives of newspapers and broadcasting outlets had long-since been co-opted by the social and economic establishments, and the media were so gutless that they had abdicated their editorial responsibility to corporate lawyers. With them, Pete had said, keeping the public informed ran a poor second to avoiding libel suits, and that's why Canadians were so surprised when somebody lifted one little corner of the rug and blew the whistle on organized crime, corrupt politicians, and cops on the take. "In Canada?" they snorted in disbelief. "Now, really!"

At first, she'd thought he was just doing his hard-bitten, cynical reporter routine, but later she realized that he believed everything he said. Still, while he took his profession seriously, the same didn't hold true for himself, and he'd howled in delight when she teased him, calling him Peter Cronkite and telling him that with a little work, he might be ready for "W5" or "60 Minutes."

Oh, to hell with him, she thought, wondering why she'd agreed when he suggested they meet at the press club and go out for a late dinner. She was in a solitary mood and he'd sounded a little hyper. Oh, well, maybe a couple of drinks would help her snap out of it, she told herself.

It wasn't as though she didn't have *anything* to feel good about. After all, she'd succeeded in booking Erica Jantzen for the Friday show, and she estimated that her coup would only cost the station about five-thousand dollars. It'd been a good pitch, if she did say so herself. Mrs. Jantzen had been effusive in her thanks, invoking god's blessing for her, Larry, and "those kind folks at the station." She'd called Elaine "an angel from heaven" for helping her to give her daughter a fine, tasteful funeral.

She looked down at the street. The pools of shadow were lengthening. She felt like getting in her Camaro and hitting the freeway, flooring the accelerator and going as far and as fast as she could. She smiled ruefully. What would be the use? The further she went, the further she'd have to return.

No, there'd be no wild ride tonight, with the wind whipping through her hair and the radio turned on full blast, for as she stepped into the hallway she was stabbed with the realization that what she wanted to get away from the most was herself.

Chapter Eight

Pete wedged the phone between his ear and shoulder and kept pecking away at his computer terminal, putting the finishing touches on a Sunday edition feature on amateur wrestling.

"Gosset here."

"Pete, my man. What's happening?"

Pete recognized the nasal, rapid-fire voice instantly. "Not a lot, Speedy. What's new with you?"

"A couple of things, buddy, and one of them has to do with you."

"Oh, yeah? Lay it on me."

"The broad you left Lexer's party with, that Linda Selden?"

"Yeah, what about her?"

"Are you tight with her or what?"

"Hey, gimme a break," Pete laughed. "Next, you'll be asking if I balled her."

"You keep hanging with her and you ain't gonna have anything to ball *with*."

Pete stopped typing in mid-sentence. At first, he'd suspected that Speedy was tripping out on something and wanted to take him along for the ride. But now, he wasn't so sure. Dropping the bantering tone, he asked: "What's the story, Speedy?"

"The story is that Lexer saw you leave with the chick, and he wasn't too happy about it."

"Oh, yeah? How did you latch onto that information?"

"With my ears, man. I wasn't standing no more than three feet away from him when he starts busting his chops to some skinny, bald dude about you being a fuckin' muckraker."

"O.K., but where does Linda fit into this?"

"I'm gettin' to that," Speedy said. "After he finishes cutting you up, he tells this wimpy-looking fuck that you put the arm on his girlfriend's sister so you could try and get some dirt on him."

Pete wanted to fire off a glib response, but his thoughts got in the way.

"Thanks for cluing me in," he said finally.

"Hey, what're friends for?" said Speedy, pausing before adding: "Uh, Pete?"

"Yeah?"

"Just one more thing," he said. "Like if I'm with somebody and we run into each other, kinda make like . . . ." His voice trailed off into an embarrassed silence.

"Like I don't know you," Pete said.

"Yeah, right," Speedy laughed nervously.

"Well, you better watch your ass, too," Pete cautioned. "Those dudes you're hanging with are into some pretty heavy shit."

"Yeah, but I ain't exactly a pussy either," Speedy bragged. "I can take care of business — been doing pretty good up to now."

The small-time rounder was in way over his head, Pete

thought, but he kept his doubts to himself, saying only: "Yeah. Anyway, take care."

"Yeah. You too."

When they broke the conversation, Pete sat at his desk, thinking about Speedy's warning. He wondered who the guy was that Lexer had badmouthed him to. Then, he dismissed that as having little consequence. What *was* significant was why Lexer was so uptight about his being with Linda. As far as Pete knew, her only connection with Lexer's organization was a social link through her sister, Cheryl Batten. How much then could she possibly know about the inner workings of the mob?

When he had escorted Linda home from the party, they'd stopped for a couple of drinks at the Bellair Café. Pete had plied her with Grand Marnier as they sat at a sidewalk table, their laughter floating into the night sky. When they had reached her apartment, she'd invited him in for a nightcap, which turned out to be more than one.

By then, Linda's vocal cords were well-lubricated and he'd been able to steer the conversation toward Jack Lexer, but all he'd been able to learn was that the latter was her nominee as North America's "Creep of the Year". She'd talked on like a broken record about what a rat-bastard Lexer was; how he'd ruined her sister's marriage, and was now destroying her life. But that was it, an outpouring of bitter anger with no details. It wasn't much to go on, Pete conceded but, at least, it was something he could build on. If he could get her to trust him. If. So many ifs. What was that saying? If wishes were horses, then beggars would ride.

They don't write them like that anymore, he thought sardonically. Of course, they probably don't make investigative journalists the way they used to, either. Face it, Gossett, you fucked up. There wasn't much to criticize in his strategy: feed her some booze, get her tongue loosened up, and lend a sympathetic ear while she tees off on everything that's made her life since puberty less perfect than it could've been.

The only problem was, she'd loosened up too much, and

when he'd left her at two A.M., she was sprawled out on the couch, dead to both the world and Pete's investigative skills. She'd nodded off in mid-sentence and he'd had to lean forward to pick up her muttered words.

"Cheryl's a prisoner and he . . . ."

He? That was easy. Lexer. But that prisoner stuff, he mused as he switched off the computer terminal and filed the original and the back-up disc, what the hell was that all about? Well, there was only one way to find out. Linda darlin', he smiled to himself, get ready to be swept off your feet like you ain't never been swept before.

"Hit me again, Stan," Larry grinned at the elderly, sparrow-like bartender. Cradling the double Scotch in his hand, he scanned the narrow, low-ceilinged room. The subdued lighting and the dark oak panelling gave the press club the look and feel of an Edwardian study. Larry liked the place. He thought it had an air of tradition and permanence about it. A helluva lot more permanence, he'd often thought, than the jobs of most of its members.

He was about to look for a table when a voice came from his left: "Hi, Mr. Chambers. Caught your show this morning. Great stuff!"

Larry turned toward the voice and saw a square-jawed, preppy-looking young man gazing at him with unabashed admiration.

"Uh, thanks," he said, studying the face, then pasting on an apologetic smile. "Gee, I'm sorry but it seems I've forgotten your name."

"Haines. Jeremy Haines," the young man replied. Looking at Larry hopefully, he added, "You may remember an interview I did with you when I was free-lancing for *The Spectator*."

"Of course, now I remember," Larry lied. "Terrific article. Got a lot of good feedback on that." He took a long sip of Scotch. "So what are you up to these days?"

Jeremy looked a little shamefaced. "Well, I'm not doing all that much writing. Actually, I'm doing the late news and weather on CKTV."

"Oh, really?" Larry tried to sound at least halfway interested as he craned his head, searching for Elaine.

"Yes. It's not really what I want to do, but at least it's a foot in the door."

"Yeah, right," Larry said. "The trouble with a lot of kids today is they think they can start at the top — go right from journalism school to anchoring a national newscast."

Even as he spoke, he wondered how many times he'd aimed the same tired platitudes at attentive, almost worshipful faces, all the would-be Mike Wallaces and Geraldo Riveras who thought that he had the key to their success in his back pocket. Hell, even if he had the formula, did they think he'd tell them? Not a chance. The only friends you had in this business were those who either didn't want your job, or didn't have a hope in hell of getting it. Everyone else was the enemy.

Haines quickly seconded Larry's sentiments and was about to launch into another paean of praise for the hotliner's work, when Larry spotted Elaine and curtly excused himself. He led her to a table and they were barely seated before he asked her anxiously: "What's the scoop on Jantzen? Is she in or out?" He leaned forward, waiting for the answer with his entire body.

"She's in," Elaine said, affecting a studied, ho-hum, what-shall-I-do-for-an-encore pose. "Now, do I get a drink?"

Larry grinned broadly and chucked her under the chin. "Sweetie, you not only get a drink but you get the number one hot-line host in the country as your personal waiter."

"Oh?" she said, swivelling her head and making a point of gawking around the room, "I didn't know Trent Ferguson was here."

Larry cocked his fist at her and glowered menacingly. "One of these days, Elaine — one of these days — he said, doing a stock impression of Ralph Kramden, "pow, zoom, to the moon!"

Bouncing out of his seat, Larry hurried to the bar and came back with a gin-and-tonic for Elaine and another double Scotch for himself. They clinked glasses and Larry carolled: "Here's to the best goddman researcher this town has ever seen."

"Thank you, kind sir," she said, batting her lashes. But, in the next instant, the giddiness vanished and her customary veneer of sophistication dropped into place. "Don't look now," she said airily, "but guess who just came in?"

He stole a sidelong glance toward the door and curiosity became delight. "Well, isn't this a happy coincidence," he gloated. "I couldn't think of a better time to run into that sucker."

Tall, slim, with a carefully cultivated tan that accentuated the whiteness of his teeth, Trent Ferguson was one of the new breed of journalists. None of this starting out as a copyboy at some small-town rag or being a relief announcer in Moose Jaw, for him. After taking Journalism at Carleton, he'd gone right into a reporting position with a major TV station in Edmonton. Within six months, he was doing a weekly interview show. From there, it had been everything from anchoring in Halifax to hosting a public affairs show in Ottawa, with his big break coming when ABC-TV recruited him to cover the Middle East.

After dodging bullets in Beirut and Damascus for a year, Ferguson had had enough excitement to last him a lifetime, so when Ben Abelson offered him a hefty five-year pact, he'd found the security and the money too good to turn down. He hadn't regretted the choice. Toronto was cosmopolitan enough for his tastes, and success had come even sooner than his supreme self-confidence had led him to expect.

Though in his late thirties, he retained his boyish good looks, including a set of dimples when he smiled, which was often. And why not? After all, he had a lot to smile about. Elaine followed him with her eyes as he got a drink, then started toward them. He had just enough grey in his dark, close-cropped hair to give him a touch of distinction, and with the tan, Harris Tweed jacket, and chocolate slacks, he looked as though he could have stepped out of *Gentleman's Quarterly*.

Ferguson smiled at Larry. Then, as though wanting to prove that he didn't play favourites, he made sure that Elaine had a chance to admire his bridgework as well.

"Hi, Larry. How are you doing?" he asked.

"Fine, Trent. Couldn't be better," Larry said, shaking his adversary's hand and then introducing Elaine.

"Is this a private party?" Ferguson asked, keeping both his eyes and his smile fixed on Elaine, "or can this lost, lonely soul impose on your hospitality?"

Elaine shot Larry a quick, uncertain look. He replied by waving Ferguson into a chair.

"Glad to have you," he said, forcing a smile. "I'm going to have to run in a few minutes but I guess I've still got time for another drink."

"You usually do, don't you?" Ferguson said.

Larry looked at him sharply, wondering if he'd imagined the insinuating note.

His eyes innocent as a choirboy's, and his voice disarmingly ingenuous, Ferguson continued: "By the way, Larry. Let me compliment you on your show this morning. That bit with the mother of the murdered girl was masterful."

"Glad you approve," Larry said dryly.

Elaine was fascinated. It was like watching a mongoose make small talk with a cobra, she thought. Each seemed to be waiting for the other to let down his defences and leave himself vulnerable. She compared the two men.

CKLB's hot-line star was urbane, charming, and laid-back. When he spoke, his words were selected carefully from an extensive vocabulary and pronounced with the clarity and precision of a Shakespearean actor.

Larry, on the other hand, was earthy and confrontational, and his delivery was an urgent staccato, à la Walter Winchell. Even when he intro'd a commercial, he made it sound as if he were doing a news flash of a hostage-taking or plane crash.

Also, while Ferguson projected no rough edges, Larry wore his like a populist badge that showed his listeners he was one of them — he understood their hopes and fears and would be their champion in a world that taxed them into the ground, let dogs crap in their yards, and delayed their mail ("two weeks, Larry, as God is my witness! Two weeks from Kingston to Toronto. It makes me ashamed to call myself a Canadian").

Elaine thought that if they were cars, Trent would be a new BMW or an Audi, purring effortlessly over hills, holding the tightest curves without skidding or squealing its tires, and ensuring a smooth ride over the roughest of roads. But Larry would most likely be a battered pickup with four-wheel drive, roaring full-throttle through the deepest mud and not caring who got spattered as long as he got where he was going.

Maybe Larry was passé, Elaine thought. Maybe his blood-and-guts, tabloid-style of journalism was on its way out and he was a media dinosaur making a last, futile stand against extinction. Well, Larry was a scrapper, she'd say that for him; he'd have to be dragged out of the studio kicking and screaming.

She realized that Larry's desperation and urgency had infected her as well. Ever since the last BBM book had come out, she'd felt constantly gripped by tension and had had to get into a deep-breathing routine to relax her jaw muscles and the tightness in her chest. The funny thing was that she loved it, thrived under pressure. It had become like a drug to her, driving her to work harder, faster, and forcing her to make decisions instantly without vacillation or self-indulgent soul-searching. She'd realized that the fewer options one had, the simpler life became, and the easier it was to get on with it.

Trent turned, looking directly at her, his eyes dark and humorous, and said: "Well, Elaine, when are you going to come and work for me? Wouldn't you like to hitch your star to someone who's on the way up instead of —" Leaning toward her, he said in a loud, stage whisper, "you-know-who?"

Larry pushed himself away from the table and stood up. "I think I'll get another drink and let you two conspire in privacy," he said. "Anybody else need a refill?"

They shook their heads in unison. Larry shrugged and headed for the bar. Ferguson waited until he was out of ear-shot, then looked at Elaine and smiled as though he were en-joying some private joke. After a few seconds, he nodded slowly, "I was serious, you know," he said.

"About what?"

"About your coming to work for me."

"But why me? There are dozens of top-notch researchers in Toronto. Surely with the megabucks that CKLB has at its disposal, you can have your pick of the best and the brightest."

"And my sources tell me that's you," he said simply.

"Well, I'm flattered. I really am. But I don't think I could possibly leave Larry. Especially now that . . . ." She let the sentence trail off.

"Especially now that Larry's in a ratings war with me? Is that what you were going to say?"

"Something like that."

"Well, let me suggest something else," he said. "Let me suggest that you think leaving Larry would jeopardize his chances of overtaking me in the next BBM survey. Am I right?" In response to her nod, he smiled benignly and said: "And let me further suggest that you think that's the reason I want to hire you away from him."

"I guess so," she said with a shamefaced smile.

"Well, let me assure you," he said, "that you're absolutely right."

Her smile turned to confusion, then shock, and finally anger as she sensed he was enjoying her distress. Who the hell does he think he is? she thought, trying to buy me like some streetcorner tart. She wanted to wipe the smug look off his face but an inner voice told her to keep her cool.

A professional woman couldn't afford to let off steam in a place as public as the press club. Doing so would be sure to set tongues wagging. Oh, yes, all those male chauvinist media pigs would have a field day, snickering asides about PMS making women too emotionally unstable to hold responsible positions. So instead, she smiled demurely and said:

"Suppose I tell Larry about your proposal, or should I say, proposition, since as far as I'm concerned, you've just asked me to prostitute myself."

He held up his hands in a gesture of dismissal. "Suppose you do," he said airily. "he knows the game. He's played it long enough. All's fair in love and ratings."

"Well *I* don't want to play your game, Mr. Ferguson," she said icily.

"It's not *my* game, Miss Steele," he said, draining his drink and standing up. "It's the only game in town in this business." Plucking a card from his wallet, he dropped it on the table in front of her. "If you change your mind, give me a call. I don't know what you're making but I'll give you a thousand a month more. Think about it."

The press club was filling up now and, on his way out, Ferguson stopped to shake a hand here, and exchange a few pleasantries there. Larry was on his way back from the bar and Elaine saw Trent intercept him. The two men chatted for a minute or two; then Ferguson took his leave with a smile, a wink, and a jovial pat on Larry's shoulder.

Elaine picked up Trent's card by one corner, holding it delicately between the tips of her fingers as though to minimize the risk of catching anything contagious. After looking at it with distaste for a few seconds, with both hands she began to twist the thin cardboard rectangle. But when it began to tear, she stopped and looked at it again, and, after a fleeting moment of indecision, quickly slipped it into her purse.

Larry was using the pay phone in the lobby when Pete arrived at the press club at about eight-thirty. Putting his hand over the mouthpiece, he told Pete where to find Elaine and said he'd be along in a few minutes. After detouring to pick up a drink, Pete joined Elaine, dropping into the chair beside her.

"Sorry I'm late," he smiled crookedly. "I got a phone call at the last minute." His forehead creased in bewilderment, "Isn't it funny how you can sit around for hours and there's not a single call, but as soon as you're ready to go somewhere, bingo!"

"No problem," she said, "I've been royally entertained this evening."

Larry rejoined the table in time to pick up on her comment. "Yeah, I'll bet," he said sourly.

Elaine giggled and Pete glanced from one to the other. "Did I miss something or is this a private joke?"

"Trent Ferguson was gracious enough to favour us with his company," Elaine said, with an expression of mock ecstasy.

"Some favour," Larry grunted. "The son of a bitch walked in here like he owns the place. The guy works for a Yankee network for one lousy year and everybody around here thinks he can walk on water."

"The colonial mentality is alive and well in Canada," Pete grinned. "You know we have to get the American seal of approval stamped on our asses before our fellow Canucks think we've got anything going for us." His eyes glinted impishly. "Yeah, it's kind of like the way they grade meat in packing houses, only *their* criterion is quality rather than geography." He shook his head in wonderment. "When you stop to think of it, it's really incredible, you know. Take the Guess Who — you know, the rock group from Winnipeg? Hell, they had to record a song called 'American

Woman' and get some airplay down south before anyone here would think of them as anything more than a glorified bar band.''

"We should get you a higher soapbox," Elaine dead-panned, "so your voice could carry farther."

"Ouch," Pete winced, hunching up his shoulders. "Was I doing it again? How gauche of me to be nationalistic. And here of all places!"

"C'mon, children," Larry said placatingly. "Let's try and make nice with each other and discuss something of real consequence, say, for example, this morning's show." He tried to keep a light tone but Elaine could detect an under-current of seriousness. "Did you manage to catch any of it, Pete?"

"A bit. I was on the run but I managed to catch some of it in the car." Both his voice and expression were noncommittal.

"What'd you think?"

"The thing with the Jantzen woman was certainly inter-esting," he said, being careful to choose a neutral term, "but it made me wonder about something."

"Oh, yeah? What's that?"

"I couldn't get a handle on the way Edwards did his thing," he said. "I mean, we both know the guy wouldn't win any mdeals for sensitivity but why did he have to do it that way? Couldn't he have waited until she at least got out of the studio before hitting her between the eyes with the news that her daughter had been murdered?"

Larry avoided Elaine's eyes as he shook his head in puzzlement. "Beats me. Said something about being in a hurry, didn't he?" he said, glancing at Elaine. His expres-sion told her that he was demanding rather than seeking confirmation.

"Uh, that's right," she said lamely.

Pete stroked his chin pensively. "Strange business," he said, and Elaine saw a speculative look in his eyes as his gaze ranged from Larry to herself. Elaine found herself wanting to be anywhere but there in the press club and the prospect of being alone with Pete and facing his probing questions filled her with dread.

"Oh God," she exclaimed, putting her hand to her temple. "That damn headache's back. I took a Tylenol this afternoon and it cleared up for a while, but now, it's just as bad as ever."

"Well, take another one," Pete said cheerily. "You want to keep the pill-pushers in business, don't you?"

She grimaced in pain. "I can't. I had a couple of drinks and pain-killers and booze are a pretty lethal combination."

Pete and Larry both looked at her with concern. "Maybe I'd better drive you home," Pete ventured.

Elaine got up and put a hand on his shoulder. "No, that's all right. I don't want to spoil your evening. I'm really sorry about this. I'll call you tomorrow and maybe we can do something next week."

Fluttering them a small wave, she swept away before either man had a chance to say anything further. They exchanged puzzled looks before Larry broke into a grin.

"You sure have a way with women, Gossett."

"So it seems," Pete said thoughtfully, "so it seems." Then, in an abrupt mood swing, he picked up his glass, hoisted it aloft, and heartily proclaimed: "Well, here's to truth!"

"Who was that?"

Holly had just hung up the phone when Speedy came out of the bedroom, buttoning his shirt.

"That Larry guy," she frowned. "He said he's coming over in a couple of hours."

Speedy stuffed his shirt into his pants, ran a comb through his long hair, and pulled on his cowboy boots. "Good. You'll have some company. I'm going out."

"Again?" she pouted. "Jeez, I don't hardly see you no more." She eyed him suspiciously. "You making it with another chick or something?"

He chuckled and popped a bennie into his mouth. "You gotta be kidding. This is Speedy you're talking to." He sidled over and roped his arms around her waist, nuzzling the top of her head. "Babe, you're my woman and I'm your man and what we got is too good to fuck up." He ground his hips in an exaggerated humping motion. She curled an ankle around his calf, pulling him closer, feeling herself getting hot.

"Oh baby," she moaned, "I need you so bad. Do you have to go right away?"

He pulled away from her. "I gotta meet Frenchy," he said tersely as though that explained everything.

"Yeah? So what's the big deal if he has to wait a few minutes?" she sniffed. "What is it with you and him anyway? I always figured he walked a little funny but I never thought he was, like, y'know . . . ." She finished the thought by making her wrist go limp.

Speedy's pinched face darkened and he grabbed her roughly by the shoulders.

"Dummy up! You remember what I told you before. I want some fuckin' respect around here. If it wasn't for me —"

"I wouldn't be balling a bunch of weirdos and creeps," she cut in.

"Shut up!" he shouted, his eyes bulging with anger and the veins in his neck standing out like pieces of string. "Shut fucking up!"

Her gaze flew to the wall separating them from the neighbouring apartment.

"Keep it down, eh," she said anxiously. "Grandma's probably got her ear pressed to the wall, taking it all in."

He smiled slyly. "You think so, eh? Well, I'm gonna give her something to listen to that'll make her crap her drawers."

Holly's expression was half-fear and half-curiosity. "What do you mean?"

"Watch this," he smiled. Circling behind a beat-up armchair, he pressed both hands against the back, aiming it toward the next apartment. Then, leaning forward and with his legs pumping, he drove it toward the wall like a football player behind a blocking sled. It struck the wall with a re-sounding thud. Trying to hold back his laughter, Speedy faced the wall, holding his mouth a couple of inches from the peeling plaster and yelled at the top of his lungs. "I've had enough of your shit! I'm gonna kill ya! Ya hear me? Kill ya!" He punctuated the outburst by slamming the wall with his fist a half-dozen times. Then he pointed to his mouth, telling Holly: "Make it sound like I'm laying a beating on you."

She didn't want to comply. The old lady hadn't done any-thing to them and Holly didn't want to hassle her but she knew if she didn't humour Speedy there was no telling what he'd do, so she let out a couple of halfhearted yelps. Then, when he shot her a hard look, she gave an exasperated shrug of her shoulders and let out a single ear-piercing scream.

Speedy gave a satisfied smile and went over to the stereo, cranking it up full-blast. Snapping his fingers, he strutted to the music, jerking his head toward Anna Janacek's suite. "Now, the old bat can get down and boogie!" he carolled.

She watched him go into the bedroom and lift up the mat-tress. When he came out, he was shoving a snub-nosed revolver into his waistband.

"Jeez, where'd you get that," she asked wide-eyed. "Is it real?"

"Naw, it's a water pistol," he said sarcastically. "Of course, it's real. What the fuck do you think?" He took it out and looked at it lovingly. "My first piece," he said, like a father admiring his firstborn in a hospital nursery. "Frenchy gave it to me. It's hot but the serial number is filed off." He tucked it back into his waistband and started for the door.

"Wait," she called.

He stopped, struck by the fear in her voice. "What's the matter?"

She stood there, looking at the floor, then glancing timidly up at him, a child-woman in skin-tight Spandex and a sheer halter-top that revealed the orbs of her small breasts. She shook her head and frowned. "I don't know. I just got this feeling. . . ."

He smirked lewdly. "Yeah? Well, I got me a little feeling myself and when I get back, maybe my feeling and your feeling can kinda like, get together."

She bit her lip, struggling to express her emotions. "It's not that kind of feeling. It's like something's gonna happen, something heavy, but I don't know what."

Speedy walked slowly over to her. "It's that Jantzen chick, isn't it?"

"I dunno," she shrugged. "Maybe it is kinda. I mean, if it could happen to her —"

"It could happen to you?" he tacked on.

"Well, yeah. I mean, I knew the chick. At least, I talked to her once on the street. She seemed really nice, y'know. And then something like that happens. . . . Well, shit, it kinda blows you away, y'know."

"Yeah," Speedy nodded solemnly. "That's why I wanted you off the street. Too many fuckin' wackos out there. You never know what the hell can happen. Now, you ain't got nothin' to worry about. All the johns are screened. Nobody's gonna hassle you because if anyone fucks you over, they're gonna answer to me."

"Yeah, well some of the dudes that've been coming up here are a little scary too, y'know," she said. "Like that Larry what's-his-face. That motherfucker almost tore my tits off." She rushed on before he could launch a rebuttal. "And that other jerk-off, that creep with the bottle. You think he didn't freak me out?"

"O.K., so maybe Chambers is a little on the kinky side," Speedy granted. "But he ain't no worse than a lot of the street trade you used to pull in. And that other dude. You know who that sucker is?" She shook her head. "A fuckin' judge, that's all," he crowed. "Hey, babe, when you got a judge dickin' you, that's when you know you got it made!"

She screwed up her face. "You mean that twisted fuckin' creep is a real judge?"

"You got it." His eyes narrowed as he said tightly: "I should know. I appeared in front of the bastard on a couple of B and E charges in '78." The bitter memory twisted his mouth. "Yeah, his worship, Alan Nadeau. The son of a bitch gave me a year."

"Oh, wow!" Holly exclaimed.

"Yeah," Speedy mused. "It's funny. First, the guy throws a fuck into *me* and now, all these years later, he's doing the same thing to *you*," he chuckled. Then the laughter built, capturing his entire body until he was almost doubled up.

Holly didn't see him like that too often — usually he was down or pissed-off — and it made her feel good, made her want to laugh along with him and share the good feeling. Giggling, she did a little disco dance step, whirling around, spinning dizzily, and finally collapsing against Speedy. They clung to each other and he kissed her fiercely.

"I love you, babe," he breathed hoarsely.

"Love ya, too," she murmured, stroking his hair.

He held her at arm's length, looking steadily into her eyes. "I know sometimes I ain't too good to you. . . ."

She touched her fingertips to his lips, "It's O.K., I understand."

He nuzzled her hair. It smelled sweet and clean and reminded him of walking past a flower store in a shopping mall. He felt a surge of anger, knowing that in a short while, someone else would be tasting her lips, wanting her body the way he wanted it now. It would all be so much easier if he didn't — it was funny how much harder it was to say the words to himself than to her — love her.

She looked up at him, blinking back tears. "You're better to me than anyone. You're the only one who gives a damn whether I live or die. And maybe that's why I'm scared. For the first time in a long time, I'm really scared. Before, I didn't give a shit about doing anything or going anywhere with anyone. It was kind of a rush not knowing what was going to go down because chances were, whatever it was would be better than the bullshit I already went through. Like, I didn't have nothin' to lose because I didn't have nothin' anyway.''

"Yeah, I know what you mean," he said. "Seems like all I've ever been doing is trying to get my shit together enough so's I don't get stepped on." He shook his head self-consciously. "Aw, hell, what the fuck are we talking about anyway? People like us don't make no plans, 'cause as soon as we stop hustling and start thinking about things, we're dead meat," he said, turning away.

As she walked him to the door, Holly pointed to the slight bulge under his shirt: "Why are you packing that?"

"Protection," he said. "Frenchy, me, and a couple of other guys are picking up some shit tonight — a couple of hundred grand worth of coke. Some guys from Buffalo brought it over the border."

"But why do you need a gun?" Her eyes were round with anxiety.

"So's we don't get burned if these dudes are playing some kind of game."

"What kind of game?"

"The kind where they rip off our bread and don't give us sweet fuck-all in return."

She nodded grudgingly. "Yeah, but be careful. You could get hurt."

His laugh was full of bravado. "As long as I don't catch a slug here," he grinned, cupping his crotch. "I already got enough lead in my pencil as it is."

She giggled, then stopped, her brow furrowing. "Suppose that Al guy, that judge, calls? What should I do?"

"What do you do?" he asked, seeming genuinely surprised. "You do what you do with any john who wants to get his oil changed. You look after him. That's your job. And this —" he patted the bulge at his waist, "— is mine."

"Yeah, I know," she said doubtfully, "but suppose he

freaks out or something? You should have seen him. I mean, the guy is severely bent, y'know?''

He scowled darkly. "As far as I'm concerned, any motherfucker who gets his kicks sending guys to the joint has got to be mentally fucked. Those bastards probably blow their stones when they look down and see some poor sucker shitting himself waiting to see how much time he's gonna have to do. That's probably why those scumbags wear those fruity robes — so's nobody can see the cum running down their legs.''

"That's what I mean," she said. "You should have seen the way he looked at me. Like he really hated me. And yet a couple of minutes before, he was all nice and talking to me like I was his own kid or something.''

Speedy shook his head wearily. "I dunno. So many of these straights are so tight-assed and totally fucked that you never know when they're gonna spin out." His expression hardened. "But you gotta look after him. Same thing with that Chambers guy. That's the way it's gotta be because that's the way it is, with you, me, the organization. But don't worry. It ain't gonna be for long. I'm moving up. Next week, we'll get us another place and some new furniture." He pulled out his wallet and fished out a twenty. "Here. Get yourself something. Some earrings, or maybe that Prince album you been blabbing about.''

She pushed the bill away. "Unh-unh. *You* get me something. It'd be better that way — mean more, y'know?''

He stuffed the twenty back into his wallet, smiled, and turned to leave. "See you later, babe," he said. "Take care and don't sweat it. Everything's gonna be O.K. from now on.''

Holly forced a smile, wanting to believe him, but she couldn't seem to get past the feeling that things were moving too fast for her — things that she didn't understand. And the feeling had intensified with the phone calls.

The calls had come within minutes of each other, with the result that she now had three clients for that evening. It meant she'd have to make sure she got rid of one before the next one showed up, because if there was one thing johns demanded it was privacy, especially after they'd drained their prunes and their sex drives had been replaced by guilt.

She hoped she'd set up everything properly, but there were more things in her head than she was used to, and it kind of hurt when she tried to remember what time each of her clients was supposed to show up. God, she thought, I should have written the times down. Maybe what with me starting to get so busy, I should get one of those appointment books or something. She giggled at the thought, basking in the glow of her sudden popularity. Then her face clouded as she remembered the way the callers had talked to her when she'd said she was kind of busy that evening. But then, she guessed she shouldn't have been surprised, because they were guys who were used to throwing their weight around. Still, she didn't like to be threatened and her hands clenched in anger as she recalled the menace in the words: "I think you should make some time for me because I got some friends who promised you'd be good to me. And I don't think you want to make them look bad, do you? Because then, they might decide to make *you* look bad, if you know what I mean."

The other guy was just as big a creep, she fumed, telling her he'd been told that she'd be available for him. What the hell was she supposed to be anyway, she wondered. Some kind of goddamn pizza that you could phone for and if it wasn't ready in fifteen minutes you got it for nothing?

With Bruce Springsteen pouring out his soul through the stereo, she painted her nails, layering the purple polish while keeping one eye on the clock. Still an hour or so before Chambers was due to show. She slid out of her slacks and halter and wandered aimlessly to the window. She leaned forward, looking out, clad only in a pair of light-blue bikini briefs. The evening air felt like cool silk brushing against her jutting breasts and firm, white belly.

When she looked at the clock again, she had a strange feeling that it was staring back at her, its ticking measuring out the minutes of her life. She had a crazy urge to grab the clock and toss it into the street where it would smash into a hundred pieces. Instead, she went into the bedroom and pulled on a sheer dressing gown. Then she returned to the living room, turned up the stereo, and resumed her perch by the window.

She thought about the new apartment and furniture Speedy had talked about. And looking down at the people passing beneath her window — the street people and the straights, punk rockers, and middle-aged matrons — she didn't feel the usual bitterness or jealousy. Finally, the sun was going to shine on her life. And as she waited, she closed her eyes and painted pretty pictures in her head of how it would be, with her and Speedy and the life they would make for each other.

Chapter Nine

Pete stabbed the buzzer, the door opened, and Linda Selden smiled and waved him into the apartment. She was wearing a pair of formfitting designer jeans, and a clinging, low-cut blouse that showed her cleavage to good advantage.

Although he'd been in her suite before, he was struck once again by its opulence. Her living room was larger than his entire apartment and it boasted a profusion of art deco furniture with a lot of chrome and glass. The walls displayed huge, metal-framed prints of surrealistic street scenes and trendy still lifes, one of which depicted a single stiletto-heeled shoe rendered in muted pastels of pink and grey.

Against one wall was a bank of expensive stereo equipment, while the centre of the room was dominated by a large, blocky coffee table with a glass top, around which an assortment of sofas and armchairs were arrayed.

He handed her a bottle of Beaujolais and trailed after her into the kitchen, where she uncorked it. "Terrific place you've got here," he offered.

"So you said the last time," she smiled.

"I did?" he said, shaking his head ruefully. "I guess it's true what they say about the memory going first."

"There are some other things I hope you forget as well."

They clinked glasses. "Such as?" he asked.

"Such as the way I acted the other night," she said. "Falling asleep like that was unforgivable."

"Oh?" he exclaimed, "how did you *want* to fall asleep?"

"Stop it," she said, "I'm serious."

"Listen, it's nothing to worry about," he said. "It was late. You had a couple of drinks —"

"More than a couple," she interjected. "And that's what I want to explain. You may not believe this, but I don't make a habit of getting bombed and passing out on my escorts. That was a rare exception. I know it's no excuse but I was really in a bad space and I guess I tried to use the booze to get out of it."

"Don't we all?" he mused, then said lightly, "Tell you what. Just to prove what a nice, understanding guy I am, I'm going to forgive you." He reached over, picked up her hand, and gave it a chaste peck.

They returned to the living room and sat down on a sofa facing the balcony. She sipped her wine pensively and then after a moment of indecision, cocked her head and looked at him closely.

"Did I say anything the other night that struck you as — well, strange?"

"No. Not that I can recall," he said. "I think we were just making small talk about Lexer's party before you subtly critiqued my conversational skills by dozing off."

She rolled her eyes toward the ceiling, "I'm never going to live that down, am I?"

"Oh, I don't know," he said breezily. "I'm sure the *National Enquirer* will bury it in one of their back pages. And who knows? By the year two thousand, there probably won't be more than a couple of hundred people still talking about it."

"I'm serious," she said, struggling to keep a straight face. "I was upset and drunk as a skunk and I could've said something I shouldn't."

"Actually, you were the soul of discretion," he said, "except for a couple of choice comments about Jack Lexer."

Her eyes widened in alarm. "What did I say about Jack?"

"Well, if you'll wait until I check my notes —" he said, pretending to reach into his jacket pocket. Seeing her anxiety heighten, he dropped the charade. "Basically, all you said was that he had ruined your sister's marriage and was now ruining her life."

She gave a slow sigh of relief and reached over and squeezed his hand.

"I'm glad I didn't go completely overboard," she said, looking at him searchingly and, finally, as though satisfied with what she found there, she smiled and said softly, "I like you too much to get you involved."

"Well," he said, returning the smile, "I like you too much *not* to get involved when it's obvious that something's tearing you up. I'm not promising I can help you, but I can guarantee that I'm a good listener."

She let her gaze roam around the room, then sighed wearily and sagged against the back of the sofa. When she finally spoke, her voice seemed small and fragile. "What I said the other night about Lexer and my sister. . . . That wasn't just the booze talking. He *really is* destroying her, Pete. Slowly, a little bit each day, he's taking control of her, turning her into his personal slave."

"Hey, I'm not saying I don't believe you, but I've seen your sister and she seems like an attractive, very together lady. What kind of hold could Jack Lexer possibly have over her?"

Linda leaned forward and picked up her purse from the coffee table. Snapping it open, she rummaged around before pulling out a thin metal vial about half the length of a ballpoint pen. Unscrewing the top, she poured some white powder into her hand. "Do you know what this is?" she asked.

He nodded slowly. "I think I can make a pretty good guess."

"I took it from Cheryl the night of Lexer's party. She went wild and we had a big argument. Actually, it was right after that that I ran into you." She got up, went into the kitchen, and washed the cocaine down the sink. She came back and stood looking down at him, a current of anger tensing her body. "That goddamn stuff has poisoned my sister's life. She started on it when she was still married to David." Catching his surprised look, she hurried to explain.

"David and Cheryl didn't exactly live in the fast lane but it wasn't uncommon for them to attend parties where there was as much coke as caviar. She told me the kind of people who were there: lawyers, judges, politicians, business leaders. Lots of big names. Hardly a week goes by when one of them doesn't pop up in some society column."

Pete was hungry for their names but, afraid of interrupting and possibly ending the narrative, he forced himself to remain silent.

"Anyway," Linda continued, "gradually, Cheryl developed quite an appetite for cocaine and it didn't take long for that appetite to become a habit around which she restructured her entire life."

"Yeah, once that stuff gets in your blood, it can own you," Pete said. "But how does Lexer figure in all this?"

"He was the one who got her started and he's also the one who's feeding her habit."

"What happened to her marriage? Surely David must've known what was going on. Didn't he try to help her?"

"We both did, but by the time we found out, it was too late. By then, help was the last thing she wanted. All she wanted was to suck that white powder up her nose and feel more beautiful, more important, and more intelligent than anyone else in this city of beautiful, important, and intelligent people."

"How about Lexer? What was his angle?"

"He wanted Cheryl," she said as though it were self-evident. "He wanted to wear her like one of those gold chains he's got around his neck." She pursed her lips, thinking, "But you know, I think there was more to it than that. I think what really turned him on was the idea of taking her away from David."

"But why? What did he have against Batten?"

"Nothing personal," she said. "I think it was less who he was than what he represented: the whole WASP establishment thing, Upper Canada College, Rosedale, and old money."

"David Batten is also a pretty good-looking dude, if my memory serves me."

"That's right," she nodded. "Now, take a look at Lexer. Flashy, crude, *nouveau riche*. His parents came over from the old country in steerage with all their belongings on their backs. And as for looks — well, his face looks like an unmade bed."

"So you think he was trying to prove something to the world by plucking Cheryl out of David Batten's nest?"

She shrugged. "Maybe the world. Or maybe just himself."

"So where do you go from here?"

"I don't know," she said bleakly. "That's the problem. I *want* to do something — I feel I *have* to — but I don't have any idea what. Sometimes I think I should get away as fast and as far as I can because it seems that with every passing day, I become more trapped by guilt and hate."

"You shouldn't blame yourself," Pete began.

"I don't," she flared, "I blame Lexer, but that still doesn't change the fact that I haven't done a damn thing to help my sister."

"Well, maybe there's nothing you *can* do," he said, adding pointedly, "at least, not alone."

She looked at him hopefully. "You mean, you'd —"

"Do whatever I can to nail that rat-bastard to the cross," Pete finished.

She shook her head. "Nobody can touch him. Not you. Not anybody."

"He's big," Pete conceded, "but nobody's so big they don't make a mistake once in a while."

"If Jack makes a mistake," she said, "he's always got someone to cover it up for him."

"Is that where Mike Edwards comes in?"

"You know about him?" she asked, admiration mixed with astonishment.

Pete nodded, hoping she wouldn't see through his bluff.

"Boy is that guy a creep," she scowled. "The police department must do a pretty poor job of screening if an animal like that can join their force. I don't think it's *possible* for him to look at a woman without leering. He's scary. There's no telling what a guy like that is capable of."

"He's probably harmless," Pete grinned. "He's probably like Jimmy Carter and just lusts after women in his heart."

"Hmmmph," she sniffed. "As far as I know, Jimmy Carter doesn't hate women and that's more than I can say for Edwards. He positively despises them, which as far as I'm concerned, is pretty bizarre considering that he seems to want them so badly in a sexual sense."

"How do you know he hates women?"

"Partly it's the things he says, but it's also the way he says them. At first, I thought it might be due to some kind of occupational fallout from working on the Vice squad for so long. Actually, that's something I can relate to because after selling real estate for a few years, I started to look at everyone I met as a potential customer.

"So I figured that it might be the same with him; that after associating with hookers and porno queens for several years, he'd begun to think of all women as tramps. But Cheryl knows him a lot better than I do and she says that he's been like that since his wife left him a couple of years ago."

Pete was too busy framing his next question to pay much attention to Linda's review of the homicide detective's hang-ups. Taking pains to sound casual, he asked: "How long has Edwards been on Jack's payroll?"

She thought for a while. "I really don't know but Cheryl

once told me that they started doing business way back in the mid-seventies, so that would make it over ten years now.''

"And nobody's ever caught on, even though Edwards seems to be a fixture at Lexer's parties?''

"Apparently, Edwards' cover is that he's conducting a surveillance of organized crime figures when he attends these 'do's'.'' She smiled wryly, "I guess his superiors believe him . . . even if nobody else does.''

Pete thought for a moment before Linda broke his concentration by saying teasingly: "Don't frown. You'll get wrinkles.''

It was like a replay of the scene in the elevator on the night they met: Both of them dissolving into giddy laughter, only this time, their mirth wasn't allowed to run its course. It was cut short by the feverish meeting of their lips and Linda whispering: "If you like this couch, you're going to *love* my waterbed.''

"Honey, don't wait up for me. I ran into some old pals at the club and we're gonna go for Chinese food.''

"Thanks for calling,'' Jane said sarcastically. She could tell from her husband's slurred speech that he was half in the bag, and she was almost relieved that she wouldn't have to confront him. When Larry drank, he generally became either abusive or maudlin and, in either case, it was impossible to talk to him. And she had a lot to say.

She'd made up her mind: She wanted out. Out of her marriage and his life. And that very afternoon, she'd taken a giant step in that direction. Where had it all gone? she wondered. It was funny, but she hadn't realized that her marriage was eroding until half of its foundation had washed away.

Now that she had decided her marriage was over, she was able to look at it in a cold, analytical way. Like an archeologist, she had picked her way through the ruins of their relationship, looking for origins and answers.

When had the distancing begun? When had they started to talk *at* rather than *to* each other? She had tried to find some watershed in their relationship, some event that might have triggered the slide from love and understanding to indifference and self-absorption.

Finally, she had given up as she had so many times before, realizing that the process had been like time itself, with no discernible beginning or end. Time. Maybe that's all it was. Time to see each other as they were and weren't. Time to see that dreams were bigger than people and you couldn't expect happiness to be handed to you all tied-up with a big red ribbon. She crossed over to the family room where Dianne and Arlene were lying on the floor, watching a late-night soap.

"C'mon you two," she commanded. "It's past your bedtime."

"Aw, Mom," Dianne moaned. "Can't we just see the end? It's only another couple of minutes."

Jane tapped her wristwatch. "By my calculation that couple of minutes is more like twenty. Didn't you say you had to get up early for horse camp?"

Grumbling, the two girls reluctantly got up and backed toward the door, their eyes still glued to the TV screen. Jane kissed them each on the cheek and watched their legs disappear up the stairs.

She flicked off the hall light and stood listening in the darkness. Above her she could hear the girls getting ready for bed. Each sound seemed strangely special, as though she were hearing it for the first — or last — time.

How would she be able to tell them? she wondered. Her throat caught and tears welled in her eyes. It would be rough on them. Not that single-parent families were foreign to them. Half of their friends came from broken homes. But she knew they'd be hurt and confused. Why shouldn't they be? she smiled bitterly, *she* certainly was. She'd have custody, of course. And if Larry put up a fight, well, that was where the private investigator came in.

She'd anguished over the decision to hire one for hours. Suppose there was still a chance to salvage their marriage, she'd fretted, and Larry found out she was having him followed? That would be the final nail in the coffin of their relationship. He'd never forgive her.

Standing there in the darkness, she tiredly shrugged her shoulders. It was too late to worry about that now. She'd crossed the Rubicon. Within a couple of days, the investigator would be reporting back to her and then she'd know what her next step should be.

She went into the family room, switched off the TV and sat staring at the blank screen. She could hear the girls' muffled footsteps overhead, and then silence. Stepping into the kitchen, she mixed herself a stiff gin-and-tonic. It would be another night of doubt and recrimination warring with bitterness and frustration. If only she'd had her Valium prescription refilled. But she couldn't face Dr. Stern's finger-wagging preachments. She decided she's have to find another doctor, someone who had a better understanding of the stress that housewives have to put up with each day. She mixed another drink and wondered if the liquor would be enough to get her through this night.

Clutching the glass, she stepped onto the patio, then wandered aimlessly toward the driveway, where she stood looking at her jaunty convertible. Thank God it's in my name, she thought. That's one less thing we'll have to fight over. Just as she was about to go back into the house, she saw the dark silhouette of someone approaching along the crescent. As the figure passed under a streetlight, Jane recognized Tod Selby coming toward her at a slow trot.

She was standing in the shadow of the house and he would have run right past her had she not sung out: "Hi, Tod. Little late for jogging, isn't it?"

He stopped at the edge of her driveway, squinting toward the sound of her voice. She stepped into the moonlight and walked slowly toward him.

"I could say the same for that drink." He smiled, his white teeth almost luminous in the pale light.

"Touché," she saluted him with the glass. "What's with the running? Surely a good-looking young man like yourself must be able to find more interesting ways of getting exercise."

He gulped down some air and his rapid breathing began to subside. He was dressed in a pair of Adidas, no socks, track shorts, and a white T-shirt. He looked at her and shrugged.

"I just don't want to get too far out of shape over the summer. I'm going out for varsity basketball in the fall."

As she moved closer, Tod could smell the liquor on her breath, feel the warmth radiating from her body. Stepping back, he glanced anxiously toward her house, and then his.

"Uh, I'd really like to talk some more but —" he began.

"Wouldn't you like to do something more than talk?" she purred.

He gave a nervous laugh. "Yeah, sure, but my mom's expecting me. . . ." Once again, he shot a glance toward his house.

Jane traced little circles on his chest with her finger. "Oh, c'mon now. You're a big boy. You don't have to worry about mommy, do you?"

Involuntarily, he pulled back as she pressed against him. "Somebody could be looking."

"Would that bother you? You didn't seem very worried the last time." She let her hand glide across the front of his shorts, bringing it to rest on his crotch. "O-o-o-h, what's that?" she chirped, feeling him grow hard.

He pulled her hand away but made no move to leave.

"You don't want to go home now, do you?" she cooed. "Wouldn't you rather go for a nice long drive and cool off that strong, hot body and loosen up those —" she dropped her eyes to his bulging shorts, "— stiff muscles?"

Wordlessly, he followed her up the driveway to her car and climbed in beside her. She felt a glow of triumph as she

backed into the street and headed for the freeway. Putting
the spirited little car through its paces, she veered onto
Bayview with a squeal of tires, then, several minutes later,
repeated the maneouvre when she turned east onto Steeles.

Neither of them spoke as the high-rises and housing sub-
divisions slipped behind them. The only sound came from
the car radio and the night air rushing through the windows.
She glanced at him out of the corner of her eye. He was far
from comfortable in the cramped interior. His long legs were
jackknifed, his knees nudging the dash, and when she hit a
bump, his head brushed against the top of the convertible.

He was staring through the windshield, nervously licking
his lips and drumming his fingers on the gearshift console.
She smiled inwardly, thinking that she had just the right cure
for his nervousness. After all, it had worked before, hadn't
it? She dropped her hand onto his well-muscled thigh. He
gave a slight start but made no move to pull away, and as she
began to lightly stroke his leg, she realized he was moving it
closer so that her fingertips caressed his inner thigh.

She slowed the car, then pulled into a dirt road leading to
the construction site of a shopping mall. On one side, concrete pilings rose out of the ground like a twentieth-century
Stonehenge. On the other, a collection of massive excavating
equipment formed a ragged silhouette against the night sky.
Pulling behind a construction shed, she switched off the ignition and leaned back against her door, sliding her right leg
onto his lap.

"These Volkswagens don't have much room, do they?"
he said tightly.

"The seats go down," she said, watching him with hidden
amusement. He wanted her to make it easy for him, she
thought. Well, let him do some of the work. Let him sweat
and want it until his balls are ready to burst.

"How about the driver?"

"Huh? What was that?" Preoccupied with her own
thoughts, she'd caught only the tail end of the remark.

"I was just asking if the driver went down, too." His

voice was still a little strained but his smile was easy and confident.

She sat up and shook her finger at him in mock reproach. "O-o-o-o-h, aren't you a naughty boy!" Then she reached down and ran her forefinger up inside the leg of his shorts. His eyes shining with desire, he leaned over, half-straddling her, pressing his mouth against hers and cupping her breast.

Their tongues met, hot and thrusting, probing each other's mouths. Then abruptly, he pulled away and yanked down his shorts. She watched, feeling her excitement mount as he struggled out of the jockstrap, then took her hand and placed it on his erect member.

She began to stroke him, gently at first, while he gave her low, moaning encouragement. The sound excited her and she began to work at him faster and faster as he writhed in ecstasy and thrust his pelvis in concert with her pumping hand. His rapt expression, coiled muscles, and intensified moans told her he was on the threshold of a climax and instantly, she pulled her hand away and leaned back in her seat, twisting her body so that she was facing him. He looked at her with a mixture of lust and annoyance.

"What's the matter?" he asked hoarsely.

"Nothing," she smiled. "I just want to make it last." She picked up his hand and brushed her lips against it. "I want *everything* between us to last." She looked deep into his eyes. "Don't you?"

"Uh, sure," he stammered.

"If you think *this* is good," she said archly, "wait until I get my own place. Dianne and Arlene will be away some weekends and we can spend day after glorious day together. And we'll do things you've probably only fantasized about. Won't that be wonderful?"

Tod eyed her doubtfully. "I don't think I understand. What's this bit about getting your own place?"

She gave a little embarrassed laugh. "Oh, that's right. I didn't tell you, did I?"

"Tell me what?"

"That I'm leaving Larry."

"Leaving him?" he said in amazement. "You mean you two are splitting up?"

"That's right," she said gaily. "And after I'm on my own, we can see a lot more of each other and not have to worry about who might see us together."

Looking at her quizzically, Tod began to chuckle. As Jane stared at him in bewilderment, his mirth fed on itself until, within seconds, the car was flooded with the sound of his harsh laughter.

"What's so funny?" she said sharply. "Will you please tell me what the big joke is?"

"The big joke?" he sputtered. "I'll tell you what the big joke is. It's you!"

Her mouth dropped open and she stared at him in disbelief.

"Yeah, you," he repeated, watching her recoil from the words. "You and this pipe dream of yours about us carrying on one of the great love affairs of our time."

"But doesn't this —" She made a vague, helpless gesture with her hands. "— mean anything to you?"

"It means exactly the same thing to me that it does to you — a chance for some quick, convenient sex, without the hassle of telling lies that neither of us believes."

"No, you're wrong," she said hotly. "You're wrong!"

"Bullshit," he spat. "I'm right and you know it. You came on to me because you wanted to prove something. Maybe to yourself or maybe to the hot-line hotshot. I don't know. But I can tell you one thing: You're not going to prove it on my time or with my cock because as far as I'm concerned, you're just another fucked-up, middle-aged housewife who thinks getting balled by some young stud is going to fill the holes in her life."

She slapped him hard across the face and pulled back her arm to strike again when he caught her by the wrist. "You want to get physical?" he sneered. "Then get physical with this!"

Reaching over, he placed both of his large, strong hands

behind her head and started to pull her down toward his still-erect penis.

"Don't! Please, Tod, stop it," she whimpered. "Don't you remember when you were small and you used to come over and I always had a treat for you?"

The more she pleaded, the more powerful he felt. Slowly, inexorably, he brought her head down, lower and lower. By now, she was crying and trying to claw at his eyes. But he was too strong. Finally, physically exhausted and emotionally drained, she stopped struggling. Doubled over, with the gearshift jammed against her side, she remained locked to him until, with a final shuddering thrust, his passion was spent.

On the drive back, they remained silent, neither of them able to look at the other. Jane felt sick and empty. Even self-delusion had been stripped from her. Now, all she had left was a sleepless night that would stretch endlessly toward an uncertain dawn.

Speedy was nervous. More nervous than he'd ever been in his entire life. It was what he'd always wanted but now that he had it, he wondered if maybe he was in over his head. His armpits felt sodden and his jaws ached from working them around a wad of gum that had long since lost its flavour.

The car wash was clammy and dimly lit and Speedy felt like he was in some kind of king-sized sewer. Frenchy was sitting on an old wooden bench, reading a paper and looking like he didn't have a care in the world. The other guys, Joey Patriarca and Bill Zajac, were in a dingy little office in the back.

The building was long and cavernous and had a track-like apparatus to which cars were hooked and propelled through a cascade of water and a forest of brushes. At the other end, a crew of attendants with cloths and sponges would wipe off the excess water and vacuum the interiors. The workforce was mostly made up of winos and transients who were happy to score a few extra bucks through some casual work that didn't detract from their more serious pursuits.

During the day the business did a pretty brisk trade, but tonight, there was only one car in the building and it was there for a decidedly different purpose. A maroon Lincoln was parked just inside the entrance and to one side, leaving enough room for another car to pull up beside it. That was part of the plan.

Speedy went over it again in his mind as he discreetly dabbed at his steaming forehead with a folded handkerchief: When the car pulls up and signals with the horn, Frenchy gives the high-sign to Joey and Bill. Then I press the button and raise the door. Once, the car's inside, I lower it. Then I just stand where I can case them and make sure there ain't no surprises.

He traced the outline of the gunbutt with his fingers. It felt cool under his shirt. He hoped he wouldn't have to use it. He hadn't let on to Frenchy, but the truth was that he'd never handled a gun before. He'd checked it out and at least knew where the safety was but, God, he wished he'd had a chance to blast off a few rounds and get the feel of it.

He wondered if he'd be able to pull the trigger and waste somebody, finally deciding that if the drug couriers pulled anything funny, he'd have no choice. The thought chilled him, turned the beads of sweat to icy droplets. They were made guys. Mafia soldiers from Buffalo. If he blew them away, it would really bring down some heavy shit. Yeah, that would be —

"Hey, lose that, will ya?" Frenchy's voice sliced through his thoughts.

"Huh? What'ya mean?"

"I mean that goddamn gum," he said peevishly. "Can it. I'm tired of listening to you chomping on that shit." He looked at Speedy with a mocking smile. "You ain't nervous, are you?"

"Who me?" Speedy said indignantly. "No way." He patted the gun and took a few swaggering steps. "This is my thing, man. I just hope those motherfuckers try something. Yeah, I'd show those bastards a thing or two."

"Yeah," Frenchy said, sounding far from convinced, "I'm sure you would. But don't sweat it. Everything'll be cool. These wops are real pros. We've been doing business with them for a couple of years and there haven't been any hassles so far. That's why you're in on this. We wanted to start you off with something easy."

"Easy or hard, it's the same difference to me," Speedy crowed. "No matter what goes down, old Speedy's ready to take care of business."

But deep inside, he wished he were back at the apartment with Holly. Holly. For the first time that evening, he thought of her. She'd been worried about something — about those creeps she was servicing for the organization. Chambers and what's-his-face, Nadeau, that twisted fucking judge. He'd never seen her so freaked. And they'd been through a lot together. She'd stuck with him when he'd slapped her out and boogied with other chicks. She was a good kid and dynamite in the sack.

He hoped he wouldn't have to lay any more beatings on her. But sometimes, he had no choice. If he didn't, she wouldn't know what was what, and the whole thing would fall apart. And where would they be then? It was a funny thing, he thought, how society pushed you into doing and being things you didn't really want. He smiled to himself. Society. Where the hell had he gotten that scam from anyway? Then he recalled the social workers who'd tried to tell him that he wasn't a bad kid when he kept getting into trouble but was just "acting-out." Yeah, he was acting-out all right. At least, he'd acted his way out of a lot of beefs and detention centres by telling the shrinks and probation officers what they wanted to hear.

He and Frenchy both tensed as they heard a car approach. The dingy panes of glass in the garage door flashed pale yellow and, a few seconds later, the engine and the light died almost simultaneously. Then the horn sounded three short

blasts and one long one. Frenchy gave a curt nod and Speedy
went over and pressed the button beside the door. It rose
with a slow, grinding sound. The higher it slid up, the more
light spilled onto the waiting vehicle: a dark, nondescript
sedan with a New York plate. There were two men in the
front seat and both were looking straight ahead, their faces
expressionless.

When they drove inside, Speedy quickly lowered the door
and took his assigned place. The men got out of the car slowly,
sweeping the interior of the building with their eyes. The
driver shook hands warmly with Frenchy and exchanged
some small talk while his partner lounged against the front of
the car with one foot on the bumper. He and Speedy exchanged wary nods.

After a couple of minutes, Frenchy waved Speedy over
and introduced him to the driver. "Speedy, I want you to
meet a helluva good guy. This here is Paul Carbone, one of
the best guys you ever want to do business with."

Speedy shook hands with the short, bull-necked man. Carbone had big, bushy eyebrows, a long, slightly hooked nose,
and a square, gunmetal chin. A thick mass of chest hair spilled
out above the collar of his white silk shirt, cushioning the
obligatory gold chain which was slung around his neck. Carbone introduced his partner from a distance, flicking his
hand toward him and announcing: "Johnny Arroya."

Figuring Arroya was the one he was supposed to watch,
Speedy cased the guy. He seemed young, probably no older
than Speedy, but he looked like he'd been around. He wore
black slacks with razor-creases and a white shirt open at the
collar, flaunted a collection of blocky rings on his meaty
hands, and had black wavy hair that looked like it had been
carved rather than styled. Speedy thought the dude's eyes
were really spooky. They were dark, deepset, and never
seemed to blink.

Frenchy called Joey and Bill out of the office and the pair
began to strip off the interior panels of the sedan's doors.
While they worked, Frenchy and Paul kibitzed and Speedy

and Johnny eyed each other over the hood of the car. Joey and Bill, both in their late forties, were old hands at their task, and within ten minutes were pulling plastic bags of cocaine from the doors and handing them to Frenchy, who stacked them neatly in a couple of attaché cases. When the job was completed and the panels were replaced, Frenchy opened one of the bags, wet his finger, and stabbed it into the white powder. Touching his finger to the tip of his tongue, he gave it a taste test, and fervently pronounced: "This is some dynamite shit."

"The best," Carbone smiled. "Personally, I wouldn't use nothing else." He pulled a vial out of his pants pocket and held it up like a talisman. "Why don't we do a couple of lines before we finish up here?"

They all went into the back office and took turns snorting trails of the powder through rolled up bills as Carbone counted the packets of currency stacked on one corner of a battered desk. When the count was complete, he gave a satisfied smile and placed the half-million, in small bills, in a leather satchel. When the Buffalo men had left, Speedy lost no time in strutting over to Frenchy.

"Fuck, that was a piece of cake, man."

"It's not over yet, buddy," Frenchy said. "The blow's gotta be dropped off downtown tonight. That's you, Joey and Bill. I got some other business to look after."

"Who do we deliver it to?"

"Never mind who," Frenchy snapped. "Knowing too many names can get you in trouble. Let's just say it's going to a distribution centre. It'd blow your mind if you knew where some of this stuff is going to end up, and the profit it's gonna chalk up by the time it gets there."

"Then the organization uses the bread to score more dope and make even more money, right?" Speedy said.

"Something like that," Frenchy nodded, "but lemme tell you, scraping up the bread to make a buy, whether it's for half a million like today or five times that much, is a piece of cake. There's all kinds of people in this town who're dying to put some of their loose cash to work and make a three-hundred per cent profit on their investment.''

"Yeah? What kind of people?"

Frenchy suspected that he was talking too much but his ego was stroked by playing teacher to Speedy's apt pupil. "You'd be surprised," he said. "Doctors, lawyers, business-men, anybody who's got some cash stashed away under his mattress or in safety deposit boxes where the tax boys can't get their hooks into it.

"Like, this one guy I know, he owns a half-dozen restaurants and what he does is skim some of the take — maybe only a grand or so a day, but it adds up. Then he takes this loose cash and helps us bankroll a big dope buy. After we turn the stuff over for a big profit, we give the guy about three times what he put up, and he's laughing."

"Yeah, but suppose there's a bust and the cops grab the dope or the money?"

"Then the guy's out some big bucks because there's sure as fuck no guarantee in this kind of operation."

Speedy's face wore a puzzled frown. "but even if the guy scores some big bucks from backing a dope deal, he's still got problems with the bread, doesn't he? I mean, like, how can he buy anything, say, like a house or something, without people asking questions and the cops getting wise?"

"That's where the organization comes in," Frenchy smiled proudly. "For a price, we help him smuggle the bread out of the country, say to Panama or the Bahamas. Then he can either write cheques on his foreign account or have money wired to his bank right here."

"That's a lot of hassle, isn't it?"

"Not if you know what you're doing," Frenchy said. "But if you've got the right connections, there's an easier way because there's a few banks right here in good old T.O. that'll launder as much cash as you want, no questions asked."

"You mean it's really that easy to wash dirty money?" Speedy asked.

"It is in Canada, man," Frenchy grinned. "The cops here know how to hand out speeding tickets and put the arm on restaurants for free meals, but they don't know shit about organized crime. And the politicians? Fuck, they're even scared to admit it exists in this country because, if they do, someone might get the bright idea to ask them why they haven't done anything about it."

Frenchy stashed the attaché cases in the trunk of the Lincoln. Bill got behind the wheel and, after Speedy let him out of the building, he and the others joined him outside. After they dropped Frenchy off, Speedy had the back seat to himself.

"Where to now?" he asked, aiming the question at the back of Bill's head. Bill and Joey exchanged stony looks before the latter replied:

"Anyone ever tell you you ask a lot of questions?"

"Hey," Speedy said defensively, "I didn't mean nothing by that. I was just asking, that's all."

"Oh yeah?" Bill said. "Well, even though Frenchy says you're O.K., me and Joey don't know you. So, I'll tell you what. For the time being, why don't you just dummy up and enjoy the ride?"

Speedy could tell from his tone of voice that it was a closed subject.

Fuck 'em, Speedy thought, sinking back into the cushioned elegance of the luxurious car. But his fit of pique didn't last long. Within seconds, he was smiling in the darkness, watching the buildings glide by, and thinking of the stories he'd be able to tell Holly. He could hardly believe it; finally, after all those years of being stepped on and treated like shit, things were starting to go his way.

Totally incongruously, he thought of the time when he was thirteen and had sliced his wrists with a razor blade. He'd sat on the edge of the bathtub, watching the blood ooze out of the narrow fissures and drip onto the tile floor. The sound of each drop striking the floor had seemed deafening.

Soon after, the biting pain had lessened and his head had

felt as though it were floating above his body. That was when
the door had opened and his foster mother's horrified face
had seemed to fill the entire room. He'd wanted to tell her
that it was all right, that he was on his way to this place
where there was this great, big, shimmering light and people
were waiting for him.

He'd never forgiven her for bringing him back. After he
had been sewn up and counselled and psychoanalyzed until
all that bullshit was coming out of his ears, he was sent to
another foster home. And then another.

There'd been many other times when he'd thought about
doing what he'd attempted to do so many years before. But
something had always stopped him, some sense that if he
could just hang in there for a while longer, his luck would
change. Now, finally, it had happened. And thinking back,
he saw that, in one way or another, all of his current good
fortune could be traced to Holly.

The sound of the buzzer zapped through her like a jolt of
electricity. She scrambled to her feet, threw on a housecoat,
and went to the door.

"Hi, you're looking good tonight," the john smiled. His
speech was slurred and he gave off a powerful scent of liquor.

She forced herself to smile back and led him into the living
room. He loosened his tie and took off his jacket, draping it
over the back of a chair.

"I guess you were pretty surprised when I called," he
grinned crookedly.

"Yeah, kinda."

"By the way, you really looked nice the other night."

"Uh, thanks," she said hesitantly.

Brushing by her, he started for the bedroom, saying: "I'm
in kind of a hurry." He stopped in the doorway and looked
back at her. "So, if you wouldn't mind. . . ."

She followed him into the room and noticed for the first
time that he was carrying a briefcase. Snapping it open, he

pulled out a navy-blue dress, a pair of white leotards still in the package, and a pair of frilly white panties. He laid them carefully on the bed as though following some preordained ritual.

"I just guessed but I think they're your size," he said, looking at her with an air of expectancy.

"Like, you want me to put that stuff on?" she said.

Wordlessly, he picked up the dress and handed it to her. She held it at arm's length and looked at it with distaste. It was a pinafore, the kind that kids wore, she concluded. She remembered seeing those stuck-up girls who went to private schools wearing get-ups like that.

With his prodding, she exchanged her bikini briefs for the frilly panties, shimmied into the leotards, then pulled the pinafore over her head and wrestled it into place. She looked at herself in the dresser mirror and began to giggle.

"What's the matter?" His voice was hard and humourless.

"Nothing," she said apologetically. "It's just that I'm not used to wearing dresses. And this one — well, the style's really different, y'know."

He sat down on the edge of the bed and waved her over. As soon as she reached him, he clamped a hand on her arm and pulled her onto his lap. Wrapping his arms around her waist, he linked his fingers just under her rib cage, tightly holding her. She felt a slight rocking motion and when she turned her head, she saw that he was staring right past her with eyes as hard and shiny as her teddy bear's.

"What's the matter?" he asked sharply, as she squirmed around, trying to relieve the pressure on her chest.

"I can't breathe," she wailed. "You're holding me too tight!"

He released his grip and placed a hand on her calf. Sliding it lightly over her knee, he brought it to rest on her outer thigh. Gradually, he began to knead her flesh with his fingers, working his way between her legs. His fingers began to stroke lightly, then probe harder and harder. She pulled back with her hips and gave a little yelp of pain.

He quickly drew his hand away, his face betraying confusion and remorse.

"I — I'm sorry," he muttered. "Did I hurt you?"

"Yeah, a bit." This trick was too rough, she decided. Kinky too. The best thing to do is make it a quickie. "Say, why don't we lie down for a while?" she asked seductively. "You can use a little loving, can't you? Isn't that what you'd like — something hot and sweet and tight?"

He was looking past her again and gave no sign that he'd heard her. When he finally spoke in a dull monotone, he seemed to be addressing some unseen audience.

"Yes," he said gravely, "the signs are all there. The collapse of the family. The lack of respect for authority. The decline in morality. They all add up to only one thing — the destruction of civilized society." He nodded sadly as though affirming some tragic truth. "Yes, there's no stopping it. It's out of control. You see it everywhere. This isn't a city; it's a moral cesspool, with lust and filth slopping all over and spreading until, eventually, it'll touch us all."

"Yeah, right," she said uncertainly, starting to wonder if it was the booze or some bad dope that he was tripping-out on.

Like a robot in slow-motion, he turned his head with a stiff, jerky movement, and stared at her. His expression was grim and his voice was hard and accusing.

"You're just like all the rest," he said, "just like all the other human garbage out there. It doesn't matter where you go. It's like a cancer and no matter how much you cut out, it keeps spreading, further and deeper."

Grabbing her roughly by the shoulders, he twisted her torso, forcing her onto the bed. She looked up at him with wide, fear-stricken eyes as he leaned over her, his face no more than a foot away.

"Do you think I haven't tried?" It was less a question than a challenge.

She nodded and started to speak but changed her mind, figuring that he looked so spaced-out that if she said the wrong thing, he might freak out even more.

"You're goddamn right, I tried," he snapped, answering himself. Then his voice dropped and he muttered self-pityingly, "Nobody cares. Nobody gives a goddamn shit." Then he paused and said tersely, "Nobody but me."

Holly glanced desperately at the clock. "Jeez, it's getting real late and I'm expecting someone else in a little while."

His mouth twisted into a contemptuous sneer. "Oh, so you don't have any more time for me, is that it?" She started to protest but his angry voice trampled her words. "Yes, you're just like all the rest of the whores. Painted-up like circus clowns and tempting decent men with your stinking bodies and lying mouths."

Even Holly was surprised by the way her anger neutralized her fear. "Hey, wait a minute," she said hotly. "Where the hell do you get off dumping all over working girls who're just trying to make a living? We don't hurt anyone. We don't force anyone to go with us."

"Ah, but you do," he said with a smile of bitter triumph. "You do it by exploiting man's weakness and dragging him down into your gutter."

With a burst of desperate energy, she pushed herself away from him, rolled off the bed, and sprang to her feet. But he was too quick for her, lunging to get his body between her and the door.

"So that's the game you want to play, is it?" he said menacingly. "Well, I've got a better one." As he started toward her, she backed up against the dresser. Groping behind her, she brushed then quickly wrapped her fingers around a bottle of cologne. He came closer and began to unfasten his belt, hissing, "Yeah, you've got to get them young and give them the right kind of discipline. That's the only way to clean up this stinking, rotten world." Sliding the belt out of his pant loops, he wrapped a couple of turns of it around his wrist, leaving the buckle-end dangling alongside his leg.

He was no more than two feet away, when Holly raised the bottle. In one quick motion, like an infielder stabbing a line drive, he caught her wrist and twisted it until the bottle fell from her hand. She opened her mouth to scream but, again, he was too quick for her, clapping his hand over her mouth before any sound could escape.

She saw his hand go up, then, a second later, felt a jarring shock and an eruption of pain in her head. There was a loud, insistent ringing in her ears and the floor seemed soft and springy. Feebly, she raised her hands, shielding her face as the blows rained down, the sound of bone striking flesh echoing through the room.

The space inside her head was filled with bright starbursts and pinwheels of vivid colours. Then some sounds. Tiny clicks and pops, the sound of things breaking and bursting deep inside her; things she sensed could never be repaired the way the doctor had fixed her nose.

She felt herself sinking deeper and deeper into some sad, lonely place and she wanted to cry but she felt numb all over and couldn't do anything but lie there and feel everything move away from her, without being able to stop it. It took all of her remaining strength to open her eyes and when she did, she saw his face hovering over her.

His lips were moving, saying something she couldn't make out, and he was smiling at her. Actually smiling. Squatting down on the floor beside her, he took her hand, patting it comfortingly. Now she could make out his words, delivered in a low, soothing tone: "I'm sorry, my sweet little girl. But you know it's for your own good."

Then she felt his hands on her throat.

Chapter Ten

"Oh, Christ," Pete moaned drowsily, reaching for the jangling phone. "Yeah?" he grunted into the receiver.

"Pete? Pete?" The voice had a desperate urgency. "It's Speedy, man."

"Speedy? Hey, what's shaking?" He turned and squinted at his alarm clock, and blinked in disbelief. It was a quarter to five in the morning.

"I'm in trouble, Pete. I'm really in deep shit. She's dead, Pete." He started to sob, and became largely incoherent.

"Who's dead?" Pete pressed. "Settle down, man. Take a deep breath and tell me what the hell's going on."

"Holly," he wailed. "Holly's dead. Why the fuck did it have to be her? Why couldn't it be me? She was the only one in this whole goddamn world who gave a shit about me and now she's gone."

"She's dead? How . . . ? What happened?"

"It's awful, Pete. It's fuckin' awful. You should see her. Her eyes, man. Her fuckin' eyes. They're so goddamn huge and scared-looking, like they saw something really fuckin' awful. And her face —''

"Where are you?" Pete interrupted, sliding into his pants.

"I'm at home," he croaked. "You know where my pad is. But I don't know if I can stay here with — with her much longer. It's freaking me out. I can't take it. You gotta hurry."

"Did you call the cops?"

"The cops!" he exclaimed, "What do you think I am — a goddamn lame? The cops show up, the first thing they're gonna do is try and hang it on me. This is some kind of set-up, man. Somebody's trying to centre me out."

"Sit tight," Pete barked. "I'll be there in fifteen minutes."

Running three red lights and half a dozen stop signs, he made it in twelve minutes. He'd barely touched the buzzer, when the door inched open and Speedy peered out. When he saw it was Pete, his clenched features relaxed. Swinging the door open, he quickly pulled Pete inside.

"Christ, am I glad you're here," he said. "I don't know what the hell to do." He slumped onto the couch and buried his face in his hands. "God, you should see what the son of a bitch did to her. Why?" Dropping his hands, and peering intently up at Pete, he repeated the question as though expecting the veteran reporter, who wrote so authoritatively about so many things, to be able to put a rational face on a violent, chaotic world.

"Why the fuck did he have to do that to her?" Speedy asked plaintively. "She never hurt anybody in her whole life." His voice, already muffled, became unintelligible as he began to cry, his shoulders heaving and his head thrashing from side to side in a violent denial of the hideous truth.

Pete walked slowly toward the bedroom door and looked inside. The room was a shambles. The bedspread lay in a tangle on the floor and there were what looked like shreds of white cloth hanging from the furniture, like ragged bunting. Then he saw her, sprawled beneath the window. She was nude and lying on her back with her legs spread grotesquely. One arm seemed to be clutching at something above her head while the other was folded across her breasts in some posthumous gesture of modesty.

Her eyes stared at the ceiling in frozen horror and her tongue, swollen and purple, spilled out of her gaping, blood-encrusted mouth. Pete pressed his eyes shut as tightly as he could, trying to blot out the gut-wrenching sight. But deep inside, he knew it was too late and that it would always be with him.

"Jesus. Sweet bloody Jesus," he moaned. He clenched his fists, digging his nails into the palms of his hands to try to keep them from shaking. But it was a lost cause and, within seconds, the tremors had captured his body. He took a deep, steadying breath, and looked again, this time with a reporter's eye.

It was not the first time he'd seen the poisoned fruit of violence, but it never ceased to leave him feeling sad and empty. He wondered how old she was. Sixteen? Seventeen? He forced himself to look at her face, something inside him telling him that there was a message, if he had the courage to see it. But in his shaken state, he saw only the fear which had been her entire world in that instant before darkness came. He catalogued the injuries: the blackened left eye, the swollen and discoloured cheek and jaw, the thin black swirl of blood coming from one nostril and linking up with the caked mass around her mouth, the livid welts on her arms and legs. Feeling drained and older than time, he stood there for a few seconds, listening to the relentless ticking of the clock, then rejoined Speedy.

"Pete, what am I gonna do?" Speedy's eyes were wild and panicky and his body seemed a mass of tics and tension. His drawn face was pale and oily with old sweat.

Pete shook his head slowly. "I don't know," he murmured, "but for a start, I think you better call the cops."

"I can't, man," Speedy railed. "They'll hang it on me for sure. Fuck, they been laying for me for years."

Pete stared at him until their eyes made contact. "What's

the matter?'' Speedy said. ''Why're you looking at me like that?''

''I've got to know the truth,'' Pete said quietly. ''If you want me to help you, you've got to tell me the whole story. What happened? Did you and Holly have a fight? Were you high on something? What's the story?''

Speedy's mouth fell open. ''Pete! You . . . . . . You don't think I did *that*, do you?'' His hand shook as he pointed at the bedroom. ''I loved her, man. She was the only thing I ever had that was worth more than it took to get it. Sure, we scrapped. Sure, I gave her a slap every now and then. Because that's the way it was with us and she understood that. But things were getting really good for us. We were moving up. And now . . . .'' He held out his palms as though to show that his life was now as empty as his hands.

But, in the next instant, his sorrow gave way to rage. ''That rotten, fuckin' creep!'' Speedy shouted, pounding his fist against the arm of the sofa. ''I'm gonna kill that motherfucker if it's the last thing I do!''

''Who?'' Pete asked. ''Who are you talking about?''

Speedy's eyes narrowed and his voice was low and murderous. ''That pervert, Chambers. He's a fuckin' dead man, Pete.''

''Chambers?'' Pete frowned. ''You mean *Larry* Chambers?''

''Yeah, that's right,'' he nodded. ''And before I waste him, I'm gonna carve him up real good.'' His voice broke and he said in a strangled voice: ''I'm gonna make him hurt just like he hurt her.''

''Never mind about that now,'' Pete said placatingly. ''The first thing we've got to do is call the cops and make sure you've got a lawyer handy, just in case they start to come on too strong.''

''Yeah, O.K.,'' Speedy said dazedly. ''If that's the way it's gotta be.''

''And,'' Pete added, ''it'd be better if you made the call instead of me.''

"Me?" Speedy stared at him blankly.

"Yeah," Pete explained. "That way it looks like you've got nothing to hide."

Speedy grunted his assent, and as he crossed over to the phone, Pete studied him closely, wondering if he were capable of the savagery that had taken Holly's life. His hands didn't look bruised but then, he could have used some kind of blunt object on her. Unable to come up with any definitive answers, Pete had a vague feeling that whatever had happened here, this night, could be his ticket back to the crime beat if he played his cards right.

On the surface, it looked like just another case of john-meets-hooker, john-loses-hooker, hooker-loses-life. Sex and violence were often just opposite sides of the same coin and, sometimes, it wasn't easy to tell where one left off and the other began. Pete had never been able to figure out how the same urge could foster both intense physical and emotional fulfillment and acts of unspeakable horror and degradation.

Oh, well, he told himself, that's probably why I'm an underpaid reporter instead of an overpaid shrink. Speedy replaced the receiver and began to pace the room anxiously, telling Pete: "They said they'd be right over." He stopped and gestured angrily, "Fuck, there she is lying there like — like that — and this fuckin' pig starts giving me the third-degree over the phone." He paused and bit his lip. "Are you sure I done the right thing by calling them instead of getting my ass out of here?"

Pete shrugged. "Seems to me you didn't have much choice."

"Yeah, I guess you're right," he said uncertainly. Then, as though spurred by an afterthought, Speedy darted back to the phone. From what Pete could overhear, he'd called his friend, Frenchy, filled him in on the situation, and got the name of a lawyer he could call if things got heavy. When he had hung up, he looked a little more relieved.

"The outfit I work for is going to fix me up with a mouth-piece if I need one," he said. "That's the beauty part of working for dudes with bucks. They make sure their people don't get fucked over.''

''Yeah, right,'' Pete nodded, but his mind was elsewhere. He still couldn't believe that Larry Chambers would be mixed up in something like this. But Speedy had been so positive. He had to know more and, after assuring him that it was all off-the-record, he got Speedy to open up.

As Speedy paced and talked, Pete listened — sometimes in disbelief — and wrote, and by the time he heard the heavy footsteps ascending the stairs, he was convinced that if even some of the leads the would-be mobster gave him panned out, he'd have enough material for a dozen exposés. He also realized that for the time being, his hands were tied, since without corroboration of Speedy's allegations, ninety per cent of what he had written down was potentially libellous.

But if he didn't yet have the treasure in hand, he now at least had a pretty good map. The question was: Should he use it? Was it worth it to start tilting at windmills again, especially when these particular windmills had the capacity to tilt back in a dangerous and possibly fatal way?

It was only when he heard Mike Edwards' voice in the hallway that he made his decision. Swiftly, he ripped the several pages of notes from his pad, folded them up, and wedged them into his shoe. Then he went to the door to let in Toronto's finest.

Larry could feel Jane's eyes boring through the darkness. He replaced the receiver and walked unsteadily to the bathroom. The light burned his eyes as he stood in front of the washbasin, staring at his face. His skin looked grey in the harsh light and the whites of his eyes were like cracked porcelain.

He filled a glass with cold water and lifted it to his parched lips. His brain seemed swollen, throbbing against the inside of his skull, and when he closed his eyes, a kaleidoscope of colours swirled in his head. He retched violently, spewing out a stream of evil-smelling bile. He ran the water faster, hoping to drown out the sound.

He forced himself to drink some more water and finished off by gargling some mouthwash. He looked in the mirror again. He was still there. It wasn't a nightmare. The bathroom and he were both real. And so was the phone call from Mike Edwards. Mike had called to tip him off that there'd been another murder, another young girl who'd been beaten and strangled. Larry had been horrified. Two in one week with the same M.O. sounded like the work of a serial killer.

Then Mike had told him the victim's name and his stomach had dropped like a runaway elevator. Holly. Holly Gains. He couldn't believe it. It had to be somebody's idea of a sick joke. Larry had been seized by a combination of shock and panic; it had been all he could do to haul himself to the bathroom and now that he was there, he was afraid to come out. Afraid of Jane's questions and of his own reactions.

"Larry?" she called anxiously. "Are you all right?"

"Yeah, fine," he replied. "Just got a bit of a headache." And he made a noisy production of rummaging through the medicine cabinet.

He wondered if anyone had seen him leave Holly's. Had there been anyone on the sidewalk? He strained to recall, to re-create the entire episode, but it was a complete blank. He couldn't remember what she'd worn or a word she had said.

He did recollect stumbling up the stairs of the press club and later, much later, mumbling his address as he flopped into the back seat of a cab. But, in between, there was nothing. He'd had blackouts before, but only for ten or fifteen minutes at the most. This was scary.

It was the pressure. The pressure and the booze. He placed his hand on the doorknob but couldn't bring himself to turn it. He stood, paralyzed with fear. Suppose he'd left something behind, some article of clothing. His fingerprints; they must be everywhere. Panic welled up in his throat. Suppose they thought *he* had done it. But no, Mike said they had a suspect in custody. Holly's live-in lover and pimp.

The poor kid, he thought. She'd never had a break and probably could have turned into a decent woman if she'd had a chance. He'd tried to help her, had given her some good advice and slipped her some money from time to time, but it hadn't been enough. Still, she was gone now and he had to worry about himself. He took a deep breath, switched off the bathroom light, and opened the door.

He could see Jane's outline in the darkness. She was lying on her side, with an arm propped under her head. "Who was that?"

"Mike Edwards." He glanced at the digital alarm clock. It was 6:30. He didn't have to get up for another half-hour but couldn't see any sense in going back to bed.

"The cop?" She yawned and rubbed her eyes.

"Yeah. Homicide." He sat on her side of the bed, looking down at her. "There's been another murder. Another girl — Mike thinks she was a hooker — was found strangled. Looks like she was beaten up pretty badly first."

"Oh, no!" Jane shot up to a sitting position. "Do the police think it's the same man — the one who killed the Jantzen girl?"

He nodded slowly. "Mike says it's the same M.O. But who knows? There's a lot of crazies out there." His voice took on a note of alarm. "Make sure you tell the girls not to go anywhere alone, especially after dark."

She reached for his hand, feeling closer to him than she had in a very long time. "I will. Don't worry about them. They wouldn't do anything foolish."

"I know, I know," he said, trying to reassure himself as much as her. "But you can't be too careful. Who the hell knows what's out there? The kind of person that would do something like this. . . ." He shook his head disgustedly, letting the words trail off.

"Have the police got any leads?"

"Well, they took in the guy she was living with — looks like he was her pimp, too — but they haven't charged him yet. He's not talking either. He's one of these street-smart punks and he said he wouldn't give a statement until he talked to his lawyer. What with this horseshit Charter of Rights and Freedoms Trudeau saddled us with, a cop can't even ask a suspect if he'd taken a crap without getting his knuckles rapped."

His voice grew louder, angrier. "And you know what? Just as Mike is preparing to sweat the punk a little, who turns up but the creep's lawyer. And not just any lawyer but Morley S. Spector, Q.C."

"Spector? But he's one of the top criminal lawyers in the city, isn't he?"

"In the *country*," he corrected. Which raises a couple of pretty interesting questions. One: Why would Spector rush to the aid of some two-bit pimp at six A.M., and two: Who's footing the bill for his services because, according to Mike, this punk, Speedy Renner, hasn't got two nickels to rub together."

"So the police couldn't get anything out of him?"

"Not a thing. But Mike's been talking to the Director of Criminal Prosecutions, who says that unless Renner comes up with an airtight alibi, the A.G.'s department is going to charge him with first-degree murder."

While Larry shaved, he could hear Jane rattling around in the kitchen. Getting dressed, he came downstairs to find a poached egg on toast and a steaming cup of coffee waiting for him.

"You didn't have to get up," he said, but Jane could see that he was secretly pleased.

"I wanted to," she said, sipping her orange juice. "By the way," she added, trying for just the right note of casualness, "I didn't hear you come in last night. Were you very late?"

He chewed his toast slowly, deliberately, wondering if the

question was an opening gambit in still another verbal chess match. But there didn't seem to be any ulterior current flowing beneath her placid surface.

"Yeah, very late," he said, adding sheepishly, "and very drunk."

"Is that why I don't see your car in the driveway?"

"Yeah," he nodded glumly. "I didn't want to take any chances, so I took a cab home."

"So where's the car now?"

"In a parking lot downtown," he said, adding, "So I was wondering if you could drive me to the subway. . . ."

He braced himself for the usual chewing-out about drinking himself to death and risking his reputation and career, and was taken by surprise when she smiled and said: "Sure, no problem. I have to go to Becker's to get some milk for the girls' breakfast, anyway."

Before they left, Larry tiptoed up the stairs and looked in on his daughters. Dianne's face was half-buried in her pillow and Arlene was curled up in a ball, with her knees almost nudging her chest. He gazed at them fondly from the doorway, fighting against an impulse to snatch them up into his arms and tell them how glad he was that they were safe and well, and how much he loved them.

Then he thought of Holly and as he started back down the stairs, he vowed that he would use all his influence as a major radio personality to see that her murderer was brought to justice.

Elaine bustled into Larry's office with a sheaf of papers clutched in one hand. "Did you go over the stuff I gave you on the anti-Spadina Expressway group?" She looked harried and her manner was uncharacteristically abrupt.

Larry didn't answer. Leaning back in his chair, his hands clasped behind his head, he was staring fixedly at the ceiling.

"What's the matter?" she asked.

He slowly lowered his gaze to meet hers and said somberly, "There was another one last night."

"Another one?" she gave a puzzled frown. "What do you mean? Another *what*?"

"Another murder," he said tightly. "Another girl in her mid-teens. The cops think she was a hooker."

"Oh, my God," Elaine gasped, "what the hell have we got here? Another Jack the Ripper?" But within seconds, she was once again the cool, efficient newswoman. "How did you find out? I didn't hear anything on the news this morning."

"Mike Edwards tipped me off," Larry replied. "It looks like a pattern on the surface but looks may be deceiving because, according to Mike, this one was probably the result of a lovers' quarrel that turned ugly, real ugly. Apparently, she was beaten to a pulp before she was strangled."

"They've made an arrest?"

"Technically," he said. "The guy's in custody but hasn't been charged yet."

"Do you know the girl's name?"

Larry remained silent for a few seconds before swallowing hard and saying softly, "Yeah, I know it. But we can't use it until Mike gives me the word that her next of kin have been notified. He should be getting back to me within the hour and I want you to take down the info if I'm on the air."

She nodded, then shot him a worried look. "What's the matter?"

"What do you mean?" he asked, growing uncomfortable under her steady gaze.

"You look kind of shook-up," she said. "This is really getting to you, isn't it?"

"Yeah, I guess it it," he sighed, wondering if her question was as innocent as it seemed.

"Uh, stop me if I sound insensitive, but you're on in ten minutes and I was wondering if you'd had a chance to look over your briefing notes."

194

He began searching through the pile of papers on his desk, muttering: "I've got them here somewhere. . . ."

All the trouble I went to preparing them and he goes and loses them, Elaine thought angrily. "Never mind," she said sharply. "It's too late now. You'll have to wing it."

"Who have I got for the first segment?" he asked glumly.

"A couple of members of a citizens' group who are lobbying to ensure that the plan for the Spadina Expressway isn't resurrected now that the Railway Lands are going to be developed."

"Hell, I know all I have to about that bunch," he snapped. "Nothing but a gang of left-leaning academics and ego-tripping bleeding hearts. They're all the same. If they weren't against building expressways, they'd be lobbying against throwing live lobsters in boiling water."

"Oh, come on. They're not that bad," she said. "There are some really top-drawer people associated with the anti-Spadina movement, and two of the best and brightest are going to be on with you in —" she checked the clock, "exactly six minutes."

"Yeah?" he said gruffly. "Well, fill me in on them."

"Well, Jerry Cowan is a professor at York University and one of the top urban planners in the province. And May Ponting has been the head of the Inner City Citizens Coalition for four years and she's done a lot to keep the developers honest."

"Hah," he snorted. "If Cowan is such a hot shot planner, why isn't he working for Genstar or Trizec, pulling in some big bucks, instead of holing up in an ivory tower at York?" He got up and began to pace agitatedly around the room.

He stopped in mid-stride. The strength seemed to have gone out of his legs. As he sagged to the floor, he groped for the desk, knocking over a tray of correspondence. His head was spinning and he shook it to fight off the dark fog that was closing around him. He blinked Elaine into focus. She was looking down at him in dismay. With her assistance, he got to his feet and made it to his chair.

"Lower your head," she commanded. He did as he was told and felt the blood pound in his temples.

"You need a doctor," she said, her eyes clouded with worry.

"I need a drink," he muttered, pointing feebly toward his desk drawer. She reached down, pulled out a half-empty bottle of Johnny Walker, and reluctantly handed it to him. He took a large swallow and gave a little shiver of pleasure. Wiping his brimming eyes with the back of his hand, he smacked his lips appreciatively.

"And people think *penicillin* is a wonder drug," he grinned. "They should try *this* stuff." He started to hoist the bottle again but Elaine grabbed it away from him.

"That's enough," she snapped, glancing worriedly at the clock. "You're on in three minutes."

He got unsteadily to his feet. His neck felt stiff, so he began to rotate his head but thought better of it when the dizziness began to return. Elaine unwrapped a stick of chewing gum and pressed it between Larry's lips.

"Chew," she ordered.

He worked his jaws slowly while she reached over and straightened his tie and eyed him appraisingly. "Hmmmm, could be worse," she said, adding officiously, "Comb your hair."

"Yes, ma'am, three bags full, ma'am," he said sardonically, running a comb through his thin locks.

"O.K.," she said, with a look that seemed to suggest she'd done as much as she could, given what she had to work with, "Break a tonsil."

Walking down the long hallway to the studio, Larry tried to focus his thoughts on the upcoming interview, but it was no use. Suddenly, the events of the previous evening had come rushing back to him. He remembered Holly coming to the door and letting him in, even remembered the colour of the dressing gown she'd worn and the music that had been playing on the stereo. He could see it all now as though he were watching a home movie with himself and Holly in the starring roles. There they were, sitting on the couch. In the next scene, she was slipping off her robe and looking invitingly over her shoulder as she started for the bedroom. And then . . . and then nothing. It was as if the film had broken and the screen went blank.

But he told himself that figured, because that was probably when he'd passed out. Christ, how much had he drunk? Ten, twelve doubles? Damn good thing it hadn't happened in the street. He could have fallen on his fucking head and ended up in some emergency ward or drunk tank. But, aside from his flannel tongue and aching head, he was A.O.K. The only real damage — and it was next to nothing — was a little brusing on his right hand he thought had happened when he stumbled going up the driveway and fell against Jane's car.

Reaching the studio door, Larry took the gum out of his mouth and, unable to find a waste receptacle, wrapped it carefully in a tissue and stuffed in it his jacket pocket. Then, putting on a set smile, he pushed open the door and strode briskly inside.

Chapter Eleven

Morley and Barbara Spector had had a late night. Of course, that was not unusual since they were charter members of Toronto's somewhat limited jet set, flitting from one opening to another, and making sure they were seen at all of the most prestigious fund-raising galas. The previous evening, though, had been rather extraordinary even by their rarefied standards. The Premier, the Lieutenant-Governor, and a half-dozen ambassadors had been in attendance at a benefit for one of Barbara's favourite causes.

Morley's heavy-lidded eyes drooped even more than usual when he arrived at the Metro police station and a plainclothes detective led him into an interview room. His round shoulders sagged as he gazed around the sparsely furnished room, waiting for the officer to return with Speedy Renner. There were just two straight-backed wooden chairs at opposite sides of a small table, and Morley groaned as he lowered his soft body onto a hard seat.

Lexer had his goddamn nerve telling him to hustle down

here and provide legal counsel to some two-bit punk, he thought resentfully. Why, he'd been tempted to tell Jack to get himself another boy, maybe some wet-behind-the-ears kid fresh out of law school, who'd be only too happy to scoop some business. But the temptation to tell Lexer off had been quickly stifled. Morley had long since laid claim to his first million but he had an unquenchable appetite for risk-taking in the stock market and in land speculation. He knew that one wrong move, one bad break, could wipe him out, so when Lexer spoke, Morley listened, not only with his ears, but his bankbook.

In return for helping Lexer place copious quantities of off-shore cash in gilt-edged investments, Morley got a healthy finder's fee; it was a source of income that he could ill-afford to give up. So he had no illusions as to why he was sitting in that dingy cubicle when the door swung open and the officer brought Speedy in. Rising, he shook hands with his client and waved him into the seat opposite him. Speedy began to speak but Morley admonished him with an upraised finger, throwing a sidelong glance toward the guard.

"If you wouldn't mind, officer," he said amiably, "my client and I would like to have some privacy."

The detective nodded brusquely and left the room, pulling the door shut behind him. Morley let his gaze roam slowly around the room, looking for a possible hiding place for a microphone. As far as he could see, the place was probably clean but he wasn't about to take any chances. Opening his attaché case, he pulled out a yellow legal pad and a small transistor radio, which he proceeded to click into life.

"What's the story?" Speedy asked, eyeing the radio.

"Just a precaution," Morley smiled. "In case the walls have ears."

As awareness dawned, Speedy grinned admiringly. "Sharp man. Real sharp."

With some heavy-metal rock as background music, Morley began his interrogation.

"Did you give any sort of statement to the police?"

"No way. All I gave them was my name and address."

"When they asked you to supply a statement, did they charge and caution you?"

"You mean that rap about 'You have the right to remain silent' and all that shit?"

Morley nodded.

"No. The head pig, that prick Edwards, just said that they had me by the balls and why didn't I save everyone a lot of time by confessing."

"But you didn't say *anything*?" Morley pressed. "You didn't offer any explanations or alibis, is that right?"

"Right on," Speedy nodded smugly. Then, his voice dropped abruptly and his bravado crumbled. "Mr. Spector, I didn't have nothing to do with it, honest."

"Well, that's nice to know," Morley smiled thinly. "That should make my job a little easier."

Speedy's eyes narrowed into baleful slits. "I got a damn good idea who did it though."

Morley held up his hand and looked at him sternly. "If you do, keep it to yourself. I'm not interested." Although he spoke softly, there was a cutting edge to his voice that gained Speedy's undivided attention. "You see, the police and I have what you might call 'a mutually beneficial understanding': I don't try and solve their crimes and they don't try to gain acquittals for my clients."

Giving Speedy a long, penetrating look that seemed to say "if you lie to me, I'll know it," Morley resumed his questioning.

"First of all, your given name is Chester, isn't it?"

Speedy's expression became pained. "Yeah, but I don't use it because it's like a real nerd's name, y'know." He shook his head disgustedly, "It was my mother that hung it on me. Named me for her brother. Some favour she did me."

"Nerd's name or not," Morley smiled, "that's the name you'll be going under from now on, so you may as well get used to it. Yes, indeed," he said, rolling the words off his tongue, "Ches-ter Ren-ner. A real straight-arrow name — something even a Methodist minister might be proud of."

Speedy glowered, half-convinced that the smooth-talking, elegantly attired lawyer was putting him on.

"O.K.," Morley continued. "Now tell me everything that you did yesterday, beginning with the first thing in the morning."

"Well, Holly and me, we aren't —" He checked himself, dropping his voice before going on, "we weren't much for getting up early. You see, we both kinda worked nights."

"O.K., you don't have to go into that. I've already been briefed."

"Briefed?" Speedy frowned. "By who?" Frenchy?"

"That doesn't matter," Morley snapped. "Let's just say that I'm aware that you and the deceased —" he paused, his eyes skimming his notepad, "Holly Gains, followed somewhat unconventional lifestyles."

"Yeah, I guess you could say that," Speedy said, warily, wondering just how much the lawyer knew.

Morley reached over and turned up the volume on the radio. "There's no need for us to fence. I know where you were last night and what you were doing."

Speedy felt his chest tighten. What kind of scam was this shyster trying to pull? he wondered. First Holly gets snuffed and now this bullshit. . . .

"Listen, man," he said shakily, "I don't know what kinda shit you're laying on me, but I thought you were supposed to be my lawyer. "Frenchy said you'd look after me. . . .'"

"And I will," Morley said matter-of-factly, "but only if you do as you're told." He leaned forward, and slowly, soothingly, like a teacher patiently explaining a lesson to a slow-learner, he said, "Now listen to me. Listen to every word very carefully. You are in serious trouble. My source in the A.G.'s office tells me that they're going to charge you with first-degree murder. As a matter of fact, they'll prob-ably do it as soon as we're finished here."

Reflexively, Speedy's gaze flew to the door. He nervously

licked his lips and his eyes swept over the walls in a desperate search for a way out of the small, windowless room.

"Take it easy," Morley said calmly. "If you're innocent, you have nothing to worry about." Nothing, he told himself wryly, except over-zealous prosecutors, incompetent cops, and a sensation-seeking press.

"Yeah, sure," Speedy said sardonically. "Well, frankly, I don't give a fuck. Holly's dead, man. She's the only one who ever gave a shit about me and she's gone. You know what I got out there now?" he said, jerking his thumb toward the door. "Sweet fuck all."

"I know. It's an awful thing to lose someone you care about, especially in such a cruel, violent way, but we can't bring her back. She's gone, but *you're* still here and we have to focus all of our energies on protecting your interests."

Speedy looked at him for a few seconds then smiled knowingly. "You know all about this whole caper, don't you? The deal with Frenchy and the guys from Buffalo last night. And you know about Larry Chambers too, right? Like, how he's been getting freebies from the organization, and how Holly was one of them?"

"What I know isn't relevant," Morley said coldly.

"Like hell it isn't!" Speedy shouted. "That goddamn Chambers had a session booked with Holly last night. He is also one weird fucking dude and he's laid some violent trips on Holly before."

Morley winced as flecks of Speedy's spittle dotted his face.

Speedy seemed to put his entire body into the force of his argument. "So what happened was that he probably flipped out and snuffed her," he said. His energy drained away with his anger and he slumped in his chair. "When I came home and seen her like that. . . ." He shook his head dazedly. "I couldn't fucking believe it." He paused, framing his words carefully as though it were important to him that someone — anyone — heard them. "I loved her, Mr. Spector. I really did love her."

Morley glanced away uneasily. He hated outbursts of

emotion — whether of anger or grief, it made no difference to him — finding them both unproductive and time-consuming. He glanced discreetly at his Rolex and groaned inwardly. He had a meeting scheduled with a couple of city councillors in less than an hour. A consortium of developers he was involved with was trying to establish some clout with the city's Executive Planning Committee, and it just so happened that Morley was personally acquainted with two of its more influential members. Considering that he and they moved in the same lofty social and business circles, and shared the same political loyalties, Morley had no doubt that he would be able to get them to subscribe to his consortium's vision of Toronto as New York North.

"I'm sure you did," Morley nodded, "but if I may, I'd like to get back to the matter at hand, which doesn't —" He looked at Speedy pointedly. "I repeat, *doesn't* involve Larry Chambers or anyone else." Before Speedy could respond, he rushed on.

"O.K. Did you ever strike Miss Gains or assault her in any way in the presence of others?"

Speedy scanned his memory before slowly replying: "There was this time at the Carousel Lounge when I gave her a backhand. . . ."

"Were you acquainted with anyone who might have witnessed this assault?"

"Naw, there wasn't nobody I knew there."

"Is that the only time you struck her in public?"

"Well," he said, frowning in concentration, "we got into a hassle in the hall outside our apartment yesterday but I don't think I hit her."

"Don't you know?"

"Well, we were kind of tusseling and I might have taken a swing at her but I don't think so. I think she just tripped or something and smacked against that old bitch's door."

"And just who is this 'old bitch' you're talking about?"

Speedy shrugged. "Some old hunky broad who lives next door. She must be over a hundred."

"Did she see you and Holly fighting?"

"For sure," Speedy sniffed. "That's how she gets her kicks. Spying on people and sticking her nose into their business."

"You know for a fact that she observed you?"

"Yeah. She had her head stuck out her door. I felt like slamming it on her scrawny neck."

"And that was the only time you physically fought with Miss Gains in or near the presence of your neighbour?"

"Well, I think that's the only time she saw us, but she might have heard us hassling every now and then because one time, the cops came and told us to keep it down. I don't know for sure but I'd make book it was her that blew the whistle on us."

Spector's raised eyebrows made Speedy feel uneasy. What the hell was this shyster trying to pull? he wondered; make him think he was in deep shit so he could sock it to him for some humungous legal fee? Well, let him try. The organization was footing the bill and there was no way they'd let some asshole lawyer fuck them over.

After another series of questions, Morley smiled blandly and said, "I think it would be in your interest to give the police a complete statement. If push comes to shove and you go to trial, we'll want to be able to show the jury that you were totally cooperative and had nothing to hide."

Speedy raised his eyebrows as if questioning the lawyer's sanity. "You want me to tell the cops where I was last night?"

"There's no other choice," he said firmly. "But remember. . . ." He raised a cautionary hand. "You must be very careful about what you say." He repeated it again for emphasis. *"Very careful.* Do you understand that?" He studied his client closely, to see if Speedy had read between the lines of the admonition.

"Yeah, I think so."

"Fine," Morley smiled, once again bending over his notepad. "So tell me where you were last night."

"I, uh, I was out with a couple, uh, three, pals of mine."

"And their names?"

"Frenchy Pouliot, Bill Zajac, and Joey Patriarca."

"Fine. And during what period of time were you in the company of these three individuals?"

"Well, I was with the three of them from about ten o'clock last night to about one this morning. Then, Frenchy had to split and I was with just Bill and Joey until about three or three-thirty."

Spector nodded encouragement as he scribbled furiously. "Fine. And what were you and your friends doing during the latter hours of Wednesday, June 26th, and the early hours of Thursday, June 27th?"

Speedy wet his lips nervously with his tongue and glanced uneasily toward the door. "Uh, I don't know whether I should say anything about that."

Spector held out his hands in a coaxing gesture. "Come now. We need to provide a complete account of your activities during this period if your story is to be believed. Do you understand that?"

"Uh-huh." Speedy felt he was being subtly coached but wasn't sure what the lawyer wanted him to say.

"All right then," Morley smiled. "Perhaps your memory has been affected by this very traumatic experience. Could that be it?"

Speedy didn't know what "traumatic" meant but he nodded anyway. "Yeah, right."

"So, maybe we should go over some possibilities. Does that seem like a reasonable approach?"

"Yeah, I guess so," Speedy muttered unenthusiastically.

"Fine. Fine." Spector leaned back in his chair, clasping his hands behind his head and contemplating the ceiling. "Now, could it possibly be that you and your friends were engaged in some sort of recreational activity?"

"Yeah, that's possible," Speedy quickly agreed.

"Yes. And could it also be that this recreational activity consisted of say, a poker game?"

"Yeah, that's right." A smile spread slowly across Speedy's face. "I remember now. That's what we were doing. We played poker until almost daybreak."

Spector immediately sat up and made some rapid notations on his pad, then looked at his client and added, "I suppose, now that your memory is jogged, you can also recall where this all-night poker game took place?"

Speedy's relieved smile turned into a puzzled frown. "Where? Uh, at this car wash on Bathurst?" It was more of a question than a statement and Speedy could tell from the lawyer's pained expression that he hadn't come up with the right answer.

"Are you sure of that?" Spector pressed, bringing his face to within a foot of Speedy's. "Are you sure it wasn't somewhere else, say at the home of one of your friends?"

Speedy blinked in bewilderment, then smiled as the cue sank in. "Oh, yeah, that's right. We were at . . . ?" He looked to the lawyer for assistance, then added half-questioningly, "Frenchy's?"

Spector nodded contentedly. "Yes, I'm sure Mr. Pouliot will be able to corroborate that." As he got up, he put his notepad and the transistor radio into his attaché case and snapped it shut. "But just to be on the safe side, I'll contact him and your other two friends to ensure that their memories are as acute as your own."

After shaking hands with Speedy, he rapped on the door, then turning back to his client, remarked: "Now that your memory has been refreshed, I'm sure you'll be able to give the police a full and accurate statement." He paused, then added, "And I think we both agree that it would be unwise to bring up Mr. Chambers' name since our mutual friends feel that any unnecessary publicity could prove harmful to their interests."

Speedy had barely finished giving a grudging nod, when the door swung open and Mike Edwards entered, followed by another plainclothes detective lugging a bulky, reel-to-reel tape-recorder.

Catching Edwards' eye, Morley said earnestly: "My client has assured me of his innocence and is prepared to give you a complete statement in the hope that any information he may be able to supply will assist you in apprehending the killer of Holly Gains."

"Nice speech, counsellor," Edwards winked, watching his assistant plug in the machine. In a way, he regretted Renner's cooperative stance. He wouldn't have minded sweating the punk a little. But what the hell, at least he'd be able to get home before noon.

After his partner had tested the machine and positioned the microphone, Edwards recited the charge and caution in a bored monotone and had Speedy acknowledge that he was giving a statement of his own free will. Speedy shot an anxious look toward the lawyer, who responded with a reassuring nod, as the detective launched into his first question. As the questions and answers wound onto the tape, Morley glanced at his watch again. With a little luck, he'd be on time for his meeting. And if he was a little late, well — he gave a mental shrug — that was the price one had to pay for ensuring that the mills of justice ground exceedingly fine.

It was close to ten when Elaine tiptoed into the studio and gave Larry a message from Mike Edwards informing him that Holly's next of kin had been contacted, and that Speedy Renner had been officially charged with her murder. It was all Larry could do to get through the remaining minutes of the segment with the anti-expressway lobbyists; before hastily ushering them out of the studio, he leaned into the mike, booming: "That's it for this segment. I'll be back after the ten o'clock news with a *Larry's Line* exclusive." His voice took on a studied note of urgency. "I have just learned that there has been another brutal slaying in the city of Toronto. I repeat, there has been another murder in Metro and I'll have a complete investigative report in five minutes. So stay tuned to the show that tells it like you want to hear it!"

Waiting for the newscast to conclude, Larry had to fight against the urge to bolt to his office and take a few anesthetizing swigs from the bottle of Scotch. Finally the on-air light flashed him his cue.

"As I said before the news," he began, "there has been another homicide in Metro. Acting on information they received, Metro's homicide squad went to 232½ Yonge Street early this morning, where they found the battered and strangled body of Holly Gains, age sixteen.

"Miss Gains was formerly of Burlington and had been residing in Toronto for the last several months. In custody and charged with first-degree murder is Chester Renner, age twenty-eight, who, police believe, shared the Yonge Street apartment with Miss Gains. The police have been reluctant to provide any further details for fear of jeopardizing their continuing investigation; however, an informed source has advised me that the homicide department is investigating a possible link between the death of Miss Gains and that of Helen Jantzen, who was slain in a similar manner earlier this week. Mr. Renner, who is represented by renowned criminal lawyer, Morley Spector, is expected to appear in court tomorrow to enter a plea.

"So there you have it, folks," Larry proclaimed. "Toronto's finest have done a fine job in coming up with an arrest in record time. Now, as we all know," he intoned earnestly, "any accused person is presumed innocent until proven guilty in a court of law, but I still think we should take off our hats to the boys in blue because, God knows, they catch enough flak when they make the occasional human mistake." Dropping the reverential tone, he said crisply: "That's enough from me. Let's hear what *you* think about this latest tragic turn of events."

Larry's first call seemed to be a prototype for others which flooded in for the duration of the program. Although the voices were many and varied, taken together, they represented a primal scream of fear and rage.

"Murderers are worse than animals!"

"If they bring back hanging, I'll volunteer to spring the trap!"

"I don't care if it's the noose, the electric chair, or lethal injection, these murderers have got to be done away with. That's the only way we can ever feel safe."

The phone console was still blinking furiously when it came time for Larry to sign off. He knew what that meant. He'd hit them hard and deep, touching a responsive chord within a huge segment of his listening audience. Now they owed him and, after tomorrow, he told himself, they'd owe him even more.

"I'm sorry to say that Thursday's edition of *Larry's Line* has come to an end. I regret that I wasn't able to respond to each and every one of the hundreds of calls that were pouring in, but that's the way the hot-line cookie crumbles. But those of you who haven't had a chance to air your views will have another shot at it tomorrow when I continue with more or less the same theme.

"We've heard a lot of raw, human emotion expressed this morning on *Larry's Line* but, to quote an old showman, 'you ain't seen nothin' yet'. Tomorrow morning, my special guest will be Erica Jantzen, the mother of murder victim Helen Jantzen. I might add that the fund we've started here at CKAL for the Jantzen family is well over the ten-thousand-dollar mark. But keep your donations coming because as you may know, Mrs. Jantzen is on social assistance and your generosity will help her provide a decent burial for Helen, and a brighter future for her four surviving children. So, until tomorrow, that's it for my time. Thank you for yours. God bless, and have a nice day."

It was mid-afternoon when Speedy was again led into the interview room. By now, he'd lost track of time. Herded from one windowless room to another, he had no idea if it was night or day.

The bare light bulb glared down at him from the high ceiling, the brightness hurting his eyes as he came down from coke, speed, and booze. It had been more than twenty-four hours since he'd last slept and his bones ached. The stale, heavy air seemed to press in on him from all sides as Spector entered the room and took a seat across from him at the small table. The lawyer again withdrew a yellow legal pad from his briefcase but, this time, instead of making notes, he kept glancing at those he'd made earlier that afternoon.

"In an attempt to corroborate your alibi, I contacted Bernard Pouliot," Morley said. "Mr. Pouliot confirms that you, himself, and two other gentlemen, William Zajac and Joseph Patriarca, played poker at his residence from approximately ten P.M., Wednesday, June 26th, 1985, to four-thirty A.M., Thursday, June 27th, 1985."

A slow smile spread over Speedy's features. With an airtight ablibi, he reasoned, the cops'd have to drop the charge. But his self-assurance began to fade when the lawyer glanced up from the notepad with a worried look. "I'm afraid we can't expect the same degree of cooperation from your other two associates."

"Huh? Why not?"

"Well, according to Mr. Pouliot, William Zajac has gone to South America to conduct some business on behalf of his employers and may be gone for weeks, or for that matter, months."

Speedy leaned forward, nervously drumming his fingers on the table. "Yeah? Well, what about Joey? You talked to him, didn't you? He'll back me up, won't he?"

"Yes, I did manage to talk to Mr. Patriarca," Morley said. "But unfortunately, he won't be able to corroborate your statement."

"He won't," Speedy yelped. "Why the fuck not? He was with me all last night."

"He may well have been," Morley said, "but the fact remains that he's not prepared to talk about it."

"What the hell is that supposed to mean?"

"It means that he's not prepared to go to jail, which is exactly where he'd end up if he came in contact with the police." In response to Speedy's bewildered expression, he added cryptically: "You see, Joey Patriarca is not really Joey Patriarca."

"Are you outta your skull?" Speedy flared. "What the hell are you talking about?"

"I'm talking about the fact that your Joey Patriarca is really one Joseph Caifano who, as it turns out, is under indictment in Florida for trafficking in narcotics and jumping bail. He's been living in Toronto under an assumed name to avoid arrest, so you can readily understand his reluctance to talk to the Metro Homicide Department."

"Well, isn't that fucking great," Speedy fumed. "Where the fuck does that leave me?"

Morley shook his head glumly. "Not in a very good position, I'm afraid," he said, flicking a glance at his notes, "especially in light of what the police have."

"Oh, yeah?" Speedy snorted. "And what have they got besides four-fifths of fuck all? They ain't got nothing' on me because I didn't do it. Why would I kill her? I loved her, for Chrissake!"

"Did you now?" Morley asked tonelessly as his eyes skipped over the notepad. "Well, let's take a look at the way you apparently demonstrated that love." Stabbing a passage with his finger, he began to read.

"Harry McWhorter, bartender at the Carousel Bar and Grill, stated that he had seen Mr. Renner and Miss Gains in his establishment on numerous occasions. He also stated that, approximately one month ago, he had Mr. Renner ejected when the latter began to slap Miss Gains and call her a number of obscene names in an extremely loud voice."

Speedy shook his head in disbelief. "Why the hell would Harry say something like that?"

"You mean it isn't true?"

"Yeah, it's true," Speedy said slowly. "But why would the dude say it? Like, Harry's no snitch."

"Who knows?" Spector shrugged. "Maybe the police

leaned on him a little. It's been known to happen. Or maybe he's trying to square himself with them from some other picture.''

"You mean the cops got this shit too?" Speedy asked anxiously.

Spector smiled slyly. "Who do you think I got it from?"

Speedy whistled admiringly. "That's great. Then you shouldn't have no trouble knocking the hell out of whatever bullshit case they think they've got.''

"Unfortunately, they seem to have more than a 'bullshit case,' as you call it.''

"C'mon," Speedy scoffed. "All they got is one goddamn bartender who saw me slap Holly around. Christ, if that was enough evidence for a murder conviction, half the guys in Toronto would be in the joint.''

"They've got a lot more than the bartender," Morley said, flipping through the notepad. "Ah, here we are," he said with a satisfied smile. "Mrs. Anna Janacek, Apartment Two, 232½ Yonge Street.''

"Yeah," Speedy said sourly. "That's the old bitch that lives next door. She's a nosy old hunky that ain't got anything better to do than stick her face in other people's business. Hey!" The revelation lit up his face. "That old bat is always listening at her door or peeking out her window to see what kind of shit she can pick up on. I'll bet *she* knows something about Holly's murder. I'll bet *she* heard or saw something.''

"Well, you'd win your bet," Morley said dryly. "According to the police, she saw, and heard, a lot and that's one of the reasons they feel they have a solid case against you.''

Speedy's face fell. "What . . . what the hell did she tell them?''

"Among other things, that she heard loud arguments between yourself and Miss Gains on a number of occasions.''

"O.K., so we argued," Speedy said defensively. "That don't prove nothin'.''

"No single piece of circumstantial evidence ever proves

anything conclusively," Morley said, "but a combination of several pieces can add up to a substantial body of evidence. Substantial enough, in some cases, to produce a conviction."

Speedy stared disconsolately at the notepad as though wondering how so much bad news could be contained in so few pages. Then, looking up, he muttered miserably: "Lemme have a cigarette, man."

Spector fished one out of a package and handed it to Speedy, watching as his client shakily tried to find the end with a match. When he finally succeeded in getting it lit, Speedy took a couple of long drags, letting the smoke out in slow trails. Then he looked at Spector and said in a flat, fatalistic tone: "I guess she told them that she saw me knock Holly on her ass outside her apartment, eh?"

"That's right. But that's not the most damaging part."

"What?" Sitting bolt upright in his chair, Speedy exclaimed. "What the fuck else could she have told them?"

"According to Mrs. Janacek, at about eight-thirty P.M. on Wednesday, June 26th, 1985, she heard the sounds of a violent struggle coming from your apartment. She said that she both heard and felt a large, heavy object strike her wall and, in answer to a question from an investigating officer, she agreed that this object could well have been the body of a young woman hurled with some force. She also told the police that, during this commotion, she clearly heard you yell 'I'm going to kill you,' or words to that effect, several times."

Speedy shook his head dazedly. "It was just a joke," he muttered.

"What's that?" Morley said sharply. "What did you say?"

Speedy look at him forlornly. "We were just jerking around, trying to put the old lady on. It was like an act, y'know?"

"Well, if it was," Morley said skeptically, "it was a pretty convincing one because the Crown now has one very frightened old lady who is prepared to testify that she heard the sounds of a life-and-death struggle between you and Miss Gains at approximately eight-thirty. Now, correct me if I'm wrong, but didn't you tell me that you didn't leave the apartment until close to nine P.M.?''

"That's right," Speedy said, "but what the hell is all this supposed to prove? So she heard a bunch of noises. She didn't *see* anything."

"Quite true," Morley said, "but the key issue is not so much *what* she heard as *when* she heard it."

"What's that supposed to mean?"

Morley answered the question with one of his own, "Do you have a Westclox wind-up alarm clock?"

Speedy looked at the lawyer warily as though sensing a trap, before finally replying: "Yeah, we've got a wind-up clock but I don't know what make it is."

"Well, for what it's worth," Morley said, "the police have recorded it as a Westclox." Leaning forward, he looked at Speedy intently. "Now *this* is important. Did you look at that clock at any time on the evening of June 26th, 1985, prior to going out to meet your friends?"

Speedy thought for a while before replying. "Yeah, I checked it out to see if it had the same time as my wristwatch because I didn't want to be late for my first . . . . . . uh, assignment."

"So the clock was functioning when you left the apartment?"

"Yeah."

"Well," Morley said tersely, "it isn't now."

"O.K., so the goddamn clock isn't working," Speedy said with a puzzled frown. "So what's the big deal?"

"The big deal is that the police think it was broken when Holly was struggling with her attacker. You see, its face was smashed and some shards of glass were found beside her body and the clock itself was on the floor nearby."

"I don't get it," Speedy scowled. "So the clock was busted up. What the hell has that got to do with me?"

"What it's got to do with you," Morley said with a long, world-weary sigh, "is that when the face was shattered, the hands were locked on the time showing when the damage occurred. And that time," he said leadenly, "was eight-thirty."

Chapter Twelve

Alec Vlassos winced as he hauled his considerable bulk up the steep flight of stairs and stopped, wheezing, in front of Speedy's apartment. Going through the motions, he tried the doorknob before reaching into his wallet and extracting a credit card. Inserting the plastic rectangle between the door-jamb and lock, he manipulated it with a practised hand, "cheating" the catch. Feeling the bolt release, he gave the door a gentle shove and smiled with satisfaction as it swung open.

The first thing he did was make a dash for the bathroom. Standing in front of the toilet, he directed a forceful stream toward the bowl and sighed contentedly as the pressure within his bladder subsided. God, he'd needed that, he told himself. Standing across the street, waiting for the cops to leave, he'd felt like his back teeth were floating.

Giving it a few shakes, he put it back in his pants then groaned in dismay as he felt the warm, familiar sensation. Shit, he'd done it again. He hadn't gotten it all out and had dribbled in his underwear. He'd known for a while that he'd have to go back to the urologist and get his plumbing reamed-out again, but he'd been putting it off. "Next week, I'll make an appointment," he said aloud. "It's got to be done, so there's no sense putting it off."

Alec had been in the habit of talking to himself for almost a year now. It had become second nature to him, so much so, that most of the time, he was totally unaware he was doing it. Had he been so inclined, he could probably have traced the origin of his muttered monologues back to the death of his wire-haired terrier, Daisy.

When he used to take Daisy for long walks through his Leaside neighbourhood, he would talk to her constantly in the tone one would use with a precocious child. After Daisy expired of what Alex concluded to be a combination of old age and bad breath, he continued to take regular walks on which he voiced his opinions, although now he no longer had an audience, four-legged or otherwise.

Stepping into the bedroom, he walked over to the outline of Holly's body that had been chalked onto the hardwood floor. Recalling a newscast that provided a graphic description of the injuries inflicted on her, he shook his head sadly. He was getting too old for this business, he decided. It was starting to catch up to him. The nightmares were turning into real life, and vice versa. How much more could he take of the tragedy and violence — the sickness of a society that wouldn't even acknowledge its symptoms?

But what else did he know aside from being a private investigator? What the hell could he do at sixty-three years of age without even a high school diploma? Become a brain surgeon? He ran a hand over his bald, bullet-shaped dome and sighed. This was going to be a tough one. Yeah, he didn't know which way to go on this caper.

It had started out simply enough. Middle-aged broad thinks her husband is getting some tail on the side. Wants to get the goods so she can: a) shame him into giving up the strange stuff, or b) get some ammunition so she can bleed him dry in a hefty divorce settlement.

Either way, it meant no difference to Alec. He'd been in the business for over thirty-five years and he'd seen them come and go — the victims and the perpetrators, the abused and the abusers. For twenty-five bucks an hour plus expenses, they got his experience and his brains. And if they didn't also rent his conscience, well, at least it wasn't as though it got in the way, because over the years, he'd developed the ability to treat his morality like his diamond stick pin — something he trotted out only for special occasions.

Letting his gaze drift over the room, he muttered with more than a trace of sarcasm: "Well, it looks like Toronto's finest have done their usual outstanding job." He could see from the light film of powder on a couple of pieces of furniture that the identification unit had at least gone through the motions of lifting some prints.

"But then why bother investigating when you've already got your killer?" he asked the empty room. "The wrong kind of evidence could hurt rather than help your case."

Alex wasn't trying to do the cops' job for them, though. As a matter of fact, if anyone had asked him, he would've been hard-pressed to explain his presence in Speedy's apartment either to them or himself. "Must be a sign of senility," he philosophized, "unlawfully entering a dwelling without even knowing why."

But if his behaviour was strange, so was this entire case, he concluded. Unable to think of anything better, he focussed on those places that he thought the police might've missed, his first targets the sofa and upholstered armchair.

Pulling off the cushions, he began to probe in the recesses between their backs and seats. His fingers brushed against the usual conglomeration of lint and dirt, but in one corner of the couch he made contact with a thin, cylindrical object. He gripped it in a pincer fashion between his fingers and pulled it free.

It was a ballpoint pen. He held it by the tip, studying the lettering on its side. In gold script, were the call letters, CKAL, and the station's frequency, 780, as well as its address and phone number. He shoved it into his jacket pocket, chuckling at the cops' ineptitude.

It was no wonder that half of the murders and three-quarters of the robberies in Toronto went unsolved, he thought. Of course, Alec had to admit he was far from objective when it came to the Metro Police Department. He'd tried to get a job on the force when he got back from overseas after the war but had been rejected. Nobody had come right out and said it, but he was sure it had had something to do with the fact he was of Greek ancestry rather than a Limey like most of the top brass in the force. Almost forty years worth of water had passed under the bridge since then, but the bitterness still surfaced every now and then like a case of mental heartburn.

It continued to eat at him that if he'd been accepted onto the force, he would have been able to take early retirement by now and would be lying under a tree with a good book, or maybe matching wits with a ten-pound pike, up north somewhere.

The truth of the matter was that Alec didn't know how much longer he'd be able to stay in business. As he got older, he no longer had the energy to maintain a heavy client load, a fact which had become obvious to many of the lawyers who had stopped using his services. Now he had to rely mainly on the fruits of his advertisements in the "Business Personal" section in the *Star* and his display ad in the yellow pages.

It was his ad in the phone book that had led to his being hired by Jane Chambers. She'd emphasized that he would have to be discreet, and he'd fulfilled that part of the bargain all right. Larry Chambers hadn't had even the slightest suspicion that he had been tailed. Of course, the shape Larry had been in when he stumbled out of the press club, Alec could have been walking right next to him, instead of a couple of yards behind without him getting wise.

After Larry had staggered up the stairs and entered Holly's apartment, Alec had followed him and had stood listening outside the apartment door. But the music — if that's what you called something that sounded like a bunch of scalded cats — had been too loud for him to make out any voices. The noise would've been loud enough to drown out almost anything, for that matter, including the screams of a girl who saw her impending death reflected in the eyes of her killer.

Alec had stationed himself in a doorway across the street and had seen Larry leave a half-hour or so later. He'd also seen something else. While he'd waited for his quarry to emerge from the building, Alec had noticed a dark-coloured Chrysler passing by at regular intervals, with its driver craning his head to look up at the window of Holly's apartment.

To help pass the time, Alec had begun to clock the vehicle. It went by every three minutes almost to the second and he had guessed the driver was circling a couple of blocks, taking the same route each time. He had not got a good look at the driver's face but he had had no trouble catching the license number, and jotted it down on the inside of a matchbook cover.

Of course, he still hadn't known for sure if the guy had, in fact, been checking out Holly's place or looking at the building for some other reason, but when it came to information, the veteran private eye's philosophy was that if you had too much, you could always get rid of some, but if you didn't have enough, you were in deep shit.

Still, he wished he could've hung around a while longer and seen what the guy was up to. But that had been out of the question. So he'd just cased him until Larry had lurched out of the building, and Alec had had to resume his bird-dogging routine, trailing the errant hot-line host to the corner of Yonge and Bloor where he hailed a cab.

Completing his brief survey of the apartment, Alec started for the door, then stopped dead in his tracks. He listened. First to the slight scratching noise, then to the metallic click of a key being inserted in the lock.

Jack Lexer was adjusting the drapes in front of a wall-to-wall expanse of glass when his secretary ushered Morley in. It was a clear day and, from his twentieth-storey suite of offices, he could see for miles. He liked the view, especially of the block of office buildings to the west, most of which were owned by his development company. Glancing over his shoulder, he acknowledged the lawyer with a nod and grunted: "Well?"

"I think I've got it under control, Jack."

Lexer turned around to face him and scowled. "You *think* you got it under control? For what I pay you, you should fucking well *know*."

Morley smiled weakly, trying to convince himself that the rebuke was some crude attempt at humour, but Lexer's baleful look quickly disabused him of that notion. As he began to explain, the lawyer found his voice becoming less authoritative, in fact, almost obsequious.

This realization filled him with a shame bordering on self-loathing. He was Morley Spector, Q.C., for Christ's sake. He'd waxed eloquent before the Supreme Court of Canada and had had the learned justices hanging on his every word. And now, here he was, bowing and scraping before a man who'd built a corporate empire on a foundation of prostitution, labour racketeering, and loan-sharking.

Morley knew enough to camouflage his wounded ego, however. In the courtroom, he felt in control of his own destiny. The arcane world of the criminal justice system might be an impenetrable fortress to the layman, but to the cognoscenti, it was a vehicle for imposing at least a semblance of order on a society that would otherwise revert to the law of the jungle.

As far as Morley was concerned, the practice of law was the most noble calling afforded to man and, even after so many years as a lawyer, he still thrilled to the time-honoured Latin phrases and the lofty precepts they embodied. But he knew that Jack Lexer lived in another world — a world that honoured only what it could buy or take.

"Jack," he said slowly, "what I have to say to you comes from a friend as well as a lawyer."

Lexer walked around behind his pool-table sized desk and leaned forward with his palms planted on the top. "Shoot."

"This is dangerous, Jack," he said. "Getting involved with a low-life like Renner. It's a dicey business. People like him have no values, no stability. There's no predicting what they'll do or say."

Lexer looked at him darkly. "You think I enjoy this? You think I enjoy paying you two hundred bucks an hour to wipe that punk's ass?" He walked over to the bank of windows overlooking the city's commercial heart. Standing with his back to the lawyer, he said thoughtfully: "You know, from here, I can pick out over a dozen buildings that I bought within the last five or six years."

"Yes, well, that's what I mean, Jack," Morley said. "You don't need this. You've got several terrific revenue-bearing properties, a lot of prime land that can be rolled over at a substantial profit, and some thriving businesses. The waste disposal company has a tremendous amount of potential and I understand the restaurants and car washes are doing quite well."

Lexer turned to look at him, his craggy profile silhouetted against the pale blue sky. "I don't think you entirely understand how the organization does business," he said with a trace of condescension. "All that stuff you're talking about is in my name, but that doesn't mean it's mine, because in this business, you only own what you buy with your own money."

He walked over to a massive oak credenza and pulled out a bottle of Scotch. Filling two tumblers, he continued his commentary as he handed one to Spector.

"Like, if I buy a building with a loan from a bank, who owns the building? Me or the bank?" Without waiting for an answer, he went on. "And we both know how I got the bread to buy the real estate and take over the businesses. So the question is: Who really owns all the stuff I sunk those big bucks into over the past ten years?" He nodded at Morley as though anticipating his answer.

222

"I refuse to answer on the ground that it might tend to in-criminate me," Morley smiled.

"Yeah, right," Lexer said dryly. "Anyway, the thing is, when I jumped into this operation, I had to take over the whole thing and that includes handling legal hassles for two-bit punks and piecing-off politicians, as well as moving as much money as I can into legitimate investments."

"That's why I've got to look after this Renner business because, like it or not, guys like him are an important part of the organization even if they are way down the ladder. They're the ones who take the risks, and they're the ones who take the fall when the cops and politicians want to get their names in the papers for wiping out organized crime."

"They're also the ones who can blow the whistle to take the heat off themselves," Morley cautioned.

"Yeah," Lexer nodded. "And that's where you come in. Renner doesn't know enough to give *me* any problems but he can make it rough on some of our very good friends, people that have done right by us."

"Well, it all seems to be falling into place," Morley said reassuringly. "The police seem to be doing a remarkably thorough job for a change."

"Yeah," Lexer winked. "I wonder why."

"Jack," Morley said admiringly, "I've known you for a long time but you never cease to amaze me."

Lexer took a long sip of Scotch and grinned smugly. "Like I always say, it never hurts to have friends in high places." Then his voice dropped and he said solemnly, "But even though I'm in the driver's seat, I never bullshit myself about being indispensible because any time the Buffalo or Hamilton family wants to kiss me off, I'm old news. Yeah, all the bosses gotta do is say 'Jack, leave the keys on your desk and fuck off' and I walk away from it all — the busi-nesses, the real estate, the stocks — the whole schmeer. And the next day . . ." he said, pointing toward the mammoth desk, "there's somebody else sitting there, pulling the strings of a helluva lot of people in this city and making sure the whole thing stays together no matter what it takes.''

"Well, that doesn't give you a helluva lot of security, does it?''

"Security?" Lexer chuckled. "The only security you got in this business is to keep on breathing." Suddenly, his face lit up and he slapped his thigh delightedly. "Hey, Morley. I just thought of something. Maybe when they dump me, they'll bring you in as my replacement.''

Spector smiled weakly. "I don't think I'd be too interested.''

"Morley, Morley, Morley," Lexer said bemusedly, "with what you know about the organization, you'd *have* to be interested.''

Earlier, Morley had felt a little chilly and had thought about asking Jack to turn down the air-conditioning. But now, there was no need to. Perspiration began to bead his forehead and his armpits felt warm and sticky. Lexer had just begun to pour some more Scotch into their glasses when he was interrupted by a light tap on the door.

"C'mon in," he barked.

The door swung open and Mr. Justice Alan Nadeau strode briskly into the room and exchanged warm handshakes with the two men.

"O.K.," Lexer said curtly, "now that we're all here, let's get down to business.''

Nadeau's thin face pinched into a worried frown. "I hope you don't expect me to discuss a matter that is currently before the courts, because such conduct would constitute a serious breach of judicial ethics.''

Spector nodded his concurrence. "Your Lordship has certainly advanced a valid consideration in that, as officers of the court, you and I are duty-bound to forgo any activity which might tend to bring the administration of justice into disrepute.''

Lexer glanced uneasily from one to the other. Then his expression softened as he snorted: "Jeez, you guys almost had me going for a moment there."

The three men convulsed in laughter, Spector's ingenuous giggle, blending in with Lexer's uninhibited roar and the judge's staccato cackle. When they finally reined in their mirth, their eyes were brimming and they were gasping for breath.

Still, chuckling, Lexer reached into the breast pocket of his jacket and pulled out a vial of cocaine, carefully laying out half a dozen lines on the desktop.

"O.K.," he said, waving an arm expansively. "Have a couple of toots to get your heads together and then we'll get down to business."

As the immaculately attired lawyer and judge bent over the desk and began to suck the fine white powder into their nostrils, Lexer stood looking down at them like a proud parent watching his child ride his first two-wheeler. Yeah, he thought to himself, as he gazed at the pair with undisguised admiration, there's no bullshit about it. I got the best lawyer and the best judge that money can buy.

Alec crouched down in the darkness and peered through the keyhole of the closet door. His stubby legs had managed to propel him into the bedroom before the apartment door swung open, but he'd stumbled over a row of shoes and almost sprained an ankle before settling in amongst a rackful of blouses and slacks.

He listened intently, hearing the floorboards in the living room creak under a heavy footfall. He could also hear the furniture being moved around and a deep, male voice muttering profanities.

It was obvious the guy was searching for something, Alec thought, but what? But, within seconds, as the footsteps approached the bedroom, he began to think less about what the man was searching for and more about what he might find.

Click-slap. Click-slap. The footsteps came closer. The guy

was in the bedroom now, he guessed, Alec's field of vision limited to about a three-foot diameter directly in front of him. He could make out only a section of the bed and the small portion of the floor which contained the chalked outline of the murder victim's left arm.

Alec's joints felt locked in place and there was a steady ache in the small of his back as he remained hunched over, hardly daring to breathe. The footsteps were slow and methodical, and he could feel their vibration on the floor beneath him.

Suddenly, his view changed as the bottom half of a checked sports jacket and a set of thighs encased in dark slacks blocked out the room. The man was right in Alec's line of vision now and he could clearly see him hunkering down on all fours to look under the bed. Again, he spat out a stream of obscenities as he stood up and slapped some dust from his knees.

Alec still couldn't see his face but he took note of the broad shoulders, pale neck, and carrot-coloured brushcut. That, together with his outfit, added up to only one thing as far as the grizzled private eye was concerned: cop.

Alec's shoulders sagged in defeat. He reasoned that if this cop was investigating the murder, he was probably doing a final sweep of the crime scene to see if they'd missed anything the first time around. This meant it wouldn't be long before he got around to the closet. It was ironic, he thought, the idea of being caught in somebody's closet, when he considered all the times he'd nailed cheating husbands and wives in identical circumstances.

Trying frantically to come up with a work of creative fiction to explain his unauthorized presence in the apartment, he heard the footsteps again. They were coming over from the other side of the room, circling the bed. Click-slap, click-slap. The size twelves were coming closer. Abruptly a dark curtain fell over his field of vision. Instinctively, he sucked in his breath and froze, realizing that the tall, red-headed man was standing directly in front of the closet door.

Alec shrank away from the keyhole and stared at the knob which was no more than six inches from his face. He looked at it in fascination as it slowly began to turn. Then, suddenly, just as he felt every taut muscle about to snap, it stopped and he heard the sound of receding footsteps.

He waited until the apartment door clicked shut, then went to the window and peered down from behind the curtain. There was a car parked directly in front of the building with its four-way flashers blinking and, within seconds, the tall, red-haired man got in and drove away. Although the vehicle bore no identifying insignia, to a seasoned observer like Alec, it was as obvious as its driver. An antenna for a two-way radio was enough to convince him that it was an unmarked police cruiser and to confirm that the big, raw-boned man with the brushcut was a plainclothes dick.

"Hmmm," Alec muttered, glancing around the bedroom one last time, "I wonder what the hell he was looking for?" Shrugging, he addressed his parting comment to the living room. "Well, it's good to see that Toronto has at least one cop who takes his job seriously."

Alec drove to his office and checked his answering machine. There was the usual couple of gag calls. One voice — it sounded like a teenager's — said: "My name is E.T. and someone stole my spaceship. Do you think you can find it for me so I can go home?" The question was punctuated by an explosion of giggling.

There was also a message from Jane Chambers, asking when the report on her husband would be ready. Alec erased and rewound the tape then stared glumly around his office. A few years back, he'd had larger quarters — two separate offices, one for himself, one for his secretary, and a small waiting room. Now, he just had a single room on the second floor of a small, rundown building on Queen Street. It filled the bill, though, especially since he could no longer afford a secretary.

Located above a secondhand furniture store, the office was sparsely furnished, containing an old oak desk, a bank of filing cabinets, and a floor safe that held his account books and some of his more confidential files. Any safecracker who had the misfortune to tackle that ancient vault would sure as hell be in for a terminal case of disappointment, he grinned.

The walls were painted a drab green and peeling badly, and the ceiling was a network of interlocking cracks. Alec was always careful not to slam the door, fearing that a shower of plaster would come down on his hairless dome. He shook his head sorrowfully. "If business doesn't pick up soon," he told the quietly attentive room, "I'm gonna have to do something drastic. Maybe even take out a bigger ad in the classifieds."

Absently, he slid open his desk drawer and pulled out a well-thumbed copy of *Penthouse* magazine. He flipped it open to the centrefold and stared longingly down at the raven-haired model, his mouth partly open.

"Christ," he breathed. "That goddamn Guccione has got it made. I'll bet he bangs every broad that poses in the magazine, and probably a lot more besides."

The model looked perfect. Everything about her was just right. The size and shape of her breasts, the perky nipples, the nice, tapered waist, with just the slightest swell of belly. And the tight, tastefully split pussy, framed with a neat triangle of pubic hair.

He hadn't banged a woman that even resembled the photograph since the Second World War when he used to frequent the cathouses in France and Holland. Yeah, he had got his share of young stuff in those days, he thought with a touch of nostalgia, but now, it was a different story.

"You got a lot of bucks and you can get as much young pussy as you want," he muttered, "no matter how old you are."

But money was something that Alec did not have a lot of, or, for that matter, even enough of. So now that he was older, heavier, and no longer had to ask his barber to take a little off the top, he had to content himself with whatever he could pick up at the Legion or old Mother Fivefingers. He sighed heavily and dropped the magazine back into the drawer.

He consoled himself by thinking that it could be worse and that he could still be living with Vera. They were both in their late-thirties when they got married; too late to start a family. But that was just as well since whatever it was that'd brought them together died a few years later, and there was nothing to hold them together.

He'd come home one night after a long stakeout and Vera was gone. She'd packed up and left without even leaving a note. Alec remembered the night well. It was the sixth game of the Stanley Cup between the Canadiens and the Rangers. He'd been listening to it while he was tailing an unfaithful husband. The Canadiens had taken it 4 – 3 in overtime on a rink-long rush by The Rocket. The next day, Alec had gone down to the city pound and bought Daisy. He liked to joke that he'd just substituted one dog for another.

At first, it had struck Alec as strange that he didn't miss his wife. The only difference he could notice was that the apartment seemed a lot roomier with Vera gone — roomy enough for him to install a little bar in the corner of the living room, a fixture which he increasingly began to put to good use. There were times, however, when he wondered where she was, and if she was cooking up those nice stuffed peppers of hers for somebody else.

He rolled a piece of paper into his old Underwood and began to peck out a report for Jane Chambers. He'd decided that he'd have to do some selective editing if this caper was going to pay off. He'd tell her that he had followed her husband to the press club where Larry had downed a lot of booze with a couple of pals. Then he's say that Chambers had stumbled off to a nearby bar and put the finishing touches on his bender. He had no intention of spilling anything about the Yonge Street walk-up or Holly Gains. He had other plans for that particularly tasty tidbit.

It hadn't come to him until that morning. He'd been thinking about the Chambers report and reflecting on how his client would be able to hit up her husband for a big chunk of dough thanks to the dirt he'd dug up. Oh, well, the big shot broadcaster could afford it, Alec had thought, remembering reading that CKAL's hot-line host was earning in excess of two hundred thousand dollars per year.

Alec had felt bitter and resentful when he thought of Chambers pulling in all that lovely loot just for shooting-off his mouth on the radio three hours a day. *All that money. All that money.* The phrase had gone around and around in his head like the refrain of an old familiar song. He was browned-off even more when he thought of how he had to bust his balls for twelve, fourteen hours a day just to eke out a living.

Then he'd started to think about destiny, and wondered if this case had landed in his lap as part of a greater design for his future. His health was going downhill and in a couple of years, tops, he'd have to pack his job in. That was if he hadn't gone bankrupt first. He had a few bucks invested in bonds but certainly not enough for a retirement nest egg. He regretted that he'd never set up a private pension plan, and realized that he'd be shitting pretty thin trying to get by on the meager government handouts he'd collect when he turned sixty-five.

All those years and all those cases, he'd thought, and he'd always played it on the up-and-up. Sure, he'd milked a case now and then when he figured a client could afford it, but he'd never really ripped off anyone, even when he had the opportunity. And that's why, he'd concluded, he was a prime candidate for the poorhouse.

He was too goddamn honest. He didn't need much either, just his old age pension and maybe an extra thousand or so a month. Then he'd be able to get a little place out in the country somewhere and pass his remaining years just fishing and taking it easy. He'd even get another dog, "Daisy II," and his — what were they called, twilight years? — would be the best years of his life.

All he needed was one big score, he decided, and then he'd

be sitting pretty. And that score was going to be none other than that hotshot know-it-all, Larry Chambers. He didn't know if Chambers had anything to do with the murder of Holly Gains, but Alec was the only one who could place him at the scene of the crime and that had to be worth something. Even if Chambers was innocent, he sure as hell wouldn't want it known that he was dipping his wick into some sixteen-year-old chippie. Not if he wanted to keep his reputation as a crusading Mr. Clean who could safely throw shit at everyone because there wasn't any chance of it sticking to him.

It was a risk. Alec wasn't kidding himself about that. But hell, if you couldn't take a risk at sixty-three years of age with a helluva lot longer past than future, what the hell was the use of even pretending it was worth getting up in the morning?

He looked-up the phone number for CKAL and dialed, asking the female voice on the other end if he could speak to Larry Chambers. He was put on hold for several seconds before Chambers' voice came on the line, smooth and in command.

"Mr. Chambers, I'd like to speak to you about a matter of considerable importance."

"Well, I'm sorry I don't have time right now. I'm just leaving but, if you like, I can switch you over to my researcher. . . ."

"I really don't think you'd like your researcher to hear what I have to say."

Larry was immediately struck by the hint of menace in the voice. Another crank, he thought, wishing he'd had the call screened.

"Whom am I speaking to?" Larry asked, making no attempt to hide his annoyance.

"*My* name doesn't matter," Alec countered, "but I'll give you one that does: Holly Gains. Does that name sound familiar to you?"

"It should," Larry said. "I discussed her murder on my

show this morning." His voice took on a suspicious edge.
"Hey, what is this? Do you know something about her
death?"

"Probably not as much as *you* do, Mr. Chambers," Alec
said insinuatingly, "considering that you were with her last
night."

Miles of telephone wire linked two pools of silence. Larry
swallowed hard and tried to re-inject a note of authority into
his voice.

"Listen, mister. You better watch what you say. There
are strict laws against slander in this country, you know."

"Yeah, I know that," Alec said airily. "And I also know
there are even stricter laws against mutilating and strangling
young girls."

"Listen, buddy," Larry hissed. "I don't know who the
hell you are, or what you're talking about, but if you ever
call me again, I'll have the cops on your ass so fast it'll make
your head spin."

"Very convincing, Mr. Chambers," Alec drawled.
"Yeah, sure. You didn't know Holly and you didn't leave
your pen behind in her apartment either, did you?"

Larry's mind raced. He *had* misplaced a pen but he
thought he'd left it at home. Who the hell was this guy?
What was he trying —

"Are you still there, Mr. Chambers?" The voice, dry and
mocking, crackled through the receiver. "I'll tell you what
I'm going to do. I'll give you a couple of hours to think over
what I've said and then I'll call you at home and maybe we
can kick it around a little more."

Larry's voice swelled with alarm. "No. Don't call me at
home. Besides," he added, "you don't have my number.
It's unlisted."

Alec chuckled. "Don't worry. I'll be very discreet. I'll be
calling you between seven and eight o'clock tonight, and in
case you're wondering, I do have your number. If I'm not
mistaken," he said, reading from the data Jane had given
him, "it's 785-2193. Is that right, Mr. Chambers?"

By now, Larry wasn't greatly surprised when the voice smugly recited his unlisted number. This guy isn't bluffing, he told himself. He knows. He knows where I was last night and he probably knows what happened in Holly's apartment. As he had earlier that day, Larry once again grappled with his memory.

Images came to him in fragments: her mouth, her hair. Her slim, white body. She'd been whispering in his ear. Some suggestive phrase. "Getting hot?" "Go for it"? Some kind of baby talk or come-on. Her tongue had been tracing little circles over his ear, down his neck. He'd closed his eyes, feeling adrift in a dark sea, beginning to sink deeper and deeper. The next thing he remembered was lurching into a dark doorway and heaving up a stomachful of steaming, rancid booze, vomiting until his eyes flowed over and his throat burned.

"I'll be talking to you, Mr. Chambers," Alec said softly. "Think about what I said."

"Hey, wait a minute," Larry panicked. "I think there's just some kind of misunderstanding here. I'm sure we could get it straightened out if we sat down together and —"

"I don't think that's the way to go with this," Alec cut in. "Don't worry. You'll be hearing from me and I'm sure we'll straighten it out . . ." He let the sentence hang for a few seconds. "One way or another."

"Wait," Larry yelped. "Let's talk about it."

But, by then, Alec had already hung up the phone and was leaning back in his swivel chair, contentedly staring up at the cracked ceiling. There'd been other times when the brass ring had been within his grasp, but he hadn't had the balls to reach for it. Not this time though. This time, he was going for the whole bundle.

Leaning forward, he slid out the *Penthouse* magazine again and riffled through to the centrefold. Miss April was still there waiting for him. She was different from the old sluts that'd passed through his bed and life — she wouldn't cheat on him.

As his mind stroked her glossy body, his hand dropped absently to his crotch. His eyes transfixed, his forehead steamy with perspiration, he was oblivious to the voices and lives beneath his window. Lost in his own melancholy mating dance, he swapped his one-dimensional life for a two-dimensional fanstasy, and, for the first time in a long while, Alec Vlassos did not feel alone.

Chapter Thirteen

When he saw Larry step onto the sidewalk, Pete eased the car forward until he was beside him. Leaning across, he yelled through the window on the passenger side: "Hey, Larry! Can I talk to you for a minute?"

Larry seemed to flinch, his eyes darting nervously as if seeking an escape route.

"Uh, hi, Pete. What're you doing around here?"

"Get in and I'll tell you," he said, shoving the door open.

Larry got in and looked at Pete questioningly. "So what's up?"

Pete looked out through the windshield as though firming his resolve before turning to face Larry. "You're really getting a lot of mileage out of the Gains murder, aren't you?"

"Hey," Larry said sourly, "this isn't going to be another lecture on journalistic integrity, is it?"

"Uh-uh, nothing like that," Pete said quietly. "I'm afraid it's something a little heavier."

Larry's eyebrows lifted but he drew his mouth into a tight line and remained silent.

"Larry," Pete continued, "this is totally bizarre, but you know the guy they charged, Speedy Renner? Well, he and I go back a long way. You know how it is in this business. You take information wherever and however you can, and when I was covering the crime beat, Speedy was a damn good pipeline into a lot of places where journalists fear to tread."

Larry began to squirm in his seat. He felt a creeping sense of dread, beginning in the pit of his stomach and spreading throughout his entire body. He had an unreasoning urge to leap out of the car, but forced himself to present a composed façade.

"You see . . . The thing is . . ." Pete began haltingly, "Renner called me from his apartment before the cops got there." As he spoke, he studied Larry's face, searching for the slightest reaction, but he saw nothing more than a fleeting twitch at the corner of his mouth.

"Yeah?" Larry's pale eyes were noncommittal.

"He was really coming unglued," Pete said, "so I went over to try and cool him out." At the memory of Holly lying there like a damaged and discarded mannequin, his voice choked up. "I saw her, Larry. It was unbelievable. Just fucking horrible." He looked down at the car floor.

"I can imagine," Larry said gravely.

Pete looked over at Larry again. "Like I said, Renner was really spinning-out," he said slowly. "He told me he came home and found Holly stone-cold dead." He paused, his eyes riveted on Larry's. "And that he knows who killed her."

Pete thought he saw a brief flicker of something in Larry's eyes but couldn't be sure if it was fear or surprise.

"So Renner's innocent, is he?" Larry sniffed skeptically. "Somebody else did the dirty deed, but the cops are railroading him because they don't like the way he parts his hair or some other bullshit. How many times have we heard *that* story?"

"More than I can count," Pete conceded. "But there are a couple of things that are different about this case."

"Oh, yeah?" Although he could feel his body tensing Larry tried to sound disinterested.

"Yeah," Pete continued. "You see, this girl meant a lot to Renner in a couple of very important ways. First of all, he loved her."

"Really?" Larry smiled cynically. "Wasn't he her pimp or something? Is that the definition of true love these days — selling your girlfriend on streetcorners?"

Pete shook his head slowly. "I've given up trying to understand what people do to each other. Maybe you've got to be there to make any sense of it. But I think they were both so screwed-up that they were the only ones who *could* have loved each other." Pete smiled bemusedly. "I don't know if that makes sense to you. For that matter, I don't know if it makes sense to *me*."

"O.K., so even conceding that he loved the girl, that doesn't mean he couldn't have snuffed her," Larry argued. "Some of the most brutal murders you can think of were committed by men and women who claimed to have loved their victims."

"That's true," Pete nodded, "and, frankly, that whole love-hate trip is something I've never been able to fully understand. I mean, if you really love someone, how could it possibly make sense to want to destroy them?"

"I always thought that love and sense were mutually exclusive," Larry said dourly.

"Maybe you're right," Pete said. "But to get back to Renner, I'm the first to admit that the guy's no choirboy but the funny thing is, when he told me he had nothing to do with the girl's death, I believed him."

"Hey, where's that hard-nosed cynic we've come to know and love?" Larry jabbed.

Pete smiled wryly. "Maybe he became a little more human." Then he said seriously, "But there are still *some* things that even a warm, giving guy like me finds difficult to believe."

"Such as?"

"Such as you being the person who strangled Holly Gains."

The grin froze on Larry's lips. Contrasting sharply with the fear in his eyes, it gave his face a grotesque, schizophrenic look.

"What . . . what the hell kind of joke is that?" he finally managed.

"It's no joke," Pete said. "That's the story I got from Renner. He says you had an appointment with Holly on the night she was killed. He also says you've been with her before and that the girl was afraid of you."

Larry took a deep breath. He knew that if he ever had to come up with a convincing performance, it was now. He spoke slowly, evenly, stirring in just the right amount of indignation.

"I'm surprised that you'd even listen to such bullshit," he began. "I've heard of red herrings, but this is ridiculous. If he wanted to ring in some big name to get himself off the hook, why didn't he go for the biggies like Walter Cronkite or David Brinkley?"

"So, you're saying there's nothing to it?"

"You're goddamn right that's what I'm saying," he said hotly. "From what I hear, the cops have the guy by the bags and it's strictly desperation time. And let me tell you something else." His expression hardened. "If any of this creep's bullshit allegations, if the slightest whiff of innuendo about my being involved with that girl hits the press, I'm gonna sue the ass off everyone involved, and that's a promise!"

"Well, I just thought I should get *your* side of the story," Pete said.

Larry shook his head disgustedly. "Christ, you really want to get off the sports beat, don't you? But don't try and do it on *my* back!"

"Well, the fact is, I *am* off sports — at least, temporarily.

Our regular crime reporter's away on holidays and since I've got the experience, and some inside knowledge of the Gains murder, they're letting me carry the ball. My first story'll have a good chunk of our front page tomorrow.''

"Well congratulations," Larry said, trying to appear enthusiastic but falling short. "Uh, this stuff that Renner's been spouting," he said hesitantly, "about me, I mean. You didn't include that in your story, did you?"

"You know me better than that," Pete said. "I've never reported unfounded allegations and I don't intend to start now. I told you what Renner said but I didn't say I believe him. I still don't think he murdered Holly Gains but that's more intuition than anything else.''

Standing on the sidewalk, watching Pete's car disappear in the midday traffic, Larry felt as though the world were closing in on him. Whatever else you could say about Pete Gossett, he was sharp, one of the best investigative journalists ever to work in Toronto. What the hell had he been up to? Larry wondered. Had Pete really wanted to get his side of the story or had he been on a fishing expedition, hoping Larry would rise to the bait by over-reacting? Larry was confident he hadn't given anything away, but how could he really be sure?

He was sure of one thing, though: No matter how much Renner mouthed off, there was no way the little weasel could link him to Holly. He conceded that he might have left a few fingerprints around her apartment but if the cops had lifted any, there'd be no reason for them to try and match them up with his. He broke into a sweat and his legs felt weak. No reason, unless they got a tip.

The voice echoed in his mind; pulsed in his temples. "You were with her last night." "There are stricter laws against mutilating and strangling young girls." With a supreme effort, he uprooted himself from the sidewalk and went back to the station. He paid no attention to the curious looks and bantering comments as he walked dazedly to his office and, with a shaking hand, began to dial Jack Lexer's number.

Jane perched on the side of the bed, flipping through the family photo album. Arlene's tenth birthday party: Half a dozen girls with party hats mugging at the camera with Dianne, just barely in the frame, sticking her tongue out.

She flipped back another couple of years: herself on a chaise longue by the pool, squinting into the sun. She sighed, thinking how unself-conscious she'd been when she wore a bikini in those pre-cellulite days.

She went back still further. Larry with a six-month-old Dianne cradled in his arms. She was dressed in a white, hand-knitted outfit that Larry's mother had made. Dianne's round, happy face peered out from beneath a little pink bonnet and her tiny, doll's feet bore matching booties. Jane felt a sudden rush of tenderness as she noted the pride and love in her husband's eyes as he gazed at *their* child. *Their* blood. *Their* life.

She picked up the white-and-gold album containing their wedding pictures, but she couldn't bring herself to look at it just then.

Sprawling on the bed she stared up at the ceiling, wistfully reviewing her life with Larry, and was conscious of the fact that she'd begun to think of it in the past tense. There had to be more than this, she thought. But then, doubt descended like a heavy cloud. Suppose there wasn't. Suppose she ended up like some tragic nomad, doomed to wander from one emotional desert to another?

She could see Larry and herself dividing up the girls' lives. This is my half. That's yours. Using Dianne and Arlene to punish each other for their own unfulfilled expectations. She could feel the sadness welling up in her chest, and finally, too great to contain, the tears came, sudden and hot.

Hearing footsteps ascending the stairs, she quickly sat up and dried her eyes, and a few seconds later, Arlene poked her head into the room.

"Mom, Karen and I are going to walk over to the mall, O.K.?" Before Jane could reply, her daughter asked anxiously: "Is anything wrong?"

Jane forced a smile. "No, nothing. I'm fine." But the quaver in her voice betrayed her.

Without a word, Arlene sat down beside her, laying her head on Jane's shoulder. Reaching up, she gently stroked her mother's hair, crooning: "Don't be sad, Mommy. Please don't be sad."

Jane kissed her daughter lightly on the forehead and said softly: "It's not always bad to be sad, honey. It depends on what kind of sadness it is. Mine's sort of a happy kind. I'm happy because I love you kids and your dad so much, but I'm sad because I haven't used my love to make your lives as good as they should be; to make this *family* as good as it should be."

As Arlene pulled away to look up at her, Jane was shaken to see that tears had traced shiny paths down her daughter's cheeks. "Mommy," Arlene said in a tiny, desolate voice, "are you gonna go away? Are you gonna leave us?"

Jane's face registered her shock. "Oh, no, honey. I'd never do that. Wherever did you get an idea like that?"

"I heard you and Daddy arguing a while back and you said you couldn't take it anymore." Her lips trembled. "What can't you take anymore, Mommy? Me and Dianne and Daddy?"

"No, no, baby," she whispered, brushing her lips against her daughter's hair. "Mothers say things like that all the time but they don't mean anything. We say things like that because sometimes we can't take *ourselves* and we end up punishing other people for what we've let ourselves become: self-pitying, whining shrews."

"You're not," Arlene said fiercely. "You're not like that at all. You're the best mother in the whole world and I love you more than anything."

"And I love you, baby," She pulled a tissue out of the pocket of her dressing gown and dabbed at her daughter's eyes. "Now, no more crying or people will start to think you're as silly as I am."

"I don't care what anyone thinks," Arlene said defiantly. "I want to be just like you."

Jane tousled her daughter's hair. "Well, from now on, I'm going to try to be the kind of person you kids and your dad can be proud of. No more tantrums. No more pouting. From now on, there's going to be nothing but sunshine around here."

And deep inside her, she sensed that, at last, there was a real chance for a new beginning.

"O.K., lemme get this straight," Speedy said slowly. "You're gonna get my case remanded to next Friday, right?"

"That's right," Morley said curtly. "There are a few things we have to straighten out before we can enter a plea."

"What'ya mean?" Speedy snarled. "I didn't do it. So why the hell don't I just plead not guilty right away and get the fucking show on the road?"

Morley checked his watch. Nine-twenty. They'd have to be in court in forty minutes and that didn't give him much time. "Sit down," he commanded, in a voice that left no doubt that he expected to be obeyed.

Speedy sullenly dropped into a chair on the other side of the small table.

"O.K.," Morley continued. "I don't have time to cite case law or debate the merits of the Canadian justice system. I'm your legal counsel and you either trust me and take my instructions, or I walk. You got that?"

Speedy nodded morosely. "But —"

Morley's hand shot up. "No buts, ifs, or whereas's. You may not be paying for my time but I can assure that it doesn't come cheaply. If I'm not here, I'll be somewhere else, but I'll still be pulling in two hundred dollars an hour." He smiled and his voice lost its edge. "Now, we have to recognize that you're not the only one with a stake in this matter. There are others who also have a vested interest in the outcome and these others are supporting you to the fullest extent of their abilities. Do you understand that?"

Speedy nodded unsurely. "I guess."

"All right. Now, let me spell it out for you. The Crown has a damn good case, more than enough to get you committed to trial on a charge of first-degree murder."

Speedy started to object but the lawyer silenced him with a look. "At this point, your only alibi witness is Bernard Pouliot, who, as you probably know, has a lengthy criminal record, including convictions for trafficking in narcotics, armed robbery, and last but not least, perjury." Morley looked at him glumly. "Not exactly a pillar of society, I think you'll agree. So, given the fact that your other two associates — each of whom, incidentally, has an equally unsavoury background — are not available to testify on your behalf, it would be a serious error in judgement to conclude that you have an airtight alibi.

"On the other hand, the Crown has witnesses who will testify that you previously assaulted Miss Gains and threatened her life. In addition, Mrs. Janacek will testify that she heard raised voices and the sounds of a violent struggle coming from your apartment at about eight-thirty P.M. on the night of the murder, at which time, according to your statement, you were in the apartment alone with Miss Gains."

"I told you about that," Speedy flared. "I told you we were just putting the old witch on!"

"Yes, you did," Morley said noncommittally. With his hands clasped under his chin and his eyes relentlessly boring into Speedy's, he continued. "And then there's the clock which, to all intents and purposes, was smashed during the assault on Miss Gains. It apparently stopped functioning at approximately eight-thirty P.M. when you, according to your evidence, were still at the apartment.''

''Hell,'' Speedy sneered, ''the goddamn clock could have stopped on its own. Maybe Holly forgot to wind it.''

''That's possible,'' Morley allowed. ''As a matter of fact, that's the tack I intend to take if this matter goes to trial.''

Speedy looked at him in bewilderment. ''What'ya mean 'if'?''

''Well, there's always a possibility we can cut a deal with the Crown, plead you guilty to a lesser charge, and avoid the necessity of a lengthy and arduous legal proceeding.''

''Forget about it,'' Speedy snapped. ''I didn't do it and I'm not pleading guilty to shit!''

''Well, ultimately, that's your choice,'' Morley said blandly, ''but with the way this case is shaping up, I have to tell you that when you get in front of a jury, it's going to be a crapshoot, with an awful lot riding on one roll of the dice.''

''Now, I'm not saying I'm gonna cop a plea or anything,'' Speedy said slowly, ''but what kind of deal do you think you can swing?''

''Well, for second-degree, the best we could hope for would be a minimum of ten years.''

Speedy's jaw dropped. ''Ten years! Fuck, I'd be an old man by the time I got out.''

''Don't worry,'' Morley said soothingly. ''That's a worst-case scenario. I'm sure we can do a lot better than that. As a matter of fact, I can just about promise you that we can get the Crown to accept a manslaughter plea.''

''Yeah? So what kind of time would I be looking at then?''

''Given the mitigating circumstances of your having been under the influence of drugs and alcohol, I think we could get you off with no more than three years, which means that you'd be out on the street in less than a year.''

Speedy rubbed his chin thoughtfully. ''I dunno. Even a year in the joint is no picnic. And suppose you and the

Crown make a deal but the judge don't buy it and nails me with five, or six years? What the hell do I do then?''

"You just sit tight while I file an appeal and pull a few more strings to get the sentence reduced.''

Spector gave a self-satisfied smile and picked a few imaginary specks of lint from the lapels of his dark-blue, three-piece pinstripe. Then he leaned forward, lowering his voice conspiratorially: "Listen, some very influential people have already been working behind the scenes on your behalf. They appreciate the fact that you haven't made waves and brought heat down on their business activities.

"I've done what I think is a pretty good job of judge-shopping, and when you enter your plea next week, you'll be appearing in front of a guy who owes some favours to some friends of ours. Plus, when you do your year, you'll have something waiting for you on the outside. Something that will guarantee you a secure and financially rewarding future with a well-established organization, if you know what I mean.''

A slow smile spread over Speedy's face. The lawyer didn't have to spell it out. The fix was in. The mob was backing him all the way. He'd kept his mouth shut and now they were going to do right by him.

"Well, what's it going to be?'' Spector asked. "Do you want to take a little pain for some substantial long-term gain or do you want to bet your future on one flip of the coin?''

"Great choice, isn't it?'' Speedy said sarcastically.

"It could be worse. At least you've got a chance to make it easy on yourself.''

Speedy stood up and ran a hand through his straggly hair. "Lemme think about it, eh? I mean, I don't have to enter a plea for another week, right? So what's the rush?''

"No rush,'' Morley shrugged. "It's just that our mutual friends want to be assured that you're prepared to do what is in their — and, of course, your — best interests.''

"Yeah,'' Speedy said knowingly, "I guess.'' Slowly lowering himself back into his chair, he leaned forward, saying earnestly: "Mr. Spector, there's something I want you to do for me. Something real important."

"What's that?"

"I want you to get me sprung for Holly's funeral. Just for like a couple of hours, y'know?"

Spector had just launched into a slow, pessimistic shake of his head when Speedy rushed on. "I don't give a fuck if they put me in leg irons, I just wanna — I *gotta* be there."

"To be perfectly frank," Morley said, "I don't think there's much chance of them letting you out for even five minutes. That's why I'm not bothering to apply for bail." He shrugged his round shoulders. "But I'll see what I can do."

"Thanks a lot," Speedy said emotionally. "I'd appreciate that. You see, Holly ain't really got anyone but me. And it'll be kind of lonely for her to go away without, like, having someone there who really cares for her, y'know?"

"I'll try," Morley said, genuinely touched by Speedy's concern. "I don't think there's a hope in hell, but I'll try."

He'd no sooner completed the sentence when a couple of police officers entered the room. One, a Kojak look alike with a shiny, clean-shaven pate and ample belly, handcuffed himself to Speedy. The other, a medium-sized man with a round face and a florid, drinker's complexion, remained a few paces behind as they walked down the hallway to the elevator that led to the main-floor courtroom. As the elevator door slid open, Spector stepped back. "I'll see you in a few minutes," he told Speedy. "I've got a little business to attend to."

But as he made his way toward the pay phone at the end of the hall, he had more on his mind than telling Lexer that everything was going according to plan. A couple of minutes passed before he could attach a name to the feeling he had, and when he did, it was with considerable surprise and not a little apprehension.

With a bemused smile, he realized that he, Morley Spector, Q.C., actually felt sorry for that little weasel, Renner.

"Isn't that something," he muttered, as he began to dial Lexer's number. "Now, isn't that the strangest thing."

Erica Jantzen smiled apologetically at Larry over her microphone. "I hope I don't say the wrong thing, Mr. Chambers."

"You'll be fine, Erica," Larry soothed. "Just relax and pretend it's just you and me having a friendly little conversation. And call me Larry."

"Well, I'll try my best . . ." She hesitated, then smiled timidly, "Larry."

"Fine. When we go back on the air, we'll just chat for a few minutes and then I'll open the line to callers for twenty minutes or so. That'll take us right up to noon. That sound O.K.?"

Erica nodded uncertainly as she fidgeted with her thin, gold wedding band.

Taking his cue from his producer, Larry leaned into his mike. "Welcome to the last half-hour of *Larry's Line*. As promised, with me in the studio is Mrs. Erica Jantzen, the mother of sixteen-year-old Helen Jantzen, who earlier this week met her death at the hands of an unknown killer." His voice became compassionate. "Erica, now I know it's not easy for you to relive this tragic event, but I think it's in the interest of parents everywhere to hear your story."

"Well, I'll do my best," she murmured, "but it's very hard . . ." Her voice broke and Larry quickly cut in.

"Yes, I'm sure it is," he said, redirecting his attention to his listeners. "Now, as most of you out there are probably aware, Helen Jantzen's battered and lifeless body was found in a field near Humber College just a few days ago, and her funeral is going to be held on Tuesday, July 2nd." He nodded at his guest. "Have I got that right, Erica?"

"Yes," she said quietly. "It'll be at 10:00 A.M. at the Westview Pentecostal Church."

"I guess you're expecting quite a turnout," Larry ventured.

"Well, with the school year being over and all, I'm sure a lot of her friends will be there."

"Yes, I'm sure they will," Larry said solicitously. "And I might add, they'll be joined by a crew from CKAL." His voice deepened, radiating a well-crafted sincerity. "In the interest of keeping you, the public, informed, *Larry's Line* will be carrying a live broadcast of the funeral service direct from the church. That's this Tuesday morning, right here on 780 on your dial."

Softening his tone, he continued: "Now, Erica, I think we both know that Helen's death, while indeed tragic, is just another statistic to the police and the other agencies which deal with the rising tide of violent crime in Metro. What can you tell us about your daughter to give us — and, in particular, all the parents of teenage girls — some insight into what made her trade her home and family for the sleazy subculture of the street?"

"Larry," she said wearily, "you can't imagine how many times I've asked myself the same question, wondering where she went wrong — where all of us went wrong."

"Yes," Larry prodded, "I'm sure you have, but you must have come up with a few answers. Surely there must have been some signs along the way that all wasn't well at home, that Helen was unhappy or emotionally disturbed?"

The rustle of Erica Jantzen taking a tissue from her purse was clearly audible over the airwaves. "As you know," she said, dabbing at her eyes, "we've been on welfare ever since my husband left us, and we've never really had enough money to feed and clothe ourselves properly.

"It was particularly hard on Helen, at her age when girls are so sensitive and all. She could never dress as well as the other girls at her school, and I couldn't give her any spending money so she could go to movies and dances with her friends." She took a deep breath before continuing. "I noticed that she had become much quieter. She stopped singing around the house like she used to, and sometimes, she didn't even talk — not to me or her brothers and sisters. I knew that something was wrong. But, if she wouldn't talk, well. . . ." She raised her hands in a gesture of futility.

"Well, I'm sure you did all you could, Erica, and I'm sure no one's blaming you because your daughter chose a seedy streetcorner life over a normal life with her family."

Listening in her office, Elaine winced. She felt ashamed and disgusted at the way Larry was badgering the distraught woman. Why did the woman take it, she wondered. The station *was* assuming the cost of her daughter's funeral but that was no reason to subject herself to such an obscene inquisition. She found herself unconsciously willing Erica Jantzen to fight back, to tell Larry to stuff his holier-than-thou act and walk out of the studio.

But Erica stayed, fighting to preserve her daughter's memory the way she'd been unable to preserve her life. But there was another reason too — Erica cared. If sharing her pain would prevent other mothers from experiencing the same tragedy, she would do her best.

"Now, before I open up the lines," Larry intoned, "and I see that the switchboard is lit up like a Christmas tree, I just want to say one thing. Toronto The Good, as it's sometimes called, is a fine, clean city, the best in the world. I'm damn proud to live here and I'm sure the same goes for all of you out there listening. But to keep it this way, we've got to get good and mad at the creeps and criminals who want to turn this city into a moral sewer. We've got to make sure they get our message and crawl back into their holes.

"Thank God for Metro's finest and an Attorney General who doesn't pander to the bleeding hearts and do-gooders who think that rapists, child-molesters, and murderers are just poor, misguided individuals who were deprived of love in their formative years.

"Well, I wish I could tell you what *I'd* like to deprive them of but the CRTC won't let me. Now, let's hear from you. This is *your* show. *Larry's Line* is your voice, your chance to show some guts and tell our city fathers what you think. Jabbing a button on the phone console, he barked: *"Larry's Line!* Talk to me!"

"Larry, I would like to speak with Mrs. Jantzen," a female voice filled the studio.

"She's right here. Go ahead, caller."

"Mrs. Jantzen, do you believe in God?"

Erica blinked in bewilderment. "Do I believe in God? Is that what you're asking?"

"That is exactly what I am asking," the woman said sternly. "Can you give me an answer, please?"

"Why, yes. I mean, I certainly do believe in God."

There was a note of triumph in the voice. "Then you must concede that it is God's will that your daughter was taken from you?"

"Well, I guess in a way that's so, but I still can't understand —"

"If you had God in your heart," the voice broke in, "you would have no trouble understanding. Search your soul, Mrs. Jantzen, and you will find the seeds of your sorrow."

Erica's eyes began to glisten. "But I tried to be a good mother to Helen. I really did. But I have other children and I have to spread my time and my love around. If I had known she was so unhappy and desperate, I would have done anything I could to help her."

"It is not you who could have helped her." The voice had the fervent conviction of an Old Testament prophet. "Only our Lord and Redeemer could have helped her but your heart was not open to Him. You have shut God out of your life and now, He has shut your daughter out of yours."

Erica's voice was muffled by sobs. "Please don't say that. It's not true. I loved her. I would have done anything . . . anything."

"It *is* true," the voice shrilled. "It says right in Isaiah, Chapter Three, Verse Two, that the blood of the Lamb will be shed for the sins of the Shepherd. Sin not, lest the blood of your blood flow like the river."

"All right," Larry interjected. "I'm sure God has forgiven Mrs. Jantzen for anything she might've done to contribute to her daughter's death. I'm sure that, as good Christians, you and I can do no less. Do you agree with me, caller?"

"I agree with you, Mr. Chambers, that as Christians we must be charitable to sinners, but I also believe that as Christians we must bear witness to the transgressions of those who do not lead lives of Godliness. God bless you, Mr. Chambers. And God forgive *you*, Mrs. Jantzen."

As he severed the connection, Larry was positively buoyant. The show had everything it took to capture and hold an audience: conflict, pathos, not to mention a little sex and violence. It was dynamite, he assured himself, and he felt as upbeat as he sounded when he led into the next commercial break with a breezy: "We'll be back with more after a few words from the people who keep *Larry's Line* on the air — our sponsors."

While waiting for the commercials to conclude, Larry smiled reassuringly at his guest and, through her tears, fear, and confusion, Erica Jantzen bravely smiled back.

Chapter Fourteen

Jack Lexer flicked his cigarette lighter and lit, first Larry's and then his own cigar. "You're gonna like that," he smiled. "From Havana. Hand-rolled."

Larry took a deep drag and exhaled, the aromatic smoke hovering over him like a halo. He leaned back on the couch and tried to relax, but his body was so tense that when he tried to smile his face felt as though he'd just come from the dentist and the freezing was still in.

"That was quite a show you put on this morning," Jack said, underlining the comment with a series of nods. "Yeah, that bit with the Jantzen woman was enough to shake up anyone, even a tough old bastard like me."

"Thanks, Jack," Larry replied. "I've got to admit I had some misgivings about putting her on because there's always a chance that someone like that — someone who's so emotionally overwrought — might go over the edge. You know, once, three or four years ago, I was interviewing a woman whose ex-husband had abducted their kid and taken her out of the country, and as soon as the woman started talking about the kid, she damn near became hysterical. We finally had to get a doctor to sedate her and, let me tell you, that sure kicked the shit out of what could have been a helluva powerful segment.''

Lexer nodded sympathetically. ''It's a bitch all right, when you're trying to take care of business and someone won't cooperate. I've had that problem myself.'' He studied Larry through the haze of cigar smoke, waiting for him to get to the nitty-gritty. After all, when the guy had called him, he was in a helluva sweat about something. And now that he was here, he wanted to make small talk. What gives? he wondered.

Larry had intended to lead up to his problem gradually but, sensing Lexer's growing impatience, he blurted out: ''Jack, I'm in deep shit. That girl who got strangled. Holly. I was at her place that night. But I can't remember bugger-all about what I did there.''

Lexer looked at him with amusement. ''You can't remember? What the hell is that supposed to mean?''

Larry said sheepishly, ''I was so goddamn bombed that most of the night's a goddamn blank and that's what scares the hell out of me.''

''Well, you're a nice fellow, Larry, and you've done me some favours over the past couple of years, but I don't know what I can do for you. Something like this,'' he shrugged, ''maybe you should see a doctor.''

''No, no. That's only part of it,'' Larry protested. ''The thing is, I got a call from some guy who wouldn't give his name and he said that he saw me leave Holly's place at the same time the cops figured she was knocked off.''

Lexer's face lit up with interest. ''Ah-hah,'' he said with a satisfied smile, ''Now we're getting to the good stuff.''

''Good stuff?'' Larry said incredulously. ''This scumbag is threatening to blow the whistle and tell what he knows to the cops. He says he can prove I was in Holly's apartment and that the cops'll be able to nail me for her murder if he points them in the right direction." He slammed his hand on the top of the oversized coffee table. "What beats me is, who is this guy and how the hell does he know where I was? Why the hell would anybody be following me?" He glanced pointedly at Lexer. "I don't suppose you'd know, would you?"

Lexer's meaty features clenched, "This ain't the time to get paranoid, pal. Sounds like this jerk-off's got you by the short-and-curlys and I'll do what I can to bail you out, but let me tell you, my friend, it ain't gonna do you a helluva lot of good to start pointing fingers."

"Sorry, Jack. I didn't mean —"

Lexer cut him short with an upraised hand and a contemptuous look. "Listen, you're a big boy. You were old enough to know what you were doing when you started chasing this young stuff. Remember when you were at the house last fall and there were all those broads around? The two sisters — the models — and those four strippers from the Casablanca? I told you to take your pick, right? And what did you do? You grabbed that little teenybopper bitch from Montreal. What the hell was she — sixteen, seventeen? And ripped out of her skull on coke."

"She was a cute kid," Larry said meekly.

Lexer waggled his cigar like a baton. "That's the goddamn trouble. She *was* a kid. She wasn't old enough or smart enough to keep her mouth shut and that's why I told you to take her and split. You remember that?"

Squirming under Lexer's inquisitorial glare, Larry nodded.

"O.K.," Lexer continued. "So you got this hang-up about young pussy. That's no skin off my ass. Me, I got the hots for coloured broads — not all the time, but once in a while for a change of pace, y'know? And give me a little Oriental snatch now and then and you've got a happy man. So, I'm not throwing stones. Whatever turns you on, y'know?"

Larry thrust out his jaw indignantly. "Listen, Jack. Just because I don't want to bang broads who've got a couple of yards of stretch marks and boxes the size of the Grand Canyon doesn't mean I'm some kind of kiddy-diddler."

"Don't get your shorts in a knot, pal," Lexer smiled. "Like I said, whatever turns you on. But don't come down on me because I had my people line you up with some steady, young tail. I did it as a favour to a friend, got it?" He didn't wait for Larry to answer. "O.K., so this Holly what's-her-face ends up getting whacked. That's not my fault and it's not your fault." His face clouded and he looked at Larry intently. "Is it?"

"No, of course not," Larry said hastily.

"O.K. then. So what's the hassle? I hear the cops got the chick's old man in custody and that he's going to be pleading guilty."

Larry stared at him in amazement. "How the hell do you know that?"

Lexer smiled smugly. "Let's just say I got friends who keep me clued in."

"Yeah," Larry said glumly. "But suppose this creep puts *me* into the picture. Maybe Renner'll figure he's got a shot at walking and change his mind about copping a plea."

"That's possible," Lexer said thoughtfully, "and I don't think we want that, do we?"

"Well, it could open up a lot of cans of worms if the guy goes to trial," Larry said.

"The guy that called you," Jack said sharply. "Did he name a price?"

"No, but he said he'll be calling me at home this evening and I'm goddamn sure he doesn't want to discuss the weather."

They sat like two brooding statues until Lexer finally broke the silence. "If you pay him once, he'll bleed you dry. You know that, don't you?"

Larry nodded gloomily. "Yeah, but what choice do I have? This blackmailing slimeball found my pen in Holly's apartment and chances are my fingerprints are all over the place.

"I was talking to Edwards and he tells me they've got a pretty good case against Renner. The punk's alibi is weak and there's no evidence that anyone else was in Holly's apartment that night. But suppose they can prove *I* was there? Then Renner has a good chance of walking, and I have just as good a chance of seeing my name on the front page of every paper in the country."

"That wouldn't be good for any of us." Lexer's voice was as soft as it was ominous. "You're doing a good job and it would really fuck us up if you got knocked off your white horse."

"Jack," Larry pleaded, "you know I've cooperated with you in the past — put people you wanted on my show, promoted your development schemes and business interests. Just get me out of this jam and I'll do anything you ask."

"O.K., this is what you're gonna do," Lexer said, his tone crisp and businesslike, "Find out what the guy's angle is — how much he wants and how he's going to take delivery — and let me know. Then do exactly as he says."

Larry frowned in disbelief. "You mean you want me to pay him off?"

Lexer violently stubbed out his cigar in the ashtray. "Yeah, for the time being." The menacing glint in his eyes contrasted sharply with the smile playing on his thick lips. "Then I'll see if maybe we can come up with something a little more permanent."

Valiantly trying to concentrate, Larry reread the paragraph but still couldn't make any sense out of it. His gaze flew to the telephone on the end table and he stared at it with a mixture of anticipation and dread. Ring, you son of a bitch, he silently cursed, dropping the newspaper onto the couch, but quickly picking it up again as Jane entered the living room.

"Care for some dessert?" she asked.

"Uh, no thanks," he said, pretending to be engrossed in the paper.

"I guess it *was* a silly question," she said airily. "After all, you hardly touched your dinner."

"Sorry about that," he said, slowly lowering the paper. "I know you went to a lot of trouble, but my ulcer's been kicking up again and it's pretty hard to tackle a big meal when your guts are on fire."

"Well, why didn't you say so?" she asked, surprising him with her solicitude. "I thought the medication and diet were working but if they're not, you'd better make another appointment with Dr. Simon."

"I already have," Larry lied. "I'm going to see him next Thursday."

Jane came over and, resting her hand on his shoulder, said softly, "I know things haven't been that good between us lately but I do worry about you, you know."

"I know you do, honey, and I appreciate it." Touched by her concern and the genuine tenderness in her expression, he patted her hand. Suddenly, he wanted nothing more than to take her in his arms and hug her so hard that she'd know she was the most important thing in his life. But he couldn't do it. Not now. Not when his future was at the mercy of a phone call. There were so many things he wanted to tell her but he was like a drowning man who was too frightened to even call for help.

"Well, if you need anything, let me know," Jane said.

"I will, hon. You can count on it."

As Jane started back to the kitchen, the jangle of the phone stopped her in mid-stride and she made a move to answer it. But Larry bounced up from the sofa and beat her to it. Plucking the receiver from the cradle, and holding his hand over the mouthpiece, he said, trying to sound casual, "It's probably for me, I told Elaine to call me right after dinner." In response to his wife's cool stare, he shrugged apologetically. "No rest for the weary."

He waited until Jane was safely in the kitchen before raising the receiver to his ear. "Hello?"

"Mr. Chambers?"

Recognizing the voice, Larry felt his stomach lurch. "Yes, but I don't suppose you're going to tell me who *you* are."

"You've got that right," Alec chuckled. "All right, now that you've had a chance to think over what I said, have you come to a decision?"

"A decision?"

"Don't play games," Alec snapped. "You know what I mean. Are you going to cooperate or do I tip off the cops that they might have another suspect in the Holly Gains murder?"

"I'll cooperate," Larry said leadenly. "What do you want?"

"What do you think? I want a little piece of what *you've* got. Not too much. Not enough to break you, but enough to make it worth my while, if you know what I mean."

"How much?"

"Fifty thousand. And make sure it's in small bills — nothing larger than a fifty."

"Fifty thousand?" Larry yelped then, glancing toward the kitchen, quickly lowered his voice. "That's almost every nickel I've got in the bank."

"It's lucky for you that you've got that much," Alec said dryly. "I wish *I* did."

Larry's sweaty palm made the phone feel clammy and repellent. Pressing his mouth to the receiver, he hissed: "O.K., but remember this is a one-shot deal. I'll give you the fifty thousand but I don't ever want to hear from you again. You got that?"

"I got it and you better get the fifty thousand by Monday."

"That's out of the question. Monday's a holiday and the banks are closed. The soonest I can get it is Tuesday."

"O.K. then, Tuesday it is," Alec said amiably.

"What do I do with it? Send it to you by courier?"

"You've gotta be kidding," Alec laughed. "What you're going to do is put it in a briefcase and take it to the airport — Terminal Two. You're going to get there at exactly three P.M. and then you're going to take a seat near the Tilden Rent A Car booth. You got it?''

"Yeah, right," Larry sighed.

"Then, at exactly three-ten, you're going to slide the briefcase under the seat, leave the terminal, and go home. Any questions?''

"Yeah," Larry said anxiously. "Suppose somebody wanders by and walks away with the briefcase? I'm out fifty grand and so are you.''

"Somebody *is* going to walk away with the briefcase, my friend," Alec said, "but that somebody is going to be one of *my* people." He wanted Larry to think that there were others involved in the scheme, so there'd be less chance of Chambers thinking he could pull a fast one. "Remember, you're going to be under surveillance from the time you arrive at the airport until the time you leave, so don't try anything funny. If you tip the cops or bring anyone with you, the deal's off and the cops get what I know about you and the girl. Got that?''

"Yeah," Larry said sourly. "I got it.''

"O.K., that's it then. Do as you're told and everybody comes out smelling like a rose. Fuck up and you lose a helluva lot more than money.''

Larry stood holding the phone against his ear, listening to the angry buzz long after Alec had hung up. Then, with a grim expression and a shaking hand, he began to dial Jack Lexer's private number.

"Oh, come on," Linda coaxed. "Just one more dance.'' Her large green eyes were both inviting and daring Pete, as she swayed to the funky beat.

Wiping the sweat off his forehead, he led her off the crowded dance floor. "Let's get a drink first, then we'll really get *down*," he whooped, affecting a soul-brother strut. "Because dancing is myyyyyy life.''

When they were back at their table, Pete raised his wineglass. "Here's to you, Ginger."

"Now, you're dating yourself," she smiled.

"What can I say?" he shrugged. "I'm a fan of old movies — anything with Bogart, Cagney, or John Garfield."

"Does that mean you like to live in the past?"

"Could be," he nodded thoughtfully, then quipped: "How much do I owe you, Dr. Brothers?"

"I'll tell you later."

"I can hardly wait," he leered. But in the next instant, he became serious. "Maybe there's something else you can tell me, right now."

"Such as?"

"Such as why you and your sister move in the same circles as Jack Lexer."

She stared down at her glass for a few seconds before replying: "I've already told you about my sister and, as for me, well, you can put that in the past tense because I'm through with that scene."

"How did you get involved in the first place?"

She tossed her head and her hair swirled around her neck. "It was better than being alone." She looked into his eyes, forcing a smile. "These days, when a woman passes thirty, she's considered over the hill. She's the one the guys hit on when the bar's about to close and they start to panic about coming up empty."

"You don't expect me to believe that about *you*, do you?" Pete asked. "Have you seen the way some of the young studs in here are eyeing you tonight?"

"Oh, they *look* all right, but they're probably thinking: There's a lady with a lot of miles on her who might be desperate enough to go for a one-night stand."

"No way," he smiled, reaching over and taking her hand. "They're probably all saying: "I wonder what a classy lady like that sees in a shmuck like him." The sound of driving guitars and a wailing sax washed over them, and Pete found himself shouting to make himself heard.

"I know exactly what I see in you, Mr. Gossett," Linda shot back.

As the music died and Pete watched the band file off the stage, he could feel Linda looking at him. When he turned back to her, her expression was a blend of amusement and irritation.

"Well, don't you want to know?"

"I think I can guess," he smiled. "It must be my earlobes. Everybody says they're my best feature."

She dismissed the remark with an impatient shake of her head. "Can't you ever be serious?"

"Sometimes, but I try not to be. I find it interferes with my digestion."

"You've really got that act down pat, haven't you?"

"What act is that?"

"You know," she said airily, "the cynical journalist who's down on everything, including himself."

"You think it's an act?" His eyes crinkled in amusement.

"I *know* it is," she snapped. "I know that underneath all the tough talk and sarcasm, there's a man who cares about things and — whether he wants to believe it or not — people." When it began to look as if he wasn't going to respond, she eyed him sternly. "Well?"

He threw up his hands in a gesture of defeat. "What can I say in the face of such overwhelming evidence but 'guilty as charged.'"

"Don't feel bad," she consoled him. "Most people can't see through that front of yours. It's just that I've been around so many people who *really* don't give a damn about anyone else — who take what they want and throw the rest away — that I can tell when someone does."

"Well, since we're in the mood to throw flowers, how about giving *me* a chance?"

A smile balanced precariously on her lips. "Oh-oh."

"You, Linda Selden," he said severely, "are a terrific person to be with."

"I've heard that before," she sniffed, "usually from some guy who's trying to look down the front of my dress."

"Ouch," Pete winced, "and here I thought I was being subtle."

"Not subtle enough to keep me from knowing what *your* game is, Mr. Reporter."

"Oh," he said innocently, "and what game might that be?"

She sighed resignedly. "Listen, Pete. I know that your interest in me is just a by-product of your preoccupation with Jack Lexer."

He was about to protest, but changed his mind and looked directly into her eyes.

"I won't con you. You're right. Or, at least, you were. But right now, my interest is totally centred on you and that's the truth."

"Just on little old me?" she asked. "You're not interested in big bad Jack even a little teensy weensy bit?"

Pete shrugged. "I think most people are interested in a guy who comes from the streets and becomes a multimillionaire without apparently ever having done an honest day's work."

"Jack Lexer . . ." her voice grew harsh, "found a better way. He got where he is and will stay there by buying people. He's damn good at it too, because he seems to have a —" she searched for the right word, "talent for knowing who's for sale, and at what price."

"Well," Pete offered, "the way things are in this age of instant gratification, it's probably a buyer's market."

"Well, it certainly was when it came to my sister," Linda said.

Studying her closely as she spoke, Pete found himself comparing her with Elaine, and wondering how he could be attracted to such completely different women. Where Elaine was ice, Linda was fire, and while Linda came across as the tougher of the two, she, paradoxically, also seemed to be the more vulnerable.

Certainly, he had a lot more in common with Elaine, but there was a wall between them they could peer over from time to time, but that they could never penetrate. With Linda, it was different. Even though they hardly knew each other, she seemed willing to trust him with her innermost feelings.

"Where did that leave Mrs. Lexer?" Pete inquired. "Jack's still married, isn't he?"

She nodded. "Roxanne Lexer runs after social acceptance the way Jack chases money and power. As long as Jack keeps his affairs under wraps, she goes along with it. If you read the society pages at all, you'd know she's up to her ears in fund-raising for about a half-dozen foundations, everything from cancer research to symphonies. And who knows?" she winked, "maybe she's got a nice young stud stashed away somewhere to look after her more basic needs."

"So Lexer has what you might call an open marriage?"

"Right. His wife is dripping with diamonds, has social standing, and his kids are enrolled in the best private schools. Jack and his family go to the right places, know the right people, and when he wants a little something on the side or a flashy woman on his arm so he can impress his less respectable friends, he calls my sister."

Pete raised his eyebrows skeptically. "And she stays home and waits for him to call?"

"She'd better if she knows what's good for her."

"What do you mean?"

"I mean that Jack pays the shot for her fancy apartment and her new Jaguar, not to mention the joy powder that she shoves up her nose. But, in return, she has to be available whenever he wants her. And she is."

"Sounds like he owns her."

"He does," she said hollowly. "And not just her. Lots of people."

"Well, I guess it's their choice."

"Not always," Linda said. "Sometimes, there's no way out. At least, there isn't for my sister. Not as long as she's pretty and entertaining enough for Jack to keep on the string."

"Has she ever tried to pull out of the fast lane and make another life for herself?"

"Once," Linda nodded. "About a year ago, she met a man named Steve — a nice guy. I think he was a stockbroker. They went out a few times but Jack found out."

"What happened?"

She laughed bitterly. "A lot. Cheryl and Steve were in a restaurant when Jack walked in with a couple of his 'associates' as he likes to call them. Cheryl found out later that he was having her followed. Isn't that something? Anyway, when she saw Jack, she turned about fourteen shades of white and started to explain that she and Steve were just friends."

"And Jack didn't say a goddamn word. He just started slapping her and he ended up by tearing off her dress, yelling that he'd paid for it and he'd be damned if she was going to whore around in it."

"And what was this guy — this Steve — doing while all this was going down?"

"He was getting worked over by Jack's goons."

"And nobody did anything? How about the restaurant staff? Didn't they at least call the cops?"

Linda looked at him condescendingly. "Get serious. You know the way people are when something violent happens. They trip all over themselves looking for a hole to crawl into. It was no trick at all for Jack's heavies to convince the witnesses to the assault that it would be in their best interest to develop a sudden case of amnesia. And when Cheryl told Steve who and what Jack was, he quickly changed his mind about pressing charges and I don't blame him. After all, who the hell wants to spend the rest of his life looking over his shoulder?"

"So he got away with it?"

"Just like he gets away with everything else," she said matter-of-factly.

"Strange business," Pete mused. "you'd think that this episode might have given your sister a hint that keeping company with Lexer could prove injurious to her health."

"Well, if it has, she hasn't shown it," Linda said. "She seems quite content to go through life being the mistress of one of the most powerful men in Toronto. Anyway, it won't go on forever. As soon as she starts to lose her looks — and all the cocaine she's doing will see to that — Jack'll toss her aside and get someone younger, and prettier. He's done it before."

"You worry about her a lot, don't you?"

"Wouldn't you, if she were your sister?"

"I guess so," he nodded slowly, "but it certainly takes some of the sunshine out of *your* life, doesn't it?"

"Oh, my life has its moments," she smiled, "like, right now, for example."

He returned her smile. "Well, I'm glad you're enjoying yourself." His brow furrowed. "But at the risk of spoiling the party, I'd like to ask you a couple of questions. I don't want to put you on the spot though," he added hurriedly, "so if you'd rather not answer them, just say so, O.K.?"

She nodded noncommittally.

"Do you know if Lexer is tight with a guy called Larry Chambers?"

"Chambers? Isn't he the guy with the phone-in show?"

"That's him. Do you know him?"

She shrugged. "Not really. I've only met him a couple of times at Jack's parties. I don't think he's into coke. The times that I saw him, he looked too drunk to snort."

"Are he and Lexer friends?"

"I suppose so, but Cheryl once told me that the main reason Jack lets him hang around is that he does favours for him every now and then."

"What kind of favours?"

"I don't know. She didn't say."

"And is that all that Lexer does for Chambers in return for these favours — lets him get a taste of life in the fast lane?"

"Something like that, I guess." She frowned in concentration. "I seem to remember my sister saying something about him, something about —" Her face lit up with recognition. "Girls!"

"Girls?"

"Uh-huh. Cheryl said that Chambers has a thing for girls — the younger the better."

"Wait a minute," Pete said, with a look of disgust. "Are you talking about kids?"

"No. He's not *that* kinky, at least as far as I know," Linda said. "Apparently, he's satisfied with fifteen- or sixteen-year-olds."

"It's a great life, isn't it?" Pete said sourly.

"Well, you remember what I told you about Jack and how he can always tell a person's price? Well, Chambers' happens to be girls. Someone else's may be coke or investment capital to either expand a business or keep it from going under." She rifled through her purse, then looked up and asked, "Have you got a cigarette?" Before he could answer, she added, "Never mind, I'm trying to quit."

"So that's how he does it," Pete said thoughtfully.

"Does what?"

"Buys influence in high places. He trades on people's weaknesses. He finds the soft spot — greed, lust, or whatever — and fastens the hook."

"Something like that," she nodded somberly, "and you'd be surprised how many people he's got dangling from that hook. You think judges, cops, and politicians don't like to have a good time? They've got influence, prestige, and social standing, but there are things they want that their education, money, and breeding can't give them. And that's where Jack comes in. Everybody's got a little dark corner inside their personality, and if that dark corner doesn't gain expression, it can grow until it consumes its possessor."

Pete smiled skeptically. "So Jack performs a worthwhile public service?"

"I guess in a way that's true," she said, "but sometimes, the cure is worse than the disease, and the price turns out to be much too high."

"I'm sure you're right about that," Pete said soberly.

"I hope I'm right about something else too," she smiled.

"And what might that be?"

"That you care for me as much as I care for you."

Even in the dim light, he could see a faint flush of colour spread over her cheeks. He reached over and gave her hand an affectionate squeeze. "I care for you a great deal. That's one thing you *don't* have to wonder about."

She returned the squeeze. "I'm glad. I'm glad about a lot of things. About meeting you. About being here with you tonight."

"I'm glad too," he said huskily. "And do you want to know why?"

"Yes." Her voice was scarcely more than a whisper.

"Because," he trumpeted, springing out of his chair, "that is one helluva hot band and dancing is myyyyyy life!"

Leading her through a maze of undulating bodies, he staked out a spot on the dance floor. As Linda shimmied her hips, her breasts swayed, and her mouth sent Pete a silent invitation. And, in that moment, amid the music, smoke, and bodyheat, they felt as if they were the only ones in the room and that the band, flashing strobe lights, and the shaking, swaying dancers were merely a backdrop for their own private drama.

Thank God, Tuesday had finally come, Larry thought, as his body swayed to the rhythm of the subway car. The long weekend had seemed to last forever and it had been one of the greatest challenges of his life to get through the past three days without revealing to his family that he was coming apart at the seams.

The fear of exposure, of having not only the police but a prurient public digging through his dirty laundry and chortling over even the smallest stain, had never left his mind. Hell, he thought, so he wasn't perfect. He'd never pretended he was, so why the hell was his neck on the chopping block? It wasn't fair, he decided. After all he'd bloody well given to his audience, his city, it seemed the cruellest irony that he should be singled out by some sleazy blackmailer.

Well, thank God for friends like Lexer, he reflected. He didn't know what strings Jack would pull to bail him out of this jam but he knew that if anyone could do it, it was Jack. He felt confident that before the day was over, he'd be home free and no longer have to worry about being bled dry by some scumbag extortionist. Larry knew the kind of muscle Lexer could call on, and if they leaned on his tormentor, there was little doubt that the slimy bastard would see the wisdom of finding a safer way to make a dishonest buck.

Although the fear was still with him, it had relaxed its grip and he was now able to see beyond the next tension-filled minute. For the first time in a long while he allowed himself to think of the future, and when he did, images of his wife and daughters flooded his mind. He'd let them down, he told himself, but that was all in the past. They deserved a good husband and father and, by God, he'd see that they got them, and that once again they'd be a family in the truest sense of the word. He'd learned his lesson and, thanks to Jack, it wouldn't be one that would cost him both his career and his family.

By the time Larry reached the radio station, he had managed to banish most of the clouds from his horizon, although his date at the airport still loomed before him. Trying to put it out of his mind, he turned his thoughts to that morning's program. He had a packed show lined up. He'd be leading off with Maude Brown, a former columnist with the *Toronto Sun*, who was heading up a provincial commission on child abuse: He anticipated an avalanche of calls on what was becoming one of the hottest issues of the day.

Then, at about ten-thirty, he would cut away to a remote, live and direct from the chapel where Helen Jantzen's funeral service was being held. After that, it was back to the studio for an interview with Mike Edwards about the progress of the police investigation into her murder. Larry was especially interested in talking to Mike, hoping that the homicide detective could also give him some inside information on the Crown's case against Speedy Renner.

Over the weekend, some of the fog had lifted from Larry's memory. Now, he could remember entering Holly's apartment, watching her slip out of her dressing gown, and then running his hands over her slim, white body. But he still had a blank spot about what happened afterward, although he was certain he hadn't done anything to harm her. Why would he?

No, the cops had the guy who did it. And he'd heard from a source in the Attorney General's Department that Spector was trying to cut a deal, which meant the chances were good the punk would be pleading guilty. That would clinch it, Larry thought. After all, no one would plead guilty to a crime he didn't commit, would he?

Absently, he pulled open his desk drawer and stared at the bottle of Scotch. With a triumphant smile, he slid the drawer shut and held out his hand in front of him at arm's length. There wasn't so much as a hint of a tremor. Over the weekend, all he'd had was a couple of beers. Not even an ounce of hard stuff and he hadn't missed it at all. Yes, he told himself, things were definitely looking up. He'd no sooner completed the thought when, after a perfunctory knock, Elaine whisked in.

"Look at this," she exulted, thrusting a sheet of paper in front of him. "These are some of the preliminary results of our independent polling. We're up five points and Ferguson is down three.'' Her voice rose with excitement, ''Isn't that fabulous?''

He studied the figures and smiled. ''I told you that sucker was just a flash in the pan. Another couple of weeks, and he'll be packing his bags for Omaha.''

''You got it,'' Elaine bubbled, flashing him a V-for-victory sign and swishing out of the office.

Larry leaned back in his chair, then sat up abruptly as something inside him triggered an impulse to call Jane. But while dialling his home, his gaze fell on his wristwatch. Five minutes to nine. Time, he told himself, to mount his white charger and do battle with the forces of darkness. Smiling ruefully, he got up, stretched, and strode purposefully toward the studio.

Chapter Fifteen

Jane picked out a pair of tan slacks and a white silk blouse and laid them carefully on the bed. She finished brushing her hair, and then checked her wristwatch. Ten-fifteen. Still plenty of time for her to do the grocery shopping before heading downtown.

She and Larry had been invited to a party at Harrison Riley's on the following weekend and she felt that she positively had to have something new if she were to hold her own with the other wives — the mates of the city's ruling class. She preened in front of the dresser mirror, tilting her head this way and that, critically eyeing the way her hair swirled about her ears, which she had never felt were her most attractive feature.

Sliding into her outfit, she again went over her agenda for the day. Lunch with Barbara Salem at Pagliacci at twelve-thirty. That would take the best part of two hours. She hadn't seen Barbara since her friend had started her new job as a Coles book-buyer and they'd have a lot of gossip to catch up on. Then she'd do a tour of the better shops — Creeds, Holt Renfrew. Surely one of them would have a nice cocktail dress — something not too expensive, say four or five hundred dollars.

She wouldn't be able to take her usual sweet time though. She had an appointment with Mr. Vlassos at four o'clock. He'd called to say that a report on his surveillance of Larry was ready, and Jane had told him that she would have no further need of his services. The private investigator had hinted that nothing had turned up to suggest Larry was having an affair with anyone. Jane now felt a deep sense of shame at having her husband followed by a sleazy professional voyeur but, she told herself, at the time she'd been angry and desperate.

Now, she was fearful. If Larry found out that she'd had him followed, any chance of making their marriage work would be destroyed. Well, she'd have to make damn sure that never happened. That was why she was paying a personal visit to Alec Vlassos. At first she'd thought of mailing him a cheque, but worried about the possibility of Larry coming across a bank statement showing the payment. She'd never be able to explain it. No, she'd decided, the safest way was to pay the investigator with cash, pick up the report, and tear it into a thousand pieces. She wouldn't so much as glance at it, she vowed, feeling that to do so would be a betrayal of Larry's trust. God, she anguished, how could she have been so petty and spiteful!

On the way to the supermarket, she switched on the radio and immediately heard her husband's voice. It sounded different — hushed and respectful instead of brassy and combative. Jane wrinkled her forehead in bewilderment. He seemed to be talking about a funeral service. What could that be about? she wondered. Then she remembered Larry mentioning something about a special segment on the girl who was murdered — a live broadcast from the church. She turned up the volume and the minister's voice flooded the car.

"We are gathered here today to say farewell to someone we have known and loved. But in spite of our heavy hearts and deep sense of loss, this is not a day of sadness. This is a day of rejoicing for one whom we loved here on earth has gone now to the greatest love of all — the love of our God and Saviour.

"Helen's mother has asked me to include a special prayer in my service and I am happy to do so. She has asked me — and all of us here today — to join her in a prayer for the soul of the man who cruelly snatched away her daughter's life. It may strike some of you as strange to pray for the perpetrator of such a vile and senseless act, but who needs our love and God's guidance more than someone so devoid of human feeling as to commit such a foul deed? Only someone who has never known love could inflict so much pain on so many. Only someone who is trapped in a world of dark despair, who has hardened his heart against God, could have done such a terrible thing to a sweet, innocent child.

"We pray to you, our Lord and Redeemer, to share Thy infinite mercy with this lost, lonely creature, to heal his tortured soul, and wash away the moral pollution that has plunged him into the lowest depths of human behaviour. With our love and Thy mercy, we can still rescue this fallen angel, this imperfect being, from the fires of eternal damnation."

As Jane reached over and switched off the radio, her hands were shaking and she felt strangely disoriented. Pulling into the supermarket parking lot, she squinted up at the sun. It was a beautiful day, not a cloud in the sky. But despite the sunshine she felt cold, as though deep within her there was a lump of ice that wouldn't melt. She could picture the murdered girl lying in her casket like a cold, pale Sleeping Beauty that no kiss could ever wake. She thought she could even make out the face. Yes. Her hand shot up to her mouth to stifle a silent scream. It was Dianne. It was *her* face on the still, waxen form. She shook her head in violent denial. No, it was just her mind playing some kind of sick joke. The bad vibes from the funeral service had fed her subconscious fear for her own daughters' safety.

Jane thought about the minister's invocation. He'd called for forgiveness for Helen Jantzen's murderer. She wondered if she'd be able to forgive the killer if the victim was Dianne or Arlene. But why such horrible thoughts on such a beautiful day? she chided herself. Was it because she couldn't stand prosperity? Because everything was finally going so well that she couldn't believe it would last? She had to get out of that mind-set and think positively. What was that saying she'd read somewhere? *Today is the first day of the rest of your life.* A little simplistic and cloying for her taste, but maybe there was something to it, she decided as she walked into the supermarket with her jaw firmly set and her mind fixed on the future.

Larry pulled into a parking stall and looked at his watch. Two-fifty-five. He still had five minutes before he was due to enter the airline terminal and make the drop. The briefcase containing the fifty thousand Jack Lexer had loaned him was on the seat beside him.

He clicked open the case and looked at the packets of twenties stacked neatly beside each other. This was small change for Lexer but, for Larry, raising fifty thousand dollars would've meant draining his bank account.

Larry wasn't the only one anxiously eyeing his watch. Leaning up against the Air Canada ticket counter, Alec Vlassos gazed across the terminal toward the Tilden booth. For the tenth time in the last few minutes, he checked his watch. Two-fifty-eight. Chambers would be here soon, he thought anxiously, if he's coming. He took a deep breath and exhaled slowly, feeling his belly sag against his belt.

Fifty thousand. And strictly tax-free. The first thing he'd do was rent a little cottage up north — take his first vacation in years and get in some fishing. It wasn't the best time of the year for that but, as far as Alec was concerned, fishing, like sex, was ninety percent anticipation and ten percent performance. Yeah, he reflected, it'd be terrific just lying back in a little boat and drifting along without a worry in the world.

Then when he got back, he'd be all rested and ready to face the old grind again. At least now he wouldn't have to worry about going belly-up or busting his ass until he dropped in his tracks. After he collected the fifty grand, he'd invest it in Guaranteed Income Certificates and let it sit for a couple of years. Then when he retired, he'd have something to fall back on.

Maybe he'd pack up and head for someplace where you didn't have to freeze your ass all winter. Vancouver, or maybe Victoria. He'd heard it was nice and quiet on the island. And so what if it rained a little in the winter? Umbrellas were a helluva lot cheaper than overcoats.

Still, he fretted, even fifty grand wouldn't go all that far if he wanted to live decently. Of course, there was always another possibility. The idea that had been whispering in the back of his mind began to clamour for attention. If fifty thou' would give him a new lease on life, double that would hand him a ticket to the kind of retirement that most people could only dream of.

Hell, what was another fifty thousand to a guy like Larry Chambers, Alec reasoned. Surely, his family and career would be worth a hundred grand to a guy who earned twice that much in a year. Of course, there was another angle to explore as well which, Alec suspected, might be worth some big bucks.

That morning, he'd checked out the license number he'd recorded on the night of Holly Gains' murder. As it turned out, the sleek black Chrysler that had continuously circled past Holly's apartment while Chambers was inside doing his thing was registered to one Alan Nadeau, a Justice of the Ontario Supreme Court, no less. Alec pulled a small black notebook out of his inside pocket and checked the data: 31

Briarcrest Road. The good judge had certainly picked a high-class neighbourhood to park himself in. Yeah, fifty grand would be chicken feed to a guy like that all right.

He put that notebook away and glanced up just in time to see Larry enter the building. Chambers was looking straight ahead and walking stiffly, a slim brown briefcase clutched in his right hand. Alec watched as he stopped in front of the Tilden booth and glanced around before crossing over to take the seat nearest the counter of the car rental agency. The terminal wasn't particularly crowded, and Larry's chair was next to a long line of empty seats.

Alec kept up his surveillance, occasionally glancing around to see if anyone else was taking an inordinate interest in Chambers. As far as he could see, there was no one who looked even remotely suspicious — just the usual collection of airport staff, travellers, and those who had come to see the latter arrive or depart.

Three-o-five. Larry slid the briefcase down beside his leg. He wanted to look around and see if he could spot the rotten bastard who was prepared to destroy him but fought against the impulse. Instead, he gazed down at the well-polished floor and waited for the minutes to pass.

Larry and Alec weren't the only ones who were waiting, however. A dark, slim man was also intermittently checking his watch. But this third player in the drama did so in a practised, subtle way that gave no sign of impatience.

It wasn't surprising that Victor Grasso wasn't bothered in the least by waiting. It came with his territory. There were times when he'd waited for hours on end for the right opportunity to carry out an assignment. And if it hadn't come, he'd been able to easily shake it off, knowing there was always another time and place.

Because Grasso never rushed things or took unnecessary chances, he was never short of work. The fact that he could kill with a gun, an ice pick, or a length of wire without his pulse rate accelerating was another reason. As his employers often lamented, stone killers like Victor Grasso were pretty damn hard to come by.

Victor was a little more grim than usual this afternoon, however. Although he tried to take things as they came, he had to admit he was a little pissed-off at having to take this contract on such short notice. He figured the fact that he was in Buffalo when his boss agreed to do the job for the Toronto mob probably had something to do with it. If he'd been in Vegas, which is where he usually hung his hat, the contract would probably have been farmed out to someone closer to home.

Victor eased over to the bank of pay phones about twenty yards to the left of the Tilden booth and pretended to leaf through a telephone book. At exactly three-ten, he saw Larry get up and walk briskly out of the terminal, leaving the briefcase behind.

Larry's breathing didn't begin to normalize until he reached his car and began to navigate the parkade maze. By then, Alec had picked up an abandoned newspaper and ambled slowly past the cluster of car rental booths. Stopping in front of the Tilden kiosk, he made a show of scanning the paper while his eyes darted around him. Satisfied that no one was paying any undue attention to him, he dropped into the chair that Larry had just vacated. Looking down, he saw the briefcase and nudged it with his heel as though to reassure himself that it was real. A few minutes passed. It was three-sixteen when Alec reached down and grabbed the handle of the briefcase. Then, heaving himself to his feet, he headed for the nearest exit.

Victor plugged a quarter into the pay phone just as Alec strode past him. Replacing the receiver, he watched the aging private investigator push through the door to the parkade before he started to follow him. As he left the terminal, he spotted Alec's bulky frame about fifty yards ahead. Instinctively, he felt for the ice pick in the specially made sheath in his waistband. He also had the option of a silencer-equipped revolver in his jacket pocket but, so far, he was leaning toward using the pick.

The parkade was about half-empty, with a large number of empty stalls interspersed among the rows of cars. Victor picked up his pace. He was twenty yards behind his quarry . . . fifteen . . . ten. Close enough now to hear the keys jingling in Alec's hand as he reached down to unlock his decade-old Ford.

As Alec pulled the car door open, Victor's hand tightened on the ice pick. He began to slide it out of the sheath when he caught a movement out of the corner of his eye and, looking to his left, noticed a young couple emerging from a car a couple of stalls away.

Averting his face, he quickly turned and walked in the opposite direction, hurrying toward the elevator. When he reached street level, he bolted for the exit ramp. As arranged, Frenchy was parked to one side, waiting for him. He climbed in the passenger side, his breath ragged and heavy. Frenchy started to gun the motor but eased off when Victor gasped: "Hold it! Wait right here!"

"Wait?" Frenchy blurted. "What the hell for? Didn't you do it?"

Victor took a deep breath. "Couldn't," he puffed. "Was . . . all . . . set . . . to . . . shiv him . . . but . . . some . . . goddamn . . . jerk-offs came by."

"Well, whattawe do now?"

Victor's breathing was returning to normal. "We wait, and then we tail him."

"You know what kind of car he's driving?"

"Dark-blue Ford sedan, '77 or '78," he growled. "He should be coming out any minute."

He'd barely completed the sentence when Alec shot past.

"That's him," Victor barked. "Count to ten, then get on his ass."

"What do we do if we lose him?" Frenchy asked anxiously. "Do you know who he is?"

"What the fuck are you talking about — do I know who he

is?" Victor sneered. "Do you think he fuckin' well introduced himself to me?" He cooled down as Frenchy kept a uniform distance behind the Ford. "Anyway, I've got the jerk-off's licence plate number. If he gives us the slip, we can get a make on that. Don't worry," he scowled, "that cocksucker don't know it yet, but when he picked up that briefcase, he fuckin' well committed suicide."

By the time they reached the expressway, there was enough traffic to keep Frenchy from appearing conspicuous, so that although Alec checked his rearview mirror a couple of times just to be on the safe side, he felt he was home free.

Before pulling out of his parkade stall, Alec had checked in every direction and hadn't picked up on anything suspicious. He reasoned that if Chambers had rung in the cops on the caper, there was no way they'd have let him get out of the terminal. Now, he was on the expressway and halfway home. Suddenly, his mind changed gears. It would be crazy to keep so much money in his apartment, he realized.

Then his worried expression softened into a satisfied smile. The office. It was about time his old safe did more than just collect dust. At the same time, he remembered something else. Jane Chambers was coming to see him at four o'clock. He looked at his watch: three-forty. Plenty of time. He smiled at the irony; he'd just picked up fifty grand from Larry Chambers and, in a little while, he'd be chalking up another couple of hundred bucks from his wife. God, Alec thought, if Chambers only knew it was his old lady who'd brought him all this grief. Chances are the poor shmuck would be up to his ass in *another* homicide.

Jane squinted at her reflection in the store's full-length mirror. She liked the material and the style of the cocktail dress, but she wasn't quite sure about the neckline. A little revealing for Larry's conservative taste, she thought. Almost by accident, she glanced at her watch. Three-forty. Only twenty minutes to make her appointment with Mr. Vlassos. On the one hand she was tempted to say, to hell with him, let him wait, but on the other, she wanted the private detective out of her life and into the past as quickly as possible. As she deliberated, the sleek, middle-aged saleslady smiled at her benignly.

"It really looks wonderful on you."

"You don't think the neckline is too. . .?" She raised her eyebrows questioningly.

"Not at all," the woman smiled. "If I was your age and had your figure, that's exactly the type of dress I'd wear to display myself to best advantage."

Although Jane suspected the line was part of a well-rehearsed sales pitch, she couldn't help basking in the glow of the compliment.

"And you don't think it's too long?"

"Mid-calf is just right for you," the woman nodded solemnly.

"I'll take it."

Within ten minutes, Jane was pulling out of the Bloor Street parking lot and easing out into the late-afternoon traffic. She was a little angry with herself, feeling that because she was in a hurry, she'd let herself be pressured into buying a dress that didn't have that special something she was looking for. Oh, well, tonight she'd model it for Larry and see what *he* thought. If he didn't like it, she could always take it back.

As she headed for Queen Street, Alec Vlassos was approaching his office from the opposite direction.

By now, Frenchy was only a few car-lengths behind, his forehead bathed in sweat. It really burned his ass that Grasso looked so goddamn cool, staring straight ahead with a twisted little smile, like he was really having a ball while Frenchy was shitting bricks.

Frenchy had to admit the dude made him nervous. He never said shit unless it had to do with the job. It was as if the slightest distraction might lead to some little mistake that could turn into a big one.

Well, fuck him if he wanted to play the role of hotshot hit man from Buffalo or wherever Frenchy thought. He'd show Grasso he could hold up his own end and that he wasn't a two-bit jerk-off. He wiped his hand across his forehead and thought he saw Grasso's smile widen. Well, let the son of a bitch laugh; it was goddamn humid today and it wasn't his fault he wasn't made of ice. But he'd show Grasso he was a stand-up guy, he vowed, as he once again turned over the assignment in his mind: As soon as the guy in the Ford parked, he was to let Grasso out and then just keep an eye on the play, making sure they were ready to roll.

Then when Grasso came back — assuming the job was done — Frenchy would drive him to the airport to catch one of the two flights the hit man had booked, for different times and under different names. Then with Grasso winging his way to Vegas, Frenchy would deliver the briefcase to Bennie Accardi, his immediate supervisor in the organization.

In a way, Frenchy felt a little offended at not being let in on the ins-and-outs of the hit, but he knew there was a reason for that. The guys up top, the ones calling the shots, wanted to protect their asses in case the thing came apart, and how could Frenchy snitch if he didn't know shit? It made a lot of sense. This way, there wouldn't be any heat on the people actually involved in the hit, like him and Victor, because they didn't even know the sucker they were going to whack. And the guys who had a motive for wanting him clipped were so far removed from the caper, and had their asses so well covered, that no one could touch them. Yeah, he told himself, it was smooth all right. That was one of the reasons Frenchy was an advocate of big business because, he concluded, a small, independent operator could never make it on his own. Too much work and risk and not enough profit.

They were on Queen Street now, heading east, and they had just crossed Bathurst when the blue Ford swung to the left into a parking lot. Frenchy immediately pulled over and let his passenger out.

"O.K.," Victor said sharply. "You know what to do.

Just keep circling the block and make sure you stay in the right-hand lane in case we gotta split in a hurry. I'll catch you when the job's done.''

By the time Frenchy pulled away, Victor was already stationed in the doorway of a tailor shop, watching as his target got out of his car and shambled down the sidewalk, the briefcase clutched tightly in his hand. Just before opening the door to his building, Alec stopped and looked around, then apparently reassured, went inside.

Victor crossed the street, quickening his pace. He got there just in time to see Alec's legs disappearing up the stairs. He stood on the first-floor landing, listening, tracking the footsteps. Stealthily proceeding up the stairs, he heard the click of a bolt retracting, and seconds later, the slam of a door. He reached into his pocket, feeling for the gun butt, then completed his ascent to the second-floor landing. He listened, picking up some muted sounds from the street below, but nothing from the dimly lit hallway.

Out on the street, Frenchy was cruising by for the second time. He'd watched Grasso follow the fat old dude with the briefcase into a small, beat-up old building, and now, every time he drove by, he homed-in on the door, half-expecting the hit man to come busting out.

Frenchy was sweating more than ever now. Suppose something went wrong. Suppose some cops came by and caught the play. Murder was a heavy beef. He didn't mind breaking legs or busting heads but whacking someone was new to him. For a brief moment, he felt like flooring the car and taking off, but the impulse didn't stay with him for long. In his business, copping out in the middle of a job was just as bad as being a snitch. If Grasso came out and found his wheel man gone, Frenchy would be dead meat. Just as he made the turn from Bathurst onto Queen for the third time, he spotted a woman crossing the street at a quick trot just up the block but he didn't pay much attention to her until he saw her enter the building Victor and the target had disappeared into only a few minutes before.

At almost the same instant, a Metro police car passed him

and, once again, Frenchy had to battle the urge to flee. But instead, he took a deep breath and began to circle the block again. And while Frenchy performed his assigned task, Victor Grasso was about to embark on his own.

Almost soundlessly, he pushed the door open and stepped into Alec's office. He stood there for a moment, watching the pudgy, bald-headed man seated behind the old wooden desk. Alex was lifting the wads of money out of the briefcase and placing them in neat little stacks on the desk. His thick lips moved as he riffled through the bills, tallying the currency. Then Victor shifted his weight and the floor creaked. Alec blinked at him in surprise, automatically shifting the briefcase to conceal the piles of currency.

"Something I can —"

The words froze in Alec's throat when he saw the revolver. At first, he thought it was a hold-up, but only until he noticed the silencer. Then he knew. He tried to come up with some of the excuses he'd always been so good at using to get out of tight spots, but all he could manage was: "Don't. Please. Don't."

And mixed in with the terror was a crushing sense of betrayal. It wasn't fair, he told himself bitterly as he stared wild-eyed into the gun barrel. This had been the only god-damn time in his whole bloody life that he'd had a chance to score, and score big. It wasn't fair.

With a sound that wasn't even as loud as a cork popping out of a bottle of champagne, the bullet slammed into Alec's forehead, the impact whipping his head back and with it, his rotund body. The back of his swivel chair clattered against the wall, jolting Alec's body and flinging it forward. He was doubled over, the blood from the small, round hole in his brow dripping steadily into his lap. Victor reached down and held the revolver about a foot from Alec's right temple and squeezed the trigger. There was the same hollow pop and a slight acrid smell. A spurt of blood gushed through the thin fringe of grey hair circling Alec's shiny pate, then slowed to a steady trickle.

Victor had just begun to slide the revolver back into his

pocket when he heard a gasp and wheeled around. Jane froze, staring in shocked disbelief at the dark man with the gun. Her eyes, wide with terror, took in the nightmarish image of Alec Vlassos, crumpled and bleeding, his hands dangling against the floor. She wanted to turn and run, to scream as loud as she could but her body refused to cooperate. She stared in silent horror, her mouth agape, as the dark man raised the gun. She was gazing right into the barrel now, wondering what the funny-looking thing on the end was. Again, she tried to scream but the paralysis that had frozen her body into a statue gripped her throat like a vise. And, in the instant before she heard the pop and her brain became a roaring inferno, she saw the sad-sweet images of her husband and daughters flit by in quick succession. Then, concomitant with the pain and deep sense of loss, came the darkness, sweeping over her and washing her toward a black, timeless harbour.

As Jane's body sagged to the floor, Victor shoved the revolver into his pocket and scooped the blood-spattered wads of currency into the briefcase. Then, stepping around her sprawled form, he stopped, letting his gaze drift over his handiwork before giving a slow nod of approval.

Gripping the satchel, he stepped into the hall and glanced down the corridor, listening intently. With a grunt of satisfaction, he closed the office door and quickly descended the stairs. When he reached the main floor, he shot a quick look up the staircase, and then stepped out onto the sidewalk. He'd covered only a few dozen yards before he spotted Frenchy's car. It was cruising along the curb, locked into a line of slow-moving traffic. Victor climbed in before it had come to a full stop.

"Well," Frenchy said grim-faced, "did it go down?"

Victor stared straight ahead, his face and voice expressionless.

"It went down." He looked at his watch. "If you step on it, I can make the five-thirty flight."

"This fuckin' traffic . . . ." Frenchy growled.

"Take it easy," Victor said evenly. "If I don't get this one, I'll grab the next. So just keep cool and stick to the speed limit. The last thing we need is to get stopped by the cops."

Licking his lips nervously as they waited for a light to change, Frenchy finally screwed up enough courage to ask: "Uh, you didn't happen to run into a broad in there, did you? I saw this chick go into the building a couple of minutes after you guys, and I was afraid she might get into the act."

Victor continued to stare through the windshield. "Yeah, she wasn't bad-looking for an older broad."

"You saw her?" Frenchy asked anxiously. "Then that means she saw you, too, and there's a witness."

Victor turned and looked at Frenchy with thinly veiled contempt. "Don't bust your balls, man. There's nothing to worry about. She ain't gonna tell no one nothing. What she saw," he smiled mirthlessly, "she's gonna keep to herself. Forever."

Chapter Sixteen

Pete was on University Avenue when he heard the call on his car's short-wave radio. He'd gotten into the habit of monitoring police calls during his first stint as a crime reporter and, even after his exile to the sports beat, he'd kept up the practice.

The clipped, coded message made the hair on the back of his neck stand up: A double homicide was no more than a dozen blocks away. Speeding to the scene, he screeched to a stop in front of Alec's building. Clambering out of his car, he almost fell into the arms of a middle-aged, heavyset woman. She was wearing a faded housedress covered by a cotton apron and her hair was bundled up in a multicoloured kerchief. She tugged at his arm, her broad, Slavic face a study in terror.

"You da poleetz?" she inquired breathlessly. Then, without waiting for an answer, she pointed to the door of the dingy building. "Upstairs. I find dem. Mr. Vlassos and lady. She on floor. He falling from chair. I don't know what be happen." She shook her head vigorously. "I not see notting. I not know notting — just what I find."

Pete brushed by her and bounded up the stairs, stopping in front of a partly opened door. Noting the attached nameplate: ALEC VLASSOS, PRIVATE INVESTIGATOR, he edged into the office, being careful not to touch anything. The first thing he saw was a pair of tanned female legs and, as his eyes traced a path to her head, he felt his legs start to buckle. Even though her face was streaked with congealing blood, he knew he'd seen her before. Then he remembered. Some event at the press club a year or so ago. Her name was Jenny or Jane — something like that. Then the rest of the connection sank in. Jane Chambers, Larry's wife.

"Holy fuck," he breathed. The first shock wave hadn't subsided when he saw Alec. By now the blood had turned the legs of the detective's pants a deep crimson. Pete reeled from the sight.

Somehow, he managed to steel himself long enough to give the office a quick once-over. It was strictly a fishing expedition and nothing immediately leaped out at him; there was no sign of a struggle or a weapon. It looked as though it had been neat and quick and he was willing to bet that the killer hadn't left any incriminating evidence behind. Dropping to his haunches, he looked underneath the desk and spotted a thin wad of currency. Could that have been the motive? he wondered. But how much money could a small-time private eye with a hole-in-the-wall office have in his possession? Then he noticed something else.

There was a small black notepad lying next to the dead man's left foot. Pete reached over and picked it up by the edges and set it down on the desk. Then, being careful not to touch the covers, he flipped through the pages, coming to the last entry: " '84 Black Chrysler sedan seen in vicinity of Gains apartment, 11:30 – 11:45 P.M., June 26th, 1985. Licence number ADM 216. Registered to Alan J. Nadeau, 31 Briarcrest Road. *Henderson* Directory lists Nadeau as a Judge in the Supreme Court of Ontario." Quickly copying the entry into his own notebook, Pete carefully returned the notepad to its former resting place.

He'd just started toward the filing cabinet when he heard the thud of footsteps on the stairs and hurriedly retreated to the hallway. The first one up the stairs was a uniformed constable; a young, beefy officer whose round face was flushed from the unaccustomed exertion.

"Who . . . who are you?" he panted, blocking the stairway with his bulk as if to prevent Pete from fleeing.

Pete flipped out his press credentials. "Pete Gossett, *The Herald.*"

By now, the young constable's partner had joined him while, below on the first-floor landing, the frightened cleaning lady gazed up at them, shaking her head dolefully and muttering in some East European language. The second, older, cop jerked a thumb toward Pete and asked his partner: "Who's he?"

"Press."

As though that was sufficient introduction, he turned to Pete and asked brusquely, "You been in there?"

"Uh-uh," Pete said. "Just peeked in the door."

"Yeah?" He looked at Pete distrustfully. "Well, you've seen all you're going to. I want you out of the building and I mean *now.* We've got enough to do without worrying about tripping over reporters."

"I was just leaving," Pete said affably. "I've got to call in for a photographer, then I'll be back."

"Not up here you won't," the cop snapped.

"You're the boss," Pete said, scrambling down the stairs and charging past the still-jabbering cleaning lady. Finding a telephone booth, he dialled the newsroom and heard the city editor's gruff salutation: "Atkins here."

"Mac, it's Pete. I stumbled onto something big. Picked it up on the police band. A double homicide at 837 Queen Street West. A man and woman. Looks like they were both shot."

"Domestic thing, I guess," Atkins said in a bored voice.

"I don't think so," Pete said. "I've got a feeling this one's going to turn out to be a little more complicated than that."

"Oh, yeah?" Atkins asked, suddenly interested. "What makes you think so?"

"The victims," Pete said. "The guy was a private detective and the woman. . . ." Pete struggled with the words.

"Yeah, what about her?" Atkins asked impatiently.

"She's Jane Chambers. Larry's wife."

There were a few seconds of dead air, and then a murmured: "Oh, my God."

Pete waited for a further response and when none was forthcoming, asked: "Are you going to send someone to pick up on this or should I go with it?"

He breathed a sigh of relief when Mac replied: "Go with it. I'll have a photographer there in ten minutes."

"Another thing. Have someone check Larry's bio file and see if we've got any shots of him or his wife."

"You got it," Atkins barked. "Any other media there yet?"

"No, but the whole mob'll be here pretty goddamn soon."

"O.K., get what you can. I'll make sure there's a hole on page one. We need a positive I.D. on the victims and, if you've got the inside track, we may get an exclusive on that."

"I'll see what I can do."

He slammed the receiver into its cradle and bolted out of the booth, almost running into a pair of plainclothes detectives who'd just stepped out of an unmarked car that was parked half on the sidewalk and half on the street. He was even more taken aback when he saw that one of them was Mike Edwards.

"Hi, Mike," Pete began.

Edwards eyed him suspiciously. "What the hell are you doing here, Gossett?"

"Same as you," Pete said tersely. "My job."

"You back on the crime beat?"

Pete thought he detected a distinct lack of enthusiasm in his voice. "For the time being."

Turning away with a disgusted look, Edwards stepped inside the building and started up the stairs with his partner at his heels. Pete followed a couple of steps behind but; when he reached the second floor, he found Edwards blocking his path.

"This is off-limits to the press," Edwards said curtly. "We've got to protect the scene until the boys from the crime lab and the medical examiner get through. You know the routine. If I let you up, all of your press buddies will want to join the party too."

"No problem," Pete said quickly. "But maybe I can be of some assistance to you."

Edwards gave a lopsided grin as though the suggestion was too outlandish to merit any serious consideration. "*You* can be of assistance to *me*? How do you figure?"

Pete pointed past Edwards to where the cleaning lady was being calmed down by the young uniformed cop. "That lady told me that one of the victims is the guy who rents the office — a private eye by the name of Alec Vlassos."

"Well, it might have taken me a while, but I think I could have figured that out for myself," Edwards said sarcastically.

"Yeah, and you can probably figure out who the woman is, too," Pete said, "but I think I can make it a little easier for you."

"Yeah? How so?"

"I know her. At least, I know who she is."

Edwards eyes narrowed with interest. "Go ahead. Who is she?"

"Jane Chambers. Larry's wife."

"Holy Mother of God," Edwards gasped, looking down and shaking his head in disbelief. Then suddenly, he looked up and speared Pete with his pale-blue eyes. "Are you sure?"

Pete nodded somberly. "It's her all right. There's a purse on the floor and you can check the I.D. but I'd swear it's Jane Chambers."

Edwards stared at the wall, murmuring half to himself. "How am I going to tell him. What the hell can I say?"

"It's rough all right."

"Well, thanks for telling me," Edwards said with what sounded like genuine sincerity. He turned and started to enter the office when Pete checked him.

"Uh, there's one other thing."

"What's that?"

"I want to run the names of the victims but I want to make sure the next of kin have been notified first."

"O.K., give me a call at headquarters about ten o'clock and I'll let you know if we got hold of the families."

"Thanks," Pete said. "Oh, by the way, I was wondering if I could have a couple of minutes with the cleaning lady. I won't ask her anything heavy, just who she is, how she found the bodies. The usual stuff." Expecting to be rebuffed, he was surprised to hear Edwards say: "O.K., you got five minutes, then get the hell out of here and don't come back. But remember one thing. If she knows anything at all about the murders, you don't even mention that she exists. We got two now and I don't want to try for three."

After Edwards stepped into the office, Pete sauntered over to the young cop. Jerking his head in the direction of the cleaning woman, he tried for an air of authority.

"Mike said I could talk to her for a couple of minutes."

The officer looked unconvinced but grunted his assent and Pete whipped out his notebook. By the time he'd slapped it shut several minutes later, he'd learned that Luba Fedoruk, age forty-seven, cleaned the offices in the building every Tuesday evening, beginning at six o'clock. This evening, she'd started with Vlassos' office and, at about five after six, she'd inserted her pass key in the door and discovered that it was unlocked.

Almost immediately, she'd seen the bodies and "the

blood, so much blood, joost like in bootcher shop.'' She couldn't remember much after that, just stumbling, almost falling, down the stairs and screaming at the manager of the furniture store next door. He'd called the police while she had waited outside, shivering in shock and terror. She hadn't seen anyone on the second floor or leaving the building.

Pete had just stepped out onto the sidewalk when two more unmarked squad cars pulled up, each bearing a pair of detectives. Pete recognized a couple of them and gave them a cursory nod as he got into his car and started back to the newsroom. But even with a deadline looming before him, he wasn't thinking about the story that would carry his byline in tomorrow's edition of *The Herald*.

His mind was focussed on a much bigger story that was finally starting to take shape. It was like doing a jigsaw puzzle from the outside in, he thought. First the border and the corners. Then the hard part — filling in the centre. That was where he was now, working toward the middle, to the heart and guts of the wanton violence that threatened a city's innocence.

Later, when he pulled into the *Herald*'s parking lot, he knew he was close to something. He started to get out of the car, and then abruptly stopped to check the rearview mirror and to glance to both sides. With a self-deprecating chuckle, he got out and walked across the lot. But even while he laughed at his own paranoia, a sobering question broke the surface of his consciousness: If he was close to something, could whatever it was be just as close to him?

Larry continued to pace the living room, stopping only to look out the window whenever he heard a car approaching. What could have happened to Jane he wondered. She'd told him she planned to shop around for a new dress, but she'd promised to be home by five o'clock. Now it was almost nine, and he hadn't even heard from her.

He'd fixed supper for the girls, telling them that their mother had probably just got caught up in a shopping spree or had run into a friend and decided to have dinner downtown. He hadn't sounded convincing, even to himself, and the worried looks stayed on their faces while they picked at their plates. The silence had grown heavier with every passing moment.

Dianne and Arlene were in the rec room in the basement now, listening to records. At least they were supposed to be. The music was a lot softer than usual, and every now and then, Larry could hear the buzz of their voices. With the girls out of the way, he was able to doff his unruffled manner. He'd immediately rushed upstairs and used the phone in the master bedroom to call everyone he could think of — Jane's friends, her mother, her sister — but no one had heard from her.

In spite of the fact that he and Jane had been getting along better, he took the precaution of checking her closet. Her suitcases were still there and there was no sign that any of her clothes or personal items were missing. Just as he glanced at his watch again, he heard the sound of an approaching car. Rushing downstairs, he darted to the living room window. His body sagged in disappointment. Instead of seeing Jane's familiar white Rabbit, Larry spotted a plain grey sedan rounding the bend of the crescent. He started to draw back from the window, but stopped when the car pulled into the driveway. Peering around the curtain, he watched the door on the driver's side swing open and curiosity gave way to surprise when he saw Mike Edwards step out and start up the sidewalk.

He had the inside door open before the detective had a chance to ring the bell.

"Mike," he boomed warmly, "what the hell are you doing in this neck of the woods? C'mon in," he said, ushering Edwards into the living room. "What can I get you to drink?"

"Nothing, thanks," Edwards replied softly. "I'm on duty."

"What?" Larry yelped. "At this hour? What's the story? Are you guys still working around the clock on the Jantzen case?"

When the detective didn't answer immediately, Larry looked at him closely, for the first time noticing the tight mouth and grim expression.

"What's the matter, Mike?"

Edwards shifted his weight and noisily cleared his throat before answering: "I'm afraid I've got some bad news for you."

Larry blinked uncomprehendingly at the detective as a jumble of thoughts swirled through his mind. Holly. Edwards was here to see him about Holly. The blackout. Maybe he *had* done it. Maybe that goddamn blackmailer had blown the whistle. But why? There was no reason. He'd paid him the fifty thousand. Anyway, Jack was going to take care of it. But suppose he hadn't. Suppose Lexer's plan had backfired. He was sure that Edwards was staring at him with a questioning concern but he couldn't speak, couldn't force even a single word out of his dry, constricted throat.

"Larry," Mike said, "your wife is. . . ." He hesitated, unable to utter the word that reflected such cruel finality.

"Jane?" Larry asked numbly. "What, Mike? What happened to her?"

"She's been shot."

Larry's legs felt weak and he stumbled backwards, trying to keep his balance. He felt the detective's large, strong hand on his wrist, heard his deep solicitous voice asking, "Are you all right?"

He took a deep breath and released it in a long, shuddering exhalation.

"She's dead, isn't she?" The tears began to well up in his eyes before he heard the answer. He could feel the vibrations of rock music beneath his feet and the horror suddenly took on an even greater dimension. How could he tell Dianne and Arlene?

Edwards nodded and, swallowing hard, said, "Yes." Then before he could stop himself, he blurted: "It would've been quick. She wouldn't have suffered."

Larry stared at him vacantly, giving no sign that he'd heard him. "I've got to tell the girls." He said it again, louder this time, as though trying to convince himself that there was no use trying to put off what he knew would be the most painful task he'd ever performed.

"Larry." The detective's hand was on his shoulder now, pressing tightly, conveying his support and concern. "Is there anything you want me to do?"

Larry shook his head. "No." The word came out like a sob.

"I hate to do this, but you know I've got a job to do. . . ." Mike began apologetically.

Larry ran a hand over his eyes and looked at the detective. "Yeah, I know."

"We're going to need you to make the identification."

"Right away?"

"Well, sometime tonight, if you can make it."

Larry nodded absently. "Yeah." Looking toward the basement door, he shivered as though a cold wind had passed through him. "I've got to tell the girls, and then call Jane's mother. She'll have to look after them for a while. I don't want them to be by themselves."

He slowly started toward the basement stairs, then stopped and looked straight into Edwards' eyes. "How did it happen, Mike? Was it an accident or . . . ."

"It was no accident," Edwards said. "It looks like the work of a pro."

"A contract job?" Larry asked incredulously. "That's crazy. Why would anyone want to kill Jane?"

Edwards shook his head dolefully. "I don't think anyone

did. I think the guy was the target and she just happened to be in the wrong place at the wrong time."

"The guy?" Larry exclaimed. "She was with a man?"

"That's right. At least, she was in his office. My guess is that she was taken out because she saw the guy get hit."

"Who's the guy?"

Edwards pulled a notebook out of his jacket pocket and thumbed through it before stopping at a half-filled page. "His name is Alec Vlassos and he runs a one-man private investigation agency at 837 Queen Street West." He glanced up at Larry questioningly. "Do you know him?"

Larry shook his head. "No. Never heard of him."

Mike stood there, torn between his personal feelings and his duty. On the one hand, he felt sorry for Larry and hated to have to question him at a time like this; but, on the other, he was conducting a murder investigation and the sooner he got some leads, the sooner he could follow them up, and maybe stand a chance of breaking the case. In the end, his investigative instincts won out.

"Have you any idea what Jane was doing in his office? I mean, can you think of any reason why she would have been meeting with a private eye?"

Larry thought a long time before replying, "I've got no idea, Mike. No idea at all." But as he started down the basement stairs, steeling himself for the task ahead, he knew he hadn't been entirely truthful. A couple of the loose ends in his mind had started to come together, but there was no pattern yet, no clear answer to any of the questions that boiled through his consciousness. And, for the moment, he was content to leave it that way.

Standing in the darkened living room, Mike Edwards heard the low voices, then the shrieks of anguish and the keening sobs. He looked down at the floor and shook his head sorrowfully. It was times like this that he hated his job.

"The bastards are getting out of hand," he muttered to

himself, summing up all the unreasoning violence and gratuitous pain he'd seen in over twenty years on the force. Jamming a cigarette into his mouth, he lit it and took a few fierce puffs, telling himself once again: "Yeah, the bastards are definitely getting out of hand."

Sitting at his desk, Pete looked at the headline and winced. "Hot-line Host's Wife Gunned Down in Double Slaying." Christ, he thought, it made Jane Chambers sound like a capo in the mafia. All the same, he couldn't help but feel a glow of satisfaction. While the other papers had only the bare bones of the story, the *Herald* had the meat. Thanks to Edwards' cooperation, he was the only print journalist who'd been able to reveal the identities of the victims. The *Herald*'s pictures weren't that bad either. Steve Daniels, one of their top photographers, had managed to sneak a shot through the open door, getting most of Vlassos' body and part of Jane's outstretched arm.

As far as Pete was concerned, Frank Wallach, the *Herald*'s regular crime reporter, couldn't have picked a better time to go on a holiday. He wasn't due back for another ten days and what with the "Hooker Murderers," as they'd been tabbed, and yesterday's double homicide, Pete had more than enough to keep him busy until then. He needed all the time he could get, too, because, in addition to doing the usual follow-up stories on the slayings, he'd decided to play a hunch and dig a little deeper.

He'd already located Judge Alan Nadeau's parking spot by the courthouse and had Steve get some shots of his car from a couple of different angles. And tonight, when he started to research his next story, he'd have the photos in his hot little hand. He was planning to do a feature on the perils of prostitution in the big city, against the backdrop of the Jantzen and Gains killings, and figured that the best place to start was "the track," the inner city circuit where most of Metro's hookers plied their trade.

It would be an in-depth report including personal profiles of some of the girls and focussing on their reactions to the current climate of fear surrounding the city's flesh-peddling trade. In the past, he'd found hookers to be surprisingly willing to talk about themselves and at first had thought this might be due to some ego-stroking impulse to be in the spotlight. But later he'd realized there was more to it than that. It was as though having their stories told elevated these "working girls" from the status of nonpersons and allowed them to reaffirm their role in a society that, by and large, either scorned them, or tried to pretend that they represented some kind of moral aberration that a little more right thinking and church going might expunge.

Using the story as a hook, Pete planned to flash around a couple of pictures of Nadeau and his car and see what, if anything, turned up. He knew it was a long shot, but then he wasn't exactly overburdened with sure things and, in his many years as an investigative reporter, he'd learned that you could never tell when even the smallest fragment of information could turn out to be the key to a dynamite story.

All in all, he felt pretty upbeat. He had a couple of good stories coming to a boil, and he was meeting Elaine Steele for lunch. It'd been almost a week since he'd seen her and even though he'd been spending quite a bit of time with Linda, he had missed Elaine.

She was tough and smart and he admired that about her even while he realized that these two qualities didn't exactly enhance their relationship. There was a constant aura of competition between them, and it seemed as though the only time that they didn't share a kind of wary *détente* was when they were making love. That was the only time they seemed able to give freely of themselves. The rest of the time, they held back, protecting some inner part of themselves — some secret vulnerability — which, if revealed, might give the other party an edge.

They'd settled on a little Hungarian restaurant on Yonge Street that had been convenient for both of them. Although the décor was simple, the small, candlelit tables gave the room a semblance of intimacy. Pete had just selected a corner table, when Elaine strode in, looking immaculately tailored and as self-assured as usual.

He stood up and prepared to give her a peck on the cheek but she seemed not to notice, brushing by and settling hastily into her chair. "We're going to have to make this quick," she said, the words coming out in a rush. "I've got tons of work to do. I'm still one guest short for tomorrow." She glanced up from the menu. "I don't know if I told you but I'm hosting *Larry's Line* this week or, for that matter, until Larry feels up to coming back."

"Have you spoken to him?"

"Yes. He called me early this morning. That was the first I heard . . ." She shook her head sorrowfully. "I still can't believe it. How could something like that have happened? It doesn't make any sense."

Pete nodded. "You're right. I spoke to Edwards last night and he can't figure it out at all." He paused before adding, "At least that's the story he gave me, but you know how close-mouthed the cops can be with us media types."

She looked at him over the ridge of her water glass. "You think they know more than they're letting on?"

"Who knows?" he shrugged. "But there's got to be some reason why a hit man would want to take out some nickel-and-dime private eye. That is, if it actually was the gumshoe they were gunning for."

Elaine's eyes widened. "You think it was a contract job?"

"The M.O. sure as hell fits. Small-calibre weapon, probably silencer equipped. All head shots. Two for the dick and one for Jane Chambers. No sign of a struggle, and the killer disappears without anyone so much as catching a glimpse of him. Does that sound like amateur hour to you?"

"Buy why? Why Jane? She was just a typical upper-middle-class housewife. Who would want *her* dead?"

"Well, it's just a theory," Pete began slowly, "and I don't know if it's one that the cops are considering, but I think we both know that Larry's made a lot of enemies over the years and that some of them are more than a few bricks shy of a load.''

"You think someone killed Jane to get at Larry?" she asked incredulously.

"Anything's possible," he said, "but given the circumstances of the killings, it's not very probable. Like I said before, these were more like executions than murders. If some wacko had pulled the trigger, chances are it would've been a helluva lot messier unless, of course, he was a total psycho, which would make it a whole different ball game.''

"Oh? Why is that?"

"Because most psychopaths are just like pro hit men. They kill without passion and, since they don't lose control, they do a neater job and are less likely to screw up and get caught.''

They'd finished their salads and were well into their Wiener Schnitzels when Pete asked casually, "I don't suppose Larry mentioned what Jane was doing with a private investigator.''

She smiled tightly. "You never stop, do you?"

Pete threw up his hands. "Hey, I wasn't trying to grill you. Honest. Whatever you tell me is off-the-record. You know Larry and I go back a long way; it's just that I'm interested. I'm not going to pretend I'm any great fan of his type of journalism, but I kind of like the guy.''

"Oh, sure," she said sardonically. "That's why you splashed his wife's murder across four columns of the *Herald*'s front page.''

"Listen," he shot back, "a double murder just happens to be front-page news not only in Toronto but everywhere else. I didn't invent the rules. I just play by them, and so do you and Larry. Look at the mileage you got out of the Jantzen and Gains killings. Yeah, and how about that ghoulish remote from the church? And you've got enough balls to accuse *me* of sensationalism?''

"But . . . but that's different," she stammered.

"Oh, yeah? You tell me how." His voice rose, turning the heads of some nearby diners. "The only difference is that now one of *us* is on the receiving end — is seeing how the other half lives when their personal tragedies are spread over front pages and aired on radio and TV." He steamrolled over her protests. "No, we're performing a terrific public service when we shove mikes up people's noses and record their pain when their kids are run over by drunk drivers or wives are shot by spaced-out punks or hired killers."

"Keep it down," she hissed. "People are looking."

"Yeah, right," he said, lowering his voice. "We don't want the great unwashed out there to get wise to us, do we? Wise to the fact that we're the goddamn Barnum and Baileys of death and destruction for Christ sake!"

"If you hate your job or . . ." she paused and looked directly into his eyes, "yourself, why don't you do something about it?"

He smiled bitterly. "Because I don't know anything else. I don't know anything except doing what I do and being what I am. So I guess I'm stuck with what I've got."

"So why not make the best instead of the worst of it?" she asked earnestly. "You're a damn good reporter. You've got a lot to say and there's a lot that *needs* to be said."

"Right," he smiled wryly. "Now, if I only could find someone to listen to it."

"There are all kinds of people out there that you could inform and influence," she said. "You could help make the world a better place — better than the hellhole you seem to think it is."

"How? By telling the citizens of Toronto that justice is served when a rapist gets off with a year because the woman he assaulted wasn't a virgin?"

Elaine's expression was a mixture of amusement and pity. "You know, for a guy who's been in the business for so long, you've lost sight of one very important fact."

"Oh really?' he asked in mock surprise. "And what might that be?"

"That it *is* a business. I may not have had all your scoops and awards, but I know that much."

"Which means?"

"Which means it's a tough business but one in which I'm damn well going to succeed."

He raised his wineglass. "Well, here's to your success," he said cheerily. "If anyone can do it, you can."

Lifting her glass, she forced a smile. "I'm going to pretend you really mean that."

"But I do," he said with studied sincerity. "I really do. After all, what journalism really needs is another good hot-line hostess."

They finished their meal in silence. Pete was aware of Elaine's smouldering anger but did nothing to try to defuse it. To hell with her, he thought. If that's what she wants, let her have it. Let her be another Larry Chambers or Trent Ferguson. A lot of sound and fury that signified nothing but higher ratings and greater advertising revenue from supermarkets and car dealerships.

As they stood in front of the restaurant and said their goodbyes, they fumbled for words, not daring to look into each other's eyes.

"Well, good luck for the rest of the week," Pete said, this time really meaning it.

"Same to you," she smiled. "I'll be watching for some of your exposés."

"Well, I don't want to overdo it," he deadpanned. "So I figure I'll limit myself to two or three a week."

"I think that's wise," she said, playing along. "You don't want to burn yourself out."

Their shared laughter lapsed into an awkward silence.

"Well, I've got to be off," she said.

"Take care."

"You too."

He stood and watched as her slim, statuesque form disappeared into the stream of pedestrians. He felt a twinge of sadness and with it, a familiar sense of loss. Yeah, he told himself, this was nothing new. He'd been here before and as he sat in his car and looked out at the sun-drenched day, he sighed heavily, realizing that he'd probably be here again.

Chapter Seventeen

It was early evening when Pete started his rounds. There was only a hint of a breeze and the inner-city air was heavy and humid; the kind of day that bred restlessness, and Pete suspected that the johns would be out in full force in pursuit of prepaid orgasms.

Rather than spook potential interviewees by pulling out a notebook, he'd opted for a micro-taperecorder in his jacket pocket and an ultra-sensitive microphone taped to his wrist. He also carried some five-by-seven glossies of Mr. Justice Nadeau's black Chrysler and a couple of file photos of its owner.

He parked downtown near the CBC's gothic complex. With its majestic brick façade, it looked more like a cathedral than a broadcasting facility. Pete had always considered that rather appropriate, however, since as far as he was concerned, most of the Corporation's on-air "personalities" tended to think of themselves as demigods if not full-fledged deities.

It was shortly after nine o'clock when he began his trek.

The hookers were already posing in the doorways of closed-up shops or lounging on the steps of shabby apartment buildings. Offers of companionship volleyed out from all sides, and the street reeked with cheap perfume and pricey sex.

A slim, black girl in a slit skirt, a see-through blouse, and stiletto heels smiled at Pete. "You wanna go out, handsome?"

He returned her smile and went over to her. "I'd like to, but I'm working."

"So am I," she purred suggestively. "And I do some *really* good work, if you know what I mean." She thrust her hips in a mini-version of a bump-and-grind and looked at him expectantly.

"Yeah, I think I do," he grinned, "but seriously though, I'm on an assignment."

Her dusky face darkened. "An assignment? Hey, you ain't no vice dick, are you?"

He laughed, "Do I look like one?"

"How the hell do I know?" she grumbled. "Shee-it, them motherfuckers doin' all that undercover jive, they can look like anything. Like, one time, this dude come up to me and ask how much I charge, and he look so raggedy that I don't believe he got the price for nothin', y'know? But anyway, I told him so much for this and so much for that, y'know? And you know what that motherfucker went and done?"

"No. What?"

Her nostrils flared and her ripe lips curled in disgust. "That son of a bitch busted me. He run me down to the station and charged my ass with solicitin'. Ain't that somethin'?" She folded her arms indignantly across her chest, forcing up her breasts and shoving her nipples against the diaphanous blouse.

Pete shook his head in sympathy. "It's a bitch all right."

"Anyway," the girl said crisply. "I ain't got no more time to jive with you. You want some of this . . ." She ran her hand invitingly over her jutting buttocks. "Or don't you?"

Pete handed her his business card and while she studied it,

he went into his pitch: "I think the public would like to know what it's like to work the streets, especially in light of the recent killings. I figured maybe I could ask you a couple of questions and, you know, let you tell your side of it and maybe change some people's opinions about working girls."

She handed back the card, sneering, "Hey chump, what makes you think I give a shit about what folks think of me. Hell," she snorted, "I make more in one night than most straight chicks make in a month. I don't need nothin' from the *public*." She almost spat out the word. "So just take your fancy-assed card and your questions and your fuckin' *public* and get outta my face."

"If that's the way you want it," he said, turning to leave. Then, as an afterthought, he turned back, holding out one of the photos of Judge Nadeau. "By the way, have you ever seen this dude?"

Taken by surprise, she peered at the picture. "I dunno. He looks kind of familiar. Why you wanna know?"

Pete shrugged. "I just got a hunch he spends some time in this neighbourhood."

She looked at him sharply. "Hey, I knowed one of them chicks who got offed. Is this the dude what done them murders?"

"I've got no proof of that but, if I were you, I'd take a damn good look at this picture and think twice before doing any business with him."

As she stared fixedly at the photo, Pete showed her a shot of Nadeau's car. "How about this car? Have you seen it before?"

She glanced at it and laughed derisively. "Shee-it, half the johns come cruising by here be drivin' Chryslers or Cadillacs." She snorted disdainfully. "Yeah, all them dudes be driving big cars and packin' fat wallets and they bitch about payin' the going rate. No matter what you tell 'em, it's always too much. Like, if you tell 'em a blow is fifty, they wanna give you twenty or thirty." She tossed her head haughtily. "Well, when they pull that shit on me, I just tell 'em to take their asses down to the women's shelter and get next to one of them bag ladies.'' She cackled gleefully; her lips pulled back to reveal pinkish-grey gums and wide, white teeth.

In spite of the woman's hard exterior, Pete could see worry in her eyes. It was the same with the other women he canvassed. There was fear on the street, and the only thing stronger than their fear was their greed or, in some cases, their desperation. Pete knew that most of them were run by pimps who viewed them as carnal cash registers. Hell, he knew horse trainers who treated their stables better than these creeps treated theirs.

Pete had covered half a dozen blocks and had rapped with more than a dozen hookers, before he found Angie. She couldn't have been more than eighteen or nineteen. Short — probably no more than five-three — she looked like a cross between a punk rocker and a *Playboy* centrefold. She had great breasts, full and firm, with no visible means of support. Her slim waist and curvy hips were sheathed in a second skin of mini shorts which came little more than halfway down her swelling buttocks, their whiteness accentuating her deeply tanned thighs.

Without the purple lipstick and the black slashes of mascara flaring out from the corner of her large brown eyes, she would've been pretty, Pete thought. She had good features: pert nose, heart-shaped face, and small, even teeth, but her hair was the real attention-getter — it was a long, feathered cut with bright red and yellow streaks running through her light-brown tresses. Cyndi Lauper looks straight compared with this one, Pete muttered to himself.

"You shopping around or what?" she smiled as Pete approached.

"Something like that," he grinned self-consciously.

"Well," she crooned seductively, "you won't have to go any further. I can give you anything you want, any way you want it."

"Well, actually, all I want is a couple of minutes of your time."

"Aw," she pouted, "you don't think Angie can make you happy and put a little excitement in your life?"

"Oh, I'm pretty sure you can do that all right," he smiled, "but I make it a point never to mix pleasure with business."

"Oh, yeah?" she said. "You doing business now?"

"Sort of. I'm a reporter and, at the moment, I'm trying to put a story together."

"A reporter?" she exclaimed. "Hey, isn't that something! And you want to interview me? Wow, far out!"

Buoyed up by the girl's positive reaction, Pete pressed his advantage. "I'm doing a follow-up on those two girls who were murdered recently — Helen Jantzen and Holly Gains." He looked at her hopefully, "Did you know them at all?"

"I knew Holly. She used to work Jarvis Street when I first started. That must've been the end of April, or early May."

"You didn't know Helen?"

"Uh-uh. At least not by that name. Course, a lot of the girls on the street don't use their real names."

"Well, how do you feel turning tricks, knowing that there's some wacko out there who may be your next john?"

"Hey, I ain't thrilled about it, that's for sure. But when you're a working girl, you're always taking chances, y'know. Like, you could get some john who's into whips and chains, or one of those creeps who gets his rocks off and then tries to rip off the money he paid you. Hey, it ain't like working at McDonald's, y'know."

"Yeah, right," Pete nodded. "But these recent killings . . . Haven't they made you think about getting out of the business, or taking a break for a while?"

"Hey, I wish I could afford to," she said bitterly. "But I got an old man who's got a two-hundred-buck-a-day coke habit and I don't have a helluva lot of choice, at least not if I don't want to get beat on."

"Your old man beats on you?"

"Hey," she grinned condescendingly, "is the pope Catholic?"

"Have the killings caused you to take any extra precautions?"

She started to answer, and then cocked her head, eyeing him suspiciously. "Hey, wait a minute. Didn't the cops nail some guy for those killings?"

"They've got Holly's old man in custody," Pete replied, "but so far, they've only charged him with *her* death."

"Do you think he did it?"

"Frankly, no. I've known him for quite a while and as far as I'm concerned, he couldn't even come close to doing something like that."

Angie looked at him gravely. "So you figure the guy who did it — the creep who killed Holly and the other chick — you figure he's still out there?" She gestured vaguely toward the street and the procession of cruising vehicles.

"Yeah, that's what I think," Pete said sombrely. "And I also think that whatever drives him to kill is still inside him, growing bigger and stronger, and that it's only a matter of time before it breaks loose again."

Fishing out Nadeau's photo, he flashed it at Angie. "Have you ever seen this guy?"

She studied it carefully before glancing up at Pete. Her face was ashen and her eyes were dilated with fear. "Yeah, I almost went with him once. He pulled over to the curb, right about there." She pointed to a spot on the street a couple of doors away. "He was staring at me, so, finally, I went over and rapped with him, y'know. But right about then, one of the other girls came up to talk to me, and he just up and drove away real fast, like something scared him off. Afterwards, I figured that maybe it was his first time and he got cold feet."

"Or," Pete offered, "maybe he didn't want your friend to see him pick you up."

She stared at the picture again. "You saying this is —"

Pete cut in, "I don't know if he is or isn't. But I want you to remember that face and . . ." He showed her a photo of Nadeau's Chrysler. "This car. If you spot either one of them around here, call me right away, no matter what time it is." He handed her his card, saying, "Use the pager number and leave a message. It'll get to me any time, day or night."

"O.K.," she murmured, adding: "You really think there's going to be more killings?"

Pete nodded slowly. "Yeah, I really do. I don't think there's an off-switch for someone who can commit such brutal murders. Most serial killers are psychopaths and that means they're programmed to kill, the same way a politician is conditioned to bullshit."

"Jesus."

"Oh, there's one more thing," Pete added.

"What's that?"

"I was just wondering if you've taken any steps to protect yourself. You know, just in case. . . ."

She put on a tough, streetwise expression, but her eyes held a hint of fear. "You better believe it. I got a razor in my purse and if any creep tries to do a violence trip on me, I'll cut his balls off."

"Ouch," Pete winced. "Anyway, if you spot the guy in the picture, you know what to do."

By the time Pete had returned to his apartment, he had what he needed for an in-depth report on the hazards of hooking in the big city. But he had something else that he considered even more important — evidence that one of the pillars of the province's judicial establishment had a darker side to his personality.

That was nothing new to Pete. He'd been around long enough to know that a lot of people led double lives — one in the sun, the other in the shadows. As far as he was concerned, if a judge, or anyone else wanted to walk on the wild side every now and then, that was their business. But now there was more in the shadows than mere lust; there was the spectre of defiled bodies and violent death. Pete felt hollow and powerless. He wished that whatever was happening — whatever he felt himself becoming a part of — was over. But, deep inside, he sensed that it was only beginning.

Elaine still had butterflies in her stomach. Today was only her second day of substituting for Larry, and Friday would be her last because he was due back on Monday. She'd learned a lot working for him, and one of the key things was that people — or, at least, ninety per cent of them — didn't phone open-line radio shows to obtain information, or engage in reasoned debate. More often than not, all they wanted was to have someone confirm their biases.

She knew that, initially, she'd been too laid-back, letting the callers dictate the tempo but after she'd gotten her feet wet, she'd felt totally in control, cutting off rambling calls with a curt ''phone me again when you've got something to say'' or ''you're wasting not only your time but mine''.

Bob Grey had told her that she handled the show like a veteran and, more importantly, she'd received a call from Harrison Riley, who had followed up his flowery praise with a dinner invitation. All good things come to she who waits, she told herself, as she straightened the sheaf of notes and headed for the studio. She was on a roll and today's show would take her further and further.

This morning, she was conducting a kind of symposium on violence, with a three-person panel of experts. She thought that she couldn't miss with the three people she'd selected. There would be Mike Edwards representing the Metro Police Department, Dr. Lionel Sanford, a Professor of Sociology at the University of Toronto, and last but not least, Paul Manko, an ex-convict who'd served twelve years of a life sentence for murder. Elaine had opted to call him ''Mr. X.'' She loved the intrigue of having a mystery man on the show and knew the audience would eat it up. But there was another consideration involved in protecting his identity. He'd been paroled in 1978 and, after working at a number of trades, he'd managed to start his own printing company and was now happily married and the father of two young children.

Because he'd changed his name after being released, no one, except his immediate family, knew he'd done time and, wanting to keep it that way, he'd only agreed to be interviewed on the condition that his anonymity was preserved.

When Elaine entered the studio he was the first one she spoke to. Short and round-faced, Manko looked almost cherubic; he hardly fit the common perception of a killer, and smiled nervously when he shook Elaine's hand.

Mike Edwards was his usual dour self, his pained expression telling Elaine that he'd had to be dragooned into representing the homicide squad. The third member of the trio seemed to be the only one who was pleased to be there. Professor Sanford, fortyish, with a thick, well-trimmed beard, was nattily attired in the uniform of academia: brown tweed jacket with leather elbow patches above and a *de rigueur* pair of meticulously faded jeans below. Puffing on a meerschaum pipe, he had the disconcerting habit of studying the ceiling before responding to a question. On television, it wouldn't have been so bad but on radio, even a couple of seconds of dead air could seem like an eternity. God, she fretted, why does he have to smoke a damn pipe? When he sucks on it, the mike will pick up the sibilance and the folks at home will think he's asthmatic.

But, as it turned out, her fears were groundless. Sanford liked hearing himself too much to miss any opportunity of filling every second of air time allotted him. So what if he was bombastic and his utterances were based on questionable research statistics. He made a perfect counterpoint to the macho straight-arrow cop and the folksy, colloquial ex-con.

"Sergeant Edwards," Elaine began. "Before we start to talk about the phenomenon of violence in our society in general, and in Toronto in particular, could you give us a progress report on the investigation of the four recent killings in our city?''

The veteran detective had a habit of speaking slowly and deliberately, turning over the implications of each word in his mind before he let it reach his lips. ''Well, I guess you're referring to the Jantzen and Gains murders as well as Tuesday's double homicide.''

''That's right,'' Elaine said crisply. ''Have there been any new developments in these cases?''

''Well, we're still following up a number of leads in the Jantzen case but, as you can appreciate, it's slow going since there are no witnesses to the killing. As far as the Gains case is concerned, as you know, we made an arrest and the accused is scheduled to enter a plea tomorrow morning.''

''Does that mean, that as far as the Metro police are concerned, the Gains case is a closed book?''

''No case is closed until a conviction has been obtained,'' Edwards replied. ''We are still continuing our investigation of the matter, although, what with the double homicide earlier this week, our resources are being spread pretty thin.''

''What about those last murders?'' Elaine said earnestly. ''All of us here at CKAL are still in shock over the death of Jane Chambers. She was a wonderful person and we all feel a deep sense of loss. What's happening there?'' Have you any solid leads?''

''Edwards noisily cleared his throat before replying: ''I can't say that our leads are solid, in the sense that we think an arrest is imminent, but I can assure you that we're working overtime on this one, and that we're confident the case will be brought to a successful conclusion.''

''Well, have you at least arrived at any possible motive for this horrible crime?''

His voice took on a hard edge. ''I think it might tend to impede the progress of our investigation if I made any disclosures at this time.''

Elaine knew better. She knew that the investigation had

hit a dead end and the cops were coasting, waiting for some evidence to fall into their laps via an informant. She'd spoken to Mike earlier and he'd told her that it looked like a contract killing, which meant that the hit man was long gone and that the chances of breaking the case were slim to none.

She debated whether she should pursue this angle, then decided not to, reasoning that if she wanted to be in the business for the long haul, it would be in her interest to cultivate the kind of cozy relationship that Larry enjoyed with the police department. Tossing curves at the boys in blue would not be exactly the best means to that end, she decided, turning her attention to the bearded academic.

"Professor Sanford, you've presented a number of papers dealing with the high incidence of violence in our society and I wonder if you could provide some insight into the causes of what seems to be an epidemic of homicide in our city."

Sanford's windy response contained a healthy dose of the academic buzzwords that passed for conventional wisdom in university faculty lounges and social science seminars. In one sentence, he managed to combine such esoteric terms as "cognitive dissonance," "global variables," and "stress-filled ambience." Elaine knew that she'd have to ease him to the sidelines if she was to hold the attention of an audience whose literary tastes ran to the backs of cereal boxes and in-depth reports on Elizabeth Taylor's latest diet.

Dismissing Sanford with a curt "Well, that's very interesting, professor," Elaine focussed on her remaining guest. "As I mentioned earlier, my third guest is a convicted murderer whom I will be referring to as 'Mr. X' in order to protect his identity." The meek-looking ex-convict looked at her with a wary intensity and his attempt at a smile more closely resembled a facial tic. "Mr. X," Elaine continued, "I think that in any discussion of homicide it's important to get the opinion of one who has been there, as it were, and I can't think of anyone who fits the bill better than someone like yourself, who has actually committed the crime of murder.

"Now, you were convicted of second-degree murder and spent a dozen years in a prison before being parolled several years ago, is that right?"

He nodded, then taking a cue from Elaine's animated gesture said, "Yes, that's right."

"Now, even after many years and paying a heavy price for your crime, I'm sure you're still haunted by the knowledge that you took the life of a fellow human being who, in fact, was your wife of fifteen years."

"Fourteen," he corrected.

"Yes," Elaine rushed on. "And looking at any crime and particularly something as heinous as murder, I think one of the key issues is deterrence. I think it would be interesting to find out how *you* feel about that." Hit by Manko's blank stare, Elaine quickly added, "I mean, looking back, do you think that any penalty, for example, capital punishment, would have kept you from killing your wife?"

"Well, actually," Manko began, "they did have capital punishment when I was sentenced and if I'd been found guilty of first- instead of second-degree murder, I probably would've been — whatyacallit — executed."

"So," Elaine said with a faint tinge of triumph, "the fact that you could have been put to death wasn't a factor when you killed your wife."

"I guess not," he said haltingly, "but —"

"O.K.," Elaine cut in, "since we know what *didn't* influence you, perhaps you could tell us what *did*?"

"What . . . ?" he frowned perplexedly.

Elaine let out an exasperated sigh. "What motivated you to kill your wife, Mr. X? Why did you beat her until every last breath of her life was gone?"

Manko shoved his hands out toward Elaine as though to ward off the question, and his pale eyes blinked in dismay. But, telling herself she had no choice, Elaine ignored his pleading pantomime. The ivory tower prof had spouted a load of soporific dogma and Edwards had been about as dynamic as Perry Como on Valium. The show was dragging. She knew she had to light a fire under someone and Manko was all she had. As the pained expression congealed on his face, she was afraid that he might dry up or bolt from the studio, but finally he sagged back in his chair and stared at the microphone.

"That was so long ago," he said in a low, choked voice. "I'm working hard and providing for my family. I'm trying to lead a good, decent life and put all that behind me. I don't even like to think about . . . that."

"By 'that,' I take it you mean killing your wife?" Elaine asked, gazing at him with wide-eyed innocence.

"Miss Steele," Professor Sanford smiled knowingly, "I think that Mr. X's reaction is quite understandable. My colleagues and I have found that many murderers tend to want to block out the details of their brutal crimes. Regardless of any perceived provocation, the taking of a human life is still one of the strongest taboos in societies governed by the Judaeo-Christian ethic. And the killing of one's spouse ranks just a little below the slaying of a parent or sibling in the hierarchy of heinous offences. Wouldn't you agree, Mr. X?"

Manko stared at him blankly, like a foreign dignitary waiting for an interpreter's translation. Smoothly picking up the slack, Elaine brightly announced: "I think this has been a super introduction to our topic, which is the horrendous growth of violence in our society. And now, I'd like to open the discussion up to our audience, which I'm sure is just raring to pick up their phones and call *Larry's Line*.

She punched a button and a middle-aged female voice launched into an angry tirade. "I just want to say that that man you've got on should be ashamed to show his face in public. Imagine! Bragging about beating his wife to death. If I were a man, and maybe twenty years younger, I'd come down to your station and give him what he should have got from the courts, and I don't mean maybe."

"Now, now," Elaine chided, "Mr. X has paid his debt to society and I don't think it's fair to punish him again, no matter how brutal and despicable his crime may have been."

Through the glass of the control booth, Bob Grey made a circle with his thumb and forefinger. She acknowledged it with a nod and a smile, and punched another button. She liked the feeling that she was pushing the buttons now. But her exhilaration was short-lived.

Jane's funeral was on Saturday and Larry would be back on Monday. Where would that leave *her*? Back to putting briefing notes together and fetching coffee? She knew that that wouldn't be easy to face after the attention and status she'd had over the past few days.

But maybe, she told herself, it wouldn't be for all that long. After all, she was having dinner with Harrison Riley that evening and he might have some ideas of his own about her future. She smiled to herself as she thanked a caller for still another venomous outpouring. Yes, her dinner date with Harrison promised to be very interesting. And it would be up to her to make it so.

Larry passed a hand over his chin, feeling the stubble. Should he shave? he wondered, then decided to have another drink instead. He deserved it. It had been a helluva week, but it would soon be over. Jane's funeral was to be held on Saturday. Larry had made all the arrangements and Jane would have the best of everything in death, as she'd had in life. He knew that many of the city's top politicians and media personalities would be there. He'd also gotten a nice call from Harrison Riley, who told him that he could take as much time off as he needed to get his life together. Yeah, the old man was one terrific guy all right.

Funny, he thought, tomorrow that scuzzball, that Speedy what's-his-face, would be appearing in court to enter a plea in connection with Holly's death. Just one day before Jane was to go to her final resting place. Somewhere deep inside him something stirred. Larry tried to make a connection between the two events, but every time he seemed to get close, his mind abruptly pulled back.

No, he finally decided, they were two random incidents and the only link between them was their senselessness. Ordinarily, he would have been hot on Renner's case, piping in a remote from the courthouse to give his listeners a blow-by-blow account of what would be shaping up as more than a run-of-the-mill murder. The buzz from the cop shop was that the homicide boys were busting their asses trying to tie Speedy Renner into the Jantzen slaying as well.

Oh, well, he thought, Elaine was probably keeping on top of it. She was doing a terrific job filling in for him. True, she was somewhat tentative at times and a little rough around the edges, but he couldn't have asked for a better short-term substitute. He was itching to get back into the studio though. He needed to be in touch with his audience — his people. They understood and respected him, and when he fielded their calls, he felt as though he were taking a warm bath in their admiration and affection. For the first time in his life, he realized how much he needed them.

"Yeah," he murmured tipsily, "good ol' Lainie. Great kid." One day, he told himself, she'll have a show of her own. 'Course she's never gonna be a Larry Chambers — not enough of a gut-fighter for that — but she'll be able to hold her own after another couple of years' apprenticeship with radio's "Master of the Morning."

He poured himself another shot of Scotch. He was starting to feel good — nice and loose. "Nice and loose," he repeated like a child reciting a nursery rhyme, "loose as a goose, and all because of this good ol' juice." Well-contented with his burst of creative expression, he gave a self-congratulatory smile and hefted the bottle of whiskey.

He felt as though he were floating on a warm cloud. But he knew that no matter how high or how far he floated, he would have to come back to earth for Jane's funeral. The girls were still at their grandmother's. They were better off there. He couldn't give them what they needed — how could he, when he was in so much need himself?

He sat up stiffly on the sofa and stared at the seascape that

Jane had bought when they were in San Francisco several years and one lifetime ago. Why did she have to die? he wondered, just as things had begun to go well between them. It was as though he'd been set up just so life could play this monstrous trick on him. But who had actually played the trick? And why?

He had to see Jack Lexer and find out what had happened. He'd called him several times and left a message but his calls hadn't been returned. There was only one thing to do. He got to his feet unsteadily and weaved toward the door. As he passed through the hallway, he caught sight of himself in the oval wall mirror. His hair stood up in tufts and his red-rimmed eyes squinted out above a heavy shadow of whiskers. He stared hard at his reflection, his lips curling in disgust.

"Jesus," he muttered. Then he thought of his daughters. He couldn't let them see him this way. Tears welled up in his eyes and his chest began to heave. His reflection began to blur as though it were submerging in a murky pool. He blinked and it started to come back into focus. But it wasn't *his* face now. It was *hers*. Holly's. Her eyes wide and staring. Her mouth agape in a silent scream. He shook his head violently and lurched out of the house, wanting to look back but afraid of what he might see.

Chapter Eighteen

Pete found a message on his desk when he got back from lunch. Speedy had called and wanted to see him right away. Rushing down to the remand centre, Pete emptied his pockets and passed through a metal scanner before he was allowed into the visitors' area.

The large drab room was separated into two sections by a long counter which was flanked by rows of chairs. Inmates sat on one side and visitors on the other. A guard informed Pete that there was a firm rule against any physical contact with a prisoner. He took a seat near the middle of the counter and waited for Speedy.

When he finally appeared Pete had to look twice to be sure it was him. Speedy's raffish moustache had been trimmed and his usually straggly, post-hippie locks had been fashioned into a close-cropped style that made him look like a street-wise yuppie.

"Hey, what's happenin', man?" Speedy bawled.

"Not too much. How're things with you?" He noticed

that there were dark circles under Speedy's eyes, and that he was a lot more laid-back than usual. But then, why shouldn't he be? Pete wondered. After all, this was probably the first time in God knows how long that Speedy's system had been free of amphetamines.

"Not so good, man," he said morosely. "Spector tried to pull some strings and get me a pass so's I could go to Holly's funeral, but it was no go."

"That's too bad."

"Yeah," he said, staring down at the counter. "It's this afternoon and I was wondering if you could . . . like, if you had the time . . . ." He gave a lopsided smile, trying to hide his embarrassment.

"What do you want me to do?"

He took a deep breath and looked into Pete's eyes. "I'd like you to get a wreath and put it on her grave. And put a nice card on it that says it's from me. I was gonna get Spector to get someone to do it, but I couldn't get hold of him."

"Sure, no problem."

They sat in silence for a few moments before Pete asked: "So what's the story for tomorrow?"

"I'm pleading guilty."

"Guilty," Pete said incredulously. "What the hell for? You told me you didn't do it."

"I didn't, but . . ." He glanced around nervously, "I made a deal."

"With whom? The Crown?"

"Sorta," he said uneasily. "Actually, there are a lot of people involved, and the word is that if I cop a plea, I'll be out in a year. If I fight it, according to Spector, the chances are I'll get nailed for the whole bundle — murder two, at the least — and get life."

"But you said they didn't have any case against you."

"That's what I thought until I talked to Spector," Speedy said glumly. "He says they've got a lot of — what'ya call it — circumstantial evidence, probably enough to convince a jury I done it." Reacting to Pete's look of disbelief, he went on. "See, I ain't got no alibi — I mean, I got one, but the guys I figured would back me up, copped out. And, like, the old lady next door heard me yelling at Holly at the time the killing was supposed to have taken place."

"They know when the killing took place? I thought they were only able to come to within a couple of hours."

"Yeah, well, that was before. Now they figure they've got it pegged right to the minute almost."

"How the hell did they manage to do that?"

"Well, there was this clock. . . ."

"Clock?"

"Yeah, our alarm clock. It had been all smashed up and had stopped at about eight-thirty. It was on the floor next to Holly and the cops figure it got broken when she was scrapping with the guy that killed her."

"And it showed eight-thirty?"

"That's what Spector says."

"Well," Pete said, "that's hardly conclusive evidence. Maybe the clock wasn't even running at the time it was smashed."

"Yeah, that's what I told Spector but, well. . . ." He held out his hands helplessly.

"So you're going to plead guilty to a crime you didn't commit?"

He stared at Pete bleakly. "I don't have much choice."

"That's bullshit. We've all got choices, if we've got the guts to make them instead of letting others make them for us."

"That's easy for you to say, man," Speedy said with a hangdog look, "but you and me, like, we're in different spaces. A guy like me has only got one choice — whether to be in shit up to his ass or up to his fuckin' eyes."

"Don't do it, Speedy," Pete implored. "You plead guilty to murder and, even if the Crown is willing to deal, you could be looking at some heavy time in the slammer."

Speedy looked around furtively before leaning forward

and whispering: "The fix is in, man. I got all kind of heavy-duty people in my corner." But, within seconds, his confident façade started to crumble. "Besides, I already said I'd do it and you don't back out of deals with these people."

As he stared at Speedy, trying to think of some new argument to keep him from taking the fall, something started to sprout in Pete's consciousness. At first it was just a bud of recognition, then slowly, almost imperceptibly, it sprang into full flower.

"The clock!"

The words and the intensity both caught Speedy off-guard. "Yeah, what about it," he stammered.

"Was that the only one you had? The one that was broken?" Pete asked excitedly.

"Yeah, that's right. Why?"

"Because when I went to check out —" He made a quick mental edit, deleting "Holly." ". . . the bedroom, it was quiet as hell. Except for one thing."

"Yeah? What was that?"

"The ticking of a goddamn clock."

Speedy's puzzled frown gave way to awareness. "You mean the clock was working when you came over that morning?"

"That's right. I'd swear to it."

Speedy's eyes slitted as he nodded knowingly. "I thought that son of a bitch would try and frame me."

"Who?"

"Edwards. Who else? That bastard's had a hard-on for me for years."

Pete shook his head skeptically. "I don't know. I'm no fan of his either, but fabricating evidence is damn serious business. I'm not saying it isn't done, even by Metro's guardians of the law, but it's hard to believe that our pal Mike would stick out his neck that far just because you're on his shit list."

"It ain't just because of that," Speedy argued. "There's other reasons. Let's face it. If he breaks a murder case, he's a big man with his name in the papers and all that bullshit, and he chalks up a bunch of brownie points with his bosses. So why the hell wouldn't he stack the evidence to make sure his case doesn't go for a shit?''

"Well, you may be right," Pete said, still not totally convinced. "There probably wasn't anyone else in a better position to doctor the clock. But the thing is, what do we do about it?"

"Fuck-all, I guess," Speedy said glumly.

"How about getting Spector to call me as a witness?" Pete offered. "I could testify that the clock was still working long after Holly was killed."

"Yeah, but that would mean I'd have to plead not guilty and I already made a deal to cop a plea."

"Well, back out of it, for Christ sake," Pete snapped. "This is your life we're talking about, not a goddamn used car."

"Yeah, well, if I crossed up my people I wouldn't have to worry about my life, that's for goddamn sure, because that'd be all she wrote."

"So you're going to go through with it and plead guilty," Pete said leadenly.

Speedy felt moved by Pete's concern as he stood up to indicate that the visit was over. I've got to, man. But I want you to know that I really appreciate what you're trying to do."

Ignoring a guard's shouted protestation, Speedy reached across the counter and the two men shook hands.

"And Pete. . . ."

"Yeah?"

"You won't forget about that wreath, will you?"

"No, I won't. You can count on it."

As Pete turned to leave, it struck him that there was almost as much surprise as pleasure in the grin that had lit up Speedy's thin, sallow face.

Larry stepped out of the elevator and walked unsteadily

toward the receptionist. The young fashionably attired woman looked at him coolly as he mumbled a request to see Jack Lexer.

"Is Mr. Lexer expecting you?"

"No, he's not," he said thickly. "But I'm sure he'll see me. My name is Larry Chambers. I'm with CKAL." He looked at her hopefully, but she gave no sign that his name had struck a responsive chord.

"I'm sorry," she said in a bored, nasal tone. "But Mr. Lexer is a very busy man and if you don't have an appointment. . . ."

Larry could feel anger growing inside him. "Just tell him I'm here," he said tightly. "He'll see me all right." He reached down, grabbing the corner of the reception desk to steady himself.

She glanced at him acidly and punched a button on the intercom. "Mr. Lexer, there is a Mr. Chambers here to see you. I've told him that you're busy but he is quite persistent."

Larry could read the disappointment in her face when she turned toward him. "You can go right in," she said, waving her hand toward the door to Lexer's office.

Larry knocked lightly, and then stepped inside. Jack was behind his desk, riffling through a sheaf of papers, and Larry had taken a couple of steps toward him before he realized that Jack wasn't alone. On the leather couch to his left a swarthy, heavyset man in a cream-coloured summer suit was stretched out with his hands behind his head. When Larry approached the desk, the man sat up and leaned forward, watching him closely.

"Jack —" Larry began.

Lexer held up his hand without raising his eyes from the desk and said sharply, "Just a minute."

Larry stood there, trying to keep from swaying. There was a buzzing in his head like some background noise he couldn't tune out, and he licked his lips, thinking about how much he needed a drink. Glancing around, he noticed that the blocky man with the deepset eyes was staring at him intently.

Finally, Lexer got up and extended his hand. "Larry, good to see you," he smiled. "What can I do for you?"

"I've got to talk to you." He glanced pointedly at the thick-chested man. "Alone."

Lexer caught the man's eye, saying: "O.K., Nick. Take five."

After the man had left, Larry shook his head admiringly. "Christ, that guy's built like a goddamn tank."

Lexer nodded. "He should be. He used to be a weight lifter. He finished second in the nationals a couple of years ago."

"Oh, yeah? What's he doing now?"

"Working for me."

"What doing? Frankly, he doesn't look that swift."

Lexer smiled thinly. "I guess you could call him a public-relations expert." He reached over and plucked a cigar out of a humidor on his desk. "You know, in the business world these days, everything is public relations, getting people to see things your way.

"Every big company, every government agency, has got some smooth-talking schmuck who can charm the birds out of the trees. Me, I got a couple of those, too, cranking out press releases about what a great guy I am, and how my different businesses are contributing so much to the city. You know the game, image-building, and you know how the right image can take you a long way and how the wrong one can put you in the dumper."

He stuck his thumbs in his waistband and puffed out his chest. "I didn't go to Harvard, but I can buy and sell a lotta guys who did. And they know it. They don't do business with me or invite me to their parties and fund-raisers because they like me. As a matter of fact, a lot of the old money in this town still won't have fuck-all to do with me. They figure that because it took them a helluva lot longer to make their pile that, somehow, it makes them better than me. But it doesn't mean shit how long it takes you to get money and power. It's what you do with 'em that counts."

He lit the cigar and puffed until the end was a glowing ember. Blowing out wreaths of aromatic smoke, he spoke slowly, measuring his words. "Guys like Nick, they represent a different kind of power — something I got that a lot of people with more bread don't have. It's the power to put fear into people's guts and get them to see things your way when words alone won't do the job.

"And you know something? Rich people are easier to scare than poor people because they got a helluva lot more to lose. Like, nobody wants to get his legs broken, right? But you take a rich guy and he's fuckin' terrified because if he's got his legs in casts up to his ass, he can't ride his fuckin' Arabian horses or go swimming in his Olympic-size swimming pool." He gave a broad wink. "And he sure as hell can't bang all the young pussy that's sniffing around after his bread.

"But you take some poor sucker, and it don't mean shit to him if you threaten to bust his kneecaps, because what the hell does he do anyway but have a few beers, watch TV, and yell at his old lady. For what the poor fuck is making busting his ass at some chicken shit job, he'd probably be better off with a disability allowance anyway."

Suddenly Lexer looked embarrassed. "Hey, listen to me shooting my mouth off when it's *you* that came to talk to *me*."

Larry looked covetously toward the liquor cabinet. "You know, Jack, I certainly wouldn't say no to a little Scotch if it isn't too much trouble."

Lexer looked at him darkly. "I don't like to say it, but you look like you've had a couple too many already. Hey, I'm the last one to preach, and I know you've been through a lot, but you've got to pull yourself together because let me tell you, as one friend to another, you look pretty rough."

Larry licked his lips nervously. "Listen, Jack. I'm really fucked up. I can't think straight. And it's not just the booze. I really think I'm losing it. This whole thing with Jane. I . . . ." He looked pleadingly at Lexer, his lower lip quivering. "Jack, I've gotta know. What happened? This thing with

Jane and that private eye. What happened? Why did she have to die, Jack? Why?''

Tears began to roll down his cheeks and he tried to push them away with the back of his hand.

Lexer shot him a warning look. "There are things that it's best not to talk about."

"But, why?" Larry sobbed. "Why did she have to die?"

"How the fuck would I know?" Lexer shouted. "I don't know nothing about your wife or this private eye you keep talking about. I'm a businessman, for fuck's sake. What do I know about people getting hit? You better get yourself together and knock off that kinda talk before people start getting hurt."

"People?" Choking back his anguish, he stared at Lexer in bewilderment.

"You got kids, haven't you?"

Larry's mouth opened and closed but no sound came. Finally, after a few false starts, he managed to croak: "Not my girls, Jack. Please, not my girls. They're all I have left."

"Then can this shit about me and your wife and this . . . this detective. They're gone and that's the bottom line. Forget about it. You had someone on your case and now he's out of the picture and you're in the clear."

"Yeah," Larry sniffed bitterly, "I'm in the clear all right."

Lexer's eyes narrowed into menacing slits. "And you'll stay that way as long as you play ball and keep your mouth shut. But if you fuck up, just remember it's your ass that's on the line."

"What do you mean?"

Lexer smile cryptically. "The word is that the dick had a file on you and that it had some pretty hot stuff in it."

Larry swallowed hard. "Hot stuff? What kind of hot stuff?"

"He knew about the Gains bitch, didn't he?" He shook his head, chuckling. "You're goddamn lucky the cops didn't get their hands on it. I hear they're going nuts trying to come up with a motive and if they had that slimeball's report, they wouldn't have to look very far.''

"What's that supposed to mean?"

"Figure it out. Guy's screwing around on his wife and she hires a private dick to tail him. The dick gets the goods, meaning the wife can cut her old man loose and get a hefty settlement in the bargain. The husband finds out and gets a hard-on for his wife and the dick seeing as how they're both part of a caper that could ruin him financially, and — if the story gets out — professionally. Hell, in a situation like that, the husband would be a total fuck if he *didn't* want to whack them.''

Larry chewed nervously on his lower lip. "Uh, this report. Where is it now?"

Lexer's face was a picture of innocence. "I wish I knew. But, you know . . .'' His mouth tightened into a thin line. "Stuff like that has a way of turning up when you least expect it, you know what I mean?"

Larry's shoulders sagged and he stared at the floor. "What do you want?"

Lexer smiled. "I just want us to work together and help each other out like we've been doing for the last couple of years. You look after me, and I look after you, right?"

Larry heard the words but they didn't register. His mind was elsewhere. At the funeral home to which he'd taken a photograph for the cosmetician and hair stylist to work from. He'd thought about having a closed-casket service, but the mortician had convinced him that Jane's hair could be re-arranged to completely cover the bullet wound. He'd also delivered the dress that his wife would be buried in — the light-blue cocktail dress that had always been her favourite — and the thin, gold, chain and locket that she always wore around her neck, with the picture of Dianne and Arlene. She'd been wearing it when she died, but it had been removed by the police.

"You hear what I said?" Lexer's gruff voice broke into his revery.

"Huh? Oh yeah, I heard you."

"O.K. then. When you get back on the show, I want you to start boosting redevelopment of Chinatown, right? My people have a lot of property in there, but right now, it ain't worth shit. We need the city to start kicking in with some tax breaks and incentive grants to make it worth our while to free up some investment capital.

"And after we get the ball rolling on that, I've got a couple of Metro councillors who've done me a few favours and could use some exposure. They're thinking of running provincially, and if their party gets in, we'll have a couple of more friends at Queen's Park."

"Right," Larry murmured absently.

Lexer glanced at his watch. "I hate to rush you, but I got a lot of work to do and people to see, so if there's nothing else. . . ."

"No, nothing else," Larry said tonelessly.

"O.K., pal," Lexer said, putting a beefy hand on Larry's shoulder and guiding him toward the door. "I'll be talking to you soon. And if there's anything I can do for you, let me know."

"Yeah, I will."

Standing on the sidewalk, in the shadow of a bank of Bay Street office towers, Larry felt empty. Where had it all gone? he wondered. Had he been that evil or merely that weak? He shook his head dejectedly and walked slowly toward the parking lot. As he sat in his car, staring sightlessly through the windshield, he thought of how his daughters would hate him if they found out why they no longer had a mother. And when he began to cry, he knew that his tears were more for himself than for Jane.

Elaine shivered with delight as his fingertips glided over her belly. Craning her head, she brushed his lips with her own and they kissed fiercely, as she opened her thighs to receive him. Afterward, as they lay looking up at the ceiling, their fingers entwined, letting their thoughts float languidly in the darkness, Elaine concluded that Harrison Riley was one of the most exciting lovers she'd ever had.

He'd seemed to know not only what she needed, but what she'd wanted as well and had brought her to a state of total physical and emotional abandonment. As she glanced at him out of the corner of her eye, he turned toward her and their eyes met.

"This has been one of the most enjoyable evenings of my life," he whispered, brushing his lips against her ear.

She nuzzled his neck, saying huskily, "I really can't believe this is happening. I always thought you were a good employer, but these fringe benefits are more than I expected."

He hoisted himself onto one elbow and smiled down at her. "It's hard to get good help these days and I'm prepared to do everything I can to keep it." He bent down and kissed her lightly on the lips. "And you."

"That's one thing you don't have to worry about," she murmured, looping her arms around his neck, and pulling him down to her.

When they stopped kissing to catch their breath, he looked at her tenderly. "Can you feel the magic — in this bed, in this room?"

She nodded, saying throatily, "I don't want it to ever stop."

He smiled ruefully. "Neither do I, but I'm going to have to risk breaking the spell because there's something I'd like to discuss with you. Something that's causing me some concern."

"Oh-oh," she said. "That sounds pretty heavy."

"I'm afraid it is," he sighed. "It's this whole thing about Larry. His . . . situation."

"Yes," she said sadly, "it's an awful thing. I still can't think of why anyone would want to kill Jane. It . . . it's so *bizarre.*"

Harrison ran a hand through his silvery hair. "Yes, it is.

And I'm afraid one could say the same about Larry's conduct the last couple of days. I'm sure he has every reason to be distraught, but Bob Grey told me he showed up at the station yesterday bombed out of his mind. Is that right?''

"Well," Elaine said hesitantly, "it did seem as though he had been drinking. . . ."

He cupped her chin in his hand and looked at her with amusement. "I admire loyalty but I think we have to face facts. Larry appears to be losing his grip and, frankly, I think it will be quite some time before I'd feel confident about letting him back on the air."

Elaine would have been hard-pressed to describe her reaction. There was surprise, of course, and shock, but there was also a sensation that was not entirely disagreeable.

"You mean he's not coming back on Monday?"

Riley shook his head. "Not a chance, m'dear. I'm afraid you're going to have to hold the fort for a while longer. He needs a rest — a long one."

"Have you told him?"

"I told Bob to let him know — to tell Larry to take an extended holiday — but he hasn't been able to reach him. He said he's phoned at all hours of the day and night but there's no answer."

Anxiety crept into Elaine's voice. "I don't think he's going to like your suggestion, Harrison."

"Oh?" Riley seemed genuinely surprised. "Why is that? A nice, long, paid holiday will be just the thing for him. Give him a chance to get away. I'll spring for some plane tickets to the continent. He can take his daughters and show them the sights, get their minds off this terrible tragedy. God, I know if it were me, I certainly wouldn't want to stay in a house with so many memories. The sense of loss would be crushing."

"You don't know him the way I do," she said. "*Larry's Line* was the biggest part of his life when Jane was alive and now. . . ." She shook her head sorrowfully.

"I'm sure the show is very important to Larry," Harrison

conceded, "but I have to think about what's important for the station as well. The bottom line is that Larry's ratings were dropping for quite a while before those shows on the hooker killings stopped the slide.

"The fact of the matter is that Larry Chambers may well have had his day. The oldsters are still hanging in but the younger people, the ones with the big purchasing buck, are going over to Trent Ferguson. We have to fight fire with fire, youth with youth, one attractive personality with . . ." He traced a finger over her lips, "one *extremely* attractive personality."

"But now?" she asked in a small voice. "Right in the middle of all this?"

"What better time? You've shown that you can handle the job. If we didn't have such a capable substitute, we might have to bide our time. But the way things stand, the transition can be made swiftly and smoothly without risking any public disfavour over replacing Larry."

Elaine fell into a moody silence. After a few moments, Harrison became concerned. "What's the matter?"

"Nothing," she said dully.

"This is no time for secrets," he chided. "Tell Uncle Harrison what's troubling your sweet little head."

"It . . . it just seems so unfair," she frowned. "He's been with the station for so long, put so much of himself into the show. . . ."

He took her hand and looked deep into her eyes. "All right then. I'll leave it up to you. You tell me that you don't want the job and, on Monday, Larry will be back behind the microphone. But remember, in this business, the breaks don't always come along to suit both your ambition and your conscience."

A knowing smile playing on his lips, he watched her struggle with herself. "Well, which is it? You can't have it both ways," Harrison said.

In that instant, she hated him, but not as much as she hated herself. "I want the job," she said, adding mockingly,

"I want to be the queen of hot-line radio and shove Trent Ferguson's microphone up his you-know-what."

"That's my girl," Harrison crowed. "In a couple of weeks, we'll put on an advertising campaign that'll have Ferguson shaking in his boots: billboards, full-page ads in all the dailies, TV spots. And by the time we get through, you're going to own the morning slot in this city."

Elaine's reply was cut short by the insistent ring of the doorbell. She glanced anxiously at Harrison. "It's almost midnight. Who the hell could that be?"

"Only one way to find out," he said breezily, starting to slide out of the bed.

She put her hand on his chest. "Stay here. I'll get rid of whoever it is and we can . . ." Her voice lowered suggestively, "talk some more."

He lay back on the bed, watching her glide toward the closet. The dim light filtering through the bedroom window gave her skin an eerie, translucent glow. His eyes followed her as she picked out a dressing gown and wrapped it around her supple body. Her pillow was still full of her scent and he breathed deeply, feeling the stirring of passion. Smiling contentedly, he muttered to himself, "You're not getting older, you're getting hornier."

Closing the bedroom door behind her, Elaine crossed the living room and peered through the peephole in the door. It was like looking at someone at the bottom of a deep pool. The eyes were huge and bulging, the nose wide and porcine, and beneath them was a loose, lop-sided grin belonging to Larry Chambers.

The question burst from her lips even before she had the door fully open. "What the hell are you doing here?" Then surprise gave way to alarm. "What's the matter? Is something wrong?"

He swayed dangerously and stumbled backwards, fighting to keep his balance. A wave of hot whiskey-breath engulfed Elaine and, instinctively, she pulled back.

"I jus' came by for a li'l drink," he slurred. "Thought y'

might wanna help me cel'brate.'' He lurched past her into the living room, where he stood rocking from side to side as though buffeted by a strong gale.

She pulled the dressing gown around her more tightly, cursing herself for opening the door. She knew how difficult it was to get rid of Larry when he was blitzed. He became childlike and maudlin and she was in no mood to hold his hand and assure him that everything was going to be all right. She wasn't *that* big a hypocrite. He couldn't have come at a worse time. Her thoughts flew to Harrison in the bedroom — waiting, wondering.

She walked over to Larry, ready to lecture him and send him on his way, but when she saw the sad, lost look in his red-rimmed eyes, she softened and put a hand on his arm.

''Larry, I know it must be awful for you, but you have to pull yourself together. It's late and you must have a lot to do before Saturday.'' She couldn't bring herself to mention the funeral but hoped he'd grasp the implication. He bowed his head, mumbling bleakly. ''I know what I have to do tomorrow but tonight . . .'' He looked up and his voice became loud and harsh, ''tonight, I'm going to cel'brate.''

''All right,'' Elaine sighed, ''tonight we'll celebrate. But would you mind telling me what it is we're celebrating?''

His features loosely arranged themselves around a look of acute astonishment. ''Yah mean ya don' know?'' He shook his head slowly as though lamenting all the woes of the world. ''Isn't that something? They didn' tell ya.'' His shoulders lifted and then fell with his deep sigh of resignation. ''Well, thass the way it goes, I guess. Hell, they didn' even tell *me* until tonight.''

''Tell you? Tell you what?'' Even as she spoke, she could feel the sense of dread building within her.

He blinked his pale, watery eyes. ''I'm finished,'' he said in a voice like the rustle of dry leaves. ''Finished.''

Elaine glanced uneasily toward the bedroom door. ''Go home, Larry,'' she said softly. ''Things'll be better in the morning. We'll talk then.''

Giving no sign that he'd heard her, he took a few wobbly steps and sagged onto the sofa. "Ken called me tonight. He said Riley wants me to take a long hol'day." He looked at her imploringly. "How the hell can I take a hol'day? I'm number one for chrissake. I'm the goddamn king of the airwaves."

He spread his arms as though embracing some unseen presence. "This city needs me. And the people . . . They . . . they *love* me. You know that." His eyes pleaded for confirmation.

"Sure they do," she nodded. "And they'll still love you when you come back; when you get things sorted out. You'll be bigger and better than ever then."

He shook his head in violent denial. "I won't be coming back. That bastard Riley's giving me the chop."

Instinctively, her eyes flew to the bedroom door again. "But why . . . why would he do that? You're CKAL's bread and butter."

Larry's mouth twisted venomously. "Because of some fuckin' numbers some hotshot pollster came up with." He smirked triumphantly. "Ken thinks he's so fuckin' sharp, but I found out that he had an audience survey run last week." He chuckled dryly. "Thought he could put one over on ol' Larry, did he? Well, I'll show him," he bawled, slamming his hand on the coffee table. "I'll show the whole goddamn bunch of back-stabbing bastards!" He took a deep breath and his eyes glinted slyly. "And you're gonna help me, right Lainie?"

Her mind raced, but seemed to be going in circles. "What . . . what can *I* do?"

His eyes bored directly into hers. "You can tell them to stick their job up their asses. I'll make a connection in nothing flat — maybe something in TV — and you'll come with me, be my right hand again." He hauled himself to his feet and faced her, placing his hands on her shoulders and smiling soddenly. "We're a helluva team and we always will be, right?"

"Wrong." The voice was as sharp and sudden as a guillotine.

Neither Larry nor Elaine had heard the bedroom door open, or seen Harrison Riley step into the living room.

Larry's mouth dropped open and he stared at Riley, then Elaine. "Well, I'll be. . . ." Then he began to laugh, softly at first, then breaking into a full-throated roar. Almost doubled over, he fought to catch his breath and, wiping his brimming eyes with the back of his hand, howled, "Holy fuck. Have I been sandbagged!"

While Elaine fidgeted and averted her eyes, Harrison casually finished buttoning his shirt. When he finally spoke, it was with a studied detachment.

"I'm sorry you're so upset about this recent development. We all thought it would be in your best interest to get away from the pressure cooker for a while." His voice became hard. "It's unfortunate that you've chosen to regard the situation in such a negative light."

Whether through shock or anger, Larry seemed more sober and his speech less slurred. "You all thought," he sneered. "That's my fuckin' life you all were thinking about, you know that? For the last twelve years I gave your fuckin' station my heart and my guts. Five goddamn days a week, year in and year out, I put my ass on the line, giving and taking shit so I could come up with big enough numbers to keep your goddamn advertisers happy!"

"Who are you kidding, Larry," Harrison sniffed disdainfully. "You did what you did because you *are* what you *are* — an ego that walks like a man. And with every year and every call from some dull normal who thinks that you're God's gift to truth and justice, your ego has gotten bigger and bigger, to the extent that it has outstripped both your ability and your value to CKAL."

Larry's voice took on a whining tone. "O.K., I'll take some time off and recharge my batteries. When I come back I'll be better than ever — lots of new ideas and energy. I don't know why I didn't see it right away, but it's a great idea."

"Larry," Riley said with an air of finality. "You're off the show. When you come back from your holiday, I'll find something else for you."

"Something else?" Larry flared. "Like what? A desk job? Shuffling papers? I'm a journalist for chrissake and a damn good one."

"Are you kidding?" Riley said derisively. "The only stories you've broken in the last decade were handed to you on a silver platter by callers or anonymous tipsters. The only digging you've done has been into your desk drawer for a bottle of Scotch." Reacting to Larry's look of surprise, he rushed on. "You thought I didn't know about that? About the liquid courage you need to fortify yourself before you can go on the air?"

Larry looked accusingly at Elaine. "Thanks for nothing."

"It wasn't her," Riley said curtly. "Your ego has bumped into a lot of people at the station and they've got eyes and ears."

"And mouths," Larry spat. "Big, lying mouths."

Riley shook his head pityingly. "Get wise to yourself. You've had your day in the sun. It's time to move on. And it would be best if you did it gracefully."

"You'd like that, wouldn't you?" Larry sneered. "Yeah, you'd like me to just hand your little girlfriend here what I busted my ass for twelve years to build, right?"

Elaine shrank from his tone as much as from his words. "I didn't know anything about this," she began.

"Oh, sure, tell me another one," Larry snapped. "You and Mr. Megabucks here cooked the whole goddamn thing up, didn't you? Well, I'll tell you, Lainie," he said sarcastically, "I didn't know you had it in you. Of course . . ." He paused for effect. "I never knew you had *him* in you either." Jerking his thumb toward Harrison Riley, he began to laugh harshly.

"That's quite enough," Riley said stiffly. "Get out of here. Now." His features tightened. "And if you intend to stay in the business, I'd advise you to send résumés to other parts of the country because you're through in Toronto." He walked briskly to the door and pulled it open, glancing sternly at Larry. "Now, get out."

"See ya around, Lainie baby," Larry snarled as he shuffled toward the door. "Good luck with *my* show." He reached the doorway then turned around, meeting her eyes. "But don't worry. If it doesn't work out, you can always go back to what you do best. After all, selling your body got you this far, didn't it?"

Pete watched the faces of the people lining the hallway as Speedy was led past. It was always the same: curious stares, smirks, and whispered one-liners. It reminded him of bear-baiting, the looks and gestures substituting for the yapping dogs.

Along with his new haircut, Speedy was wearing a dark-blue suit and matching tie and Pete guessed it'd been a long time since he'd looked so straight. All Speedy needed was a briefcase and he could be taken for an up-and-coming executive, except for one thing. Most upwardly mobile executives didn't wear scuffed-up cowboy boots. Pete pulled away from the wall so Speedy could spot him. Catching Pete's eye, he stopped and smiled.

"Hi, man," he said cockily. "You come for the show?"

"Something like that."

"Uh, the wreath . . . Did you, uh. . . ."

The guard who was shackled to Speedy took a step, tugging on the cuffs.

"It's done," Pete said.

Speedy was hustled away but he called back over his shoulder, "Thanks a lot, man."

"Good luck," Pete called back.

Pete found a spot at the press table and opened his notebook. He glanced toward the defence table where Morley Spector was unloading his massive briefcase, neatly stacking up thick binders and law books. Then the lawyer went over to the prisoner's box where he had a whispered conversation with his client, his mouth no more than a couple of inches from Speedy's ear.

All of the supporting cast had filed in and the courtroom was awash with the usual symphony of coughs and rustling.

"All rise." The bailiff's resonant command brought the assemblage to their feet. All eyes swung toward Mr. Justice Alan Nadeau as he strode purposefully toward the bench, his black robe swishing around his legs. Pete caught Speedy's look of alarm and his anxious glance toward his lawyer, but Spector was poring over his notes, oblivious to his client's discomfiture.

While the courtroom gradually fell into an expectant silence, Nadeau rifled through some papers, adjusted his black horn-rims, then ordered the accused to stand.

"Mr. Renner, I see that the indictment against you has been amended, and that you now stand accused of manslaughter in the death of Miss Holly Gains, in that you did unlawfully cause her death, contrary to Section 210 of the Criminal Code of Canada. Do you understand the charge, Mr. Renner?"

"Yes, I do."

"Are you prepared to enter a plea at this time?"

"Yes, sir."

"And how do you plead to this charge? Guilty or not guilty?"

The spectators held their collective breath as Speedy cleared his throat and said in a strong, clear voice: "Guilty, Your Lordship."

A buzz of voices swept through the courtroom, dying only when Nadeau cast a stern eye over the gallery. Hiking the loose-fitting robe a little further up on his bony shoulders, he looked at Speedy with the clinical detachment of a bacteriologist examining a slide containing a rather unexceptional germ culture.

"Mr. Renner, ordinarily, I would reserve judgement, but I have had the opportunity to peruse the submissions made by your counsel and the Crown and I feel, therefore, that I am in a position to hand down a sentence this morning.

"Defence Counsel and the Crown have jointly recommended that you be sentenced to a term of three years and it is customary for a judge to consider such a submission to be a proper basis for sentencing."

Speedy felt the tension drain out of his body. Involuntarily, he nodded his head as though seconding the judge's remarks. Three years, he told himself. He'd be out in one and the organization would look after him, make it up to him for the time he'd spent in the joint. But he no sooner had started to build his castle when he began to see the foundation crumble.

"Although the Crown has accepted the defence position," Nadeau intoned, "that the offence was mitigated by your having ingested a large quantity of alcohol and mood-altering drugs, and has accordingly allowed a reduction of the charge from second-degree murder to manslaughter, this in no way diminishes the seriousness of your crime. You have committed a particularly heinous act. You have deprived a young lady of her life in a most brutal fashion. There is no evidence of provocation, but there *is* evidence that your relationship with the deceased was marked by a pattern of physical violence."

Speedy began to object but was checked by Spector's upraised hand and admonishing expression.

"She was a young girl," Nadeau went on, "confused and frightened, and you preyed upon her to further your own selfish ends. You forced her to sell her body to provide you with money. You used her with no regard for her physical or emotional well-being and then, in a blind, chemically induced rage, you snuffed out the life of a defenceless human being who was little more than a child.''

Speedy had been worked over by cops and had the boots put to him in street fights, but none of those beatings had ever inflicted as much pain as Nadeau's vitriolic tirade. Frustrated and shaken, Speedy tried desperately to catch Spector's attention, but the lawyer sat staring straight ahead with an impassive expression.

"Mr. Renner, as I have said, I generally consider a joint recommendation by counsel very strongly but, in this instance, I am unable to conclude that the interests of justice would be well-served by my sentencing you to a term of three years. Violence is of epidemic proportions in our society and a strong message must be sent to those who would contemplate the taking of a human life. In the interests of both punishment and deterrence, therefore, I hereby sentence you to serve a term of seven years in prison.''

Speedy's mouth opened and closed but no sound came out. Spector came over to him, speaking earnestly but his words couldn't get past Speedy's shock and anger. A pair of sheriff's officers closed in on him, one of them dangling a pair of handcuffs, as Speedy shrieked: "It's a frame-up! I didn't do it! I want a trial!''

Bolting out of the prisoner's box, Speedy dashed past the officers, channelling all his anger and fear into a desperate attempt to reach the hallway. But the aisles were clogged with exiting spectators and he found every potential escape route blocked. Frantically trying to ram his way through a cordon of bodies, he got only a half-dozen yards before the guards jumped him and wrestled him to the floor. Speedy thrashed around violently as one guard dug his knee into Speedy's back while another tried to get the cuffs on him. As each of the guards outweighed Speedy by a good fifty pounds, the struggle was short-lived. When they hauled Speedy to his feet with his hands manacled behind him, his tie was askew and the back of his jacket was split. Blood bubbled out of his nose and onto his upper lip as he continued to scream, his face contorted with rage.

"Let me go ya bastards! Let me go! I'll kill ya! It's a fuckin' frame! I didn't do it!"

By this time, the sheriff's officers were joined by a couple of constables and they carried Speedy out of the courtoom. As they dragged him toward the paddy wagon for the trip to the penitentiary, he made one last attempt to break free, but by then, his energy was spent and his effort was as feeble as it was futile. When the door of the van slammed shut behind him, he huddled in a corner on one of the benches that ran along the walls. Across from him sat a sheriff's officer, looking at him with more distaste than interest. He felt the vehicle start off. As the van turned a corner Speedy's body swayed and his head bumped against the smooth metal wall.

But the next meeting of bone and steel was not an accident. Curling into a ball, Speedy uncoiled his body with a fierce burst of energy, hurling himself backward. His head struck the wall with a sickening crack and he slumped to the floor as if in slow motion.

The guard lit a cigarette, peered at his wristwatch in the dim light, and wondered when they'd be stopping for coffee. Shifting his position, he felt a twinge of pain in the ankle he'd twisted in the scuffle with Speedy.

"Bastard," he hissed at Speedy's moaning form. "Goddamn low-life bastard. They shoulda' fuckin'-well given you life."

Chapter Nineteen

As Pete sat at his kitchen table, sipping on his third cup of coffee, he wondered if it was all worth it. He had two stories in today's edition but knew that neither of them was anything to write home about. However, he was relatively contented with the feature on the city's hookers, in which he'd been able to introduce a little humanity along with the obligatory sensationalism. Yeah, that article was at least passable.

The report on Speedy's court appearance bothered him. Technically, it was O.K., well-written and informative in terms of what had happened in court. But that was the problem. Pete knew that what had happened in the courtroom was only the tip of the iceberg and that he hadn't even managed to hint at what lay below the surface. Consequently, he'd told *a* story rather than *the* story.

The *Herald*'s readers would read that a violence-prone pimp got seven years for killing his girlfriend in a drunken or drugged state. Confirmed in their belief that the system worked and, therefore, required no concern or involvement on their part, they could, in all good conscience, then turn to the funnies and/or Ann Landers. But what about his own conscience? Pete wondered. What was he supposed to do with his recognition that, instead of being a part of journalism's solution, he was as much a part of the problem as anyone else?

Ah, well, he sighed, things weren't totally black. At least he had today off and wouldn't have to cover Jane Chambers' funeral. Even thinking about it made his stomach churn. He hoped Larry had laid off the booze and gotten himself together. It would be rough on him and his daughters and, of course, the media would be out in full force to record every nuance of their sorrow.

Still, Pete thought, the funeral would be a kind of watershed for Jane's loved ones to start putting the tragedy behind them. Time heals all wounds. Too bad time couldn't solve all mysteries too, Pete mused, because it sure as hell doesn't look like anyone is going to be able to explain the execution of Jane Chambers and Alec Vlassos. He had no doubt that Larry, Jane, Vlassos, and Nadeau were all links in a chain leading to Holly Gains' broken body. The trouble was that the chain had a lot of twists and turns and some of the links had huge gaps between them.

It seemed obvious that both the hot-line host and the eminent jurist had both been dipping their wicks into the teenage hooker and it seemed equally apparent that one of them had gone off the deep end and killed her. But which one? The entry in the private eye's notebook pointed to Nadeau as the last person to see Holly alive.

That, combined with his performance in court yesterday, indicated that he had a vested interest in the case. With Speedy in the slammer, Holly's murder could be marked "solved" and there'd be no chance of any embarrassing evidence turning up to implicate a Justice of the Ontario Supreme Court.

Of course, there was very little chance of Vlassos'

notebook showing up anywhere since, according to one of Pete's sources at police headquarters, the private investigator's little black book was missing. Oh, it was on the list of seized items all right, along with the detective's files and the contents of his safe but, unlike the other items, it was no longer in the possession of the homicide squad.

Pete had smelled a few cover-ups in his time, but this one reeked. Someone had deep-sixed the notebook and that someone had to be Mike Edwards. But why? To gain some brownie points with the judge? Or just to make sure that nothing muddied the waters and kept him from wrapping Speedy up in a nice neat package?

It was just a hunch but it was getting stronger all the time. Nadeau. It had to be him. The notebook entry and the feedback from Angie both pointed to Nadeau having the hots for young hookers, and from there, it was just a short leap of logic to Holly's murder. But if he really believed that, Pete wondered, why did Larry Chambers' image keep popping into his mind? Why did he keep thinking about how shaken Chambers had looked when Pete had confronted him with Speedy's accusation? Before he made still another futile attempt to provide some answers, his pager beeped. Taking down the message, he grabbed for the telephone, dialed and heard a single ring before a voice answered with a soft, silky "hello."

"Angie? It's Pete Gossett."

"Oh, hi," she said excitedly. "I just wanted to tell you that that was really an awesome story you did. Like, all the girls are talking about it."

"I'm glad you liked it. I hope I did you justice."

"Oh yeah, it was great, especially that part where you quoted me." There was a pregnant pause and the sound of rustling paper. "Oh yeah, here it is," she said, reading haltingly, "Hooking's got a lot of fringe benefits but it's also got a lot of fringe weirdos." Finishing the quote, she added: "Did I really say that? It sounds really far-out, almost like poetry, y'know?"

"Oh you said it all right," Pete assured her. "I noticed right off that you had a way with words," he added, tongue-in-cheek.

"You did?" She sounded flattered. "Wow. Y'know, I used to write poems when I was in high school but I never showed them to anyone. I was afraid they'd think I was some kind of nerd. But maybe . . ." She hesitated and Pete could almost feel her inner struggle through the telephone. "Maybe you could look at them sometime? Y'know, tell me if they're any good or whether I've got any talent or anything?"

"Well, I'm no expert on poetry but if you think my opinion's worth anything, I'd be glad to look at them."

"Hey, great. Thanks," she bubbled. "Maybe next week —" She cut herself off in mid-sentence with an angry "Christ!"

"What's the matter?"

"You know what?" she asked sheepishly, "I almost goddamn well forgot what I called you about. It's that guy. You know, the one in the picture you showed me?"

"Yeah, what about him?"

"I saw him again."

Pete felt a surge of excitement. "When?"

"Last night. He cruised by a couple of times, then stopped across the street. He was parked there for at least ten minutes and he was staring at me the whole time."

Pete's excitement turned to anxiety. "He didn't try to proposition you, did he?"

"I think he wanted to," she said gaily, "but it looked like he needed a little encouragement."

"Well, you better not give him any."

"I won't," she said, adding coyly, "unless you're around to protect me."

"The best protection is to steer clear of him," he said. "Of course, it wouldn't hurt if you called me as soon as you spotted him instead of waiting till the next day."

"Well, I was going to but. . . ." She broke into a nervous giggle.

"But what?"

"Well, this john in one of those fancy foreign cars called me over and y'know, he wasn't all that bad-looking either. And by the time I got back, that creepy guy in the Chrysler was gone." Sensing Pete's displeasure, she added lamely, "A girl's gotta make a living, y'know."

"I know," he said sourly, "but if you see our creepy looking friend again, call me right away. If you've got some john coming onto you, make him wait a couple of minutes. It won't kill him."

"Maybe it won't kill him," she giggled, "but lots of guys don't wanna wait a couple of minutes. Some of them are so horny, they start to come while we're still talking price."

"Isn't that something." Pete said, feigning interest.

"Yeah, really," she said earnestly. "That's why I never even touch a guy, like, anywhere until after I get the bread, y'know? 'Cause, like this one time, this john grabbed my hand and put it on his dong while we were heading for a spot where we could do it. And you know what happened?"

Pete could almost feel his eyes glazing. "No. What?"

"The motherfucker blew his stones right in his goddamn pants!"

"How about that!"

"And you know something else?"

"No. What?"

"I never got paid," she huffed. "Not a goddamn cent. After the guy drained his prunes, the only thing he was interested in was changing his laundry, so he dumps me out on the street and I had to walk twenty blocks back to my corner."

"It's a helluva thing," Pete sympathized. "A helluva thing."

"You know it," she said bitterly. "Never again, that's for goddamn sure. If I don't get the money in my hand, I sure as hell ain't gonna put anything else in it."

"I don't blame you," Pete said, biting back a chuckle.

"Anyway, I'll call you for sure if I see him again and I won't wait or anything, O.K.?"

"Great. I'd appreciate that. And take care of yourself."

"Hey," she squealed delightly, "are you starting to worry about me or what?"

"Something like that."

"Well, don't. I'm a big girl now and I can take care of myself."

But long after they'd hung up, her words echoed in Pete's consciousness. A big girl. Beneath the paint and sleazy plumage, that's all she really was. A *girl* in a big, dangerous city.

It was obvious that Nadeau had singled Angie out for attention. But why? It could be that he considered her a sexy, attractive candidate for some C.O.D. sex. But there was also the possibility that Angie's look of tainted youthful innocence had made her the lightning rod for the man's homicidal hatred.

Pete was back at work on Monday morning when he got an agitated call from Angie. They arranged to meet for lunch at a King Street diner she'd suggested, but when he arrived there, he had to wait for almost twenty minutes before she put in an appearance.

"Hi, sorry I'm late," she said breathlessly.

"No problem."

She was wearing a purple tank top and faded, formfitting jeans, and without the theatrical makeup and streetwalker gear, she looked much like any other attractive eighteen-year-old girl. Although her face had the unhealthy pallor common to those who work by night and sleep by day, she had good skin and delicate, well shaped features. He found himself staring at her, thinking that he might have had a daughter close to her age if his marriage hadn't fallen apart.

"Whattya looking at?" she asked. "Do I look so freakin' fantastic that you wanna do another article on me?"

He grinned sheepishly. "Yeah, something like that."

A waitress with a sagging body and personality to match took their orders and they studied each other for a few moments before Angie looked down at the table and began hesitantly, "Uh, I got kind of a problem."

"Yeah? What is it?"

"My old man, Bobby. He got busted on Saturday, not long after I talked to you."

"What for?"

"Possession of stolen goods," she said. "This guy owed him some money so Bobby was holding onto some of his stuff until he paid up, y'know?"

Pete nodded. "And he didn't know the stuff was hot?"

She started to shake her head then, changing her mind, nodded slowly. "He knew all right. The truth is, he was going to sell the stuff for the guy."

"Well," Pete frowned thoughtfully, "I think Bobby could use a half-decent lawyer right about now."

"Yeah," she said with a worried look. "Well, he's got one but the guy is coming on like it's gonna be a tough case to fight and he wants a lotta bread up front."

"Most of them do," Pete said wryly.

"Well, what do you think? Should I give it to him?"

"Jeez, that's a pretty hard question for me to answer. The question is: What does Bobby think?"

"He thinks he'll walk easy — that they can't prove he knew the stuff was stolen."

"Well, what kind of stuff did the guy leave with him?"

"A dozen cameras and twenty or thirty tape decks."

Pete had taken a swallow of coffee and had to gulp it down in a hurry to keep from spraying the room. "Holy Christ," he gasped between bursts of laughter, "what did Bobby tell the cops? That he figured all that merchandise was just the guys' personal possessions?"

She gave him an annoyed look. "Hey, it's not funny. Bobby's got a record and he could go up for a year."

Pete forced himself to become serious. "Sorry about that, Angie. I know you're worried and, on the face of it, I'd say you've got something to worry about. Unless Bobby's associate happens to own a department store, it looks as though the cops have a pretty good case against your old man."

"So you think I should front the money to the lawyer?"

"I don't think you've got much choice. Who knows? Maybe he can make a deal — a guilty plea for a fine or a suspended sentence."

She smiled gratefully. "Thanks for the advice. I really didn't have anyone else to turn to."

"That's O.K. Maybe you can do something for me some time like, for example, right now."

"Oh yeah? What?"

"Well, for a start, you could tell me why an attractive, intelligent young lady like yourself is peddling her ass to a bunch of frustrated degenerates."

She stuck out her lower lip in an exaggerated pout. "You tryna hurt my feelings or something? I don't go out with just any old frustrated degenerate, y'know." She giggled. "Just the ones with money."

"That's really funny, Angie," Pete scowled. "But I don't think you'll be able to get out any one-liners when some wacko has his hands around your throat."

She raised her eyebrows mockingly. "Yeah, but think of the story you'd have." She grabbed his hand and stared fiercely into his eyes. "Promise me one thing. Promise me that if I get snuffed, you'll write a whole bunch of stuff about what a nice person I was and how my being killed is such a loss to the world and all that crap. And maybe you could slap on a headline that says something like . . ." She traced an imaginary caption in the air with her forefinger. "Glamorous Hooker Meets Tragic Death." Her eyes sparkled with merriment. "Wouldn't that be far out?"

"Yeah," he said sourly, "that's one way of putting it." He was surprised to realize how much he cared about this wise-assed kid who seemed to care so little about herself.

"Seriously, though," he said. "Why do you do it?"

She thought for a moment. "I don't know. I guess I just want to be somebody."

"And you can be somebody by turning tricks?"

"It's hard to explain," she said, screwing up her face in a concentrated frown, "but, yeah, in a way, you can because at least you're noticed, you're somebody special. You're . . . you're . . ." She groped for the right word. "wanted."

"Yeah," Pete sniffed. "But for what, and for how long?"

She answered the question with one of her own. "How many people out there," she said jerking her head toward the street, "walk around every day without anybody even noticing them, like they're part of the scenery or something, like a goddamn lamppost?"

"Maybe they couldn't care less that no one knows they're alive. Maybe it's enough that they know it themselves."

"Hey," she said, eyeing him suspiciously, "are you saying that I don't know I'm alive? 'Cause if you are, you are way off base because I am into more shit than you can believe. Listen, I've got a full goddamn life and it's just gonna get better and better."

Pete smiled apologetically. "Sorry about that. I guess I came on a little strong. I usually don't sermonize like that until I've downed about half a twenty-six of Scotch."

"That's O.K.," she smiled. "I kinda like it that you care enough about me to stick your face into my business."

After leaving the restaurant, they stood on the sidewalk amid the flow of pedestrians. Angie looked up at him with a searching gaze. "You really want to get the goods on that four-eyed creep with the Chrysler, don't you?"

"Yeah," he said. "I really do."

"Is that because you want to keep more hookers from being wasted or because you want to get a real bitchin' story out of it?"

Pete thought for a while. "A little bit of both, I guess," he said, surprised at how easy it was to be honest with her.

"Well, I'm gonna help you get it."

"What?" he asked, genuinely perplexed.

"That big story you want."

"What do you mean?"

"You'll see," she chirped.

He grabbed her roughly by the wrist. "Don't do anything foolish. If my hunch is right, there's a nutcase out there — a guy who gets his jollies from wrapping his hands around girls' necks. Be careful." His fingers pressed the admonition into her flesh. "You hear me? Be careful."

"Hey, I can look after myself," she said, patting her handbag. "I got protection."

"I don't care what you've got," he said heatedly. "I don't want you ending up on a slab."

She started to walk away, and then stopped and turned back. "Anybody ever tell you that you're a worrier?"

"Only my ex-wife," he said, "but that was when she was screwing around on me."

She began to giggle, and then they were laughing together in a time and space so right in a world that had gone so dangerously wrong.

Pete helped Linda clear away the dinner plates, setting them on the kitchen counter. "Let me help you with the dishes."

"It's O.K., I've got a dishwasher. All I have to do is stack them in it and modern technology does the rest."

"I know," he grinned. "That's why I volunteered."

While waiting for the coffee to perk, they sat on the living room sofa, sipping liqueur and watching the rain shimmer against the night sky.

"So what do you feel like now?" Pete asked. "A movie? Dancing?"

She wrinkled her nose. "I don't know if I feel like going out in that downpour."

"But there's a great band at the Bamboo Club and dancing —"

"Is yooooooouuur life," she broke in, fixing him with an indulgent smile.

He frowned ruefully. "I'm going to have to come up with some new lines."

"Your old ones are all right," she said, giving his hand a consoling pat.

"So you really want to stay in on a Saturday night?"

"Maybe we can go out later, but right now, I'd just like to relax and feel mellow and have a nice conversation with my favourite man." She dropped her hand onto his and smiled dreamily up at him.

"A conversation?" he said, feigning deep concentration. Then suddenly, he snapped his fingers and his face lit up. "Oh yeah, I remember now. That's what people used to have before they invented TV."

She rolled her eyes toward the ceiling, murmuring: "Give me strength." Then, becoming serious, she said: "There *is* something I want to talk to you about."

Caught by the gravity in her voice, Pete looked at her closely.

"I'm leaving Toronto," she said quietly.

"Leaving Toronto?" He shook his head in disbelief. "You've got to be kidding. This is the greatest city in Canada. Where else could you find such overpriced glitz and such condescension toward other regions of the country?"

"Probably nowhere," she smiled. "But I'm going to Vancouver anyway."

"Vancouver?" he howled. "Lotusland North? What're you looking for? A place to retire to, or a secure supply of drugs?"

She sighed wearily. "I guess in a way, I do want to retire. I want to retire from being my sister's keeper and from all the other things that are making it too much of a hassle to stay here."

"Such as?"

"Such as Jack Lexer."

"What the hell's he got to do with it?"

"He knows we've been seeing each other and he doesn't like it."

"He doesn't, eh?" Pete fumed. "Well, screw him. Does he figure he can just snap his fingers and you split for Vancouver and I go and club seals in Labrador?"

He squeezed Linda's hand. "Don't worry about Lexer. He's not going to do anything to you. The stakes have to be a lot higher than this before he'll turn his hoods loose."

"It's not the physical stuff I'm worried about."

"So what's the problem?"

"The problem is that I get most of my leads through Lexer and his friends and if you don't have clients, you can't sell real estate."

Pete smiled caustically. "Lexer's got all kinds of ways of putting the squeeze on, hasn't he?"

"You'd better believe it."

He tried to keep his voice light. "Well, good luck."

"Thanks."

The silence yawned between them until she spoke again. "You could probably get a job with a paper on the coast, couldn't you?"

He shrugged. "Maybe. I know a few people out there."

"But you don't want to leave Toronto, right?"

"Something like that, I guess."

"But why Toronto? Can't you be an investigative journalist in Vancouver, Edmonton, or Winnipeg?"

He thought for a while. "Probably, but it'd be a different scene. Toronto may not be the big time but it's the closest thing to it that we've got in this country. This is where the action is, where there's enough money, power, and excitement to create an illusion that we're more than an American ant farm with Uncle Sam tapping the side of the terrarium whenever it looks as though we might we getting out of line."

She was poised to respond when Pete's pager emitted an electronic squeak. She watched his features harden as he monitored the message. He sprang to his feet and bolted toward the door, calling back over his shoulder, "Sorry, my love, but duty calls."

"Business?"

He stopped and turned toward her, his face dark with anxiety. "Yeah, business," he said tightly. "I'll give you a call later and let you know what's shaking."

"Don't bother," she said, then, in response to his quizzical look, added huskily, "Just come back. I'll be waiting."

He tried to smile but all he could manage was a twisted grimace and a hoarse "take care" before the elevator swallowed him up on a swift descent to the rain, the night, and to a race with death.

Pete gripped the steering wheel tightly, staring past the windshield wipers as they swept away the pelting rain. The message Angie had left with his answering service had knotted his stomach with fear: "The creep in the picture is cruising the strip."

Cursing the traffic and the rain, he barrelled toward the inner city, unconsciously leaning forward, urging the car on with his body as he shot away from stoplights. Careening onto Jarvis, he braked sharply and pulled over to the curb, squinting through the downpour. The rain had discouraged the usually brisk trade but there were still a few cars cruising slowly by, the drivers gawking at the half-dozen hookers who'd had the foresight to equip themselves with umbrellas.

Pete put the car in drive and let it creep forward. Then he saw her. Parading seductively beneath a multicoloured umbrella and bending slightly at the waist in a kind of semi-curtsy, Angie was peering into the interiors of the slowly circling cars.

He was still fifty or sixty yards away when a sleek, black, luxury car passed him and pulled over to the curb directly in front of Angie. Pete shut off the engine and sprang out of the car in one motion. He splashed down the sidewalk, the rain pouring down his face. He was within forty yards of the car now, close enough to see that it was a Chrysler. And close enough to see Angie give him a brief smile of recognition before she pulled the door open and slid inside. Pete was sprinting but the Chrysler had already begun to pick up speed. He raced back to his car and gunned the motor. The tires whirred and spun before getting traction on the slick pavement, as he hunched over the wheel, straining to pick out the car's taillights.

He knew he had to pick up the trail right away or the car, and Angie, could be lost forever. Spotting a set of taillights half a block away, he prayed they were the right ones. A right turn and they disappeared. Pete followed and picked them up again, guessing that Nadeau was doubling back onto Jarvis. But why? Maybe he'd changed his mind and was going back to drop Angie off. But no, when the Chrysler hit Jarvis, it turned left, instead of right, heading north.

Breathing shallowly, Pete followed, keeping a good hundred yards behind them and trying to decide what to do next. His first impulse was to cut Nadeau off and drag Angie out of the car. But what the hell would that prove? He had no hard evidence that the judge was guilty of anything beyond lusting after young hookers and, if that was a crime, he told himself, the jails would be a helluva lot more crowded than they are now.

No, he decided, if Nadeau was the warped son of a bitch who was getting his jollies from strangling teenage hookers, confronting him could do more harm than good. It would tip him off that he was under suspicion; he'd be that much more cautious and the chances of nailing him would be reduced. No, if he was going to be run to earth, it would have to be tonight, before some other streetcorner angel of mercy had her last breath squeezed out of her throat.

The Chrysler turned right onto Bloor, then a short time later veered left onto Mount Pleasant Road. Where the hell was he going? Pete worried. They'd reached the outskirts of Balfour Park before it hit him. The route they were following would take them right through the heart of Mount Pleasant Cemetery. Sweat began to bead his forehead. It was probably the most scenic cemetery in the city with its rolling hills, arching trees, and winding lanes. But tonight, the driving rain and starless sky would turn the serpentine thoroughfares into a labyrinth and turn the trees and hills into an obstacle course for prying eyes.

Pete's attention was jerked back to the taillights. They were bigger, closer. Much closer than he wanted. He glanced down at the speedometer. He'd maintained the same steady speed which meant that the Chrysler had slowed down. He hadn't been paying enough attention and now, he had no choice. If he slowed down as well, Nadeau couldn't help but realize that he was being followed. Accelerating slightly, he came up beside the Chrysler, and then quickly passed, making sure he kept his face averted even though the dense rain and inky night would have made it almost impossible for anyone to recognize him.

Now, he was in the lead. It wasn't what he wanted but he felt that as long as he kept Nadeau's headlights behind him, Angie was safe. But suppose the judge was wise to him and tried to lose him? Suppose — Pete froze in mid-thought. The glare in his rearview mirror had vanished. The headlights had disappeared.

Pete jammed on the brakes, and making a frantic U-turn, raced back down the road, scanning the dark, headstone-covered tracts on both sides. His mind raced wildly. Angie had trusted him. Risked her life. And he'd blown it. Cutting sharply to the right, he followed a narrow, winding lane that took him deeper into the graveyard, past bleached crosses and grey, granite headstones. Nothing. No sign of them. Not a trace of the car. The road ended in a circular cul-de-sac and he found himself returning the way he'd come.

Where now? What should he do? Call the police? No, it'd be too late. Maybe it already was.

There. Another road. Veering to the left, he swivelled his head frantically from side to side, sweeping his gaze over rose-coloured crypts fronted by black lattices of steel. He gulped back the panic. Oh God, let me find her. Oh God. Then he saw it. The Chrysler.

If he'd been driving any faster, he might have missed it. It was about fifty yards up a service road, and pulled off to the side. The lights were out but Pete could clearly make out the silhouette and the gleam of the rear bumper. He shut off his lights and turned into the lane, stopping a dozen yards behind the parked vehicle.

As he got out of his car, the rain whipped against his face, momentarily blinding him. Blinking the water out of his eyes, he crept forward. Within seconds, his hair was matted and he felt a cold trickle down his neck. He was at the Chrysler now, brushing against the rear fender, crouching slightly and trying to see through the back window. Nothing. There was no sign of anyone.

Instinctively, he wheeled around, scanning the rows of headstones. When he turned back, he still had the feeling that someone was watching, waiting. Momentarily lifting his eyes toward the car roof, he recoiled in fear; staring down at him was the face of an alabaster angel with spreading wings poised for flight. Wrenching his gaze from the towering monument, he began to creep around to the passenger side, and then stopped in his tracks, listening. It was a couple of seconds before he realized that the monotonous whirr and click was coming from the car's windshield wipers.

He was beside the front door now, raising his head, straining to see through the rain-pebbled glass. Suddenly, his legs felt weak. His hands, and then his entire body, began to shake. He looked up and again found himself staring into the face of the stone angel. Rain was coursing down its face like rivers of tears shed for the suffering of all God's creatures. He forced himself to turn back to the window, to wipe the rain off the glass with his palm and look again.

The nightmare crystallized. The pale splash became a chalk-white face. The dark smears became wide, terror-filled eyes. He grabbed at the car for support, his fingernails scraping against the glossy metal surface, as a single, strangled cry burst from his throat: "Angie!"

Chapter Twenty

They sat in the airport lounge draining the last of their drinks. "Funny how things work out, isn't it?" Linda said, frowning.

"Hilarious."

"I'm serious."

"So am I," he said sourly.

"C'mon," she scolded, "at least try to make an effort. Who knows how long it'll be until we see each other again."

He pushed up the corners of his mouth with his index fingers. "There. How's that?"

"Oh, that's just marvellous," she said sarcastically. "You really brighten up a room with that cheery personality of yours."

"That's the kind of guy I am," he said breezily. "Warm, giving, and —"

"Full of crap," she cut in.

"You certainly have a way with words," he said. "Have you ever thought of going into journalism?"

"No," she shot back. "Have you?"

"Hey, that's good," he marvelled, pointing to his heart. "Went all the way through without drawing any blood."

Pete paid the tab and as they walked through the vast terminal holding hands, he caught her checking her wristwatch. "I guess you're pretty anxious to start winging your way westward, eh?"

"I'd be a lot more excited if you were going with me."

He glanced away. "Maybe one of these days. . . ."

"That's a crock," she snapped. "You'll never leave Toronto. This is where you've chosen to make your last stand and fight a war no one else knows or cares about. You're like those shrivelled old Japanese soldiers who turn up from time to time on South Pacific islands. Even though the war's been over for forty years, they're still willing to die for emperor and country."

"Just call me Kamikaze Gossett," he grinned.

She shook her head pityingly. "Don't you remember? You're the one who's always saying that TV newscasts are geared to those with attention spans of less then fifteen seconds and that newspapers should be printed on toilet paper so they'd serve at least one useful purpose."

He smiled sheepishly. "Sounds like me all right."

"It sure does," she said.

"It's funny," he said thoughtfully. "Every year, I tell myself I'll give it just one more shot. Then the years go by and I realize that there are a helluva lot more chances behind me than there are in front."

She looked at him searchingly. "I know you don't want to talk about it, and we don't have much time, but you never really told me what happened that night."

"What night is that?"

"Don't play the innocent with me," she shot back. "You know what I'm talking about. What you've tried to avoid even mentioning for the past week. What happened when you rushed out of my apartment that night — the night of the murder?"

He chuckled mirthlessly. "You really want to know what happened? Well, I can tell you in three words. I blew it." He nodded slowly, staring into space. "Yeah, I guess there's no getting around it. I blew it, all right."

"But how?" she pressed. "What went wrong? Wasn't that message about the killing?"

"Uh, no," he lied. "It was something else. A tip about a big drug bust that was supposed to be going down at one of the mob's nightclubs. The word was that there were a lot of big names involved and I'd get the story of my life if I hustled my buns down there."

"So what happened?"

"That's the problem. Bugger all. I went into the club and waited for the narcs to show but the tip turned out to be a bum steer. The only thing that went down was a lot of booze into yours truly. And that's why I missed out on the biggie."

"You mean the murder."

"That's right. I was so pissed off that I got dragged away from you for a wild-goose chase that I kept knocking back the Scotch and got kind of bent out of shape. Somehow, I managed to shut off my pager, and the newsroom couldn't reach me when they picked up the report of the murder on the police band. So, to make a long, painful story short but no less painful, that's how the *Post* managed to get a front-page story of another sensational murder and I managed to get shipped back to the sports beat."

"That's why they put you back on sports? Just because you missed a story?"

"Well, the thing is," Pete explained, "it wasn't just *a* story. It was the fifth killing in Toronto the Good within two weeks and city editors tend to consider something like that fairly newsworthy."

"Do you think they'll give you another chance?"

"In the jungle of big-city journalism, nobody gives you anything," he said bitterly. "If you want something, you've got to take it and usually from someone who already has it."

They remained silent for several seconds. They both felt

the sadness, the sense of impending loss, closing in around them and knew that nothing they could say would change things. Finally, it was time for her to leave. She forced a smile.

"You know, I just might have stayed if . . ." Her smile fluttered. "If you'd asked me to."

"I know," he said softly. "And I just might have asked you if I thought I could give you what you need and deserve."

Her expression was a combination of surprise and anger. "Did you ever stop to think that what I want and need is you?"

He blinked at her in bewilderment. "To tell the truth, no, because I always figured that there was a limited demand for guys with big ideas and small prospects."

Her eyes were full of hurt. "You could have let me decide that."

He shook his head. "I have enough trouble dealing with my own decisions, let alone someone else's."

They kissed, and as she pulled away, she whispered, "Will I see you again?"

He held her at arm's length and tried to smile. "You never know. . . ."

"That's not much of an answer."

"It's the best I can manage right now."

With a flash of temper, she pulled away. He followed her to the departure gate where she stopped and turned to face him. "Would it be a waste of time if I wrote to you, and let you know where I'm living?"

"No," he said softly. "I'd like that."

They kissed again and then she was gone. As he watched her pass through the scanner, then round the corner toward the departure lounge, he could hear the slam of a door somewhere deep inside him. It was the same sound he'd heard so many times before.

Then his expression softened. This time, it was different. This time, there was no click of a lock; no sense of finality. And as he turned and walked slowly out of the terminal, he heard her question echoing in his mind. "Will I see you again?" And now he knew the answer was a resounding, smiling, "Yes."

The young, gum-chewing waitress hovered over him, pencil poised over her pad. "What would you like?"

"Just coffee," Pete said.

When she returned with the steaming cup, he spooned in some sugar, then sat staring at the murky liquid. It was black and impenetrable and, given his present mood, he felt it could serve as a metaphor for human existence. He sensed her presence before seeing her, and looking up, he nodded a greeting as she flopped into the seat across from him. She sent him a smile across the narrow table and, dropping his spoon onto the saucer, he returned it.

"Hi, Angie. How're you doing?"

"Not bad. How about you?"

"Could be worse." He signalled the waitress and Angie ordered a Coke and some french fries.

Between mouthfuls of fries and swallows of her drink, she hit him with a barrage of questions. He silenced her with a warning look and a shake of his head. "Wait'll we get out of here."

When she was finished and he'd paid the cheque, they walked down Bathurst Street, past the motley crew of bargain hunters waiting for Honest Ed's to throw open its doors and admit the faithful to kitsch heaven: old women with kerchiefs in spite of a temperature in the mid-seventies; middle-aged men in workclothes; washed-out looking housewives who'd raised stoicism to an art form.

Although Angie had been hard-pressed to contain her curiosity when they were in the restaurant, after they were seated in Pete's car, it was he who led off the questioning. "Have the cops been questioning the girls?"

"Not as far as I know. At least, none of them have said anything to me about it."

He gave a long sigh of relief. "That's good news."

"Yeah," she nodded. "It's bad enough having to be out on the street without them coming around because, y'know, I really don't know if I could handle that. That's why I wanted to pack it in for a while."

"I know," Pete said. "But it wouldn't have looked good if you'd suddenly disappeared. Even the cops can put two and two together and come up with four, at least fifty per cent of the time."

She nodded solemnly and looked at him with a shyness that belied her street-wise image. "It was really awful this past week, wanting to talk to you and see you and not being able to."

"Couldn't be helped," he said. "I thought it would be best if we kept away from each other for a while — at least until things cooled down a bit and we could see which way the wind was blowing."

He started the car, aware that she was staring at him. A disquieting thought flew into his mind and he shot an anxious look toward her. "You didn't say anything to anyone, did you?"

Angie shook her head. "No way."

"Not even your old man?"

She made a face. "Are you kidding? He'd be the last one I'd tell. Besides, he's in the bucket. He got three months for that possession beef and there's no way I'm gonna visit him. And when he gets out, I ain't gonna see him any more."

Pete's face brightened. "Does that mean you're going to pack in the whole scene and stop tricking?"

"Yeah," she smiled proudly. "Things have changed. Maybe *I've* changed. But all I know is that I don't want to turn tricks any more." She frowned pensively, struggling to find the right words. "The thing is, I always used to think that I was just selling my body, but I found out that when somebody buys your ass, they also get everything else, even that part way deep inside — the real you, the one you think

you can keep safe, just for yourself no matter what's happening with the rest of you."

Pete's ear-to-ear grin crinkled the corners of his eyes.
"That's great," he said, adding: "Hell, that's better than
great. It's freaking fantastic."

"Well, I want you to know," she began slowly, feeling her
way, "that like, why I'm getting my shit together and everything? Well, it's got a lot to do with you — with the way you
cared about me."

He grimaced painfully. "Hey, gimme a break. Keep that
up and it's liable to get around that I'm not the cynical,
unfeeling rat-bastard everyone thinks I am." He feigned a
wounded look. "It took me a long time to cultivate that
reputation, you know."

Angie ignored his banter. "Thanks," she said simply.
"Thanks for doing what you did and putting your ass on the
line for a ditzy, spaced-out hooker."

He resisted the impulse to toss out another glib retort, instead saying quietly: "You're welcome."

"You wouldn't have done it for just anybody, would
you?"

"No," he said huskily. "Not for just anybody."

Her smile was open and ingenuous, a different kind of
smile for Angie; free of guile, greed, and ersatz lust.

He let her out on Parliament Street. She took a few steps
then stopped and called back. "Is it all right if I call you
every once in a while? Y'know, just to, like, see what's going
down?"

"Sure," he shouted back. "I'd like that."

She flashed him a quicksilver smile and headed down the
sidewalk, switching her buns from side to side. Then suddenly
she slowed down, straightened up and, checking the exaggerated sway of her hips, continued on her way.

As Pete eased the car into the stream of midday traffic, he
felt so proud that if he hadn't been so repressed and macho,

he might have cried. Instead, he contented himself with swallowing hard, blinking a couple of times, and muttering to himself: "Strange business. Yeah, definitely strange business."

Pete dropped the receiver on its cradle, got up and switched on the TV. He was disappointed, but not particularly surprised, that Elaine had turned down his dinner invitation. He'd heard via the media grapevine that she and Harrison Riley were — to use a phrase popularized by gossip rags — an item.

Well, good luck to her, he thought, his sour expression belying the wish. Not that Elaine hadn't already had more than her share — a boyfriend with big bucks and a station manager position at CKAL. Not bad at all. It had struck Pete as somewhat odd that she'd taken an administrative job, even one so high up in the station's hierarchy. When Elaine had filled in for Larry a few weeks back, she'd really seemed to thrive on being a hot-line guru and Pete had thought that she'd fallen victim to the star syndrome. It'd also been rumoured that Larry was on his way out as the station's hot-line host and that Elaine was the heir-apparent. Yet, this morning, there was Chambers back on the air, as abrasive, combative, and opinionated as ever. Oh, well, he mused, so much for rumours.

He poured himself a shot of Scotch and settled in to watch the evening news. The funeral had been held that morning and Pete figured that it was newsworthy enough to command a spot high up in the line up. But even though his eyes were fixed on the screen, his mind was turned inward.

No matter how hard he tried, he couldn't stop himself from reliving that horrible night, and flashing-back to the episode that continued to torture his sleep with hellish hallucinations: fountains of gushing blood, gaping wounds — the flesh peeled back, showing pink, shiny tissue purple tendons and jagged bone.

Like a projectionist showing the same movie over and over, he saw himself getting out of his car. Creeping through the rain. Reaching the passenger side of the black sedan. Seeing Angie's face, pale as a shroud, her eyes mirroring unspeakable horror. Pulling the door open. Smelling the musky scent of blood. Hearing it gurgle and listening to the hiss of breath seeping out of dying lungs like air from a rapidly deflating tire.

The body had been sprawled across the car's front seat with the back of his head resting against the window, one arm draped over the steering wheel and the other shielding his face. That was when Pete had seen the throat and the dark fluid spurting from what had looked like a second mouth.

The sight had put Pete's stomach on a roller-coaster. He'd reeled away from the gory scene, and had retched violently at the side of the sodden road. By the time he'd pulled himself together and returned to the car, Angie had emerged from her catatonic state and her scream had exploded the silence, flooding the cemetery with a rising tide of hysteria. He'd had to slap her to jar her back to reality — a reality that still made his body shake and his mind rebel against what seemed like an obscene caricature of violence.

Pete had lugged Angie to his car, where he'd managed to coax the story from her, one halting word at a time. While Angie had continued with her sobbing recitation and Pete had made some sketchy notes, he'd been torn by conflict. One part of him had wanted to hold her and comfort her while another looked and listened with cool detachment, cataloguing facts and storing quotes. When Angie was halfway through her story, he'd already composed the lead paragraph of an exclusive, eye-witness account that he was confident would catapult him to the top of the journalistic leap. This was it, he had thought, the big one he'd been waiting for.

Now, all he could do was pick through ruins and wonder how so much could have gone wrong so quickly. He absently picked up his notebook and thumbed through it until he came to the notes he'd made that fatal night — fatal to his career, as well as in a more literal sense. Keeping one ear tuned to the TV, he started to read some of Angie's quotes.

"He said that I was just like the others. Just garbage, and that no matter how much perfume whores like me splashed on, it could never cover up the stink. He said I was stinking up his car the way tramps stunk up the whole world and that there was only one way to clean up the city. Then he turned down this road and stopped. It was dark, but I could see his eyes real good and they looked like they were on fire. Then he started asking me about the girls who got killed — Holly and the other one — and asked if I had any idea who done it.

"I felt cold all over. I couldn't even think, I was so scared and I don't remember hardly anything about what happened after that. I just remember him sliding down the seat toward me with this real ugly look on his face. Then, somehow — I don't know how it got there — the razor, the straight razor I carry for protection — was in my hand. And I just closed my eyes and kind of swung out with it.

"I never even felt it hit anything but all of a sudden, I heard this sound, kind of like an 'uuuuuhhhh,' and I opened my eyes. He had his hand over his throat and he was staring at me like he couldn't believe what happened and his hand was turning all dark from the blood coming out between his fingers.

"He reached over to start the car but then just kind of fell back, real slowly. Then everything got real fuzzy and I felt like I was falling, deeper and deeper and faster and faster. The next thing I remember is seeing your face, only it didn't really look like you. It looked kinda like *him*, and that's why I freaked out."

After she'd finished, Pete remembered reaching for his two-way radio, and then quickly drawing back his hand. He'd gotten his story — probably the biggest one in his entire career — but he'd suddenly realized that he'd never be able to tell it. He'd run over the facts in his mind: one of the city's most prominent citizens has his throat slashed by a teenage hooker. Hooker pleads self-defence but the victim hadn't laid a finger on her. Who would believe that one of the city's pillars of society had a compulsion to stalk and strangle young prostitutes? Who would believe that Angie had sliced away the judge's life while desperately fighting to save her own?

The answers had been obvious to Pete. Even in the feverish state he had been in, he'd realized that neither the police nor the Attorney General's department would come close to buying Angie's story. They'd gloss over the fact that Nadeau had picked her up and focus on his death, depicting it as a nice, simple case of murder. Since there'd been no witnesses, the jury would have to take the word of the razor-wielding prostitute that she'd acted in self-defence. She wouldn't have a chance. The only question would be whether she'd be convicted of second- or first-degree murder and spend ten or twenty-five years in prison.

At that moment, with his rain-soaked shirt clinging to him like wet seaweed, he'd known he couldn't let that happen. Angie had been victimized enough already and he wasn't about to deliver the *coup de grace*, especially when the only crime she had been guilty of was being so goddamn eager to please that she'd risked her life to hand him a good story.

At least, that was what he'd believed as he left Angie huddled on the front seat of his car and made a return trip to the Chrysler. By then, he'd regained his composure and had known what he had to do. His first move had been to search for the razor. He'd found it on the floor on the passenger side and, after wiping off both the blade and the handle, he'd wrapped it in his handkerchief and shoved it into his pocket. Then he had set to work wiping off every part of the car's interior that he thought Angie might have touched. He'd finished off by vigorously rubbing the handle on the passenger side with his shirt-tail.

Then, just before he'd left the vehicle, he had forced

himself to take another look at the corpse. The arm covering the face had shifted slightly, showing some of his features. Enough for Pete to realize that the dead man behind the wheel wasn't his nominee as the perpetrator of the hooker murders. To his shock and horror, he'd discovered that the sprawled body and the throat that had looked like half a pound of chopped sirloin did *not* belong to Mr. Justice Alan Nadeau.

The anchor man's intro to the next news item jarred Pete back to the present. He listened intently as an earnest young reporter did a stand-up at the gate of the cemetery with the cortege slowly passing in the background. Then the film cut to the obligatory shots of the bereaved family and friends at the graveside and followed with some wide shots of the police honour guard and close ups of local and national dignitaries. Finally, after a short clip of the minister celebrating the deceased's entry into a better world, the item ended with another stand-up by the reporter, whose voice was charged with emotion.

"Today," he solemnly intoned, "has been a sad day for law-enforcement officials both in Toronto and across the country. Police officers from all parts of Canada have come to pay homage to a fallen comrade, a man who gave his life in the line of duty, a man by the name of Detective Sergeant Michael J. Edwards, who will not soon be forgotten by the citizens of Toronto whom he served so well."

Switching off the TV, Pete poured himself another drink, and then left it untouched as he stared bleakly at the wall. God, he thought, he'd had his share of screw-ups over the years, but this time, he'd outdone himself. All of the meticulously crafted scenarios he'd devised had turned out to have as much substance as an anorexic ghost. While he'd been plotting to trap Nadeau and entertaining suspicions about Larry Chambers' part in the murders, he'd completely ignored Edwards. Ignored what Linda had told him about the cop's twisted mentality. Ignored the caper with Speedy's clock. Edwards hadn't doctored it just to nail Speedy. *He'd done it to cover his own ass.*

Free to continue his murderous campaign against the city's prostitutes, Edwards had come close to tallying another victim: Angie. Even now, it was hard for Pete to come to grips with just how far off the mark he'd been. But it had been a lot worse when it had first hit him, when he'd looked past the dead man's shielding arm and seen Edwards' distinctive eyes, pale skin, and rust-coloured brushcut. He'd almost collapsed from the mind-shattering revelation. It was only later, after Angie had recovered enough to speak coherently, that he'd gotten the full story. And he found that he'd been wrong about some little things as well as a lot of big ones.

He shook his head with disgust. Some hotshot investigative reporter he was, he told himself derisively. Thanks to him, Angie had been on the lookout for Nadeau and that was why she'd thought nothing of taking off with Edwards. Hell, she'd figured he was just another john in a fancy car. She hadn't been trying to trap a killer, but to turn a fast trick.

He sat listening to the sounds of the city, then suddenly shot to this feet, strode into the kitchen, and poured the shot of Scotch into the sink. Then he went back into the living room, walked over to the window, and leaned against the sill. Looking down at the street, he let his mind drift. How many violent fantasies would be transformed into tragic reality tonight? he wondered. Where and when would the demons appear again? No matter how well you know them, violence and death are forever strangers, and no matter how much you love the city, it doesn't always love you back.

He checked the yellow pages then picked up the phone and dialled Air Canada.

"I'd like to book a flight to Vancouver for next Wednesday, please."

"Return?"

He paused before answering. "No. Make it one-way. I'm

not quite sure about my plans yet. But that's the good thing about life, isn't it? You've always got choices.''

"Pardon me?'' the young female voice answered.

"Oh, nothing,'' he laughed. "I was just thinking about life.''

"Oh . . . yes,'' she said vaguely, as though the concept were new to her.

Later, he phoned Linda. She seemed excited to hear that he was coming to the coast. Hell, so was he. He'd never been much for the great outdoors but he was really looking forward to seeing the mountains and the ocean. Who knows? He might become a beach bum. And if he never managed to learn how to swim, he told himself, he might at least finally get the hang of staying afloat.

Larry pulled up his coat collar as he stepped into the crisp, fall night. The contrast between the cold, clean air and the close, smoky press club shocked his senses. But that was what he needed to clear his head. God, he mumbled to himself, it'd been a helluva long time since he'd drunk this much.

He'd pretty well gone on the wagon since Jane's funeral but had felt that, tonight of all nights, he was entitled to knock a few back and let loose a little. The trouble was, now he was *too* goddamn loose, particularly his legs. Still, it really wasn't his fault, because how the hell was a guy supposed to stay sober when his buddies wanted to celebrate his success by pushing drinks on him?

Buddies. That was a laugh, he sniffed. They were the same ones who'd been laughing up their sleeves a couple of months back when it'd looked as though he was going to be given the old heave-ho. Yeah, everyone loves a winner all right.

And that's what he was. He was the king of the airwaves again, crowned by the latest BBM ratings book. And that fucking pretty-boy, Trent Ferguson, was where he belonged — in second place. Second place for a second-class journalist, he smirked.

Goddamn sidewalks, he grumbled, as he stubbed his toe on a ridge of concrete and had to struggle to keep his balance. Gotta do a show about the piss-poor job the city is doing maintaining the public infrastructure. Yeah, he'd tear a strip off those deadheads at city hall, all right.

Larry's car was the only one left in the parking lot but, after all, it was almost one A.M. Fumbling his car keys out of his pocket, he fleetingly wondered if he should be driving. Ah, what the hell, he finally concluded, as he slid into the Cadillac, all the cops are probably sitting in donut shops anyway.

He inserted the key in the ignition but made no move to start the car. Instead, he leaned back, staring through the windshield with a fixed, euphoric smile. He hadn't felt this good in — he didn't know how long. Funny the way things worked out. A couple of months ago, he was going down for the third time and now, he was on top of the world. He couldn't take all the credit though. There'd been a little luck involved.

When Larry had told Lexer that Riley was giving him the chop, he'd had no idea that Jack was a silent partner in Harrison's corporate empire. His smile widened as he recalled Lexer's words: "Don't worry. You're staying where you are. When I make a suggestion to Riley, he don't say no."

Jack had been as good as his word, which meant that Harrison had been forced to find another cushy job for Elaine. He wondered if Ken Jessup was still out of work. It must've really hit Jessup hard to be tossed on the scrap heap at his age but that, Larry observed, was the way the world wobbled. It was amazing how high the turnover was in this business. Why, even Pete Gossett was now on civvy street. That had really surprised Larry since he'd always figured that the only way Gossett would leave journalism would be feet first. But now, he was supposed to be on the west coast somewhere, doing public relations work for a forestry company and writing a book.

Oh, well, he sighed contentedly, some of us can hack it and some can't. Still, at least Pete was alive and kicking. That couldn't be said for the scumbag who'd killed Holly, that fucking Renner. Just that morning, Larry had received word that Speedy Renner had been knifed to death in his cell at the Kingston Penitentiary. An investigation was being conducted but, so far, there was no indication of who did it, or why. The scuttlebutt was that Renner had been shooting his mouth off and dropping the names of some important people. Larry surmised that that wasn't the best way for a two-bit punk like Renner to assure himself of a long and happy life.

Larry started the car and eased out into the deserted street. Dianne and Arlene would be sleeping when he got home. There'd be no one to talk to; no one to share his triumph with; no one to make him feel important and wanted. Suddenly, he felt hollow inside. He still missed Jane so much, it hurt to think of her. She had been such a large part of his life and, now that she was gone, he had nothing to replace her with. A fierce yearning crept up on him; the combination of loneliness and desire coursing through him like a quick-acting drug.

Instead of heading for home, he found himself driving aimlessly through the inner city. The car seemed to have a mind of its own and he was almost surprised when he realized that he was cruising down Jarvis in a slow-moving procession with several other vehicles. He glanced toward the sidewalk and spotted the usual array of hookers, standing or strutting along the curb, and miming a sexual menu.

He shook his head disgustedly. They never learn, he thought. A couple of months ago, they'd been in a panic, wondering if death had drawn their number, and now, it was as though nothing had ever happened, as though the two slain prostitutes had never existed. Larry started to press down on the accelerator, then felt something stir deep inside him. It wasn't so much a desire to be with someone as an intense need not to be alone, he thought, as he pulled over to the curb and braked. He rolled down the window on the passenger side and waited for the blonde in the red spandex slacks to slink over. She bent down, smiling at him. The heavy makeup did little to camouflage the fact that she was still in her mid-teens.

"Wanta go out?" she inquired seductively.

He looked up at her and smiled.

"Sure. Why not? I've got a couple of hours to kill."

We hope you have enjoyed this KNIGHTSBRIDGE book.

We love good books just as you do, so you can be assured that the KNIGHT ON THE HORSE stands for good reading, every time.